# Beyond A Darkened Sky

Dana Alexander

Beyond A Darkened Sky is a work of fiction. Names, characters, places, and incidents either are the product of the author's imagination or are used fictitiously. Any resemblance to actual persons, living or dead, events or locales is entirely coincidental.



ISBN-13: 978-1733300544 (paperback)

First edition ISBN: 978-0615938448 | 2014
Library of Congress Control Number: 2014906536
Beyond A Darkened Sky, Arizona
Printed in the United States of America

*Cover design by Bespoke Book Covers*

*For Ethan, and all who believe there is more that
exists than what you see.*

# ACKNOWLEDGMENTS

*The author would like to thank:*

*Caroline Tolley, editor, for the encouragement and direction that helped this first story find its way beyond the hard-drive of my computer, the She Writes members for their support, the FF&P Chapter of RWA for the assistance with critiques, my son Ethan, for his patience, and my husband Mark, for his honesty and enthusiasm.*

# 1

"I can feel you, but I can't touch you," I whispered, extending an open hand to the empty space in front of me. "Where are you? Who are you?"

"Right here, my love," came a whispered reply.

It had been my voice that had awoken me to the scent of pine trees spanning as far as I could see, which wasn't more than a few feet with a sky lacking moon or stars or any explanation for the bluish-gray hue of night lit without them. Only moments before, I was certain someone was standing beside me. The sensation of fine hairs rising on my neck traveled the length of my arm in response.

At first glance, the space around me appeared gloomy, as if I'd been caught in a shroud of soupy, black fog. I rubbed the blurriness that plagued my pupils while considering if I'd been drugged and dumped in a forest. That notion seemed as ridiculous as the reality that faced me now, but it was the only plausible explanation for how I'd gotten here. The last memory I had was the high-pitched beeping sound of an alarm and heaviness in my body just before falling into a well of darkness. I stood alone in the emptiness of the forest for another moment before starting off with no particular direction in mind.

"This is madness," I said to myself.

After hiking for what felt like an hour, I gave up trying to recall just how I'd arrived. My latest struggle was trying to keep from screaming out in fear. My heart echoed the call as it began to race at the thought of never finding a way out of this obstacle of gray and green.

*Stuff it, Sara.*

I'd learned long ago the best way to escape a difficult situation was to think one's way out. Giving in to the easy wave of panic that threatened to crash over my senses was a sure death sentence. My foot caught at a tree root that had risen above the dirt path and twisted slightly. I fell hard, landing on my hip and forearm. A curse slipped from my lips. I needed to find higher ground. From there I might find city lights or a campsite to suggest some direction to go. I'd settle for any sign of life right now. I rubbed my ankle and pushed myself up.

One lousy survival class was all I had under my belt, pressed upon me as a New Year's resolution by a friend who insisted on having a partner. "Maybe it'll come in handy if you ever try camping," she'd joked. I never thought I'd actually have to use it.

A drop of cold sweat rushed down my back, sending another chill through me, as though an icy fingertip teased along my spine.

My memory seemed intact. I began ticking off each one from a mental checklist. *My name is Sara Forrester. I'm thirty—no, thirty-one, just last week. I'm a psychiatrist with a successful practice. And I have zero interest in committing to that kiss-ass Tyler Mason no matter how close or how wealthy our families are.* He was nothing more to me than a family friend who lately had been pressing for more of my time and attention.

*What was my last memory before the alarm bells?* I shook my head as a vague thought attempted to push through. I was supposed to attend the benefit for the Forrester Foundation with Tyler. *Did I go?* I couldn't remember. Just the way I couldn't remember how I'd arrived in a damn forest. *Could Tyler have had anything to do with me landing here?* Not likely. He wasn't capable of doing harm to me. I was sure of it. It wasn't because he cared enough, though he pretended a good game. There was too much financially for him to lose. But at least there was a chance he would pull a search party together. Maybe.

I pressed on, forging through soft ferns, over boulders, and past a thicket of constant trees, while a nagging feeling that I wasn't alone picked at my conscience. *It's nothing.* But I could sense the presence of someone lurking in the shadows. My eyes argued against the sensation, not finding a shred of evidence to prove it. I could panic but I wouldn't. I was a survivor, having come through a lot worse than this and at a much younger age. A whisper of white fog brushed between the trees immediately in front of me. I whirled around, following it with my eyes. It returned this time, slowing its pace. I held my breath as my heart began to pound heavier, until it was the only sound I could hear. In the transparency, the image of a face transformed in the mist, taking in my appearance much as I was of it, until the entire ghostly figure flitted away. That was the confirmation my eyes needed to prove I wasn't alone.

"What the hell is this place?"

The sensation of watchful eyes from somewhere in the darkness remained. But this time the hairs had not risen on my arms with the fleeting image.

"Show yourself!"

I despised a coward and suddenly remembered I had nothing to fight with, save whatever jiu jitsu I could remember.

"Why won't you face me?"

I was losing it, shouting to nothing in the depth of darkness to rid a feeling. If I was meant to die, better to get on with it. As if in answer, a piercing pain shot through my head and I closed my eyes, pressing my palms to my temples.

Behind my eyelids, I saw the image of a group of five, maybe six people with swords, battling fiercely against a cloud of black that swept in multiple directions. I couldn't make out the faces before the scene began to fade. Another immobilizing pain ripped through my head and sent me to my knees. This time the world spun around me and my stomach began to dance into nausea. I swallowed it back, as the hairs rose up my arms and neck. I opened my eyes and was startled to see the figure of a man squatting beside me.

"Jesus!" I gasped, extending an arm behind me to prevent falling backward. "What the…? Who the hell are you?" The pain subsided, and I stared, frozen with fear.

Few features were visible in the dim light. His wavy chestnut hair hung at his shoulders. But it was his eyes that held my gaze. They were blindingly white, like the headlights of an oncoming car at night, leaving me unable to read anything in them.

"I don't want to frighten you," he said, extending a hand slowly toward me as if approaching a scared animal.

*Too late.*

I was, I supposed, as frightened as I'd ever been. Fear kept me immobile, while a little voice in my head screamed, *Move!* I let out a small breath I realized I'd been holding in one gasp. He smiled past closed lips.

"Will you take my hand?"

"No." My voice was almost a whisper. "Who are you? What do you want?" I began inching backward ever so slowly, as the signals from my brain strained to reach my muscles.

"Does this help?" He brought a hand over his face for an instant, and when he removed it, the blinding white in the irises of his eyes had been replaced with a beautiful shade of cobalt blue. I stopped my backward retreat and rested on my bum. The only slight distance between us was that of my knees pulled up to my chest.

"I won't hurt you. Please, take my hand."

I cast a cautious eye at him and his open palm. If I was going to die, it was either alone in a forest or quickly by the hand of someone else. I made my choice for the latter, turned my head, and closed my eyes.

His gentle grasp enclosed my hand and he didn't move. "Sara," he said, waiting for me to look at him. "I know you're scared. I can feel it. There's no need to fear me."

I breathed in an ounce of strength and turned to face him. "I don't know how you know my name or how you got here. Hell, I don't even know how I got here. And I definitely don't want to be talking to people I don't know, unless they can tell me how to get home. Can you do that?"

"You're not going to die here." He paused, stroking a thumb over the tops of my fingers, unsettling me further. I tried to pull my hand free, only to find his grip tighten slightly in a squeeze before releasing it. He stood, as I pushed myself up, brushing remnants of dead leaves and a few pine needles from the knees of my pants.

"It's surprising that not a single recollection of who you really are has returned since you arrived," he said, eyes fixed upon me. He folded his arms and leaned against a nearby tree. "And I suppose if you don't know who you are, you wouldn't remember me, either," he said, more to himself than to me. His eyes narrowed, and his head tilted slightly, as though I was a puzzle he was trying to figure out. "I find it fascinating."

The fear he was going to kill me disappeared like a fallen leaf in the wind. "Oh, I know who I am. And you're right, I don't *remember* you because we've never met."

He laughed lightly. "We have a long way to go."

"I'm not going anywhere with you."

"Not yet but soon."

Before I could argue, he took steps to meet me, standing a few inches taller than my own five foot ten. "I'd like to put at ease all of your worries and provide answers to your questions, but I cannot. Not yet."

"And why not?"

His eyes softened with a look of understanding but remained fixed in a penetrating stare. "We must adhere to a sequence of events previously planned by the Alliance. You do remember the Alliance?"

I shook my head. "What are you talking about? What Alliance? Who are you, anyway?" I began to wonder if I was hallucinating. His index finger traced my jawline, causing me to stiffen.

"Never mind. You'll remember." He paused. "You're a skilled fighter, Sara."

He turned, took a few steps, and stopped, glancing over his shoulder. "And you are in your right mind. Perhaps open it a bit wider to other possibilities." And with that, he proceeded in the opposite direction, disappearing behind the trees.

I glanced around, turning in a full circle. "Are you kidding me?" I asked up to the sky. *I finally find someone who might have the answer to getting out of here but doesn't even tell me his name, and then he's gone.* Frustration rose to the surface as my eyes began to fill with tears, but I forced them away, faced with the need to focus. My life depended on it. No time for fear.

*Okay. Just think for a moment.*

I surveyed my surroundings. The tall clusters of pine and maples seemed familiar enough. Still, I was fairly certain I wasn't anyplace I had ever been. The strange visitor and apparition had already convinced me of that fact. The fear of being lost and facing possible demise rose to the surface, refusing to be ignored and threatening to make me fall over the teetering edge of sanity. There was enough light to see several feet ahead and behind me, outlining a path. Judging by the fading shades of darkness in the sky, I guessed the time to be somewhere around nine p.m. But who really knew? I continued pushing through the brush, climbing higher over the enormous rocks as though they were a rigid team of defensive linemen intending to hold me back.

The incline was growing steeper. By the way my muscles were straining, I had to be edging toward the summit. It was unusual that my breathing did not change from the exertion, nor did I feel any fatigue from the higher altitude. I was certainly no hiking expert but worked out enough to know that trekking across a mountainside was no easy task. Instead, I moved with little effort, feeling almost weightless.

Every detail of the environment began to sharpen, as did my awareness of the complete stillness that settled around me. I couldn't hear anything now but the crunch of my own footsteps over the dead foliage covering the rocky floor, until I stopped to listen. There was no breeze that should have been present at this altitude. Silence echoed in my ears. As if to fill the void, a faint ringing crept into the space. I sat down, sinking my head into my hands as tears began to well. I was as alone as I'd ever been or ever imagined anyone could be.

*Don't lose it. Just hang on. If there's a way in, there's got to be a way out.* The tears dropped one by one down my cheeks, dampening my shirt in dotted patches. I pulled my knees to my chest and wrapped my arms around them, brushing the wetness from my cheeks.

"I've got to clear my mind," I whispered. "There must be a rational explanation."

It was possible I was in the Adirondack Forest, a six-million-acre parcel of forest, wetlands, and streams that included areas of human settlement. I was bound to find a trail leading to civilization eventually.

"Even if you were in that forest, why is there no moon, no familiar nighttime sounds?" I asked aloud. "Why am I dressed in this unfamiliar clothing?" I glanced behind me. "And men with pure white eyes don't come out of nowhere and talk to you." I sat for several minutes, staring into the darkness, wondering if the man was indeed a figment of my imagination. The fresh scent of pine needles and musty dead leaves rose up through my senses, reminding me how real this environment appeared.

All I wanted was to leave, to go back to my comfy home on the outskirts of New York City and to what was familiar, not to be captive. With that thought, I shifted abruptly to my feet. *A crunching sound. Footsteps? Not mine.* The fact that I saw no one didn't stop me from quickening my pace in the opposite direction of the sound.

The feeling of being watched had returned. Had it ever left? Was I being tracked? I shot glances on either side of me. *No one.* Still, the footsteps could be heard, urging me to move faster.

I shot a glance upward. Twinkling lights? Why hadn't I seen them before? Was that a small house? In the trees? I continued my race forward, my feet grateful for the less rocky and root-filled terrain. The pounding of my heart and sweat-soaked shirt the only proof I was running for my life. But from what? Why?

I risked slowing my pace, as the trees began to thin, welcoming a deep breath at neither hearing nor seeing any sign of the owner of the footsteps.

To my surprise, lit cottages were sprinkled about. Tiny tree houses with roofs covered in moss. A small sense of relief came and went. Was this find good or bad? My heart skipped a beat, uncertain if it should gear up for fight or flight.

"Hey. Hello?" I called out to no visible person. "Is anyone there? Please. I need help."

The light was a comfort in a sea of darkness. Calling out couldn't be any more detrimental than dying alone in a forest.

I stopped picking my way through the thin tree saplings, closer to the village, startled by a figure standing behind a few soft ferns. Any lingering thoughts in my head escaped.

There was just enough light to set off the features of a tall man with a well-defined build. His hair was the color of toffee and hung neatly groomed past his shoulders. He stepped from behind the cluster of ferns. His clothing was a fitted, durable material, similar to mine but ending with a leathery boot that tied up the length of his calf just below the knee. Large almond-shaped eyes were perfectly spaced upon a smooth oval face.

"Sara, do not be afraid. We have been waiting for you. Please, follow me."

*We?* I stood in place, willing my legs to move but uncertain if I should follow. *No other choice but to go, I suppose.*

I watched as he climbed up the nearest tree, grabbing branch after branch, toward one of the small dwellings above.

I waited a moment longer, as my eyes tracked his movement before grasping that first branch. I climbed with amazing agility and ease, proving that gravity was not as effectual here as I would have expected. I was clearly not in the Adirondack Mountains. As I traced his path branch by branch, I was slowly giving up the internal battle that fought against my current reality.

Arriving at the entrance of a little cottage, I stepped through a tall, slender door into a room lit by the glow of several burning candles. I followed the man to a table in a small kitchen. Another person, whose back was turned to me, was busy preparing something. She turned to greet me, a warm smile extending across her face. Her movements were graceful as she angled her head in greeting. She appeared to be close to my age, despite hair of pure white that contrasted with her clear blue eyes set upon a flawless complexion, like that of a china doll. My eyes absorbed their extraordinary features as though quenching a thirst.

*My name is Eldor and this is Seria, my companion.* As he spoke, Eldor's lips did not move. Instead, his thoughts entered my mind clearly. He gestured for me to sit at the table and I did.

"Can I communicate like you?" I asked, deciding to be sure to prevent looking like the fool for trying.

*You're welcome to communicate in the manner most comfortable for you. However, you will find in time, telepathy is a much faster way to convey thoughts and feelings,* Eldor replied, glancing to Seria.

"Why am I here?" I asked, getting to the point.

"You are on a predetermined path, chosen by the Soltari, a powerful and ancient spiritual order," he replied. "You are able to bring light to people and places that have only seen darkness."

Seria brought a small, steaming pot to the table.

"We are here to aid you in your quest," she said, smiling. Her eyes dipped to the cup as she poured the hot liquid and handed it to me. The steam rose up through my senses, tantalizing with the light scent of jasmine.

"What quest? The only quest I'm on is to get home. And what predetermined path? I don't understand. What do you mean I have the ability to bring light?" I flicked a glance between them. "How did I get here?" I tried to refrain from asking so many questions, but I had found someone who had knowledge that could satisfy my need to know.

"We understand the confusion upon your arrival. Trust that all will be provided in due time. For now, we are simply guides on your path, Sara."

"Can you tell me where I am at least?"

"You're in Ardan. A world very different from your own," Eldor replied. "This is a parallel world to Earth but one that allows you to practice your abilities, to strengthen yourself from within." His words rested on the surface of my ears. Doubt kept them from sinking deeper.

"Even as a child, you knew more existed than what you experience in your physical world," he said. I searched my memory to find what he meant, to when I was a child, remembering the spirit in my room at night that would often visit and speak only in a whisper.

At the time, it had appeared friendly enough, talking to me as one child to another. "You are a much older soul than your current age. Your knowledge of the past, the memories of alternate realities have been withheld so that you could function on Earth until the time was right for the quest ahead. Extend yourself beyond what is familiar and look deeper to what you know in the depths of your soul. You are being reconnected to your true path. A path you have always known."

I wasn't sure how much of what I was hearing and seeing I believed and resisted the distinct urge to discreetly pinch myself.

"You see," Eldor continued, "evil is the action created by those who have chosen to follow the path of darkness that stems from fear. Many in your world are not yet ready to see the truth that comes from light, or what we call awareness. This fear creates weakness that plagues your world, allowing a very dark force to enter."

"I don't understand what you mean," I said, shaking my head slightly. "What dark force and what true path?" My gaze darted between them.

"We know the questions are many, and as the need arises, you will be aided by us and others," Eldor said.

"Others? What others?" I sucked in a breath, struggling to find patience.

"If information is revealed too soon, it will alter the path. And you must succeed. Trust that your confusion is temporary."

"There is a shift occurring, a battle to obtain the energy found in humanity," Seria explained. "Energy is the force that is manipulated to create the change. In this manner and in your world, a shift of darkness over light is taking place."

"So, what does that have to do with me?" People were angrier than I remembered, but times were tough. Life was about ups and downs. Always had been. Granted, there seemed to be a longer time of being down than up.

"We have knowledge, insight into your world. Ardan and other worlds were transformed into enlightened states millennia before now. We live in a higher dimension. You, Sara, are one of those beings who has traveled to the physical world to reset the balance and keep the light in the physical world."

His eyes were full of depth and locked with mine as he spoke, holding my attention as though I was under a spell. Despite the explanation being provided, as one question was answered, another sprung forward.

"Is this your purpose for all who enter here, to instruct them?" I asked.

"We are guides on your path, Sara," answered Seria.

"The others I saw when I arrived, the homes in the trees, who do they belong to?"

"Guides assist those seeking information on their path. Each is specific to the seeker. You are in the company of the elves. We are enlightened souls like you," Eldor replied.

There was something familiar about what he was saying, but I couldn't explain why. The information sounded both new and old as it filtered to my ears, as if the knowledge he provided to me already existed as a memory he was awakening.

"I caution you to watch that the dark energy does not lure you into believing it is a companion. You are strong and can move with swiftness and accuracy. Your strength and ability are like nothing you know in the physical world. The dark energy is also strong, just as quick, and very deceiving. Remember, this is a place of discovery and practice as you strengthen and recall your abilities," he explained.

I wanted to know more, to stay in the comfortable little home, but felt the strangest sensation that our time was up. Some inexplicable force was pulling at me to leave. Eldor stood and took a few steps toward a long, intricately carved wooden table that stretched the length of the wall. My eyes followed him as he leaned over to pick up a rather large object wrapped in cloth. Holding it at chest level, he brought it to me. I stood and held out my hands as he placed the heavy object in them and began unfolding the cream-colored linen, revealing a glimmering blade and, with it, a sheath and strap to hold the beautiful creation.

"Remember, fear is your enemy. Intuition is your guide. You will need this. It will aid you through your practice and further through your mission. Take care, for it is crafted especially for you." As I placed a hand on the hilt of the sword, a soft white light began to glow across the blade as though it were awakening. To my surprise and under the weight, I held it quite comfortably, admiring the sleek, smooth steel for a long moment before placing the sword safely in its sheath.

"Thank you for your guidance, and for this," I said, glancing from the blade to Eldor. "Though I'm not sure I know how to use it."

"My dear, the use of this weapon will not be a question for you when called upon to unsheathe it."

"How do I leave Ar—" Before I could finish the question, a surge of energy ran through me as the warmly lit hut went completely dark. I found myself no longer in the small cottage in the trees but on a clearly defined dirt path. Only now I was armed. For what, I couldn't know.

# 2

Daylight was beginning to show its colors, as the sky subtly lightened to a brighter shade of bluish-gray haze. I continued on, only at a much quicker pace. If I could just fulfill whatever I was called to do, maybe I could finally get home.

The face of the man who'd startled me upon my arrival flashed again in my mind's eye. *How does he know me?* He and the elves and their messages were as real as the weight of the sword that hung at my side, and still, logic urged me to consider other options. This time I did pinch my forearm rather hard. Feeling the pain of it and hearing the sound of dead leaves crunching beneath my feet were reassurance I wasn't dreaming.

The path ceased to continue, ending at a cluster of prickly brush. "Well, great," I said under my breath. I stepped to the side and pushed through into a large, empty, grass-covered field. The tips of the thorns tugged at my clothing as if to hold me back. I glanced in every direction. A circular cutout had been made in the middle of the forest, leaving a blank canvas of grass and rock. I turned around, catching a movement out of the corner of my eye. Three black-cloaked figures with no faces mysteriously approached from the opposite end of the field, crossing the border of trees that encircled the field. They separated to form a triangle around me. Each held a sword that was drawn and stood in a guarded position. Why? I had no plan to attack.

Strangely, I also had no instinct to run. Instead, I pulled the sword from the sheath and took a stance to defend myself as though I'd done so many times in the past.

"Move swiftly and with great force," said a deep voice that came from one of the faceless apparitions. I stood in a guarded, middle-stance position with my sword aimed at the chest of the black-shrouded figure closest to me. The outline of the shadows grew eerily more distinct against the white mist that had begun to form overhead and fall between us. One at a time, they took slow steps in my direction, until one of the figures reached an uncomfortable distance within my personal space. I raised an arm and swung, bringing my arm down in a diagonal slash. The cloaked figures and I shifted around each other, alternating positions and stepping sideways and back, as blades connected in a chime of steel upon steel.

One of the remaining two shadows glided closer but stayed just out of reach, while the other waited. A strike directed at my left flank, mid-section, missed by no more than an inch. Holding the sword firmly in both hands, I extended a right foot and threw my body forward, flipping headfirst over the first shrouded figure so that I was facing his back. Raising both hands, I quickly brought my sword up and into a horizontal left-to-right crosscut, striking the left side under what should have been the shoulder blade. I stared in stunned amazement. The sword hadn't connected but instead slid through the black fog. The tip hit the ground hard as the figure quickly faded and the next wasted no time coming forward.

I swung around as another shadowed man moved in a circular motion around me, spinning a hazy black mist that surrounded my entire body and made it impossible to see. I lifted the sword, prepared to strike. *Where was the damned creature?*

I gazed into the cloud, willing my eyes to see past the illusion. As I did, I began to sense the location of the shadow. I pulled the sword back, holding it upright and close to my body. Saying a quick prayer, I plotted the precise moment and lunged forcefully. A solid outline of a jaw and red eyes fell in front of me as the blade sank into the center of darkness and an ear-piercing scream rocketed through the air. Again, the sensation of accomplishment, of firm body against the end of my sword was denied. The energy, however, had not been wasted. The image slowed, stopped, and collected the black mist into its being. The dark figure began spinning again as it rose into the air and disappeared into the haze of white mist.

I shifted my attention from the sky to the last black form, more ominous in appearance than the other two, as it turned to face me. The sword it held disappeared, as did mine.

*Now what?* My senses told me to listen and focus on the energy I felt from this one. *Fear is my enemy.* Eldor's words echoed through my mind.

The figure stepped back and drew up its arms. Its long black fingers and palms aimed toward the sky, making it appear that much more threatening as the sleeves of the cloak hung in a long sweep on each side of its body like draped wings. With a flick of a few sparks, a sphere of light danced like a circle of fire between its hands that lowered to shoulder level. I shifted my weight to the right foot, then left. The black figure matched the movement. I crouched and pushed off, springing over it to face its back as I'd done before. But the hooded, wraith-like figure was in front of me again, already anticipating my movement.

*Is it waiting for me to do something different? Why isn't it fighting?*

As if in answer, the spinning circle of light was sent flying in my direction. I dodged, but the fireball's path remained fixed on my movement, hurling toward me. Again, I leaped in the air, flipping over the cloaked form of my opponent, facing its backside with the ball of energy now targeting the figure. I stepped back, turned, and ran for the forest, flicking a glance over my shoulder. The rolling flames, not slowing, blew through the figure, still seeking me. I wasn't going to outrun it. Out of some dark corner of my imagination, the image of a shield of light appeared in my mind's eye. I turned again, pressed my palms outward to brace the impact, and turned my head away. Ducking wasn't an option with the tracking feature set to "hunt and kill." An intense force pressed against the palms of my hands. The ball had been stopped in its path by a visible shield of white light.

*That worked?* I didn't know how to dismantle the energy, only how to stop its movement.

*What does it want?*

The dark figure extended an arm, pulled the sphere of blazing light back, and stood still, gazing at me. Only then was I aware of my breath flowing quickly in and out. On a single exhale, all three shadows appeared in front of me. My sword, abandoned somewhere in the fight, had been returned to its sheath.

"You asked to be ready. You are being prepared," one of the figures said in a deep voice. "Learn and strengthen your abilities. Focus on the energy you possess and your power to control it. You have done well but the challenges grow stronger."

All three ghostly figures faded into the shadows behind the trees. Had my thoughts really created a force field to halt the ball of energy? If so, what else was I capable of doing?

As I started to move off the field and back to my search for the path out of Ardan, a heavy, dark cloud fell over the terrain like smoke from a fire, blinding me. *Very wrong, very—* I searched for the words to describe the feeling that consumed my senses. *Ill intentioned.* That was it. The skin along my spine prickled in response to the worst feeling of dread I had ever known. I drew my sword, sharpened my focus to see through the smoke, and heard a voice I didn't recognize. Not at first.

"It's Sara the Soltari call you in this life," a gravelly voice said. There was a pause. "You cannot win the challenge ahead."

*What challenge? This exercise or the mission?*

"They have made you weak."

"Who are you?"

The cloud lifted. My gaze shifted to the boundary of the field as movement drew my attention back. An army of people who looked like Eldor and Seria surrounded me. *What the hell?*

The name Tarsamon resonated in the air above. I stiffened. I shouldn't know this name, but somehow, I did. The voice taking residence in the dark cloud above me was the truest sense of evil that existed in the spirit realm. The army of elves that surrounded me was indeed here to battle. Bows were fitted with arrows in unison and aimed at the center of the field. *Shit.* My deepest intuition told me two things—this was very real and I already knew who this entity was.

"Your will and desire for the survival of that world you call home are strong but not strong enough. Not now and not by the time my forces are in position. As you know of me in the darkest corners of your conscience, Sara, you know this to be true."

"Your words are poison, meaningless to the powers that govern spirituality and the immortality of souls," I said to the sky. "And you have no vision for what is to come. What is it you want from me now?"

I didn't recognize the thoughts that entered my head or the words that fell from my lips as my own. *Have I left my body, risen to another level of being? Am I dead?*

"To provide a warning. Do not interfere with the inevitable path to consume the world you call home, and peace for you and the beings of light will remain."

"Your threat falls on deaf ears. You know nothing of what it means to bring peace and can't promise to retain it for anyone. It's not within your power." The ominous sensation still remained heavy around me.

The cloud shifted, combining its mass into several pitch-dark upright figures with glowing pea-sized yellow eyes holding swords. Their eyes beamed at me like a thousand tiny lights as they slowly started toward me. Sword in hand, I leveled those closest to me, right then left, spun and repeated the same motion, as if guided by a puppeteer. I didn't remember my knowledge for battle. It was just present, available at will. I extended a level crosscut, removing the head of one of the figures. It hit the ground with a thud, dissolved into a black mist, and rose into the air above me. I pulled my elbows close to my sides, gripping the sword with both hands. Arrows flew past me to their targets. *Damn me if I should move.*

*Are the beasts getting faster?* Most had fallen to the arrows. I whirled, ducking as a blade skimmed over the top of my head, just before I thrust my sword into the demon entity. *This is too real to be practice.* A flicker of light rested in the center of my vision and I remembered the ball of light. *Could I create this from nothing?* I imagined a white spark of energy evolving into the sphere and, with little effort, found it float-ing beside me, waiting to meet its mark. I stepped back, out of the immediate reach of my enemy, and hurled it into the group, unsure if it would do any damage. I breathed a heavy sigh at the success and knelt down, resting both hands on the sword staked in the ground in front of me, and leaned my head against the hilt.

I lifted my head to see the elves had gone. So, too, had the demon creatures, those that had met my sword and the elves' bows along with any lingering gray mist. *My God, what's it going to take to get out of here?*

Having regained a relative state of calm, I moved across the field and in the direction of the trees I'd been headed before Tarsamon had interrupted.

The rolling sound of thunder broke the silence, as the fresh scent of rain filled the air. I glanced to the sky to see an array of pink and green hues scattered off in the distance and watched as they blended together and were carried off through the air like sea spray over an ocean. *How strange and beautiful this place is.*

Several minutes passed while I took cover under the canopy of a large white cedar to wait out the downpour. A movement several feet ahead drew my attention away from the rain. A spinning figure darted first in front, then behind me and circled a few other trees. Rising quickly from under the soft foliage, I stood with my hand on the hilt of the sword, prepared to draw. The cloud of blackness ap-peared to be some sort of energy form similar to the cloaked figures I'd battled earlier. It couldn't be anything physical, I thought, not the way it swirled past, until it stopped in front of me.

The features of the shadow transformed into that of a woman with long, wavy tendrils of fiery-red hair and deep blue eyes that floated like small pools against her fair skin. Feeling safe, I let my hand drop from the sword.

"So, you're Sara. I heard you would be coming." She leaned against one of the tree trunks, pulled a couple of pine needles, and began twisting them around a finger as she glanced up at the rain beginning to slow. "My name is Aria. I'll be joining you in the mission ahead."

"Who told you I would be coming?" I asked, remembering Eldor also knew of my arrival.

"Guides, of course," she replied with a bewildered expression. "Oh, I see. You haven't yet awakened to your true identity. You're being reintroduced to energy. It must be terribly confusing." She paused, flicking the needles to the ground. "You can be sure that feeling will pass."

"How did *you* get here?"

"Hmph. The guides said you may need to be reminded but I didn't think…" Her voice dropped off. "Never mind. Everyone's first arrival to Ardan is different. Come to think of it, I can't quite recall my first visit. It was so long ago," she replied. "I travel in the evening to practice. How long have you been here?"

"I don't really know. Not long, I suspect."

"Not to worry. When you're here, you're never really alone. The guides on your path will prepare you for the mission." She pulled her fingers through her long red hair and tossed it behind her shoulder. "It seems our energy is on the same wavelength. I'd love to see what we could do together combining our strength. It's been ages since we fought together."

"I've met you before?"

She tapped an index finger to her head. "That memory thing. Don't worry about it. You'll become familiar again. We'll need to join forces against the evil coming."

I remembered Eldor cautioning me about dark energy being deceiving. How could I be sure Aria wasn't like one of the dark-cloaked figures I had recently fought? I just wouldn't allow myself to trust anything here, not until I had some concrete answers first.

"What proof do I have that you are who you say you are and not a form of darkness that is masking as some sort of companion?" I asked.

She flashed a quick smile. "You always did think too much. I understand your inability to trust. Only souls on a path of enlightenment can remain in Ardan. Well, this side of it anyway. You'll meet many who are here to test your ability, to show you what you can accomplish and what you need to build upon."

"And how is it that you move like a spinning cloud?"

"My energy is different from yours. It shifts differently. Still, I think we have similar strengths. I can't really explain it any more than that right now."

"How did I arrive here? I don't recall…" I began.

"You chose to come here. No one is forced into Ardan or any of the other worlds." She shook her head slightly.

*Other worlds?*

"Let's go," she said.

"Go where?"

"An exercise." She started off in one direction, and I followed. "Let go of your worry. You'll see what can happen." Aria glanced up to see the rain had stopped, leaving only a billowy dark cast above us. She led the way to a lake. Her hair caught a breeze, sending it flying in a blaze of red fury about her head.

An image formed in my mind of the water shifting; the movement to match the vision followed. The calm tranquility began to tremble in its center, mirroring the rippling effect of an earthquake, as the water grew into wakes that attempted escape from confinement along the embankment. In a force so strong that it grabbed hold of the entire body, it combined its mass into the center and slowly began rise into a vertical array that held together in an enormous tornado-like shape.

The massive funnel came to life, spinning in a circular motion and gaining speed. My thought had joined with Aria's energy, lifting the water out of the shell of the lakebed it had rested in moments ago. The water rose higher, until it was a single body of water spinning in the sky above us. A deep, growling *whoosh* filled the air as it rotated faster and faster. Light sprays of water escaped, landing on my face in a cool mist.

"Careful," Aria said more to herself than to me, as she concentrated harder on the movement. I watched in amazement at what was occurring, while focused on holding the image of its movement in my mind. I was cautious not to be distracted as I started a slow trek forward, right foot, then left. To my surprise, the funnel of water began to move with me. A single noise and all focus would be lost, sending a flood of water crashing like thunder into the landscape.

*How is this happening?*

"Let's set it down," she said. I turned, shifting my body in the direction of the hole in the ground, keeping the image of what we expected glued in my mind. When the funnel was hovering safely over its original vast area, Aria reduced the spin until all of the water sunk low into its bed and original state of calm. I breathed a heavy sigh of relief.

The dark clouds appeared over the field again above us, creating a threatening shadow.

"It looks as though you can move energy by keeping a thought of it in your mind. Let's try again with another type of energy," Aria said.

"Is this really happening or just some elaborate dream?"

She laughed. "Real as you make it. Thoughts are energy. All energy can be transformed into the physical."

If I could manipulate natural forces, how much more capable was an experienced traveler to Ardan? When the practice was through, a friendship had begun to sprout.

"Can I find you again in this place?" I asked.

"Of course. Did you forget we're on this mission together?" She tucked one side of her hair behind an ear. "Or are you still a nonbeliever?"

"I don't know what to believe." And it was true. I was a logical, reasonable person and these experiences didn't fit into either of those categories.

"Remember, you will find that your thoughts are more powerful than you have ever considered. In fact, I bet you'll have a whole new respect and control over what you think by the time you're done."

Among the many unusual events that had happened that I could not explain was a sense when it was time to leave. And the familiar pull to move on crept back to me as it had with Eldor and Seria, urging a parting with Aria.

I was gaining knowledge of my abilities quickly. But one thing was certain, I wasn't in control of what happened or when. It was the game plan of someone with a much deeper knowledge and understanding than anything I could imagine. Every experience set off another explosion of questions, quietly taking residence in the recesses of my mind. The more time I spent here, the more I was convinced this was reality. But if that was so, what and where was the life I had known for thirty-one years?

# 3

The beeping of the heart monitor and the steady rhythmic *hush, click* of the ventilator echoed in the otherwise silent room as Dr. Kevin Scott glanced over the peaceful form of the woman he'd been waiting his entire life to find. He knew that, while Sara's body healed, she wasn't resting.

When the moment arrived to meet her, he'd imagined it would hit him with all the force of a Mack truck at a hundred miles per hour. And it had. But for some reason, he always assumed he'd meet her perhaps by accident, under circumstances where they might have bumped into each other getting coffee or some other mundane encounter. Instead, *she'd* been rolled into the ER on a stretcher following an accident and he'd fought to bring her heart back to life, willing it between each chest compression and every breath he'd given her before utilizing the defibrillator. The instant he touched her, the familiar energy of her that he'd known over thousands of years raced through him like a live wire. He'd never expected her to land in his hospital but should have with the power the Soltari had to plan the mission to the finest detail. He'd come to this world to find her, to connect with her soul as he had in so many other lifetimes. But Kevin had never known how that would happen this time around or when the mission would be initiated. And now, here she was. As she lay in the bed catching up on her responsibility for the quest ahead, his task at ensuring her safety caused him to feel as helpless as she was in that bed. A hospital was no place to guard the one woman who had been called to save the world from an approaching evil. He doubted if Miss Sara Forrester was even aware of what would soon be hunting her.

Did she know her strength yet? Had the guides in Ardan granted her that knowledge? Surely, he thought. And it was that knowledge that would make his task that much more difficult.

"Arwyn," he whispered. It was her real name. But he knew she wouldn't remember, just the way she wouldn't remember she had always been a fighter, or his love. His gaze moved over her helpless form. He knew her true identity and the roles they had chosen together for this life. And still she would be completely unaware of him. He'd have to use all of his strength and finesse to get close to her again in a new life together on Earth, and before they could stop fighting the evil of the dark shadows forever. What if she didn't want him this time? It was possible. She'd agreed with the Soltari in planning this life that it would be best to remove all emotion to concentrate on the task.

Could she put on hold their centuries-old bond and forget him for one short lifetime? Not if he had anything to do with it.

He skimmed over the notes the nurse had made one hour earlier. With the exception of the occasional increased heart rate, all was normal. He had upgraded her status. Tomorrow the medical team would be bringing her out of the medically induced coma and move her to a room with slightly less oversight from the staff.

"Oh, Dr. Scott." The nurse for the evening shift distracted Kevin from his thoughts. He turned, pressing his lips into a tight, professional smile. "I thought you would have gone home by now." She moved to Sara's bedside with an IV bag in hand.

"Just a few last-minute follow-ups."

"Dr. Surray will be assuming her care in the morning. You should go home and get some rest." The nurse plugged the IV line into the new bag and flicked it with a finger to get the drip started. Kevin glanced up from the chart.

"Still catching up on documentation. I'll be around a while longer." He couldn't tell her there was no way he was leaving Sara in the care of anyone else, especially a rotating medical staff. They had no idea this patient wasn't any other they would eventually discharge. "The notes should have been updated to reflect this patient will be under my care until she is discharged." *And further still.* "Can you please see that the chart reflects the change? And if further documentation is needed, I'll finalize it tonight."

"Of course. I'll check it now." The door to the room closed with a hush behind him. Kevin's thoughts returned to his task. *How to guard a fighter?*

She'd have stubborn will. He'd run into Sara's adoptive mother, Mary Ann Forrester, a handful of times since she'd come to visit at the hospital, a woman of strength and grace. His love couldn't have landed with a better family, couldn't have planned her life any better, despite the pain she had suffered under the hands of her biological parents early in childhood. That pain was meant to strengthen her, to build the emotional barrier she would need to fight the darkness ahead. That block would also make it harder for him to ease into her life, and more difficult still for her to trust enough to love him again.

The Forresters were well known as philanthropists, supporting worldwide charities, and for their money. Lots of money. Robert, Sara's adoptive father, was a billionaire who dealt in acquisitions overseas. Mary Ann had come from a wealthy family, too, with a father who had acquired and sold desirable works of art. As such, Sara had been provided with an Ivy League education and cultural experience that would allow her to carry on the same responsibilities and expectations of her parents.

Last week's tabloids reported that, at the age of thirty-one and having never been engaged, "The billionaire beauty may have wedding bells in the future." Kevin recalled the magazine cover at the market as the cashier rang up a handful of grocery items. A picture of a man with perfect hair and airbrushed skin was plastered on the page, flashing an *I'm all that* smile. But he hadn't seen the guy once visit Sara. Perhaps he'd missed the man's visit while on his hospital rounds. That was best, anyhow. Kevin had one goal in mind—staying as close to Sara as he could. Having a clear path to do so would make things much easier.

Getting details about Sara had come with ease with Mary Ann growing a bit more talkative with each visit. As someone who could read another's thoughts and sense their feelings, Kevin was well aware Mary Ann not only approved of the care he was providing but also understood what a lovely friend he would make for her daughter. If only she knew just how close they had been long ago. His thoughts jumped to the last conversation he'd had with her earlier that morning.

"She's got such a desire to ease the pain of others," she'd said, referring to Sara's career as a well-respected psychiatrist. "I can't believe this has happened to her. She suffered enough as a child." She sniffed once. "I really think that's why her passion is in helping others." She picked up her purse and dug a hand to the bottom, searching. "Ah, well, I'm saying too much." Mary Ann paused to wipe her nose with a tissue. Kevin read her thoughts and received the image of abandonment and neglect Mary Ann and her husband had pulled Sara from, along with a quick view of the stark adoption agency with a younger Sara sitting at a table clutching a ragged, dark brown teddy bear to her chest, its blond ear hanging by a couple of threads. "It's just that she didn't deserve this." Mary Ann held Sara's hand in her own and stroked it with the backs of her fingers.

Kevin smiled with knowing. Sara was exactly the kind of soul that would give back to others, help anyone in need. Money would be used as the tool to accomplish the task.

"She's recovering quickly. Doing quite well, in fact," he told her. "The surgery to repair her leg was successful, and her last CT scan"—he paused and flipped a page—"shows excellent results. No signs of brain damage." *Miraculous considering the trauma sustained.* "We'll be able to reduce the medication in the next day or so, allowing her to wake on her own."

"Thank you for caring for her so well."

Kevin turned to the computer in the room to finish typing the instructions for care and listened while Mary Ann spoke. Her voice resonated with fear and loneliness without her daughter.

"She would never listen to anyone. Always having to do it her way," she continued. Kevin glanced over his shoulder. Her eyes were distant as she floated back to a memory. "Never would take any help."

He'd been informed of key elements about Sara by his guides in Ardan—the city she resided in, her profession, personality traits. All very vague information, and not enough to find her if he'd wanted to. What he cared to know, like her name, where he could find her, and what walls she had put in place to guard from feeling too much for anyone, wasn't shared by the Alliance that handed down the Soltari's directive regarding the mission. But he'd known for sure it was Arwyn in the ER that night nearly two weeks ago. He'd breathed her. Her energy. Their connection. It flowed through him like the blood in his veins from the moment their souls had bonded, millennia before now.

Standing alone with her now, Kevin looked up from the notes and rested his tired eyes on her face. *God, she's lovely.* She was in every life she had chosen with him. Her flawless skin, long dark hair with wisps of deep red blended throughout. The jade-colored eyes that hid under those almond-shaped lids were vacant for now, while perfectly angled brows framing them suggested the focus and intensity he expected to find when she woke. The soft beauty was a mask that hid the emotional strength as well as the exceptional skill she possessed. He swiped a hand over his face and glanced at his watch. It was nearly midnight and he'd already put in fourteen hours. Still, this was only the beginning of his time with her. His job had just begun. He stepped beside her, gently lifted one eyelid and then another, sweeping his light across her pupils. The beeping of the heart monitor was like soothing music to him, tangible proof that she was still here.

Kevin wondered if he could break through the barriers she had built to keep anyone who dared come close at bay. He could sense the hardened edge she used as a protective cover for her feelings, even as she lay unconscious. But he also understood a softer side existed behind the brick and mortar. "No limits," he said under his breath, considering his otherworldly abilities. All the skills he possessed would aid him well in this difficult case.

There was always the hope she would remember him. In planning their quest, the Soltari had refused his request to grant her the memories they'd shared. He'd fought hard for it. But in the end, the decision was final if he wanted to join her. She was not to remember him in this life and certainly not to become distracted from the quest by him.

"So, Ms. Sara, how *does* a man reach your heart? Will you let me in or only allow me to protect you?" he said quietly. Her mouth twitched at his words. His eyes moved down the length of the sheet and blanket covering her as he considered her injuries from the accident, one by one. She was doing well, sedated thoroughly, but well.

She'd found her fascination in this life with fast cars. Pity what had happened to the sporty Mercedes SLS. Someone who had been texting his way through the intersection, in the rain, had totaled the car. Still, he was sure it was the least expensive of the collection of racy exotics she kept in that hideaway outside the city. They would be put to good use again as soon as she was healed. He scratched his signature on the electronic chart and decided he'd sleep in the physicians' quarters one floor down from Sara's room.

As he left, he made a mental note to bring the members of the team together. Most, if not all of them, had to know by now she'd been activated for her task to find the symbols that would give them access to the location of the keys. He rubbed a knuckle over his upper lip, knowing that if the team was aware, so, too, was the evil that would hunt her. Kevin knew better than anyone that she would recover quickly from her injury, but now she was anything but safe.

# 4

For someone whose idea of camping was cozying up to a laptop with a plate of food and a couple of drinks for a few hours, being stuck in a forest of unknowns I couldn't leave was pure misery. What I wouldn't give for a fully charged cell phone and a strong signal right now.

I stood, brushing leaf debris from my pants and greeting the day with the hope it was my last in Ardan.

No concept of time existed in this place, except to try to gauge the hour by the location of the sun, if only it would show itself. Lighter shades of blue mysteriously changing at different points in the day were the only indication the hours were moving along. My gaze swept across the sky. *Might be early morning.* The hint of yellow peered over the edge of what I assumed was the eastern horizon, mingling in the middle with deeper hues of gray.

I shoved past a couple of tall ferns and bent down to get a better look at an unusual red flowering plant that had appeared like a patch of blood spilled in the midst of my green and gray world. It was the first sight of anything flowering. The remarkable beauty brightened the dead foliage of the forest floor in clusters of red flowers, a drop of gold in each small center, cradled by a sparkling hint of silver on velvety leaves. I touched the delicate petals to be sure they were real. This particular plant looked like yarrow, and if so, the forest should be full of the particular vegetation that liked to spread itself across a landscape. I glanced around to spot only one other plant a few paces ahead of where I was crouched and set off in the direction of it as though it were a sign of where I should go. Within minutes, I reached a path that split and stared down at the fork lying at my feet, as it patiently waited for me to choose the way.

By now, the illusion of choice provided no option not to travel one of the paths. If I stepped into brush and headed through the numerous trees attempting to skirt the trail, another inevitable route would emerge to follow. Settling on one of the dusty lines marking my way, I walked only a few feet before seeing another bunch of cheery red flora and, just beyond, rays of light that were split by the branches of a tree as though beckoning me to discover the source. A quick glance behind me revealed all I'd just left had grown shades darker, consumed in a gray mist urging me forward.

As I approached, a lighted tunnel proved to be the source of illumination. I stepped into it with the sound of voices taking up residence in the space around me. The trees and small scrub faded behind the blinding white illumination, leaving a framework of faint, shadowed outlines of trees. The muscles of my body melted into relaxation. I was warm, completely comfortable, and at peace, as if I'd just awoken from a long, deep, and restful sleep. The voices grew in number, reminding me of being at a large party with tidbits of recognizable conversations that could be overheard among others but scrambled. *How far is it to the end of this tunnel?*

The voices softened to more like a radio that could not be tuned to one station as I moved deeper into the tunnel. *White noise.* The sound muffled any chance of clarity, until it faded to a whisper. I kept my hands close to my sides, trusting faith to guide my steps. Though I was blind in the face of the bright light, I could feel I wasn't alone. I was getting quite used to the accuracy of that particular sensation.

A few more steps and I stopped to zero in on the shadow of someone approaching. As his image became clear, I guessed his height to be about six foot two. A few loose waves softened the medium-length, truffle-colored hair that rested behind high cheekbones and a squared chin. His build was lean, with muscle, not bulky but fit. His eyes reflected a quiet, wise strength in the pools of clear blue. His clothing was rugged with pants tucked into leathered boots and a shirt that hung loose. I took quick notice of the sword tucked away in a sheath that hung at his side beneath a long coat.

He extended an open hand, palm side up. *Why does he seem familiar? Could he be the same person I saw when I first arrived?* This man looked different somehow. I studied his face for recognition but found nothing to attach to memory. Without any hesitation, I placed my hand in his. *What the hell am I doing?* But I could not stop or resist the connection occurring. Our eyes were fixed on each other and a sensation of love flowed over me in tingles that ran the length from shoulder to fingertip. The feeling was almost hypnotizing. I forced my gaze away from his to take in the changes of environment.

The landscape behind him came into view as the blinding light of the tunnel faded, replaced with flowering trees flanking each side of a gentle stream. A waterfall in the distance cascaded down an enormous cliff, sprinkling onto boulders at the end of its fall, and was captured in a pool that meandered along the bank. The branches of enormous willow trees linked arms and hung in a canopy over us in a screen of shadow and light. Fingers on my cheek gently guided my eyes back to his.

"I'm Cerys," he said. "I was hoping you would find your way here again." Stunned by the prickling sensation still running over my skin, I struggled to find my voice.

"I'm Dr. Sa—" I began.

"Sara. Yes, I know," he interrupted, eyes searching mine.

*Why should I be surprised? Everyone else has known who I am.*

"What did you mean by finding my way here 'again'? I haven't been here before now."

The corner of his mouth turned up and he blinked once. "You have, and many times. You don't remember, but it will all come back to you. Come. I have something to show you and explain in a short time."

He let go of my hand and turned, forging a path across patches of dirt and grassy terrain.

"I thought time wasn't a factor here," I said as I followed behind him.

He glanced back. "It isn't when considering development and practice. However, your time here is getting shorter by the moment. This is why there is an urgency to move forward."

*That's a relief.* "You mean I will be going home, right?"

"Yes. But first there is business to attend to."

*Business? In a forest?*

I glanced upward. The sky was now as brightly lit as if the sun was out, beaming somewhere. Missing were the echoes of nature—the sounds of birds, the rustling of leaves from a gentle breeze. The faint trickle of the waterfall was the only sound that broke the silence, along with our footsteps. Even the air was still. And I wondered, if I really listened, could I hear a feather floating on whatever current moved, that was, if birds did exist in Ardan? The smell of the air was clean. Not like after a fresh rain but instead like purified water, ionized. Without the sounds of nature, it was a noticeably quieter environment and it felt as though something was indeed missing without them. It was also a reminder that everything was not as it was trying to be portrayed, not like the world I knew. Not like, and I hesitated, Earth.

My attention was directed away from the details of the environment to the intense feeling coming from Cerys and an even stranger sensation that I knew him. I didn't know how exactly, only that I did. Nothing was plainly obvious and it bothered me to the core of my being.

A matter of minutes passed as we made our way through the lush landscape and stopped at an area where a group of larger rocks, some carpeted with vibrant and muted shades of green moss, rested. One massive willow tree hung its shadow over two of the largest of the stones. A warm, tingling sensation ran down my neck and across my shoulders again. I lifted my eyes to Cerys. With the slight wave of a hand, he invited me to sit and I did.

The gentleness in spite of strength so evident in his face made me feel completely under his power. I flashed a quick smile as he caught and held my gaze. The intensity in his stare should have made me uncomfortable but it didn't. Instead, it drew me in that much more. How was it that I could be having such strong sensations, feelings of love, a yearning almost, without knowing who he was? Did those emotions belong to me or was I sensing his emotions? I didn't know and I damn well wanted to.

"Close your eyes," he said in a low, soothing voice. He held both of my hands in his as I followed his request without question, as though I were a child putting complete faith in a stranger. *Why would I do that?* But I couldn't stop. At his request, I saw myself holding a circle of light, with no defined edge, in the center of both palms. The light then opened up and surrounded me as if it were a cocoon I walked in. "This light is yours. It's your strength and a healing power that you can bring to others. It is a light not visible in your physical world except to those who can see auras. However, even those who cannot see can sense its presence, something they might define as different about you." I thought for a moment I might be dreaming, except that I could still feel his hands, warm and gentle, enclosed around mine.

"What does it mean, that I am a healer?" The only thing I had ever known of anyone carrying light was found in a few readings I had come across in a search to understand my own abilities to hear the thoughts of others and feel their emotions. But that search was unproductive and a very long time ago. Only one book made a reference to the idea that individuals who could heal were believed to be those who carried light. I had dismissed the notion at the time and never gave it another consideration.

"Not exactly," he said. "It's a power you carry to bring light to those who have chosen to see the truth of all things. Many walk through their lives in darkness, by carrying insecurity or fears of the unknown. These fears hold them down from progressing beyond and advancing to a more enlightened place or, as some might describe, freedom from their pain. Your ability to feel another's emotion gives you insight into the truths they carry. And for you, this light protects you."

"Why do you show me this?" I asked, blinking open my eyes.

"To help you understand. Maybe to help you remember why you chose this path." My eyes dropped to our hands.

Cerys asked me to keep my eyes closed. As he continued to explain, I began to see other pictures of people crying from the emotional pain they suffered, whatever the cause. Tears welled under closed eyelids for them. Fear rose to the brink of screaming, while worry settled over it, numbing my other senses as I felt the emotions from the images as though they belonged to me.

The sensation brought the memories I'd carefully hidden for the last twenty-three years to the forefront. My early childhood experiences had already provided enough opportunity to experience emotional struggle directly. I'd been neglected by my divorced mother and forgotten by my father, only to be given up for adoption at the age of eight, soon after the school learned I was left at home unattended for an extended period of time. My mother wanted to travel more with her new boyfriend and to see to her own needs without a thought for those of her child.

The transition to my new family had been no easy task, either, despite the wealth that came with it. Mary Ann Forrester was warm and receptive from the moment I met her in the cold, stark meeting room of the adoption agency. For her husband, Robert, it was as though I was a new puppy he was bringing home. Even now, I remembered the smile he pasted on his face while the distance between us felt miles wide as we sized each other up. I suspected if things didn't work out, he felt he had the option to bring me back. I held firm to that fact as the reason we had never bonded. Despite the lack of closeness, we always respected one another. Unlike Robert, Mary Ann and I had grown close immediately, with my need for a mother and her overwhelming desire to have a daughter. I sensed her love the moment I saw her and imagined being read to under the comfort of soft, warm blankets, held close by caring arms.

I learned later she had suffered loss as she tried to have children of her own and felt the disappointment from Robert. He never trusted a surrogate. He was good to me, in any case, providing for me in ways I otherwise could only have imagined. Yet I never accepted a gift without feeling a twinge of guilt or thoughts of possible disappointment. Still, there were a few good memories with him, especially those where he included me in his fascination with cars.

The reflection of memory brought me back to Cerys. I failed to see what benefit there was in showing me the pain of others or my own. A stroke of his thumb over mine sent another tingle racing up my arm.

"I'm not responsible for the choices made by others," I said, eyes still closed. "I'm available in my profession if they seek help. That's all. Why are you showing me this?" I opened my eyes to his watchful stare and remembered Eldor's comments. "Do you mean to tell me the choices made by people have opened the path to the Dark Lord, to Tarsamon?"

"Yes. Humanity has stalled in its growth to become a more enlightened and compassionate world."

"Maybe the world needs to hit rock bottom before it gets moving again."

He smiled. "There isn't time to find the bottom, and the price isn't worth the loss."

"I wouldn't know."

"But you do."

I shook my head. "Sorry, I really don't."

I felt a strong connection to him, like no other person I'd ever known before, but why couldn't I identify it?

*His eyes.*

"I know you. You're the man I saw when I first arrived, aren't you?" The color of his eyes was different, his features more distinct. How had he changed his appearance like that?

"Yes. But you're confused. Our meeting, your return to Ardan, is not all there is between us."

"What?"

He was right. Confusion was setting in and quickly. The overwhelming sensation of knowing him, strong feelings of connection with no root, and the inability to grasp the enormity of the location I was in joined with a desperate need to get home. I felt myself beginning to panic. Inside my head, a steel wall went up, blocking everything out. *Survival.* My breath began to move in and out faster as my heart raced to keep up. I just couldn't hold on to my patience and try to reason anymore. I'd had enough of this place and now the unexplainable strong sensations between us. I pulled my hands from his.

"I can't take this place anymore," I said louder than I intended. "The questions. The answers that sound like riddles. It's enough!"

"Sara."

I bolted from the rock with the feeling I was running for my life, fighting to get back to it.

This time the path ahead was clear in the streaming light of day. I set a direct course back to the tunnel I had come through, tracing the same steps Cerys and I had taken. I blew past the sweeping willow branches, glancing once behind me. He wasn't there. *Good.* As I turned my head back, the tip of a low-hanging branch etched across my cheek. The sting of it was followed by a trickle of warmth against cool, damp skin. I ran until I was out of breath, stopping to glance once more behind me. Nothing.

I hiked down the bank toward the stream, hidden under the canopy of another willow, hoping to catch my breath before I continued to where I thought I'd seen the tunnel. *Had I missed it?* Bending over the clear, reflective water, I could see the panic staring back at me. *What am I supposed to do?* I cupped my hand and took several sips of the cool water before splashing my face and rinsing the blood from my cheek. The scratch stung again. If this experience wasn't real, it sure as hell felt like it. The air was silent, with only the sound of my breath, still fast but slowing as drops of blood-tinged water fell into the stream.

"Stop running," came the smooth, deep voice from behind me, "from who you are."

I never heard Cerys's footsteps, only felt him behind me. I lifted my head, pushed to stand, and turned to face him. I opened my mouth to speak but the words caught in my throat. I glanced in the direction I'd been running and returned my attention to his stare. He was only a couple of steps from me. I gauged the possibility of escape again, but something kept me planted firmly in place, as if my feet had rooted to the bank.

"None of this is clear to me. Do you understand?" The tears were coming, and I couldn't stop them this time. I fell to my knees, burying my face in my hands. Fear and frustration poured out of me. I felt a hand on my shoulder and pulled away.

"What is this place? What's happening?" I cried.

"You're shifting away from the physical nature you have known."

"God." I sniffed. "Is there a God? I need to understand." I gulped air in short, quick catches.

"Just breathe," he said quietly.

*Am I dead? I can't need to breathe if I am.* I didn't know what to do except tremble. I lifted my head and gazed up at him. His eyes softened. My head felt lighter as the world behind him started to spin. His appearance faded behind a sea of black closing out my vision.

In the darkness, an image formed of several important figures, sitting around a large oval table. The voices were muffled, their expressions stern, indicating perhaps some sort of disagreement.

"It's time to engage her." One voice could be heard above the others. "We cannot wait any longer to initiate the mission." A man with very long, sleek hair the color of driftwood and large, dark eyes was speaking. "I should not have to remind you that the dark forces are moving to enter that world."

"If we wake her too soon, she may be overcome with shock. Her awakening must be handled carefully." Another voice, this time calmer, had spoken. But I couldn't see who it was. "The last warrior has been sent. He is already aware of her location and will handle the shift from her world appropriately."

"Sara, wake up." It was the calming voice I'd heard moments before I'd seen darkness. I didn't want to open my eyes for fear that more of the same panic might return. His hand stroked over the top of my head and down my hair. I opened my eyes and glanced around without moving my head. I was still resting on the bank near the stream, cradled into one side of Cerys's arm.

"Don't be frightened," he said as my eyes met his. The warmth of his body soothed me in a strange and unexplainable way, and the sensation of love returned. I moved to sit up, still feeling light-headed.

"I need answers," I said. "How do I know you?"

"All in good time."

"No. Now," I pressed. He studied me with concerned eyes. "You are being awakened to your true identity."

"Which is?"

"The leader of a powerful alliance. I can't say any more."

"Ha. I have lost my mind." I sat up, swaying slightly. His gaze didn't shift, nor did his concentration.

"You may feel that way. But as I've said before, you're in your right mind."

"No, no. I'm a psychiatrist with a list of patients a mile long. I live in the suburbs of New York. Not a forest. I came from a screwed-up family and landed with a caring one that gave me every opportunity to succeed, and I have. I can play piano. I speak three other languages, not fluently, but I manage well enough. And yet none of this"—I splayed open palms—"rings a single bell."

"Yes, that's the life you've chosen. But it's not your true identity as a spiritual being."

"Okay," I said, inhaling a deep breath. "Go ahead and explain what you can. But first tell me how I know you." With the explosion of emotion out of the way, my mind had cleared enough to allow new information to be digested.

"I'll remind you later," he said. Taking my hands in his, he sent a new wave of tingles up my arms. "You must first understand what is occurring in your world that has caused you to be activated for this mission."

*Activated?*

"Fear is intended to promote learning for an individual in your world. But if one doesn't seek to learn from their fear, it manifests in different forms of pain and evil. This pain resonates throughout humankind, passed on from one person to another and so on."

"Isn't that the intention of whoever created the world?"

"In a sense, yes, to allow light or clarity to the darker areas of the conscience. But the balance has become too far weighted on the side of darkness, blinding individuals from embracing truth and preventing humanity from moving to the next level of being. They can't grow in understanding and compassion for each other."

"And that has something to do with me?"

*More than you know.* I heard the thought, but it wasn't mine. "With a path open for the Dark Lord, his intention is to consume it by killing off humanity, using its fear as a means of destruction. If he succeeds, he will become stronger than the light that exists in the world, extinguishing all illuminating sources, including your own, Sara."

"What am I supposed to do about it? Hell, I'm not even completely convinced this isn't all nothing more than a very vivid dream." I closed my eyes and took in another deep breath.

The very idea that I must be part of a calling to prevent some evil entity or darkness from building a shadow over my world and consuming it was unfathomable. I almost laughed at the absurdity of the thought. All I wanted was to get home, back to my comfortable life.

I opened my eyes to see his head angled down, staring at my hands resting in his, strong and gentle. With a deeper urgency, I wanted to know why I had come, what was expected of me. "All in good time," he'd said. I paused, suddenly aware Cerys was listening to my every thought.

"You must bring the light back to your world for humanity and set the balance between good and evil. You are chosen to fulfill this destiny. In order to accomplish this great task, you will be aided by several guides in Ardan and companions on Earth. You must find the three keys of enlightenment, carefully hidden from Tarsamon. Humankind is too drawn down by fear and negativity for the light to build between each person, as was intended. Your intervention is required to save your world."

"There must be some mistake, I'm sure. Why was I chosen? I'm no savior. The task I believe you are asking of me, of anyone, seems impossible."

"You aren't anyone," he said, imparting patience into his words. "But you are the only soul who is gifted with the ability to hold the power of the keys and who is also pure of heart." There was definitely some mistake. "Your memory may not be present just yet, but the knowledge remains as a guide to you and the companions who will aid you."

*Companions? What companions? Aria?*

"If, and I mean if I take this mission, if it's real, where or what are these keys you speak of?"

"There are symbols that will lead you to them. They have been left by the Soltari, a powerful entity that, in planning the development of your world, has provided a safe measure to assist the pure of heart with one last opportunity to prevent darkness from consuming the energy of Earth." He paused, scanning my face for understanding beyond the bewilderment I was sure was plastered across it. "Don't worry, you're guided. All that you require will be provided on the mission."

*Well, I hope so or the world as I know it is doomed.* I certainly wasn't confident in my abilities to handle the insurmountable task just heaped upon me and a few unknown companions.

"And if I refuse?"

"Then your world is given over to the Dark Lord and his forces. And all life as you have known it comes to an end."

I shook my head in disbelief and glanced up at him. My hands rested in his, unwilling to break free of his grasp.

"Please, close your eyes once more," he said.

As I did, flashes of memory blinked into my vision, playing in sequence. The pictures were so brief I might have second-guessed what I'd seen if it hadn't been for the feelings that were attached at the moment I saw them. The energy of the man who now held my hands was the same as those in each image. And the woman, could it really have been me? Every bone in my body said it was.

The first image was of us running horses up the slope of a grassy landscape containing huge and ancient-looking stones. I felt the sun on my face and the brisk air of early spring brush over my nose and cheeks as we rode. There was laughter, as I clicked my heels against the horse's side and bolted past him. The location was unfamiliar to me, but in another country or time perhaps. And yet in another vision, I was staring into his eyes while he held me to him. My hands extended over his shoulders, while my fingers reached up and stroked the nape of his neck. Behind him, I could see the warm glow of candlelight everywhere and stained-glass windows in hues of purple, blue, and green. Pictures etched into them I could not quite make out. My skin turned to gooseflesh and his hands squeezed gently around mine.

"You are, were—" I whispered. A gasp of breath and further words escaped me. I was wearing a simple ivory gown that was, at best guess, made of satin. I recognized myself in the vision, felt the feelings as though they were from my memory, but where? When? My eyes flew open to see the corners of his closed lips turning upward into a slow smile. His eyes were drawing me in once again. He stood then and, with one hand in mine, lifted me to face him, never breaking his gaze. We had been partners in another time, another life, in which I had loved him so deeply that the feeling remained even now between us, never really lost, just forgotten.

He let go of my hand and brought both of his to the top of my head and let them glide down over my hair as he cupped my face. His lips, soft against mine, lingered like someone who had been away for too long and had missed the delicate sensation of skin upon skin. One hand moved behind me and remained on the small of my back, gently urging me closer to him. I could feel the warmth of his body pressed against mine. *This can't be happening. I must be dreaming.* Never had I recalled a dream with emotions as strong as the arms that embraced me and as vivid as the hand at my back.

Tenderness. A feeling I had missed in my current lifetime was expressed in the gentle touch of his lips as he began searching along the outline of my jaw and ended in a single deep kiss at my lips. A warm sensation began to grow from the center of my being, rising to my chest and radiating heat like the desert sand in the middle of summer. A tear fell from the corner of my eye, then another, at the rush of sensations that poured over me, like a wave crashing to shore. Surprised by my response, I quickly brushed the wetness away. It took a great deal to ever move me to such depths of emotion. I could count the number of times it had happened on one hand. Yet I could not ignore the love that had just been reintroduced, rising to the surface and falling over the edge. I felt so entirely…his. And for a moment, I didn't care if I found my way back to my real life. Whatever this was, it was certainly not forgettable again. He'd been my love. I was certain. Yet somehow in this place, we'd found each other again.

"Why have you come? What happened to us?" I asked, easing backward.

"We live in different times, different worlds. It is a brave and difficult task ahead and I have come to help you." I felt as though my mind and heart were turning somersaults to process the information against reality with the emotions that were undeniable.

"Help me? How? You're a vision. Right? I mean, I saw you fade into the trees." But I'd felt his hands covering mine, and the kiss. That had been no illusion.

"Am I?"

I shook my head.

*God, not now.* The sensation that it was time to leave pulled at me, and my heart began to sink at the realization that I had to go. He gently released his hand from my lower back. Cerys wiped a lingering tear from my cheek with his thumb as he gazed over my face.

"You must go now. We'll see each other again," he said.

For the first time, I felt a weakness in my body and the fight against the pull to leave.

# 5

As I exited the tunnel of light back to the forest, I found myself in the presence of a few individuals, one of which was Aria.

"Sara?" a tall, dark-haired man asked.

"Yes," I replied.

He smiled as Aria stepped closer. "This is Juno and Elise," she said. "They are allies in the mission ahead."

"My companions," I said, remembering Cerys's message. I didn't know whether to welcome them or apologize that they, too, were burdened with the insurmountable task ahead.

"You remember us?" Juno asked.

"Sorry, no. Should I?"

He laughed lightly. "I suppose not. But maybe in time."

Juno was the tallest of the four of us. His hair was jet-black, cropped short, and spiked on top. His eyes were cat-like with a deep brown color and intensity, alert to every detail. He studied my appearance, sizing me up for my strength and ability.

Standing beside Juno, Elise appeared fragile with long, fine bones emphasizing a lean, fit body. Her thick, dark hair, olive skin, and full lips gave her an exotic appearance. Long black lashes framed soft brown pools. Together, she and Juno looked like the perfect match, straight out of a travel catalog to the Bahamas.

Elise's brow shot up and she mouthed, "Never," hearing my thought.

"Let's go. We need to find the Professors," Juno said.

*Professors? And to think I felt so alone when I arrived.*

While we hiked to the next location, I discovered the others had been here longer than I. With the exception of Aria, who couldn't remember how she first arrived in Ardan, they had entered by way of an accident. Juno was in the military, Special Forces, and had taken friendly fire that left him with a head wound. Elise considered her entrance more of a mistake, but one that was "meant to be." Her ex-boyfriend had gone berserk and, in a jealous rage, tried to choke the life out of her one Friday evening after work. Thinking he had, he'd left her for dead on the floor of her quiet little home by the lake. A friend drove out to her house after she didn't answer her phone for girls' night out. Ever since their first experience, each of them had been returning to Ardan to strengthen their skills. They traveled here, they said, when they slept.

*So, I'm asleep and this really is nothing more than an elaborate dream?*

"Things will have to change, now that you've been called to duty," Juno said, interrupting what felt like my first attempt at a logical connection to being in Ardan. "Our focus will have to shift from our work to be entirely on the quest for the keys. But first we need the symbols that will lead us to them."

"Does Tarsamon know Sara has been engaged?" Aria asked.

"He does," I answered. "He found me soon after I arrived, spoke to me."

"That's not possible. Only peaceful energy is allowed in this area of Ardan," she replied.

"Sara must have a connection with him that isn't blocked, even here," Elise said. "No one would claim to be Tarsamon in this place if they weren't."

"That's a problem," Juno said. "If he has the ability to reach you, the mission becomes much more dangerous. You'll have to block him from your thoughts and from being able to see where our quest takes us."

"If I knew how, I would." *Besides, I'm going to be waking up soon and this won't be a problem any longer, for anyone.*

"Hmph. Interesting," was his short reply. With it, words never spoken floated through my mind—*the Last Great Warrior.*

*Whatever that means.*

Our casual conversation as we hiked led me to information about the members on this mission. Like me, as a child each of them had felt the gentle tap on a shoulder or leg while they slept as their names were whispered, all in an attempt by a spirit to wake them and converse. Juno said it had been a reminder of our connection to the spirit world, to help us to not forget our true identities. I had been singled out as "weird" by my birth mother for my abilities, even ridiculed for such *lies*, as she had called them. I'd learned quickly not to speak of the misty-white apparition that appeared at the foot of my bed and tried to ignore my abilities. As I grew older, I had begun learning all about people simply by standing in close proximity to them. If they knew just how much truth I heard in their thoughts or that I could feel their emotions, I wouldn't have had the few friends I did.

My new acquaintances were also closer in the physical world to me than I might've expected. Aria and Elise were from South Carolina, while Juno lived in California. *Some dream. If I ever get last names, I might look them up when I wake.* They discussed what particular abilities they had been strengthening while they were in Ardan. Aria manipulated natural forces of energy. Elise had the ability to see an individual's past and control the emotions of others. "Both fascinating and useful," I'd commented, considering arguments that would be much easier to win by shifting another's emotions. Juno could sense coming events. And similar to me, all were experienced in broadsword.

The forest floor beneath my feet had been replaced with a cobbled path of round stone, and the scenery had shifted from one dreamy environment to another. Ivy hung from the massive stone walls, ancient in appearance, with broken edges and partial standing walls, like that of the Roman temple ruins. We stepped up the tiered stairs that were crumbled in several places, admiring the grand yet deteriorating structure. Inside were additional stone benches flanking a long hallway with great pillars on either side. The hall opened to a grand room with additional tables and benches scattered about, al fresco with a missing roof. I glanced around, taking in the cracks and crevices of the wall, and lifted the tip of my finger to touch the sandy mortar between two stones. *Feels real enough.* I jerked my hand back at the flexing of the wall beneath my touch.

The color of green flitted in the corner of my eye. I angled my head toward an elderly man with a long white beard draped in a robe the color of pine. He appeared through an open doorway close to where I was standing, distracting me from my preoccupation with the moving wall.

"Energy. It's all about energy," the man answered before I had the chance to ask why ordinarily still objects were mobile. "Everything is energy. Matter, you see, is created from a thought, a form of energy not visible but real enough. It may take many of the same thoughts to create a large material object, such as the environment that sur-rounds you now, or in the physical world in which you live.

"The walls that move, the ivy, and the colors you see are created by us, the Professors, as part of this particular environment." He lifted a hand in the direction of a length of the wall, then returned his atten-tion to our group of four. My gaze extended to the height of the stone that still remained. Despite missing key architectural pieces, it was a beautiful building. Before I could wonder about the other Professors he seemed absently referring to, another aged man in similar dress appeared at the doorway. "We hope you find it a peaceful place in which to absorb information. Come and sit, I invite you," he contin-ued. His face reflected the features of an old and wise intellectual with soft lines around the corners of his eyes and mouth.

"You have arrived at a place of theoretical teaching."

*Not what I was hoping for.*

He opened his arms wide in welcome. His long robe moved about the floor as if floating across it, and he paused to pull the bottom edge around a corner as he turned. "Others will be joining us shortly to share information you will need to proceed on the quest."

His demeanor was a cheery sort of fellow, with a certain air of confidence in his presentation. We gathered at two curved stone benches that faced each other, nearly forming a circle but with enough room for passage between them.

"Ah, here we are." The man stood behind Elise and Juno. As I watched him, two more individuals of equal age and similar appearance arrived. All were cloaked in robes, one in black, another in a deep navy blue, and one man, no younger-looking in the face but with a long salt-and-peppered beard, wore a dark red cloak.

*Are these the others he was referring to? Could there be more?* God knew how many guides and whatnot were in this forest.

*Indeed, these are the other Professors I mentioned.* My head snapped toward the old man who had spoken earlier and whose thoughts I'd just heard. *There is a respect shared between those of us who can hear each other, where no thought can be heard if it is intended to be private. Another rule of telepathy is that internal conversation with the self is usually kept quiet in the presence of others.* The Professor continued without moving his lips, the faint color of his eyes peeking through wrinkled lids. *Let's continue, shall we?*

I smiled politely, though more careful about where my mind wandered. I didn't care for the intrusion of thought but understood why he provided the example. It would be too easy for anyone with the ability to listen to thoughts to discover more than I might care for them to know.

The man in navy shifted position, redirecting my attention. "As fear increases among your people, so does anger and intolerance. As you are well aware by now, the Alliance has called you forward to rebalance the energy in your world. To rescue humanity."

"The people in our world have been fighting for centuries. Intolerance is nothing new to them," I said. "What makes this time different from any other?"

The man in the navy cloak pressed his lips into a patient smile and glanced down. He tapped an index finger twice on the stone table.

"What makes this time different is that the level of evil has been too great for too long," he said. His eyes shifted across the group.

"Simply put, there hasn't been enough balance of good to go around. The energy has become stagnant and comfortable, if you will, in the muck of negativity, opening a passage to permanent darkness." He nodded once to another of the cloaked men, who lifted his hands and separated them as if he was pulling open an invisible rolled map in thin air for our viewing. As he did, a faint white cloud of mist revealed three images. Each seemed tangible, as though I could pluck them from the air.

"Pay close attention. Though you see these symbols now, they will be blocked from your memory once you leave Ardan as a means of protection against the Dark Lord or his followers learning of their specific design. Not to worry. The symbols will be provided to you at a time determined appropriate by the Alliance. Protect them at all costs."

"How do they work?" Aria asked.

"When brought together, they will open the initial gateway to the first key of enlightenment, but only if they are held by the Light Carrier."

I studied each of the beautifully engraved images set in stone. The first had symbolic lettering circling the outer rim with three swirled shapes that formed a triangle in the center. An image of a tree and sun lay beneath the swirled design. The second medallion looked to be Mayan, with a symbol of a bat in the center. It, however, contained hieroglyphs around the edge. The third was Egyptian, with an image of an eye that included additional slight markings extending above and below the eye. It was explained by the man in the red cloak that the eye was an Udjat, symbolizing healing and protection.

"But the true power lies with the keys?" Juno asked, stretching his legs out and crossing his ankles.

*How can he be so comfortable? Because you're the only one questioning reality, Sara. They've been here before, remember?*

"Yes. That's why the keys have been hidden in three separate locations," answered the man. "The keys of enlightenment will bring knowledge and understanding to humanity, freeing the world from its negative state of fear."

As the man in navy spoke, he paced between us, hands clasped behind his back. "Evolution of the mind or thought processes is required to be a more enlightened and peaceful society. Fear is what you will battle against and all that comes from those who live by way of a fearful existence, often following the old teachings of your world. You must find the symbols and have in your possession the three keys of enlightenment before the Dark Lord consumes your world." Another quick glance in my direction from the man in navy caused me to shift slightly on the bench. "Proceed carefully and quickly," he explained, moving toward his peers. The symbols still hung in the air for us to study.

"A word of caution to you," continued the Professor. I looked up from a spot in a random stone beside my foot that was drawing me into deep thought. "Those who live in fear cannot destroy the light. The purity within that light is carried by you. You must, however, be careful that they not drain you of the energy you carry and weaken you by their own fear and darkness that can be put upon you. It is the only way you can be defeated."

"How are we to protect ourselves from the weakening effects?" asked Elise.

"First and foremost, don't get caught by the dark forces. If you do, there are several ways to fight. You will each find the one that works best for you in practice here. Some of you already have. Every thought is more powerful than you can imagine."

Questions of creation, human and spiritual, were forcing their way into my mind.

*I must be crazy.*

*Why do you think so?* The thought pierced through my own, and I shot a glance toward the one professor outside my peripheral vision. Without moving his head, his eyes shifted to mine.

*Because the concepts here are not taught in our world. They aren't even considered.*

*There will come a time for that, further into the future and long after you have left Earth. For now, the quest will not wait for your Earth to catch up to the reality you will come to remember. You and the members of your team are part of the select few granted the knowledge of truth to lead you.*

As the professors moved toward the exit in single file, the man in the green cloak paused and rested a hand on my shoulder. I glanced into his weathered, serene face. "Sara, you are well-guided," he said. "All of your questions will be answered, and strength in knowing will be yours. For now, it's a simple matter of trust." He smiled and continued toward the doorway. The black cloak of another Professor whirled as he turned to us.

"As you proceed through this door, more will be revealed that is specific to each of you. You will share similar instruction, experiences, and purpose as necessary, but not always together." With that, each of the men disappeared one by one through the doorway.

We stood and headed toward the door in quiet contemplation before Juno broke the silence. "We should try to stay connected somehow while we're here."

"How can we do that if we are separated on another path?" asked Elise.

"I can sense your energy in any realm."

"What you sense is a sheer..." Her voice dropped off, to Juno's pleasant surprise. He liked taunting her. The flame was burning in her eyes as she glared at him. But something told me it wasn't all fury. And he knew it.

"When we do leave this place, how will I find you?" I asked, providing a distraction from their exchange.

"It's all arranged, isn't it?" Juno pulled his eyes from Elise and cocked a head at Aria, who gave a quick nod.

"What's arranged?" I asked.

"We'll find you in New York, Sara. With the mission engaged, it's our responsibility," Aria answered.

We said our goodbyes and stepped through the same doorway as the Professors, disappearing to the next location.

"Last stop for you," Juno's voice called out.

I turned as he kicked up some of the dead leaves a few paces behind me. "Is this a vision you have? Are you sure? Because I wouldn't want to get my hopes up and be let down."

He smiled. "Yes, a vision, premonition. Whatever suits you. And before you ask, I'm never wrong."

Finally, the first thing I could look forward to since waking up here—leaving.

"Do you see that?" I asked, wondering if my eyes were playing tricks on me. I could swear the trunks of the trees were growing.

"I do." Juno scanned the vast number of trees flanking either side of us. "I can't imagine the purpose."

I pressed my back firmly to the solid trunk of one tree and began to feel as it pushed outward. An odd sensation came over me and I closed my eyes. I felt light-headed, almost drunk. I peeked under my lids, and instead of the expected ground spinning around me, I was soaring above the trunk I'd leaned into. Juno was still where I'd left him when I'd closed my eyes, shooting glances in multiple directions.

"Did you...? How did you just shift into becoming part of that tree?" he asked.

*I don't know*, I replied in thought. *I just leaned against one of them and closed my eyes.* I was swaying with the movement of the branches. *You should try it.*

"I'm no shapeshifter. No way have I ever borrowed the energy of an object to use as my own."

This was the first time I'd felt a breeze in Ardan. Was the reason for it due to the change in location when we stepped through that door? How many possibilities existed?

The bend and sway of long, majestic branches responded to each casual gust that lifted beneath them. Graceful arms swept through the sky, leaning one direction then another as if the tree was a musician under the direction of the conductor, wind. Each leaf that fluttered that much more in the breeze was like a tickle on my arm. And the strength in the enormous trunk and roots that penetrated the ground was an anchor allowing me to rock gently forward and back and yet remain securely bolted to the solid foundation beneath me.

I mingled in their strength until it became gradually quieter and calm, then rested with the tranquility and absolute beauty of the stillness while every current of air settled. I imagined closing my eyes, and as the world closed to the darkness, I found myself standing beside the trunk again, separated from the massive bark.

"I wonder if you can do that with anything," Juno said, picking up a large, jagged stone, one of several scattered across the forest floor. "Here," he said, handing it to me.

"Why would I want to be a stone?" But I lifted it from his extended hand, anyway, held it between both of mine, and closed my eyes. A soft rustling distracted me from the heavy mass. Something was approaching. Juno picked up on it, too.

I tossed the rock to the ground. "C'mon, let's go. We need to keep moving."

"Don't you want to know what it is? Let's wait here."

"I thought you could see coming events."

"Only if it pertains to me or the quest. The gift has its limits."

"If it's here for us, it will find us. I don't want to battle in the trees." I kept walking. "You can stay if you'd like," I said over my shoulder.

Juno hesitated. I stepped up my pace, heading toward a row of trees that should have an open area on the opposite side. The many footsteps that followed grew louder. Angling myself between a few trees, I encountered the open field. Small stones mingled with blades of grass, scattered everywhere. I turned to find Juno now only a couple steps behind me.

"Change of heart?" I asked.

"You ran. No fear, remember?"

"I remember." *Now that you mention it.*

We stood back to back, watching the trees for some sort of sign of what might approach. I felt Juno's hand reach back and touch my forearm, and I turned to see a large gray wolf emerging from the trees.

"I've never seen a wolf in Ardan before," he whispered.

"It's okay, I think. I'm not sensing any negative vibe from him." The great wolf crossed the field in a few strides to stand only a couple of feet from us. He was larger than any wolf I'd ever seen, standing almost four feet high with fur that was yellow-brown and flecked with white. His eyes were the color of burnt sugar.

"We caught the movement of your energy nearby," the wolf said. Juno had formed the thought, *Who is "we"?*, but before he could ask, a pack of seven wolves appeared from the edge of the forest.

"I'm Karshan, leader of the animal kingdom in Ardan."

"I'm Sara and this is Juno."

Karshan's lips pulled back slightly to show a fine set of sharp teeth. "My dear Sara, all of Ardan knows of you and your team. We are allies as you bring light back to your world and have trained to serve in your mission as defenders of that light."

"I'll need all the help I can get."

He nodded once and lifted his muzzle into the air, directing the rest of the pack to follow. I stared after him, awed by his size and the graceful way he moved. Something flickered in the corner of my vision as Karshan left us.

I turned to Juno. "Did you see something, over there?"

"You may have been imagining it."

"Funny. I may be imagining all of it."

"Hardly." Juno smiled as we stepped into the forest.

*Another path. How soon did Juno's vision show me leaving?*

"Think of them as a mode of transportation. They'll automatically take you where you are supposed to go."

"I guess they do," I said. *Where's the one that will take me the hell home?* "This is no Oz," I whispered to myself.

"What was that?" he asked.

"Nothing important."

A few minutes passed. I glanced up and noticed the huts in the trees. Had I come full circle? I didn't think it was possible. Juno had stopped several yards back and was in discussion with individuals who also appeared like elves. As I turned back, I nearly stumbled over a large piece of brush, surprised by Eldor's ability to appear out of nowhere.

"Eldor," I said, releasing a breath as I reached out a hand and grasped at the nearest tree for balance.

"Your time here has come to an end. Remember, I can and will provide you with additional tools as necessary." With that, he left as quickly as he had appeared.

I stood in silence among the trees that hung like overprotective adults. *Am I supposed to walk out of here? Tried and failed.* I glanced back for Juno but he was gone.

No sooner had I asked the question than the trees and brush began to fade from view, causing me to want to grasp anything for security. There was no transition as there had been through the tunnel when I'd met Cerys. Instead, I found myself standing in a large, brightly lit, and empty room with no clue how I was to get back to my life.

"Feel and you can move on," a voice from nowhere said, tempting me.

*Feel what?* Frustration began to set in again. *Just let me go already. Please.*

I turned at the sound of a low growl to see a floating dark image resembling an inkblot hovering a few feet from me. I detected a sensation coming from it that was pure evil. And unlike the three shadows I'd fought earlier, this one wanted to hurt me.

Was this really practice? Could one of Tarsamon's shadows have found a way past the elves to reach me? I moved to draw my sword, but the entity was faster. A scream ripped deep from the center of my chest and pain spiked through my left thigh. There was no blood to justify the searing sensation of metal piercing skin and muscle. But I'd felt it as real as if it had. The effect quickly consumed my mood, changing it from determined focus to anger as I sank to the ground. The black figure hovered above me. I pushed away, trying to remain out of reach of another strike. I couldn't be hurt here. Wasn't that what Aria had said? Or was it that I couldn't die?

I struggled to stand. The weakness took me to the ground again. The pain, dark mood, anger, and fatigue pressed upon me, wearing me down. I hadn't come this far to be defeated. Sweat dripped from my forehead as the pain sliced through me again. *Fight it, Sara.* With every ounce of strength I had left, I bit through the torture in my leg and brought my arm up and swung crosswise. The sword slipped from my hands and slid across the floor as my body grew weaker. I tried to light the ball of fire in one last desperate attempt to save myself and felt my heart begin to sink with defeat as nothing more than sparks lifted into the air. *Resist the negative energy that can weaken me.* The words of the Professors flashed in my memory. I moved toward my sword, with each stretch, every step feeling like slow motion. Every movement heavier than the last. The black cloud shifted and settled in a barrier around me.

*Release fear to free your strength.* At the thought, the room that had no walls shifted from a purely empty and illuminated white space back to the familiar, natural environment. The shroud of black lifted, but I could still feel the traces of ominous presence. The sweat-soaked shirt I wore was plastered to my chest, the beads of effort dripped from my temples, and a heartbeat that was as fast as a frightened rabbit's tried to slow. As I lay on my back gazing upward, I heard the familiar voices of Aria and Elise, but I couldn't see them.

I forced myself to stand, ending up on my knees instead, and called to them. No reply. Shadows moved eerily between the trees as faint whispering grew louder. From a distance, I saw Cerys walking toward me. I stood to meet him and felt my leg protest with a throbbing sensation that sent waves of pain down it. I took one step toward him and fell into the brightest, harshest light I had ever seen, realizing there wasn't any ground on which to stand.

# 6

I began choking, struggling for a breath of my own as the weight of my body felt remarkably heavy and the pain in my leg was as though a thousand knives had found their mark. I tried to speak, but nothing flowed except gags and coughs. Movement was limited to my arms and torso. I squinted through closed eyelids to see a blur of navy-blue color rushing toward me.

"You're okay. Calm down," I heard someone say.

*Easy for you. You're not the one fighting for a breath or against tremendous pain.* Something was in my throat and someone was standing over me with a hand at my face.

"We've got it. She's just trying to breathe," came another voice with a bit of urgency. I blinked several times, trying to see past the thin film covering my eyes. Several people stood around me, all staring. I wanted to yell at them to stop. The heaviness I felt in my body was contributing to more of the agony shooting through me. It clashed with harsh, unwelcoming light and urgent voices.

I was asked to cough once more, and hoping it would help, I did. I felt something slide out of my throat and my own breath come in one quick gasp, comfortable and natural, freeing me from the bonds of the ventilator. My heart was racing from the shock of returning to consciousness and the discomfort. After a few minutes, a man leaned over me.

"Welcome back. You've been missed." A voice as smooth as melted toffee floated into my ear. So far, it was the smallest, most pleasant experience yet. I, however, was only distracted from the pain for an instant and managed enough strength to formulate the only words that mattered.

"The pain, please," I cried out.

"Administer ten milligrams of morphine intravenously, stat. Lorazepam on standby," came the same calm voice in control of this situation.

Within seconds, the throbbing subsided and I settled into myself, trying to make out the faces in the room. My head was swimming in relaxation. Sweat had soaked my hair and was now cooling against my skin. What happened that had landed me in the hospital with such pain and immobilization in my left leg? A memory of a blade cutting through my skin flashed through my mind.

My eyes shifted about the room. A couple of people in scrubs were attending to a machine. Standing beside me was Mary Ann and a man with dark brown hair who must have spoken to me. Must be the attending doctor, I surmised through heavy eyelids. Mary Ann turned away, while someone gently brushed a cool washcloth over my eyes and another person took my vitals. I hated all the attention. And though I wanted to be left alone, I also had questions. They'd have to wait, as questions began flowing to me from the doctor, who had pulled up a seat next to my bed. I eyed him through my drug-induced state, noting perfectly set brown eyes, a long bridge to his nose that fit with the chiseled jaw and high cheekbones on a rectangular face. *Is there an edge I detect beneath that striking appearance?* On second thought, I shouldn't trust my senses since the administration of morphine.

"Can you tell me your name?" he asked. All I wanted to do was sleep, but his questions forced me to focus.

"Sara," I replied in a groggy voice. I tried to swallow and found it difficult. "And if I was missed, why do you ask?" I added with the flash of a tiny smile, hoping to soften the somewhat raspy reply.

"At least she hasn't lost her humor or sarcasm," came a reply from the foot of my bed. *Mary Ann.* And as my eyes dropped to her, I could see tears welling. Her brows were raised in concern or concentration. I couldn't quite tell which.

"Everything is all right, honey." She squeezed my foot gently through the covers. "I knew you were just taking your own sweet time coming back." Mary Ann took a couple steps closer, grasped my hand, and stroked it with the backs of her fingertips.

*Sweet time? How long had I been gone?*

Most of the staff in scrubs had cleared with the exception of one assistant who stood beside the doctor. "Sara, I'm Dr. Scott. Do you feel like answering a few more questions?" It was the calm, controlled voice that spoke again and drew my attention back to him.

"Of course. I'm no trouble. I promise. I have one condition if I may, that you answer a few for me?"

"Agreed." I thought I saw a brief smile escape from the serious expression.

He proceeded to ask all the usual questions to be sure I didn't have amnesia and was in my right mind—if I remembered the woman at my bedside, the name of our current president, what year it was.

"Do you remember what happened to you?" he asked.

"No. I was hoping you could enlighten me to the events that brought me here," I said in as clear a voice as I could muster.

"You remember nothing?" he asked again.

I paused, thinking. I remembered the forest, the energy, the elves, and the wolf pack. My memory was very intact, but if I said anything of the sort, the doctor would be requesting a psychiatric consult for me in short order. *Was that another smile? Why?*

"No, not about how I got here or what that terrible pain in my left thigh that you so kindly eased for me is about." I took a long, deep, relaxing breath in and released it.

"You were in a terrible accident in which another driver ran a red light, slamming into the driver's side of your car. The door was jammed into you and metal twisted. A piece of the door's frame ended up cutting deep into your upper thigh, severing most of the muscle. There appears to be nerve damage. We saved the leg and have been waiting to see what feeling and mobility you have. You've been in a medically induced coma for nearly two weeks. Do you remember any of that or anything prior to the accident?"

*Two weeks? Really? Medically induced meant there had to have been trauma to the brain.* The information was quite a lot to digest being that I had not considered anything of the sort happening to me. I tried to remember but only flashes of getting ready in the morning, fastening my seat belt, and rain were all that came to mind. For some reason, Tyler Mason's face skipped through my head, followed by a sick feeling.

"I recall only a few things prior to the accident but nothing about the crash itself," I explained, giving the doctor the recall of my flashes of memory.

Once Dr. Scott was satisfied that I was completely present with a working memory, I followed instruction for wiggling toes and sensory stimulation using pinpricks, checking to be sure of what receptive nerves existed in my damaged leg.

"I'll be in charge of your care during your stay. If you need any-thing, this is Amanda and she will be taking care of you for the next twelve hours or so." He gestured to the nurse. "Now, what questions may I answer for you before I go?"

"You answered the most important one. But can you tell me when I might be released?" Though I understood the necessity of the hos-pital, I detested being stuck in a bed. I was eager to get back to being mobile, willing the two weeks I'd already spent in bed to provide the leap to a quicker release date.

"You may have forgotten the pain you were in just minutes ago. I'm glad the morphine is doing its job. I don't think you understand the severity of your injury, though. You were fortunate, but you were hurt badly. We'll have to give it some time. I hope you understand." I nodded reluctantly. "I'd like to see if you can move that leg and sched-ule rehab before considering a release." He paused to write some-thing in the chart before handing it to Amanda. "Don't worry, you're all set for pain meds as long as is necessary." His eyes softened with some understanding behind the mask of professionalism.

I couldn't be sure if it was Dr. Scott or the drug, but it was difficult to look away from the beautiful eyes that studied mine as he spoke. His features were strikingly attractive for a doctor who spent hours in a hospital setting. Weren't doctors supposed to be tired from all the rounds and patients to see, charts to note, and the little sleep they received for the incessant time they spent tending to hospital duties? Dr. Scott's face didn't reflect fatigue or a strained life. He was simply beautiful. *What do you know, Sara? You're riding the wave of morphine comfort, free of pain and light as air.* Perhaps my trip to Ardan could be attributed to nothing more than the induced coma. I nodded and thanked him under the ever-increasing weight of my eyelids.

Dr. Scott turned to Mary Ann. "Try not to visit too long. The drug is making her tired and she should sleep while she's able. Hospitals can be quite loud." He and Amanda left the room as Mary Ann walked over to take his place beside me.

She pressed her lips into a firm line and grasped my hand. "How are you feeling, honey?"

"Tired but much better without the pain. How long have you been here?"

"Not long today. I come every day. I'm so happy you are back, darling." Tears began to well again in her eyes. "Robert has been asking about you every day. He's been stuck in England on business and is due back this weekend."

"It's okay. Being that I was unconscious, he might as well finish his business." Mary Ann blinked a few times. "You better not cry. I haven't got the energy to make us both feel better," I said under a pitiful attempt at a smile. "I had quite a dream while I was out. I'll have to share with you later." I wanted to be sure I could remember everything, if I didn't fall asleep first. "Go home and rest. I'll be fine."

"You're sure? Is that what you prefer?" At my nod, she picked her purse up from the chair. "All right. Your friends will want an update, anyhow."

"Would you mind telling them I'm not ready to see visitors just yet?" Better to be seen after I'd recovered, and I knew Mary Ann would understand.

"Of course. Don't worry about any of it," she said, brushing a hand to dismiss the notion. "I'll make up something to throw some of the press off the trail. Damn bloodsuckers have been camped out for the last week."

It was nothing new for the Forrester family to expect press at an event, whether it was one of the lavish charity events or, in this case, a personal medical emergency. The media was keenly interested in any shred of information or a picture of a billionaire's daughter nearly dying. Mary Ann tapped her chin, the evidence of a plan beginning to develop.

"Whatever you think will work." I despised attention. I'd had to accept and adjust to it since being adopted by the Forresters, who were very much in the public arena not only for their wealth but their generosity. Mary Ann was gracious and kind to most anyone. But when it came to protecting family, she was as fierce as any inbred pit bull with an emotional disorder. I found comfort in that and in the thought that I would find some peace to contemplate my recent experience in Ardan, after a little rest first. Mary Ann stared for a moment. Her brow wrinkled over her brown eyes, emphasizing dark circles and creases in the corners. I felt like a caged animal that she didn't want to leave behind.

"Please, go home and rest. You look like you need it more than I do right now. I'll see you tomorrow."

"Okay, you're sure?" she said. I nodded. "I love you. I'll be back early." She turned and took two steps toward the door.

"Oh, wait. Can you please bring me a toothbrush when you come back?" I could feel the pastiness in my mouth that was almost nauseating.

Mary Ann turned toward a cabinet in the room and smiled.

"Of course. Now, let's see. I'm sure there's one in here somewhere," she said, tossing her purse in the chair as she began rummaging through a box of basic hospital toiletries that had been placed in the room. "You even have toothpaste." She gleamed over the box and glanced in my direction. "Hmm. Let me help you before I go." She handed me a plastic cup of water and an empty cup to rinse the toothpaste residue away. I thanked her as she kissed me on the forehead and said goodbye.

Though my frame was thin, my body felt very heavy, and I was stiff from not moving. The desire to turn myself in a different position battled with the need to just close my eyes. I settled on shifting my weight slightly to the side. As I did, I remembered being struck by a dark and evil presence in the same leg, a fight that had seemed so real, causing a strong inclination to look at my thigh under the bandages. I lifted the gown.

The thought of not being able to walk was frightening. Healing might take time, but every patient's ability to do so was different. There was no doubt in my mind I'd be walking again. Being a determined woman, I opted to put the fear and fatigue aside, lifting the bandage enough to see the first two staples before changing my mind. *What's my hurry? There'll be plenty of time to get used to the damage.*

The names and details of Ardan were still fresh in my mind. Ardan… I closed my eyes, attempting to retrieve all of the memories. Gradually, each one came forward, from the misty figure first appearing, then Eldor and Seria, to the Professors and the symbols. Three medallions, but the details of each were unclear. The swishing sound of the door of my room opening blotted out any further recollection.

"How are we doing? Can I get you anything?" Amanda asked. I was jolted out of deep thought.

"Everything is fine, thanks. I think I'm just going to sleep."

Though annoyed by the interruption, I knew it was good to have allies in the hospital. They made the stay a little nicer. Telling Amanda I was going to rest would at least provide a bit of uninterrupted time to reflect, unless sleep came first.

"You'll get plenty of rest. Dr. Scott has another dose of morphine scheduled for you in a few hours. It's almost the dinner hour. Soft foods are on the menu tonight. Are you interested?" She raised an eyebrow in my direction.

"You probably don't get many takers, given the option." She wrinkled her nose and shook her head. "I think I'll pass tonight and shoot for breakfast," I said, forcing a smile at the thought of soft hospital food and the potential for runny eggs.

"That's fine. We have nutrients going into your IV, but the more progress you make, including swallowing, the faster you'll move out of here."

"Got it."

"Buzz if you need me," she said, pulling the door closed behind her.

The sun was setting outside my window. I could see it through the cracks in the blinds that someone had tilted, flaunting vibrant colors of deep orange scattered with a sweep of purple and blue across the early evening sky. I had missed that and the moon. And of course, Cerys.

Beautiful Cerys. My heart sank. I wanted to hear him again, have him touch my hands and show me his visions. I could still feel his lips on mine, even as the memory was fading, replaced with the realization that I'd become a sap in two short weeks. Caving to emotion was so unlike me. But I'd done so in that moment with him. And here I was, missing a ghost. Pathetic. What was it he'd said about the mission? My eyes began to close now in longer increments. I clung to every word I could remember, until I succumbed to the weight of my eyelids and the welcome of a drug-induced rest, minus the dark shadows.

I was awakened early the next morning as the resident began his rounds in my room. It was still dark outside my window, and the clock on the wall showed four thirty a.m. I decided I'd spend as little time in the hospital as possible and planned to order the detestable soft food required to get me to the next phase of leaving. I didn't know where it had come from, but a renewed sense of determination and focus filled my body this morning instead of the searing pain. Something had shifted since yesterday, leading me to believe what I'd experienced in Ardan was a real purpose I needed to fulfill and not just a dream. Still, I didn't yet understand how that would translate in this physical world. Lying in bed wasn't going to get me to that purpose. Dozing once the resident doctor left, I accepted another two hours of sleep before the door of my room swung open and Dr. Scott came in for his morning rounds.

"How are you this morning, Sara? Less pain?" His eyes searched mine, trying to read my expression. I'd doubted my recollection of his attractive features and smooth voice shortly after he'd left, chalking it up to the effects of morphine. But I had been without a dose since midnight. He was indeed as strikingly handsome as he'd first appeared. The light blue collar of his shirt and darker blue top of his tie extending above the white coat set off the hint of color, copper or gold, in his brown eyes I hadn't noticed yesterday.

"Much less, thank you. I'm hoping you're here to tell me it's time to go," I said optimistically, not breaking his gaze.

The left corner of his mouth turned up in a half smile as he looked down at his notes. "You're in such a hurry," he said. *I can't blame you. You would be much safer under my protection than in this hospital.*

"Excuse me?" I heard his words about being in a hurry, but did I actually hear him say I would be safer with him? *No, you didn't because he didn't say that.*

"I said you're in such a hurry." His radiant eyes came back to mine.

"I've, uh, never been a sedentary person," I stumbled.

"You just woke from a two-week nap yesterday. You might want to give yourself a little time."

*Oh, yes, time. That impediment that is keeping me stuck.* "I suppose there is little choice in the compromise for recovery."

He flashed another smile and shifted his attention to my leg. "Let's take a look at this," he said, gently lifting the hospital gown to reveal the heavy bandage around my thigh. He reached for the scissors from a tray that had been placed in the room. I watched as long fingers and smooth, strong hands slipped into sterile gloves and proceeded to work meticulously at freeing the bandage. I shifted my eyes away, remembering I didn't want to see. And yet out of curiosity, I started peering at the gash. Free of the bandage, I could see how bad the wound was with all the staples in place. A colorful array of purple and red clustered near the immediate wound, while older bruising in shades of green and yellow lingered over the skin several inches from the staples.

"Good. This is healing quite well and quickly," he said. I gazed at it another moment and then turned away, trying to nullify the effects creeping into my throat. Having an MD behind my name had strengthened an already tough skin by providing a strong stomach for most things. I'd watched surgeries in the past, even assisted with a couple. It was one thing to see injury or trauma to a patient, to work on a cadaver in med school. But to see the gash on my own leg was, well, nauseating. And the thought of the size of the scar? I didn't even want to consider it.

"We'll have to leave the staples in for a couple more days, but you won't need this heavy bandage. Let's wrap it in a gauze cover and then we'll put a supportive wrap on it when we begin movement. The wound is healing very well. You're lucky it wasn't broken." He tapped a finger on either side of the staples. "Since it has been a full two weeks, I think you can try to stand, with assistance, of course." His eyes lifted from the staples to my face. "I'll write the order for a walker to be sent down. We'll start very slow with some rehab to get you going first. Does that help satisfy your desire for leaving?"

"Rehab sounds exactly like what I had in mind."

I brushed a few tears away that had formed at the sight of the gash with a quick swipe of a finger before they were seen.

Dr. Scott looked up from further inspection and wrinkled a brow. *Did I miss a tear?* Mary Ann had told me many times that my face displayed every emotion, like a pond she could see straight to the bottom of.

"Don't feel too bad. The skin will stretch so the scar won't seem so deep and they make very good creams now that help hide scarring. I expect it to look nearly normal in about a year." His eyes locked on mine, as if he was still searching for something. I could only guess he was looking to see if what he said brought any relief.

"That's good news. Thank you."

"Someone will be in today to get you out of this bed." His tone was still so smooth, and I wondered what it might be like to listen for hours to him giving some boring educational lecture to a group of colleagues. Would I tire of it or be pleased to listen to him drone on? I knew the answer.

"Okay," I nodded. He gave my ankle a reassuring gentle squeeze and turned to leave.

I was sure his female patients forgot their ills and their names the moment he entered their rooms. He didn't carry the ego that many doctors often had, only enhancing his attractiveness. His manner was extremely compassionate and not hurried, a rare quality in a doctor. And from my limited experience of his bedside manner, he had chosen his profession well.

Before my thoughts could return to the awful laceration, Mary Ann peeked in and shoved the door open. A cheery wash of color filled one of her hands. She set the vase of fresh cut flowers beside my bed. As beautiful as they were, I never understood how anyone could enjoy watching something die over a few days and get joy from it. I suddenly wished I were viewing them from her enormous garden.

"Good morning," she said. Her elated, singsong tone joined the clatter of a breakfast cart passing outside the door, shattering the quiet of early morning and signaling another busy day in the hospital. "The nurse said I could bring these for you."

I smiled at her happiness. "You shouldn't have brought flowers. I'm not going to be here that long," I said.

"Don't be silly. You need something to brighten this drab room. Anyway, these are from my garden and I thought they might cheer you up, no matter how long you're here. How are you this morning? I saw Dr. Scott leaving. He said the wound is healing well."

Amanda interrupted us just then with a bucket containing gauze and tape to cover the exposed and unsightly wound.

"Oh, can I see it?" Mary Ann asked. She looked from me to Amanda.

"Are you sure? It's rough, especially this early in the morning," I said.

"As long as it's all right with you," Amanda said, glancing at me.

I shrugged my shoulders. "Sure, if you're up for it. Don't say I didn't warn you." Mary Ann's bottom lip fell at first glance.

"The lovely doctor said it would look much better in about a year." Mary Ann's face twisted. Her gaze shifted back to my face and the wrinkled face gave way to a determined expression.

"We're already going after the guy who hit you and his insurance company. Fortunately, he had insurance. Turns out he had been texting and says his light was green." She rolled her eyes. "A half-dozen witnesses came forward stating otherwise. My God, Sara, you could've been killed. The investigators say the guy never hit the brake or anything."

"But I wasn't killed. Still, he should be paying attention before he does kill someone. Maybe if he has to pay, the message will sink in."

After my leg was bandaged and Mary Ann and I were alone, she was eager to know what I had to share after being asleep for two weeks. It surprised me that she asked. I didn't remember mentioning anything about the visit I'd taken to Ardan. The lapse of memory was likely due to the morphine.

"What did I say?" I asked.

"Nothing yet. I've heard many people in an induced state have vivid recollections. So, tell me, did you have anything like that?"

"Oh, well, it was really nothing more than a good dream, I suppose, with wolves and elves." Her eyes were large with interest and she leaned into me, waiting for more. "Do you really care about a dream?"

"If it's important to you, I'd like to hear it." She paused. "I've heard that people who are in comas can hear the people around them, you know, as if they were floating around in the room or something. Could you see or hear us?"

"No, nothing like that. Besides, I probably wouldn't want to hear how you would be demanding that the hospital staff do more for me, even pulling your own carefully chosen doctors for a second opinion." I laughed a little at the thought of her doing just that, while also hoping to redirect her from the subject of my so-called dream.

She leaned back into the chair and tucked a lock of soft brown mid-length hair behind an ear. The ends caught in the fold of a bold printed scarf draped over a cream-colored knit top. "Of course I would have done that, but the team that you have had has been extremely good, especially Dr. Scott."

"What do you mean, especially Dr. Scott?" I asked, relieved the deflection worked.

"Sweetheart, you know I've done volunteer work in this very hospital, right?"

"Of course."

"That experience provided an opportunity to work with the follow-up and patient-care procedures the hospital staff uses. I've noticed your doctor has been particularly attentive. I think he's visited you more often than any other patient on this floor." Her eyebrows lifted.

"I don't want to know how you obtained that information since you haven't been part of the volunteer team here for, what, two years or so?" *Had she bribed someone?* Mary Ann shrugged a shoulder and kept her expression blank. "If you're suggesting there is more interest than just a doctor-patient relationship, that is utterly ridiculous. He's my attending doctor. Nothing more. For God's sake, I wasn't even able to talk. Maybe I was just in worse shape than his other patients and that's why there were more visits. Honestly, you are a hopeless romantic." She smiled at the notion. "In fact, it's more likely that he wanted to be sure you didn't lodge any complaints. And I'm certain you checked his credentials the day I arrived." She angled her head and smiled. "Of course you did." I shook my head, glanced toward the window and back to her. "I've got a new project for you—getting me out of here."

"I've already started, by getting you into the best rehab facility so you don't have to stay here. But you'll have to do your best to impress the therapist when she comes to visit today."

"I promise."

We talked for about an hour longer about current events in the world and what business Robert, my adoptive father, had been working on before I was moved to another room.

I didn't have much more thought of Ardan during the day, but that night I dreamed in a deep sleep. I was standing in a field, the same one where I'd met Karshan, the enormous gray wolf. Someone was walking toward me. I reached for my sword but it was gone. With no protection, all I could do was wait. As the image came into focus, I could see it transformed from a ghostly transparency to the figure of a man I quickly recognized as Cerys.

"Am I dreaming you?" I could feel the rate of my heart increasing at first sight of him. It was unlike me to react like that to anyone. Ever.

"I'm not a dream. Remember, the parallel universe allows travel between worlds." His voice drew me in deeper with the sound of each syllable. "What applies here can apply there, with limitations of time and space found in the physical world. I have come to remind you to not forget the teachings and experience you received. Healing is taking time, but do not lose sight of the task. The experience was and still remains quite real."

He reached a hand toward my left thigh. A bright white light appeared that stretched the length of his hand as he placed it on the wound. I watched the light sink into my skin and remain glowing just beneath the surface, highlighting the red laceration and staples. His eyes met mine. "Remember your mission to find the symbols." He paused and lifted a hand to my temple. His fingertips stroked down my cheek to my chin. "You are so loved." And I knew I couldn't forget. I had to follow the path in my world to pursue the symbols. But where was it?

"I won't forget." The words cracked as I spoke them. I woke instantly. The field was gone, replaced by the dimly lit hospital room. Hanging on the wall in front of me, the clock read three a.m. sharp. A sensation passed through me that someone was standing outside my door. I turned my head to see the remnants of a shadow pass quickly on the other side of the window, leaving me alone.

# 7

"You're quite the healer," I recalled Dr. Scott saying on my last day at the hospital. His fingers glided over the scar that had already formed as he pressed gently on either side. "I haven't seen anyone recover from such a traumatic injury so soon." I flashed a quick smile and saw something behind the gaze that caused my breath to catch. I hadn't noticed the intensity before, but maybe I hadn't been looking.

"Well, that will make my physical therapist's job that much easier," I said. "Besides, there's a life I need to get back to."

The deep injury had healed with so much speed it left me wondering. Did the recent dream with Cerys have anything to do with it? Doubtful. Whatever the reason for the quick recovery, I was grateful to be back in the comfort of my own home over the past few days. In the last month that it took me to regain full mobility and after much consideration, a sabbatical from my practice was at the forefront of my thoughts. I took only a few appointments in the last week and made the decision to investigate the medallions, though I had no idea where to start. I'd had several vivid dreams with messages and reminders to not forget my visit. Even if I'd wanted to, the dreams wouldn't allow me to abandon the task of finding them. Besides, no one would question time away from work, not this soon after such a severe accident. My thoughts returned to my last visit with Dr. Scott.

He'd called to see how my progress was going and had even visited once during the rehab sessions, mingling a few jokes with a bit of discussion about the work to strengthen my leg. While follow-up care was completely out of the norm for an ER doctor, it had felt strangely comfortable, as though we'd been longtime friends. And yet I knew so little about him. He was just three years older than my thirty-one and had only been in practice a few years. He hadn't been converted to the mechanical-type physician that buried a personality behind the lifeless drudgery of the job.

Those few encounters had introduced me to his witty and considerate nature. I naturally assumed he must have someone he was serious about with his attractive features and warm personality, so that when he asked me to dinner, there was a surprising weakness in my legs not attributed to any recovery. He was drawing me in a little more each time I saw him, asking me to call him by his first name instead of the more formal Dr. Scott.

"No more formality please," he'd said early on. "Would you do me the honor of celebrating the end of your recovery by having dinner with me?" he later asked.

"I'd like that." This time I met the penetrating stare that held me captive in those deep brown eyes flecked with gold.

The ringing of my phone jolted me back from my thoughts of Kevin and that last visit with him. I glanced at the time on my laptop. Ten thirty p.m. *Who's calling me this late?* The name Tyler Mason flashed in a separate window on the screen. My heart sank. I felt no connection to Tyler, especially since the accident. Thoughts of him occurred only when he did call. I debated letting voicemail pick up, but I'd already put off talking with him, saying I was too busy in rehab and helping Mary Ann plan the next charity event. I had to face him sooner or later to have the inevitable conversation about ending our relationship, something I dreaded because I knew how he would react. Tyler was a highly emotional man, showing little if any self-control, especially when it came to him not getting his way.

"Hello?" I said in my best tired voice.

"Hey, I finally caught you. Where have you been?" he asked. "I stopped by, but your security guard said you were out."

Tyler had called my cell phone a few times over the past week but never left a message. At the time of his call, I'd been occupied, never remembering or desiring to call back.

"I've picked up a few more days working at the crisis center and I just finished therapy last week." It was true. *Oh, crap. Why did I have to mention stopping therapy?* I balled my fingers into a fist and winced.

"Yeah, I heard about that. Your father has been keeping me posted on your progress. So, how are you feeling?"

The only thing I detested more than small talk was Robert sharing anything about me with Tyler. The relationship was one of convenience Robert wanted for financial reasons more than happiness, or so it seemed. It had been increasingly difficult to see Tyler since my accident, not only because of the lack of time I had but more because I was not interested in making time for him anymore. It was a chronic problem in any relationship I had and why I'd chosen never to commit to anyone.

Tyler's expression of self-importance during a dinner shortly after I'd been released from the hospital was too much, talking about himself and the latest cases the law firm had just handed him, and how big the clients were that the firm now trusted him with. He absorbed every conversation. While I was happy for his success, he was just plain arrogant, which spelled i-n-s-e-c-u-r-e in my book. It was over scallops and linguine I'd decided to talk with Robert and Mary Ann and tell them how I felt. There just hadn't been time to attend to those particular details.

"I'm feeling better all the time. Stronger, you know?" I could sense he wanted to ask me something and I jumped in before he could. "I'm considering a few projects at the crisis center that need a little attention," I said. It was true, but it was also true that I had recently been invited to a private meeting related to the mission and was not at liberty to discuss the details with anyone, especially Tyler. I settled on a partial truth being better than complete dishonesty.

"Something you're used to, being quite busy," he said with some annoyance in his tone. "I'm glad that you're feeling stronger. I was wondering if you were free this weekend for a night out? I thought you might like a change of pace." There it was, the question I couldn't, wouldn't say yes to. No matter what plans I had or not, I wasn't going out with him.

"Oh, I have this weekend booked. I've promised a friend of mine I'd keep her company since her husband is away at a sales convention. She's feeling a bit lonely," I replied, trying my best to sound sincere.

*So am I. Always putting everything and anyone ahead of me.*

I heard the thought as if he'd spoken it directly into my ear. Ignoring it, I thought about my friend and how she would kick me square in the shin if she knew I was describing her as lonely. She did quite well without her husband.

"When can I see you then? Because if I didn't know better, you seem to be making a sincere effort at avoiding me."

*Oh, I've only just begun my effort.*

"You're a good friend, too. There are just several people that have wanted to see me since I'm more mobile now." I tried to smooth over the awkward turn the conversation had taken, but I knew Tyler well. He never took no for an answer.

"I'm not several people, Sara." I let out a quiet breath of frustration. "I thought I was supposed to be first."

*Where would you get that idea?*

"And I'm determined to be more than a good friend," he added. "I might not be first in your life, but I intend to be somewhere in it. Put me on your calendar for next weekend, okay? I'll call you during the week to lock down the details. I've got to run but rest up."

"Sure." *Whatever.* I pressed the button to hang up and wondered if he had even waited for my response. Setting the phone back on its cradle, I grumbled under my breath about his choice to become an attorney suiting him well.

He had to know I was an equally determined woman, one who would spend time with him if and when I chose. Mistake number one: underestimating me and my calendar. I needed an amicable solution, but now wasn't the time. I was tired and I'd already been losing concentration on the notes I started putting together before Tyler's call. In a way, I was grateful that the conversation had not erupted. The words wouldn't have come out right, not this late. Besides, I always believed in parting on good terms when possible. As time went on, however, being amicable where Tyler was concerned was drifting further away.

I closed my laptop and headed upstairs to bed, brushing off the irritation clinging to my shoulders in what felt like small, knotted dough balls. I forced my shoulders back and cocked my head to the side, releasing some of the tension.

As I slipped into my favorite soft T-shirt, a nagging sensation to obtain the symbols settled again on my conscience, as if I was being shoved by an unstoppable force toward the goal line. But where was I supposed to start?

Over the last several days, my ability to sense another person's feelings had grown much stronger with the need to uncover answers about the medallions. I wondered if both were in any way connected to my dreams or visits to Ardan. As I settled in under the covers, my mind went to work analyzing the dreams and how they might be connected to this life, ticking away one by one like the mechanical workings of a clock, until my eyelids grew heavier and drifted closed in longer increments.

It couldn't have been more than a minute or two since I'd slipped into my dreams before a small light began glowing in the dark. The illumination grew larger until the soft white glow filled the previously dark space of my bedroom. I sat up in bed to see the flawless features of the elf I'd met in Ardan. "Eldor?" I whispered.

"Sara, prepare for the darkness that comes. Locate the clues to the symbols in your world."

"Yes, but how?"

"All that you feel compelled to do will lead you to follow the path of the keys. Your visions, your abilities to feel what others feel and to know the truth of all matters will become much clearer to aid you in this quest. Remember." Eldor looked at my thigh that had been injured and was now just a deep and ugly scar. He extended a finger to touch it. "You are stronger now and guided as you move forward."

I woke instantly at his touch. The familiar images of furniture around my room returned. I switched on the light beside my bed, Eldor's words etched in my mind.

"The symbols," I said to no one. "If you want me to find them, you might consider throwing me a bone." I glanced at the ceiling as if a clue would drop from thin air. *I better be aided. How else can I find something meant to be hidden without a single clue?* I switched off the light and drifted back to what I hoped would be a restful sleep.

"Don't speak to me about your ghosts. Do you hear me? It's all in your imagination," my mother said. "You're such a weird little child. I swear I don't know what I should do with you." I stared up at her through the eyes of an eight-year-old, willing her to care enough to listen. A stab in my heart at her rejection cut through me, no less painful than the other times. I fought back tears threatening to cloud my vision and reveal weakness. I was training myself to become stronger by denying any feeling. Pain would be my crutch. A reminder not to be weak. I watched as she packed again for another trip with her new boyfriend.

"When will you be back?" I asked. The little voice slipped from my control and cracked at the thought of another week, possibly two, of being alone.

"I don't know. When I feel like it. There's food in the fridge and you better get yourself to school and home on time. Do you hear me? Don't be late for the damned bus."

I nodded. "I'm scared."

She stopped packing and looked at me through blank eyes. That scared feeling left, chased away by an icy chill through my body and the wish that I'd not let a moment of weakness slip. "You're old enough to take care of yourself. Don't try to give me a guilt trip, you little shit."

The tears stung, fighting their way upward and over. There was no holding them back this time. I turned as two of them spilled over.

She couldn't see me cry. That would mean more pain. Without a sound, I stepped away to hide in the one place I knew she wouldn't go—my room.

Everything faded to black and Tyler was standing in front of me. His mouth moved fast, but I couldn't hear the words. The palm of one hand was splayed open toward the ceiling and he waved it in an *I don't get it* manner as he shook his head. His eyes narrowed, and his mouth curled in fury. He took a step too far into my personal space and I shoved him back, then stormed past him, slamming the door. The rain pelted me in heavy sheets as I raced to my car.

*Finished.* I jammed the seat belt into its latch and threw the car into reverse, peeling out of the long drive. "Calm down," I said to myself. I took a deep breath and headed for the light, still green ahead.

The Formula One training Robert had put me through on my pleading was in full gear, every sensation as alive as an electric wire, as I carefully steered through rain-soaked streets. All I had to do was pull my temper in line. I cursed him one last time, for good, took a deep breath, and eased off the gas as I entered the intersection. A quick glance to my left. *A truck. Too close. Can't make it.* A flash of light burst into my vision followed by another before everything went dark.

"The symbols, Sara. Begin the quest now." An unknown voice drifted through my head.

My eyes flashed open from the nightmares, too frightening to allow rest. My heart was thumping like a tribal drum and sweat soaked the back of my shirt. I sat up to catch my breath, as though I'd run a marathon in the dead of sleep. Sliding a hand across my eyes, I felt the wetness on my lashes. I hardly recalled crying as a child. The eight short years I'd spent with my mom were often pain filled, now buried under a solid wall of protection. I wouldn't be hurt like that again, by anyone. On another inhale, I realized I had all the clarity of what had caused me to land in Ardan that rainy night. *But what had Tyler and I fought about? Fat chance falling asleep with my brain at full throttle.*

After I'd whittled away the early-morning hours with patient notes, email, and internet shopping from bed, dozing a couple of times, Friday morning arrived with the message of the symbols sticking like paste in my brain. I wouldn't rest until I put some effort forward. *I'll need some tools.* I shoved the covers aside and headed downstairs, glancing at my office as I passed by. *Tea first, then research.*

I recalled the term "parallel universe" from a documentary I'd watched, presented by a well-known physics professor. It had aired shortly after I'd questioned whether there was a link to connect my experience in Ardan with any scientific theory.

I poured the steamy hot liquid that would awaken me to my full senses, stepped into my office, and Googled *parallel universe.*

Initial search results revealed science was discovering particles don't just exist in one universe but in many at one time. Was this enough confirmation of a connection between dreams and the real world as I knew it? Did this mean that I could be in more than one universe at the same time? I was a skeptic about a lot of things. While I looked to science to help prove or disprove certain claims, I understood that science had not caught up to the very unexplainable yet very real circumstances in life.

There simply was no scientific proof, not yet, to confirm what I had experienced in Ardan. Which meant all that was happening boiled down to whether I believed Ardan to be real or just a fantastic recurring dream based on a healing head trauma. If it was real and I did nothing about the quest, it meant the end of the world as I knew it. Who had decided I was the one to harbor the heavy responsibility for the future of this world, settling like an anchor on my shoulders, anyway? I straightened at my desk, feeling the implied weight.

The mission, the Professors, the symbols, all of it sounded dreamlike to me, bordering on crazy to anyone else. Yet it had all felt real enough, much more than any dream might. Without a clue where to start and the growing doubt about the reality of it all, I was as immobile as when I was lying in the hospital bed. A tone chimed, indicating a new email message had arrived.

I clicked back into my email to find a confidential message waiting, asking me to connect through a secure network using a list of instructions provided. *Curious, but I'm game.* A trusted tech guru at the center had installed on my laptop the most complicated security. My files were encrypted with layers of protection. Logging in to a secure network didn't give me pause. The unknown sender, however, did.

Once in the network, the message was coded, for which I also had a separate set of instructions. The information turned out to be a location where I was to meet someone by the name of C-05, with a note that their "team" was well aware of who I was and my abilities. Further, that they had a connection to Ardan. This was the first tangible evidence of a reality-based quest. But how had this person found me?

*I could ignore the message.* A feeling as though I'd told a lie I shouldn't have rushed through me. *No, I couldn't.* Nor could I decline the invitation, especially given the curiosity it invoked.

As public as the Forrester Foundation was, it was easy enough for someone to follow my family through the press, discover my role at the events or information regarding my career. But my abilities were not something I broadcasted or even spoke of lightly to the people I knew. Mary Ann was aware of them and saw proof of them enough to be convinced. She had told Robert when I was much younger, only to have them dismissed by him as a child's fantasy.

I accepted the invitation and sighed as I glanced over this week's calendar full of appointments. When did I realistically have time for solutions in my personal life? I scanned the details and selected the two that needed the most attention: the sabbatical from my group practice that included a meeting with the partners and an appointment at the crisis center with a troubled mom and her young son who had just escaped from under the control of her abusive husband.

Tyler was right. He was never first in my life and I couldn't blame him for being irritated by it. It still didn't change the fact that I wasn't interested in reorganizing the priorities in my life to make time for him. Dinner, perhaps drinks here or there, was about all I could give to a man right now. I just didn't need the complication of a demanding relationship and the work that went into it.

Though Tyler wasn't first in my life, he was a top priority to get off my plate. I spotted Wednesday evening open and remembered Mary Ann had asked me to come over for dinner this week to visit while Robert was in town. *Perfect time to close out the old and start something new.*

# 8

The pungent scent of recently sautéed garlic and spicy sausage mingled with the sweet aroma of fresh basil in the air of Mary Ann's kitchen. I lifted the lid and stirred the pot of simmering red sauce as my stomach sounded the alarm of hunger.

Mary Ann attended to every detail when cooking, right down to the homemade crusty bread. I had abandoned any hope of being able to cook long ago and envied her ability to throw together a sensational dinner on a whim. I took in one last deep inhale, remembering she had been hoping I would be in the company of a friend for tonight, likely Tyler. Oh, well, I thought, replacing the lid over the pot. That hope was about to be squelched for a longer time.

I mixed drinks for the two of us and went to the living room to get on with the social part of the evening that had the potential of turning into an inquisition, depending on Robert's mood.

As I leaned back into the plush sofa, cocktail in hand, I eased into conversation over Mary Ann's latest charity event theme she was working on for the next benefit in October. I flicked a glance to Robert sunk into one of the overstuffed chairs a few feet away from us, eyes narrowed as he leaned into his newspaper. He may have appeared outside the immediate conversation but was always close enough to add an opinion should it be necessary, or not.

He never liked discussing business matters, be it acquisitions or the details of one of the numerous charity functions planned over the next year. Business was his life. Immersing himself in anything else was his idea of a vacation.

The vodka was quickly lulling me into relaxation. How I wished to avoid the topic of male friends, romance, and Tyler altogether. But my senses told me the subject was as much on their to-do list to address as it was mine. I took a deep breath and another sip. Mary Ann scanned color schemes and table placements for next month's event, flashed a panel containing several shades of blue and cream at me, and asked my opinion. I pointed to the two selections I liked.

"So, what do you hear from Tyler these days?" she asked, picking into my innermost thoughts. At the last dinner Tyler and I attended, Mary Ann had leaned into me and whispered that my despondence was greater than my effort to hide it. I had flashed a smile and straightened in my chair, not caring too much about how I looked at the time. I would rather have been treading knee-deep in Mississippi mud than listening to Tyler pontificate.

"Not a whole lot," I replied. "I'm glad you asked because I wanted to talk to you both." I skimmed an index finger once around the rim of my glass in thought.

"Oh? What's on your mind?" Robert asked, folding the paper down with newfound interest.

"I know he and his family have been friends of yours, ours, I mean."

"For years," interrupted Robert, looking over his reading glasses bridged halfway down his nose.

"Yes. Well, concerning things between us, Tyler's been more interested in money and career than in what it takes to support a relationship and..." I hesitated, trying to find the right words. "I just don't want to keep something that feels empty going with him." It was a load off to finally let out my true feelings. I knew what to expect from Robert but was betting Mary Ann would understand and smooth it over with him later.

"I thought you liked attending the events with him. What's the problem with that?" Mary Ann asked thoughtfully as she shifted to set her drink on the table.

"Nothing *was* wrong with it until I became aware he wanted more than a friendship. The bigger issue is that he seems to have changed in the last couple of months, so much that I really can't stand to be around him anymore. He's superficial and always more interested in pleasing both of you."

"He's just a driven man," Robert said. "He sees what he wants and doesn't wait for it to come to him. I really think he's just proud of all the work he's done. I mean, the law firm appointments are impressive."

"Of course they are, and I'm happy he's doing well." *You did help him get the job, after all.* "However, I don't care for his cavalier attitude or the way he has become, I don't know, controlling. Nothing with him is a mutual agreement."

"He's a born leader, Sara. You wouldn't want him any other way," Robert said.

*I don't want him at all. And a "born leader" wouldn't hang on your shirt-tail.* "He's a pretentious ass."

"He's crazy about you. Told me so himself. He's just got a lot going while he tries to make a good life for himself. That should suit your busy schedule fine."

I pressed back irritation racing to the surface. I wasn't there to be convinced about Tyler's intentions. He'd had plenty of time to show me who he really was and I was no longer interested.

Even if Robert wanted to, I wouldn't debate the matter. I was old enough to decide for myself who was best suited for me, regardless of the number of dollars in the bank or how much more those dollars brought to the equation. Family ties were not going to determine my future. Besides, I was only telling Robert and Mary Ann out of consideration for them and our connection with the Mason family.

"I respect that you like Tyler, but I won't be dating him anymore. I will, however, be civil, even pleasant when our families get together so that you don't have to deal with any recourse or answer any uncomfortable questions."

"Thank you," Mary Ann said. "We'd like to keep a pleasant

connection with the Masons. They were so hoping you and Tyler would eventually be arriving at the discussion of marriage." She lifted her voice at the end in optimism.

*I hate to disappoint them, but the Masons obviously don't have a clear picture of this relationship, either.* Mary Ann, always the diplomat, was trying to smooth over the growing tension in the room.

I knew that Tyler was speaking to his parents and mine about his intentions and how much he said he cared for me. He was doing more talking about us to them than he was to me, making it another sticking point I had. Even if Robert and Mary Ann couldn't see what was really going on, I certainly saw through Tyler's smoke and mirrors. Marriage was the furthest thing from my mind. Why was Tyler painting one picture for them and quite a different one to me? I stifled the outrage that was brewing in my blood at Tyler, or perhaps Robert, I wasn't sure.

"Tyler operates on one set of rules," I added, *whether he lets you know them or not,* "but really, this is a decision I've already made." I felt a sense of calm begin to settle in the pit of my stomach at my ability to cool the fire that had begun welling up.

"So, who's the new guy?" asked Robert. I shot a look at Mary Ann, who grimaced at Robert, trying to signal a *not now* response.

I was caught off guard, not prepared to discuss Kevin. My mind did a quick review of the previous discussions with Mary Ann. I didn't think I'd said anything about Kevin, except that he had come to visit me during my therapy.

"No new guy," I said, careful to keep my feelings from plastering a mask of truth over my face.

"Well, I've heard the happy in your voice when you've mentioned your new doctor friend," Mary Ann said with a wink. I wasn't giving anything away. We hadn't even been on a date.

"He just stopped in on a therapy appointment to see how I was doing. He's just a friend." I took a long sip of my drink.

Robert smirked, dismissing any further communication regarding Kevin, and stood from his chair.

"I just don't think you've given Tyler a fair chance," he said. "How can you dump him when you used to like going out with him?" He paused by the counter and snaked a piece of bread.

"Going out with him *was* giving him a chance. He blew it with his arrogance and need for control."

"Well, no one's perfect, darling," he said. "And if you're waiting for that, you'll never be married, or satisfied for that matter."

The simmer boiled over then. "I'll never settle for the sake of money. Not because I don't have to but because I deserve better." I stood from the sofa, set my glass on the counter, and strolled past the French doors onto the patio. I had to expect some argument on the subject to rile me up. But why couldn't Robert see past money? Why was that the primary reason one should settle? How did Mary Ann, a loving, sweet, and giving woman, ever put up with him?

*Because he's hardly ever home.*

"Well, I'm starved. Is the sauce ready? Smells wonderful." Robert's voice carried to me on the breeze and I stepped farther away, down three steps into the softly lit garden, where several cascading flowers of white Pieris Japonica hung cheerily over the edge of the wall. The sweet fragrance lightened that of the rich, hearty sauce that lifted on a current from the kitchen.

"Dinner isn't quite ready, darling. Why don't you take a look at those notes I left on top of your briefcase? The gentleman from Harbors said he's hoping to have an answer from you by tomorrow morning," Mary Ann replied. I glanced over my shoulder to see Robert leaving the room. He reached a hand back to rub his neck, grumbling something about being pushy.

"Do you think it was a good idea to mention Kevin to Robert?" I asked Mary Ann as she joined me on the patio.

"Not to worry, honey. He's got other things on his mind." Mary Ann shot a quick smile at me over the rim of her glass before swallowing the last of her drink. "Between you and me, your doctor friend is playing his cards carefully with you. I'm just interested in how you'll respond."

"That's silly. He's just being nice. Why do you think he's being careful?"

"No particular reason, darling. I give him credit. I like a man who calculates the odds and isn't afraid to approach. C'mon, I want to show you some of the new flowers I've just planted before the sun sets." Mary Ann put a hand on my elbow, guiding me forward.

"Wait a minute," I said, turning to her. "What is there to calculate?"

"Sweetheart, you aren't the easiest person to get to know. You tend to be very guarded. And all I'm saying is it's nice to see that he's interested."

"Leaving Tyler has nothing to do with Kevin, in any way. So, put that right out of your mind and out of Robert's. Tyler owns that responsibility alone."

She put an arm around my shoulder, giving me a quick squeeze. After she set her empty glass on the ledge of the brick-bordered flower bed, we walked out onto the terrace toward the garden.

I knew that I had a tough outer shell. It protected me from feeling too much for anyone or being hurt by them. On the other hand, it might also prevent me from letting someone I cared for close or allowing something good to flourish. I felt a pit of emptiness the size of the Grand Canyon open up in my soul upon the realization that there was indeed a part missing from my life. And damn Robert and Mary Ann for making me think of it now, when I was about to put everything in my life on hold to chase after the precious symbols. In coming here to tell them of my decision to end things, I knew there would be a price to pay, believing it was an argument about Tyler. I hadn't expected to be handed a mirror of self-reflection in a few sentences.

The drive home from Robert and Mary Ann's felt longer than usual. Since I was lost deep in thought, my foot wasn't as heavy on the pedal as I generally preferred, and I found myself at times slipping just under the speed limit. Besides, having lost one of the cars from my collection in the accident, I was in no mood to risk doing it again. Not that anyone would be traveling the back roads at this time of night.

I sighed and put the window down for more of the cool evening air. The currents lifted my hair and the residual muck from the earlier conversation.

Upon entering the foyer, I saw a blinking light reflected in the mirror opposite my office. I placed my coat over the chair back, slipped off my shoes, and pressed the button.

"Healed and already on the run. Good. I'm looking forward to dinner and wanted to see what your availability was Saturday evening. So, when you have a spare moment, please let me know if you're free." There was something in Kevin's tone that was so comfortable, easy, no pressure. It contradicted Tyler's *put me on your calendar* approach.

I glanced at my watch to see it was nearly ten. His message had been left sometime before dinner and I wondered if it was too late to return his call but dialed anyway.

"Hello, Ms. Sara." Caller ID killed any element of surprise.

"Hello, Kevin," I said, feeling a nervous sensation knotting in my stomach. "I just received your message and I, uh, am hoping I'm not calling too late?"

"Of course not." I felt my heart skip a happy beat.

"I didn't know if I would have a chance to reach you tomorrow and wanted to let you know I'd love to have dinner with you Saturday. What place did you have in mind?"

"Excellent." He paused. "Oh, not to worry. It's just a little spot that, I believe, if it's not already, might become a favorite. However, I can't reveal it until Saturday night, say around seven thirty? Will that work?"

"Sure, but may I have some idea so I know the attire?"

I could almost hear him smiling. "I'm afraid not. It would take all the fun out of it. Cocktail or whatever the black dress covers would be perfect."

My curiosity spiked. "Well, thank you for the tip. I wouldn't want to embarrass you."

"Never."

As we said good night, I couldn't help the feeling of joy I'd missed in recent days settling over me.

*What are you doing, Sara? You can't start something and leave it hanging while you pursue the quest. Maybe not. Maybe I shouldn't go on a date with him.* A pang of emptiness raced through me. There was no doubt, I had to see him, even if only for a single date.

Thoughts of Kevin and what Robert might say to Tyler rolled through my mind, keeping me alert. I hadn't technically broken it off with Tyler yet. That could haunt me if I didn't take care of it soon. *Uncheck "task completed" from to-do list.* I sat down at my computer in an attempt to distract my busy mind.

A few clicks into research, a page of reading, and I leaned back into the chair and closed my eyes. Thoughts of Tyler were pressed to the furthest recesses of my mind as I considered taking on the mission. Something told me once I met with the mysterious C-05, there would be no turning back. Did I fully believe in this quest? Because I had to. And somewhere in the center of my being, I did. But I wanted an iota of confirmation. This meeting would provide the tangible proof I sought.

Usually, as part of the sixth sense I carried, concentrated focus on an issue or person would result in a related emotion or a visual image, like looking at photograph. But right now, the energy was blocked. I gave up, pushed away from my desk, and dragged my tired body upstairs.

As I sunk into the soft mattress and pulled the covers over my shoulders, a feeling of being watched kept me from drifting to sleep. *I'm just overthinking again.* To prove it, I opened my eyes. I drew in a quick breath of surprise as fear raced to a peak just before my eyes reached Cerys's face. The soft glow of pale moonlight outlined his figure. Shock was being replaced by a soothing calm as each tense muscle gradually relaxed. And still, I could feel the thump of my heart trying to adjust to the fact all was well. I pushed myself to sit, facing him, and looked past him, making sure I was still in my bedroom.

Doubt about parallel universes had been my latest consideration. With Cerys now sitting beside me, it was getting harder to tell when I was dreaming and when I wasn't. The visits from Eldor and Cerys and the dreams of Ardan began to meld into one world. All the shadows of the furniture were familiar, including the giant armoire that stood like a dumbfounded linebacker against the wall, the pictures that hung across three walls, and the overstuffed chair in the corner with the towel I had placed on the arm earlier. I'd swept my gaze across the room before returning to Cerys. He touched my hand and held it in his.

"I'm sorry to have startled you."

"No worries. I'm getting quite used to functioning on little sleep."

"Your soul doesn't need the rest your physical body does and therefore spends time in other dimensions as you sleep."

"My soul should understand if it wants to use this body to function, it will need at least eight good hours of actual rest."

He stroked the top of my hand, holding my gaze with his.

"The members of your team are being brought together to accomplish the mission ahead."

"And this man I am to meet with next week, C-05, is he connected to Ardan?"

Cerys nodded. The same warmth, kindness, and strength reflected in his face exactly as I remembered it from Ardan. He leaned close and placed a soft kiss on my lips. Again, the touch sent a tingling sensation racing along my neck, across my arm, and down the side of my body just before his lips left mine. He let go of my hands, reached into what looked like a small leathery pouch, and held his palm open for me to see.

"This is of great importance as you continue your mission. Protect it by wearing it always." I watched as he placed the ring on the fourth finger of my right hand, a simple silver-colored band that glimmered momentarily in the single stream of moonlight that reached my bed. I glanced back to him.

"What significance does it carry?"

"It identifies you as the chosen Light Carrier who will open the gateway to other realms, but only to those pure of heart and those who will aid you in the future. To others, it's nothing more than a simple band," he replied. "Expect additional tools to be provided to aid you as needed." His hand stroked my cheek and remained, holding my face close to his.

"I've missed you for a longer time than you know," he whispered. "You have important work to do." There was a pause, as our faces remained inches apart. "I will return again, my love."

I closed my eyes, seeking to preserve the moment. When I opened them expecting to find him, he was gone.

I switched the light on to see if the ring was really on my finger. I stared down at my open right hand and the silver band. Pulling at the ring to inspect it better only led to it feeling tighter, failing to release its grip. I held my hand under the light to inspect it and could see some sort of inscription, Sanskrit perhaps, that encircled the entire ring. There were also two tiny symbols. I narrowed my eyes to get a better look and saw a U shape with a sword through it and a small flame.

I switched off the light, wide awake with curiosity.

The visits from Eldor and Cerys confirmed the reality of the messages and the experience. But until it connected with me in my world, I hadn't been completely convinced. Now there was a ring on my hand, tangible evidence of the reality of Cerys and my experience in Ardan. I turned the ring on my finger as I lay awake in the dark, staring at the ceiling. A sensation crawled up my spine and I shivered. It was the same feeling I experienced just before Tarsamon had spoken to me. I bolted upright and glanced around the room. Nothing was visibly different, but a new sensation filled the empty space where Cerys had been, one that felt as though someone else had an interest in me seeking the medallions.

# 9

The almost-knee-length black dress draped dangerously low down my back. It would suit almost any attire Kevin might have in mind for dinner this evening. My long hair was swept into a perfectly knotted piece at the nape of my neck with a few small wisps dangling at one ear. As I put away the toiletries on my vanity, the doorbell sounded the beginning of the evening along with a surprisingly nervous feeling in my stomach. "Get a grip, Sara," I told myself. "You've known this man for more than a month. Nothing to be anxious about." I took a deep breath and enjoyed the momentary sense of relaxation that washed over me.

With the exception of the security guards Robert insisted on hiring to keep watch from a detached office on the property, a personal assistant and a cleaning person were the only help I had on the payroll. Mary Ann and Robert had wanted a full staff on the premises complete with chef, but I had refused, despising the lack of privacy that arrangement brought. Yet, on evenings when I was fresh out of Mary Ann's leftovers or just plain out of any food item, it would have been a welcome comfort to have a chef on board. The lack of cooking skills in my repertoire of knowledge certainly wouldn't sustain me for any length of time, should sushi become unavailable.

My assistant invited Kevin into the foyer to wait. I took one last look in the mirror on the wall of the second-floor hall and made a quick adjustment to the shoulder of my dress before heading down the staircase to meet him.

Kevin was stunning in his fitted martini jacket and pants, outlining the lean silhouette of his body. The crisp blue shirt was perfectly matched with no tie. He had slightly tousled his normally conservative chestnut-brown hair. I smiled at the image in my mind of him doing so. He turned at the sound of my footsteps as I reached the end of the stairs.

"Hello," I said, smiling. My eyes did a quick once-over beginning at his eyes, consuming the length to his feet and back again, fixed by his own stare.

"Sara." He paused. "You're lovely."

"Thank you. And you look strikingly handsome this evening." He flashed a quick smile. His eyes remained locked on mine for a second more. *Such intensity.* It sent a tingle down my back, as if invisible fingertips had just danced along the length of my spine.

"Shall we go have some fun?" he asked, taking my hand into the crook of his arm as he opened the door.

"Absolutely."

I stepped into the silver Audi R8, wondering about his usual driving machine, the ever-conservative BMW 7 series.

"New car?"

"Not exactly. Do you like it?"

I liked anything that handled well and hit top speed when you wanted it to. "Yes, it's very nice. I'm used to seeing you in the BMW. It's a pleasant surprise. Do you have a thing for speed?"

"Occasionally. I thought you might like something a little more exciting for tonight."

I smiled. *Exciting. Must be the theme for the evening.*

He turned to glance at me.

"How would you guess I'd prefer speed and handling over luxury, given the choice?"

"I know a few things about you that might surprise you." He turned his mouth up in a devious smile, this time keeping his eyes straight ahead.

"I'm intrigued. What do you know?"

Instead of answering, he stepped on the gas and took off on the long road leading to the city, leaving me to wonder.

I recently purchased a Ferrari 458 Italia that was being shipped in a couple of weeks. But as far as I knew, the press hadn't caught wind of it, and if they had, it wouldn't be interesting enough news to report. Could he know about my quiet collection of fast cars or that my favorite was the McLaren F1 and, soon to be added, the McLaren P1, with its ability to hit 124 mph in seven seconds? I might not be able to drive the P1 around town, not the way I'd like to, but that's why one lived in the distant suburbs of New York. I shifted one leg over the other and stared at the road ahead.

I'd learned to appreciate a car's performance from the time I was young, going with Robert to the track to watch tests of new vehicles and visiting several car shows over the years. While Robert preferred to stick with the classics above the top performers, my thrill was a perfectly tuned and feisty engine combined with torque and handling performance, begging for someone daring enough to attempt to tame it. The thrill of driving was a passion I sought any chance I could. Though I hadn't driven the R8, I read plenty to know its performance was nothing to scoff at.

The drive into the city was much too short, as I was lost in the feel of the car and its smooth purring engine under the controlled hands of Dr. Scott. A few polite exchanges were all that was shared as the electricity of anticipation raced between us like the blur of scenery past the windows.

Our destination was an intimate restaurant decorated with dark-red painted walls and heavy, coordinating floral drapery with dim lighting. A perfect escape. The tables were covered in cream-colored cloth with sparkling glassware, inviting one to sit and savor elegant tastes and exceptional scents of pancetta and garlic lingering in the air. It was the kind of place I could lose hours in and never think twice about what I had lost. Kevin squeezed my hand as we followed our escort to the table. The host bypassed the main dining area and led us up a flight of steps to a smaller second level that looked out over the restaurant's first floor. Four tables moderately spaced apart from each other provided for a more intimate setting.

As we were seated, the comment about Kevin knowing a few things about me that would surprise me pressed for attention. I was going to have to be very careful not to accidentally mention the unusual invite I had received or the dreams of Ardan that weren't dreams at all. It was nothing to relax and be comfortable over dinner and wine, making it all the easier to let something slip.

One glass of wine turned quickly into two as we discussed the latest more restrictive hospital policies limiting a doctor's time and attention to patients. It was the first time I'd seen him frustrated.

We moved to discussion of cases at the crisis center and how it had been difficult to set aside the concerns for those struggling when I left for home at the end of the day. The conversation switched to a much lighter note during dinner and more wine as we laughed and joked over Mary Ann's persistent attitude during my hospital stay.

A moment of quiet passed between us after we finished eating, contrasting the noise of the many thoughts running through my head. I tried to tune in to him and what he might be feeling, to no avail. It was the first time I could recall not feeling any sensation from a person so close to me. And why not? Something wasn't right about it, not him per se, just that I couldn't sense anything from him. Wine had the effect of blocking such feelings, and that was why I'd not hesitated on more than one occasion to use it as a tool. As I was wondering just how I could break the brief silence, he did.

"So, what do you think of this place? Is it a favorite yet or too soon to say?" He turned the stem of his glass once and locked eyes with me.

"It's beautiful. No doubt about that." I blinked and glanced down to the first floor and then back to him. "The food was some of the best I've had in quite a while." I paused, taking notice of his gaze that had dropped to my fingers, now wrapped around the glass I held. "I think it's too soon to say favorite but it's definitely up there." I smiled as his eyes returned to mine. The intensity of his focus was distracting, as though he was looking straight through me. I relaxed into my seat and lifted my glass for another sip.

"Too soon. Well, we may just have to visit again so you can be sure." He raised a brow.

"I'd like that." I set my glass down, my thumb and index finger resting on the stem. The candle on the table highlighted the flecks of gold dancing among the deep brown hue of his eyes, entrancing me. That sort of connection should have evoked feelings from him I could tap into, but still nothing.

"That's a lovely ring you're wearing." He dropped his gaze to the ring again. "May I?" he asked, extending a hand to see the silver band I wore.

"Of course." I placed my fingers in his hand for a better look and felt the gentle caress of his hand beneath mine, igniting heat that sent blood pulsing up my arm. He studied the ring, turning it on my finger a full circle before releasing my hand, to my dismay. I imagined those fingers extending to other areas of my skin and wondered if that same feeling would travel with them. *Damn it, Sara. Get a grip. You don't want what comes with this lust.*

"May I ask how you came to receive it?"

"It was a gift from a friend."

He smiled. "You must have good friends to give you a ring as lovely as that one."

From the moment my hand left his, a tension began growing, an odd feeling that he knew something more than he was willing to say. Could I finally be picking up on his energy? To anyone other than those who would aid me in the future, the ring would be nothing more than an ordinary silver band. Wasn't that what Cerys had said? The ring was, in fact, a perfectly shiny silver band with squared-off edges. Nothing fancy, to the ordinary person. From what I'd already gathered, Kevin wasn't someone to artificially stroke an ego. Had he seen the inscription?

"I have a few." My eyes softened, but my guard was now up. I was beginning to wonder about the depth contained behind the warm and intense eyes of this man, who had reached again for my hand. I resisted the small urge to pull it back, as introspection began to overlap his affection.

"So, what's new beyond the scope of your practice and your work at the crisis center now that you're healed?" His thumb gently stroked across my knuckles, grazing the ring. I was nearly three glasses into this evening, and the recent unsettling feeling had me second-guessing the friendly conversation. My senses told me to be cautious. But why?

*New?* "What is it you really want to know?" I asked, careful of my tone while getting directly to the point. I studied him through sharp eyes but with the warmth of a foggy wine cloud that had settled over me.

"Many things, I suppose. It's a broad question. Don't you think?" He didn't wait for an answer. "I only want to get to know you a little better, beyond your professional title."

"Mm." I nodded slightly. *Put up the wall.* "I'm afraid there's not much more than my profession." I needed a distraction and smiled. "I'm sorry. Will you please excuse me for just a moment?"

"Of course." He released my fingers from his gentle grasp.

The ladies' room was not only necessary but also a convenient escape from the unnerving sensation quickly consuming me. I suspected if he was searching for information, there would be little I could do to thwart any effort on his part. I needed to pull myself together. Something in the way he looked at me, the way his voice spoke to me in those buttery-soft tones was rattling me in a way I had never been. Men didn't cause me to react this way, to be unnerved. I'd dated attractive men in the past. What was so different about this one? What was it that was drawing me closer to him as each moment passed, like some poor fool who'd been bewitched by a spell?

The phone in my purse chimed once to indicate a text message was waiting. I dried my hands and thumbed a finger across the screen to open the message. *Danger is close. Be guarded.*

"What? What danger?" *I said under my breath.*

The sender of the message was blocked. I tossed the phone into my purse and opened the door of the restroom.

Returning to the table, I smiled at Kevin as I sat down. "So, where were we?" I asked, hoping for the chance we might take the subject of conversation off of me.

"I think you were about to tell me what keeps you busy outside of work now that you're healed?"

*Could you mean is there room for you?* As disarming as he was, I wasn't about to let distractions like love into my life, creating discord where I didn't need any.

"Well, I really wish I wasn't such a bore, but there is nothing new per se. I lead a relatively quiet life. I still do quite a bit of work with the foundation to raise money, and that often requires travel at times. My work keeps me tied up with little time for other things. As a physician yourself, I'm sure you must experience similar demands of your time."

"Mm-hm." He nodded in agreement and sipped his wine but did not take the invitation to shift the conversation to himself. There was something that had stalled in our communication from the moment he had noticed the ring, causing my curiosity to rise. Could it be he wanted to know who gave me the ring or if I was involved with anyone? I wasn't opening up about my abilities, my dreams to parallel worlds, or the mission. And I sure as hell wasn't ruining the evening by mentioning Tyler Mason. But the longer I was with him, oddly, the more I felt like I could trust him with the most personal information.

*I might be falling into the comfort of an intoxicating ambience of soft lighting, wine, and attraction.* The waiter arrived with coffee just in time to break the lapse of silence before it could get awkward.

"Are you enjoying yourself?" he asked as the waiter stepped away.

"Yes, very much. Does it seem as though I'm not?"

"Not at all. I was just wondering about the sudden silence and if it was associated with the pink hue rising in your cheeks."

"Ah, well, the hue must be the wine. And I'm rarely caught speechless." This time I felt the heat flood my face.

"I'm leaving you speechless?"

*Breathless is more like it.* I smiled. "I'm really enjoying the ambience, and your company." My stomach started to knot. I picked up the coffee and sipped, then set it down and nearly choked. On the first floor, within my line of vision, was a man resembling Juno. *It's not possible. He lives… Where is it?* I tapped an index finger twice against the cup, with the hope it would jar my memory. *It's not in New York, anyway.*

"Are you all right?" My gaze shifted back to Kevin. "The color seems to have left you."

"Yes, I'm fine. I thought I saw someone I know. A friend." I shook my head, trying to dismiss it.

"Really? Would you like to say hello?" He glanced over his shoulder, the one I had been looking past. My eyes followed to where I had seen the man, only to find the table was now empty.

"No. I'm mistaken." But I didn't think so. I never mistook a face, especially one with distinct features like Juno's. Kevin reached for my hand, drawing my attention back to him.

Heat from his fingers passed through me at his touch and my blood warmed again in response. A connection. A picture rocketed through my head of two people wrapped in the heat of a passionate kiss, and one of them looked like me. But I couldn't make out the man. The thrill of it sent the heat racing up the back of my neck and as though the temperature in the place had jumped twenty degrees.

*Do you not know?* The question followed the image. I blinked and felt the corner of my lip turn up, realizing the image and the thought were not my own. Was I picking up something from him, finally? I shifted my gaze away from his penetrating eyes to our hands, stunned by the connection. There was no easing the passion that had begun to assault me. Desire ran through my body as sure as I was the one in the image being backed against the wall, locked in the embrace as lips crushed to mine. I had to cool this thing and fast. But were these my feelings or his? Or perhaps both? He released my hand then, leaned back in his chair, and gazed coolly over the scene of people enjoying their food and conversation. A silent gasp of air escaped me as the effect of the fantasy departed.

No one had ever been able to unravel me quite like Kevin was this evening. Even with the bustling waiters and busy first floor below us, it was as though we were the only two people in the restaurant. In the past, any person I felt guarded with hit my wall and understood the boundaries. I was in unfamiliar territory with the unusual effect Kevin was having over me. Being aware of the effect, however, only kept me more rigid. I could feel another layer of brick being added to my defensive wall to protect the soft and vulnerable self that wanted no part in feeling exposed.

Kevin's elbow rested on the arm of the chair. His index finger curved over his mouth, concealing what appeared to be a smile. His eyes returned to mine. There was a long, uncomfortable pause, and I could swear the heat that was in my face had traveled through to my seat, getting hotter by the moment.

"What is it?" I asked. My senses were sounding alarms bells, warning that he knew much more than he was willing to disclose, but what the hell was it? I couldn't tune in to any more detail than the warning and it was beginning to annoy.

"I nearly forgot," he said, dropping his hand and gently closing his fingers around mine. His eyes moved over me once and returned to their fixed position on mine. "We're celebrating your recovery, remember? Congratulations on healing so quickly." He raised his cup to toast with me and smiled bigger.

"Yes, I'd forgotten. I owe you a great deal of thanks," I said, returning the smile. "For saving my life and for keeping in touch. It helped make recovery a more pleasant experience."

"It was my pleasure. You've done very well."

The heat in my body settled and I refocused, pleased to set aside an irresistible urge to be closer to him, beneath him. *Get a grip on yourself, Sara. Do not become emotional.* I wondered what it was he thought when he stared so intensely and what he could be hiding in the depths of those brown eyes. I cast a glance across my cup at him, then away as I sipped the remaining coffee. Although my conscience was telling me to be careful, my feelings were all too ready to dismiss the warning.

As we stepped down the staircase and through the door of the restaurant, a small cry redirected my attention. I zeroed in on a boy no more than four or five years old standing alone in the light from a shop window across from the small parking lot of the restaurant.

"Just a moment," I said to Kevin and squeezed his hand before letting it go. I reached the boy in a few strides and crouched beside him.

"Where's your mommy, sweetheart?" He sobbed louder and

pointed a finger in the direction down the sidewalk. "Let's go and find her, okay? Everything will be okay, I promise."

"Sara," Kevin said. His tone dropped, and I sensed a warning. I stood to meet his six-foot-two frame. In my heels, we were nearly eye to eye.

"He's a lost little boy. I can't leave him standing here." The little boy clutched my leg and peeked at Kevin.

"No. Something is wrong with this. Let's call the police and let them handle it."

"Something's very wrong with this. Who leaves a little boy on the street? I'm just going to check a couple of these shops, and if his mom isn't there, then we'll go with your plan.

"Give me your hand, darling." I crouched beside the boy again. "Let's find Mommy."

"Not him," he mumbled through choked tears and glanced at Kevin, then threw his arms around my neck with such strength I nearly fell over backward. I had to admit, for a child who didn't know me, he was a bit too trusting. Were parents still teaching their kids about Stranger Danger?

"I'm not leaving you," Kevin said. I nodded, wondering what his reaction was all about over a small child.

"Let's take a short walk to see if we can find Mommy, okay? And we'll play a game, too." *A little distraction to keep from being afraid.* "Tell me all the green items you see in the windows, okay?"

It was a short walk, as he spotted his mother talking with the owner of the market in the second shop we entered. Having delivered him safely, I turned to Kevin, who had kept a few paces behind us.

"See, all is well."

"I suppose you're right," he said, clasping my hand in his. He shot a look over his shoulder as we rounded the back side of the R8. Kevin opened my door, and then I saw it; the child was standing outside the same door, alone again. In place of the tears, an evil glare was etched across the once helpless, innocent face. And good God, were those yellow eyes? Kevin blocked my view as he held the door open. *Did he see the same thing?*

"What was that?" I asked as we started down the road. "Was that child really lost, or was that—?" My voice trailed off as I realized I'd almost walked into…a trap? *The text message.* But who had sent it? And why hadn't I sensed the danger?

"I suppose anyone can have kids, but not everyone can parent," Kevin said.

*That was no kid.* Maybe Kevin hadn't seen the evil glare or the yellow eyes.

"And you would know that well enough," Kevin added.

"What?" I said, still working out the scene I'd witnessed. "Oh, yes, in my practice I've seen plenty of deadbeat parents." Had a couple of them myself somewhere in this world. He squeezed my hand and released it to shift gears and replaced his hand, covering mine.

The drive back seemed faster than when we had left for the restaurant. We only spoke a couple more times, providing a distraction to the image of the little yellow-eyed devil frozen in my mind.

Kevin opened the car door and offered a hand to assist me. It was a gesture I was unaccustomed to receiving. I was reminded what I had missed in the brief action—being treated as a lady in an age of independence. As we approached the steps to my front door, I turned to see Kevin close behind me.

"Thank you for a beautiful and intriguing evening."

"It was entirely my pleasure," Kevin said, taking my hand and bringing it to his lips. His warm breath on my fingers sent a chill up my arm. He lowered his hand, my fingers still in his grasp. I wanted both to shake the attraction and devour it at the same time. His index finger began to glide along the length of my jawline and might have caused me to tremble except that my senses forced me to focus. "We still have the unanswered question about the restaurant being a favorite," he said.

"So we do." I tilted my head, considering for a moment, and pressed my lips into a smile. "I suppose we'll have to go back to be certain."

*If you only knew.* The thought flitted through my head and was gone as quick as a heartbeat. I couldn't be sure if it was mine. And then I considered, if I only knew what? No, it hadn't been mine. And that meant I had picked up on another thought from him.

He leaned in, kissed my cheek, and paused without drawing away, his lips still close enough that I could feel the heat of his breath against my cheek. I felt the beat of my heart quicken as I turned my head slightly toward him, my lips meeting his. Our eyes locked for a brief moment before I closed mine and pressed my lips gently to his. Slowly he moved, drawing me closer to him. His hand rested on the lowest part of my back, touching both the skin and the edge of the dress, while his lips softly molded mine into the contours he chose. My fingers glided to the back of his neck and up, curling into the soft waves of his hair. The gentle press of his hand urged me against him without crossing any boundaries. Though if he tried, I might have forgotten myself and let him. He pulled back with a whisper of a groan, eyes smoldering with the heat of shared desire. I released a breath, suppressing any sound, and swallowed the taste of him.

"Good night," I said.

"A very good night." He turned toward the car.

I waited behind the closed door, listening as the engine sped off down the long mile outside my house before shutting the lights off and making my way upstairs to the bedroom. The feel of him pressed against me lingered, as did the sensation that he awakened a passion I had never known, not in this lifetime. A flame had been lit and it wasn't to be extinguished anytime soon. A single kiss had never consumed me the way that one did. He was completely addictive. But what was it he was holding back?

"If only I knew what?" I said aloud, repeating the thought that had interrupted us setting another date. It might take time, but I was willing to get to the bottom of that mystery. Then again, love was complicated and I had no room for it. But a little lust? Maybe.

I slipped out of my dress and into a soft black chemise. It was a perfect evening with some curious questions, like why that child looked demonic, or if the warning that I was in danger was tied to the experience. *Could I really fight like I did in Ardan if I had to?* I laughed under my breath. "Your imagination is running wild, Sara," I said aloud, picturing me in a battle with shadowed demons in the heart of New York. I stretched out comfortably in bed and quickly crossed over to the edge of my dreams.

# 10

"They'll only rage against each other. The humans and their world are primitive. You understand."

The deep voice I had heard once before came back to me as Tarsamon's. He was pacing in front of me. The sun hung low in the sky behind him, and its rays filtered through the pine branches, giving his outline an even darker impression against the light. He didn't appear menacing, but quite civil, even attractive in the form he'd chosen to meet with me. His dark jeans and a black mock sweater made him seem almost human. But I knew better. My senses were reading him, too. And although he didn't mean any harm to me, he had death on his mind and a good deal of it.

"Do you see?" He parted his hands just as the Professor had done to show me his vision, a premonition of the future, as he saw it. "They'll kill each other with their anger and violence anyway. You know this."

"It matters not how they choose to end the world, but you will not end it for them."

A low laugh erupted from deep in his chest that could easily have been taken for a growl. I stood still, watching him. His eyes glowed like red beacons behind the shade of black hanging over him. They never looked directly at me. His thoughts were too focused on plotting his strategy. His energy was like that of a hurricane, spinning wildly but in control of its direction. The purpose of our meeting was a last attempt to reason, or rather convince me to give in and abandon the mission for the keys.

"The destruction is inevitable. Allow me the energy contained within it, within their souls. It can be harnessed for the power rather than wasted in an empty death."

"The power to serve your demons and grow your dark forces? No good can come from you consuming such energy," I said.

This time an audible growl was released. "It should not be wasted."

"It should not be utilized to grow evil. No matter how slow the process, their development to become enlightened is necessary. Earth provides the only physical environment for specific lessons. Given the chance, the humans could continue to evolve." *If they don't destroy their world first.*

"But they will destroy it," he said, hearing the thought. "You know it, too, or you wouldn't need the keys to rescue them."

"I seek the keys because I know the damage you can do."

"I grow tired trying to appeal to your usual reasonable nature. Your weakness is that you care too much for them. They'll regenerate in other worlds."

"This one, Earth, is most ideal. The Alliance can't have you eliminating places of development for your selfish desire."

"This world means nothing to the humans. The elements the Soltari created to sustain life, those of love, compassion, generosity, are all but dead. They don't value such an existence."

"Not all of them are able to. As I said, it's a place of development."

"You and the Alliance will fall. The balance between our opposing sides has been weighted too long on the side of enlightenment. The rise of a darker strength is long overdue."

"Do what you must. But know the Alliance will defend any path you try to take to interfere with the humans and their world."

"Only if you can get the keys can you save them, and I'm already ahead of the game."

A flash of white blinded my vision and pain sliced through my head. I rolled over, peeked under my eyelids to see the furnishings in my bedroom still shrouded in darkness, and fell back into sleep.

Shadows that clung to walls and others that slid under any solid form began creeping out to battle, moving like wraiths. I slashed at several and ran a good length as they matched pace with me, until I stumbled…and woke again. A hint of sunrise filtered along the edge of the window shades, refusing to be ignored.

I was drained from the nightmares and wished a few more hours were left of dark to give me a chance to catch up on lost sleep. *Going to need the help of Ms. Ambien or some other potent sleeping aide if I can't get this worked out.* I dragged myself from bed and went into the bathroom. A splash of cold water held the possibility of rinsing away the residual muck of bad dreams that still clung to me.

With my assistant and cleaning person off for the day, the morning was quiet and delightfully peaceful as I made breakfast. I sat down and curled one leg beneath me while I scanned the Sunday news. "Thugs Hit Market in Swanky Downtown," the heading read. It was the very market I found the little boy in the night before, and according to the article, the robbery occurred sometime after we had left. The picture of the evil face was etched in my brain alongside the one of fear riddled with tears that needed soothing. The contrast of which was disturbing. I scanned the article. No mention of a lost child or frantic mother. It was a curious night in more ways than one. I scraped the remnants of eggs into the sink, along with the ill memory from my mind.

It was autumn and the air still mild, with highs reaching into the seventies. Warm enough to plant a few late bloomers or herbs. One area of the property was reserved for the effort I sought to sort out complicated issues or take my mind off them, depending on what mood I found myself in. And though I was no expert at growing flora, I found toiling in the soil and taking care of the life that sprang from it, when it did survive, to be therapeutic.

Before I could step outside to experiment with the innocent specimens on the patio, however, the phone rang. Tyler's ring had its own annoying tone to it. "Damn it," I said under my breath, yanking my gloves off. I'd forgotten that he had wanted me to put him on my calendar this weekend. Possibly because I'd considered the whole matter resolved after speaking with Robert and Mary Ann.

"Good morning, Tyler."

"Hey. Did you get my messages yesterday?"

"Sorry, no." I'd never thought to check for messages since returning home late last night, not that I would have returned them anyhow until sometime today. Maybe.

"We're still on for today, right?" I was surprised that he asked.

"Actually, I'm working in my garden today."

"Great, I'll come over and keep you company. I wanted to talk with you, anyway."

"Well…" I paused, trying to think how best to decline the non-invitation. "I was planning on plowing through the dirt in my garden. I know that's not quite your thing. Can we talk later this evening?"

"What exactly is the deal? You aren't even interested in letting me visit you. Jesus, you really have been avoiding me, haven't you?"

*For a smart guy, he's a little slow.* Good. I'd wanted to tell him a week ago but wasn't in the mood. Nor was I now, but I wasn't about to let this chance slip away.

"Tyler, I've been wanting to speak with you, too, and there really hasn't been any time, so I'm just going to say this. I don't want to take our relationship any further. Quite frankly, you have been a bit pushy about doing things and it has kind of put me off." There. I'd finally said it, and with doing so came the welcome relief I'd anticipated.

"You really can be such a damn snob. You know that?" he shouted. "I've been working like a dog trying to make time to see you and it's you who have been avoiding me. No comment, no honesty, either, until now."

It was the response I expected, hurt followed by fury from rejection.

"Honesty? Tell me why you've decided to pursue my parents regarding our relationship instead of keeping it between us." I could feel the rage pressing past all other emotion, along with some relief in hitting the issue square on the head. "I understand your anger toward me, but I have been furious since I discovered you brought our relationship to their attention knowing full well they would get involved, as they have. What was your motive in doing that, anyway?"

"Don't psychoanalyze me, Sara."

*Too late.*

"Answer me, Tyler," I said steadily.

"I don't have to justify my actions to anyone. You're not interested in us, so what is there to talk about, anyway?"

He couldn't have been more right about that. Now I was sure he had been working Mary Ann and Robert because he hadn't denied it. But why? What did he want? Their money? To gain status or power from marriage? Whatever it was, that plan was blown all to hell. I was satisfied at my ability to hold my rage in check, for the moment.

"Thankfully, nothing." Any further comment would have resulted in an unleashing of my building rage. I wasn't interested in satisfying his anger by revealing he'd brought me to the boiling point.

"Maybe we'll talk later. For now, I'm in no hurry," he said.

"Should you change your mind in the near future, rethink it."

A click followed by silence.

*Good.*

Reaching for my box of tools and some of the cheery multicolored chrysanthemums and basil I had bought a couple days ago, I headed toward the garden to replant the life springing from the small containers. A cool breeze glided over me, lifting my hair and resting it on one shoulder. It was as if the wind had cleared the ugly little cloud that had settled over a minute earlier.

I plunged the spade into the dirt as though Tyler's words and face mingled in the soil. A little harmless therapy. The man I suspected was hiding behind Tyler's clean-cut facade had come forward as if standing on a stage and singing at the top of his lungs, "I've Gotta Be Me." His only concern was for himself, not what could possibly have been wrong or how he might resolve it by explanation or offering an apology for any ill feelings caused by his insensitivity. That was okay. I didn't want an apology or to work anything out with someone who was careless or self-centered in a relationship.

The irritation began slipping away with each stroke and movement of dirt, and I soon found my focus transitioning to the small plantings developing in the ground around me.

A nudge and the surprised sensation of cold wetness pressing my arm up nearly knocked me over from my stooped position over the flowers and shook me from my thoughts. A black and tan furry head pushed through and extended a long pink tongue over my cheek. Ares, one of the Dobermans that roamed the property, had escaped from the watchful eye of Tom, the security guard who was working to train the newest pup.

"Ares, looking for love, sweet boy? Where's Tom?" Ares shot his ears back up from their previous playful, laid-back position and looked behind him. Not seeing the security guard, he put his nose back into my hand. "He can't be far behind," I said, grasping his head with both hands and rubbing behind his ears. He reminded me of the Doberman, Gretchen, I had when I was a little girl. She, too, would bolt from my father as Ares had from Tom for a brief respite from the yelling and commands and seek refuge in the friendly hands of the little girl, certain of finding unconditional love. At the time, the dog and I understood each other well enough to provide comfort to one another, if only for a brief moment.

Ares was named for the Greek God of war, violence, and bloodshed. He was only one of the newly trained security dogs on the premises and, put to the test, would live up to his name, eventually. Right now, he was as lovable as any puppy without the challenge. I dug into my pocket for a treat I kept for the dogs if they came over for a visit. "Find Tom," I ordered, "before you get into trouble." He gulped the treat and turned, racing in the direction he had come.

I returned my attention to the garden and the last appointments for the week, mentally scrolling through the itinerary waiting on my desk that included a list of patients to be seen in my office in the city. I was booked from nine to three handling couples' therapy, a meeting with the partners at three thirty, and then I could finally set my sights on the task of finding the symbols. With an index finger, I began drawing three circles in the vacant soil. Something in the center, bolder than the edges. *What was it? An L? An S, and…? No, no. That's not it. Damn it.* I smothered the images I'd started.

By the time I finished plugging the last of the bright red flowers into the ground, the sun was low in the sky. The yarrow I encountered in Ardan flashed once in my thoughts, along with Cerys's face. I dismissed it as nothing more than another reminder of my task and headed inside to clean up.

I tied wet hair into a loose knot at my neck, pulled some sushi from the fridge, and headed for my home office to check email and phone messages, deleting the two from Tyler without listening. A ping signaling an incoming message sounded. The sender was marked *Undisclosed.* "You are not forgotten," the first line read. *Curious.* "Clues will be arriving to bring you closer to the symbols. Build your strength to prepare. Contact will come soon."

The message had to be from C-05. It had the same tone as another communication I'd received from him, and I was scheduled to meet with him early next week. *Clues. What clues should I be on the lookout for?*

I took the remaining sushi to the family room, flipped on a movie, and curled up on the plush sofa, kicking some of the large square pillows aside. I woke a couple hours later to heavy knocking at the door.

*Who has the nerve to beat down my door at this hour? Did security call and I didn't hear it?* In a state of grogginess, I dragged myself to the front door and listened for any sounds. The knocking had stopped. *There's no way anyone would have slipped past the security guards. Did I dream it?*

My mind was on the first appointment of the morning—a couple I had counseled a few times trying to avoid a divorce. As I stepped into the garage, my heart leapt into my throat.

"Jesus, Tom. You startled me. I don't expect people coming around from behind the car in my own garage."

"Sorry, Dr. Forrester. Just making sure things are secure. We had something come up on the monitors last night but couldn't track it."

"On the property or outside the gates?"

"On the property. We think it was a couple of kids, just couldn't make out their faces on the screen and couldn't track them last night."

"I see." *So, all that noise wasn't a dream.* "And the dogs? Did they find anyone?"

"They caught a scent that led to the front door, then went nuts up the wall as far as they could jump. But we found nothing."

"Hopefully, they didn't make it into the garage. How did they get past the gate?"

"That's still a mystery. There's no sign of them on the monitors at the gate."

*Slim chance kids would be here.* It was a long trek this far out of the city for kids to be looking for mischief. And the security on the premises was locked down pretty tight, making it almost impossible to get to the front door without coming through the main gate or the twelve-foot-high wall surrounding the area.

"It's not going to be a problem. I've got two other guys on it and tightened security in the evening."

"That's why I trust you. Thanks." I slipped into the buttery leather seat of the car and backed out of the drive, wondering what scent would have led the dogs up the wall.

By the time I pulled into the parking garage of the downtown office, I'd forgotten about the security issue.

"Good morning, Emma," I said, smiling as I approached the lobby desk. "Can I meet with you in my office?"

My assistant, Emma, stood behind the desk arranging files with a look of mild irritation, waiting for a couple engaged in some sort of minor disagreement at the counter to move along.

"Sure, right away," she replied.

After setting my briefcase on the floor next to my desk, I settled into the large chair, opened my laptop, and pulled up a list of clients. Emma closed the door and took an empty seat in front of my desk with her laptop in hand.

"We've got to transition my clients to any of the available docs here. Do you know offhand which ones are accepting clients right now?" I asked, turning from my laptop to face her.

"All of them, Dr. Forrester."

"Good. I have some unresolved and pressing issues that need to be dealt with that are going to require all of my time. I'll be taking a sabbatical for the next year. This will be my last week. I'll send a formal email notification about my departure to my colleagues and ask that they keep you on due to the additional workload." I paused, catching her stare and realizing I was throwing a lot at her. "Sorry, I don't mean to unload this on you all at once. I'm just in gear to get things handled." I smiled and turned back to the screen.

"I hope everything is all right."

"For now, yes. No worries, though. I just need to attend to some pertinent issues and can't do it while dividing my time between the office and the crisis center. I'm meeting with the partners this afternoon. The notice I'll send out will advise my colleagues to contact me in the event of an emergency or changes in the practice, though I don't expect any. However, the managing partner will be Dr. Leighton. I'll copy you on the email."

"Got it. What do you need me to do?"

"If you could, please contact all of my clients today and let them know this is my last week. Give them the option of who they would like to switch over to, and I will get the email to my colleagues right now."

"I'm on it."

I had every confidence my patients would be fine in Emma's capable hands as she tried to find the best match of doctor to patient.

I sent off the notice to the partners and went through documentation prior to my next client's arrival, noting I'd suggested a technique for anger management for Chad and for Robyn to refrain from following Chad, carrying on the fight.

For the entire hour, their thoughts, some shared with me and some kept silent, were as clear as if all had been spoken to me directly. To be able to hear such truth was indeed a useful tool in my profession, but I wasn't interested in it for that matter. In fact, I'd even tried denying the ability existed in an effort to find normalcy, to no avail. That meant there was no reason I shouldn't have been able to hear Kevin during dinner. And by the look in his eyes, there was plenty to uncover. I was willing to put Vegas odds on it.

The day continued much the same from one patient to the next. It surprised me how tuning in to the thoughts of my patients and feeling the hostility or the sadness each came more readily than before the accident. The strangeness of it had increased, too, as if two feelings, the client's and mine, were occupying the same space in my mind and body. By the end of the day, I was drained of all energy the same way the last fight in Ardan had robbed me of my energy. I needed to find the right balance of listening to others and also be able to block the effects of doing so, like a life-sized filter I could wrap around myself. But such a filter couldn't block Tarsamon and the warning of dark forces seeking to absorb the energy of the people of Earth. Without the ability to block the evil, how would they survive? *They won't,* came a thought I wasn't sure was entirely mine.

# 11

Rush hour had snuck up on me sometime between document-ing final notes and the meeting with the partners. I wasn't about to head into traffic until the congestion eased. Perhaps I could stay at the small apartment in the city I kept for the days when I worked late.

*Nah, need my space, out of the city.* My fridge often looked like a bachelor's after a football game, wine instead of beer, and not a single leftover. I'd scavenge for anything to prevent having to shop. Mary Ann scolded me regularly for it, too. "You're the daughter of a billionaire, who lives off of peanut butter and honey if there's nothing else in your kitchen. It's shameful," she'd said on more than one occasion. She'd threatened to hire someone to shop for me and deliver the food. But I told her that would be a waste when they wouldn't know what I liked to eat. Today, I declined my assistant's offer to handle the task and began making a mental list as I headed down the elevator.

The market was packed with other businesspeople with the same intent. I took my time, mulling around the store for fruit, things for a salad, and a few other items that would get me through the week. With a basket loaded with more than I intended, I headed for the checkout line and noticed it had grown rather long since I arrived. I sighed, reminding myself there was plenty of time to sit behind another car on my way out of the city. The man behind me grumbled once and again a little louder.

"Who the hell writes a check anymore? C'mon, let's move already," came the voice of frustration from behind me.

People glanced around but I was too tired to care. I rolled my eyes and thought I caught the movement of something on the wall or was it the ceiling? I looked up again. *What the hell?* A shadow crept at the edge of where the wall met the ceiling. The dark image had wings spanning about three feet in length and with visible shadowed claws that crept upwards and along the edge of the ceiling.

Looking for some explanation and without finding one that would justify such a sight, I turned to a portly man behind me with a tool belt hanging below the four inches or so of exposed belly. From the wrinkles at the hem, the royal blue T-shirt he wore had once been fixed beneath the belt but had struggled free, leaving the hairy belly button exposed to catch a breeze.

"Do you see that?" I asked, lifting my eyes to the ceiling and back to him. He stared for a minute, as if to say, "You talkin' to me?" before glancing up.

"That water stain the size of freakin' Texas?" His gruff voice slapped me awake. "Yeah, this place has had leaks forever. I've done repair work so many times but the owner"—he shook his head—"he just won't fork over the money to do a proper repair job on that plumbing. Whata ya gonna do, huh?"

"Let it leak, I suppose." Obviously, he couldn't see the thing that was now making its way across the ceiling and over the heads of people in the produce area.

Every moment the line had to wait just resulted in the angry man behind me becoming more vocal about his impatience so that it was getting the attention of everyone within earshot. My attention was pulled between the man and what crawled above me.

"Some people," said the frail white-haired woman—the culprit check-writer—then turned to finish her statement, "are like small children stomping their feet."

"So true." I flashed a quick smile.

"Yappin' ain't helpin', lady," the man added. The clerk had already shot a look back at him once with a halfhearted smile.

I turned my head in the direction of the annoyance and quickly back toward the register. What I saw was almost as alarming as what I'd seen on the ceiling, but I couldn't be sure of what it had been. I wanted to turn back and look again but instead stepped up to the credit card machine. An eerie feeling was settling over me, followed by the sudden urge to get out of the store. As I ran my card through the machine to pay, curiosity won out and I glanced back. There it was again, another dark shadow that dodged back behind the man making the loud derogatory remarks, as if hiding behind him.

"Ma'am, just push the yes button to indicate the transaction is complete," the clerk instructed, trying to hurry me along and get the mouthy offender out of the store.

I punched the button with an index finger and picked up my bags. Glancing over my shoulder, I caught sight of the black shadow on the ceiling. It cocked its head at me. Red eyes, not apparent before, hung on me until I stepped past the threshold of the door. Because I had seen two shadows, I was quite certain my eyes were not playing tricks on me. Hallucinations were not generally part of being fatigued, I reminded myself. But I supposed it was possible. If it wasn't a hallucination, why couldn't anyone else see it?

As I stepped onto the sidewalk from the market, the traffic looked as though it had improved some. I found my car and tossed the two bags in the front seat and set off to join the rest of the business folks headed home, with one thought on my mind—only two days earlier, I'd seen a demonic-looking child, with eyes as piercing as the shadow's.

I threw a salad together and headed down the long hall to my office. Sitting at the desk, I placed the food off to the side and flipped open my laptop to find an emblem in a circular design with an inscription. Was that Gaelic? The image was floating across my screen as though it were a screen saver. Within seconds, the picture broke into several pieces before I'd ever touched the mouse. I clicked on the pieces of broken image, attempting to get it back, but each piece began to dissolve, leaving the usual icons as if the image had never appeared. "What was that?" I said. But I knew very well. What I wanted to know was who had sent it.

Just as the Professor had said, I knew for sure the medallion was one of the three symbols I was seeking. Why then would it disappear? Maybe it was some sort of safety precaution. I grabbed a blank piece of paper and pen and frantically tried to rough out the image from memory, only succeeding in a partial recollection with little success in capturing the Gaelic lettering. "Damn." I leaned back, holding the paper in one hand, studying it. There wasn't enough information to research meaning. But I'd felt as though I'd captured the shape in the center well enough, a spiral of some sort. I searched the web under Gaelic symbolism and found the same image, known as a triskelion. By the time I'd finished researching, I had determined the symbol was Celtic and the meaning encompassed everything from mind, body, and spirit to a symbol of eternity, as well as a reference to otherworldly realms.

"I need the letters," I said aloud, tapping the corner of the computer as if to make them appear. With no luck at recalling them, I shut the laptop. Raking fingers through my hair, I looked to the ceiling. "Need a little more help."

That night while my body slept, I paced the empty field in Ardan. The sword that was usually present on my hip was gone. There was a slight rustling of bushes and a vague figure appeared along the edge of the field.

"Why have you called me here? Show yourself," I called out. Without hesitation, the faint image of a man floated from one corner of the field to the other, opposite of where I stood. The image faded and reappeared as one of the Professors in a blue cloak, standing a few feet away.

"You have come quite far in your ability to move energy here. But are you prepared to fight should you have to on Earth?"

"Can the shield and other defenses utilized here protect me on Earth?"

"Yes. Understand, though, you have the weight of gravity to contend with on Earth. You move swiftly in Ardan and in any other realm you choose to travel. But you will not be able to move as easily in your physical world should battle begin. The shadows are upon you, Sara. They have come into your world, seeking strength in your human companions, and they will not hesitate to challenge you when Tarsamon gives the order. Strengthen your body so that you are as flexible, strong, and agile as possible. Make this your focus."

"I understand."

He dropped his chin in acknowledgement and reached into a pocket in his cloak and pulled out a disc. When he opened his palm and held it for me to see, it showed the same image as the one that had floated across my computer screen. As I reached for it, the medallion turned into smoke in his hand and lifted upward.

Before I could ask him why he would dangle the item in front of me, he smiled. "I don't have the symbol you seek, only an image should you need a reference. And I don't have the power to deliver it to you if I did have it. Only the Soltari can do that. But I will tell you that to keep the power from falling into the wrong hands, one of the symbols will remain in Ardan. The letters you requested will be provided to aid in deciphering the location. You will understand their meaning in time. What's important is keeping them safe."

"But where can I find them? How will I know when to bring all three together?"

"Each contains direction to the location of the guardian of the key. Together the symbols will open your passage to the key's location. The symbols will find you when the time is right. With the shadows upon you, be assured it will be soon."

"Wait. What do you mean the symbols will *find me*?"

"With the danger closing in, the Soltari have decided it's safer if they are provided to you.

*Faster, too.*

"The keys, however, are yours to obtain." He balled his fingers into a fist. "Now, would you like another look before you leave?"

I glanced from his face to the fist that began to widen with the replacement of the disc.

"Of course."

He lifted his fingers to reveal the Gaelic lettering engraved around the outer edge.

Before I could speak, I found myself staring up at the black empty ceiling of my bedroom. I had come to believe that waking following a message was an aide to remembering them. I turned my head to the glow of the bedside clock that read three a.m. I flipped the light on, went to my office, and sketched the few letters I remembered from the dream to the roughed-out drawing I'd made earlier. There weren't many, but there might be enough to help identify the message. I was finally in motion, but with a new consideration—a dark lord who might find new information provided to me to be a threat. What would it take for Tarsamon to put out an order to kill?

# 12

A couple of weeks had passed since I'd seen Kevin. Scheduling conflicts made it impossible to set a date for me to try and unravel the mystery of Dr. Scott. But I would, because I couldn't get him out of my mind. Since that kiss, he had infiltrated my system, my wall of protection, leaving me not only with questions but with a heat that was taking its own sweet time to cool. With both of us traveling in the near future, we agreed to put off a date until we returned, or another two weeks. Perhaps a little distance would clear my head and shake the spell I was under since having dinner with him. I shook my head at the thought. Who was I kidding? The space between us had only increased my desire for him.

I switched focus to the top I'd selected to wear and opted for another in deep blue as I finished getting dressed. It was my last day at the crisis center to tie up unfinished business before pulling away from that responsibility to search for the medallions. The decision to leave my life's work, my passion, to follow a quest where no tangible evidence the end of the world was near pulled at me. I craved to help the abused, those innocents who had been under the thumb of the bullies of the world, who always left scars and pain in their wake. Yet chasing a warning about the end of the world somehow felt right.

Today, I would set aside the thought of Armageddon to handle one more task closer to home. A new family, a mom and her two boys, had made the brave and daring exit from the dangerous environment they had been locked into for the last three years. All my focus today would be on how to prevent the family from returning to the abuse that was so often the outcome for many victims. I slipped on my heels and stopped to retrieve my laptop, skimming through the morning email before packing up and heading out the door.

It didn't surprise me to find a message from Mary Ann waiting. It had been days since I'd spoken with her and I felt an urgency to respond this morning before getting tied up for the day. I scanned the message to see it was a request to go with her to Europe this Friday for an event that would raise money for agencies working against domestic violence. She wanted me to give a speech the following Saturday evening.

*I'd love to attend with you and I'm happy to give the speech. I'm running off to the center. No time. Thanks.*

I quickly typed out the response before slamming my laptop shut, making a mental note to get current stats on the rate of victims returning to their abuser to incorporate into the speech.

This was an event that hit close to home for me. My brief but intense upbringing with my biological parents and the abuse suffered was still a scar on my soul. I wouldn't miss an opportunity to help people who fought vehemently against it.

As I backed out of the driveway, my thoughts drifted back to Kevin again, as if they refused to leave me alone until I resolved to meet with him. I was surprised at how much room he had begun to take up in my thoughts lately. I liked the mystery of it, like some code I needed to crack. At the same time, it wasn't like me to lose my perspective with confusing emotions. I wanted to keep my distance and not get caught in the hidden quicksand of a relationship that particular desire was luring me toward.

A trip away. Just a few days to relax, not to think or have to feel for a week or so. Mary Ann and Robert kept a small place on a tiny private island. I had only been there a couple of times. I'd forget every troubling thought, maybe find clarity sprawled in a beach chair, toes dug deep in the sand. Yeah, that was exactly the place I needed right now. If what I'd been told about the coming evil was true, there might not be another chance for rest. A flash image of the shadows that had taken up residence at the local corner market skipped through my head at the same time. I could be back within a day if necessary. If the symbols would find me when the time was right, they could find me as easily on a solitary beach as they could in busy New York City.

I jumped at the ring that came over the Bluetooth system, yanking me from the respite of my daydream. I glanced at the number and name that popped up on the screen. It was as if my thought of Kevin had been carried on a breeze straight to him.

"Good morning. This is a pleasant surprise," I said, noting the only time we'd ever spoken was in the evening, when things were much slower and quieter.

"Good morning. Have I caught you at a bad time?"

"Not at all. I'm on my way to an appointment at the center for a few hours. What's on your mind?"

"I'd really like to see you again and two weeks was too long to wait. I had something open up and wondered if you were free this Saturday."

*Open up?*

"I just agreed this morning to go to Europe for a charity event. I'm leaving Friday with Mary Ann."

A pause. Had the call dropped?

"My apologies if this sounds presumptuous, but would you happen to need a date to this event?" His polite nature was as attractive to me as the other numerous reasons I'd found him so magnetic.

"I was planning to attend solo, but I would be pleased to have you join me if you don't mind a turnaround trip. And it'll be a little bit of work for me." *So much for establishing some distance.* I felt myself sink one step further into the quicksand I feared.

"I don't mind at all. I'm on call, but I'm sure I can work something out," he said with confidence.

"Shall I go ahead and reserve a place for you on the plane?"

"Yes, please do," he replied. "I'll look forward to it."

"So will I. I'll send you the itinerary."

"Sounds good. Thank you, Sara."

"Talk with you soon," I said, my mood elevated. I cursed myself for giving in so easily to my desire. Any involvement would only complicate things. And yet I wouldn't say no. I slammed the car door a bit harder than intended as I turned toward the entrance. I needed to be sharp and focused on this mission for the keys, not distracted by the lure of tall, dark, and mysterious. For now, the symbol I'd seen didn't require much more than a bit of research. There would be time to work out the enigma that was Kevin afterward.

I made my way down the long hall of the administrative building toward the tiny office at the end of the corridor. It was going to some lengths to call it an office. A space not much bigger than a ten-by-ten room, it was a place to lock up a briefcase or purse and use a laptop. The only furniture was a well-worn steel desk and a lightly cushioned chair. At first glance, the area reminded me of the stark adoption agency I'd sat in when I was a child. It was a perfect space. I didn't need fancy in a place where people were hanging on to hope by a few threads.

"Dr. Forrester," came a voice from behind me. I turned to see Francis, one of the administrative volunteers, two steps behind me. She was a sturdy woman in her early sixties who stood about five feet four inches tall. I hardly recognized her with her newly dyed red hair that hung in loose waves just below her chin.

"I like the red. Looks wonderful with your skin tone."

"Oh, yeah?"

"It sets off your eyes, too." *Did I ever notice they were green?*

"Thanks. I wanted to try something different. Was getting bored with a mop of gray. This sort of kicks it up a bit. Cheery, don't you think?" She patted the side of her head and smiled. I nodded as she began to riffle through a stack of papers she held above a clipboard. "Here it is. This just came for you over the fax. For heaven's sake, though, I can't imagine what it could be. There was no cover sheet, so I'm sorry. I don't even know who sent it. Luckily it had your name typed on it or it would have been added to my wastebasket today."

She handed me the single page with my name that had been

printed at the top. It was the same image of the symbol that had been on my computer last night, before dissolving across the screen.

"Thank you, Francis. People send me all sorts of things." I smiled, tucking the paper neatly into my briefcase to review later.

"Oh, I'm sure," she said. "I've got to get the rest of these copies out in the next few minutes." She waved a hand and turned toward another office in the corner.

Arriving at my desk, I pulled the fax out and eyed it, looking at the number it was sent from before taking note of the details of the image. The fax number was a series of ten numerals of seven. Other than that, not a single identifying mark of the sender could be found. Was this from the Professor? Maybe the Soltari? Did they have eyes everywhere, at all times?

Friday arrived much faster than expected. The past few days had been a blur prepping a speech, transferring responsibilities. Through practice, I'd managed to master the filter to block the feelings I received from other people, too, avoiding sensory information overload that killed the necessary energy to get through the day.

Mary Ann was taking a much greater interest in the possibility of a developing relationship with Kevin. A hopeless romantic, she'd grown concerned about me finding a partner for life. And because she liked Kevin from her first couple of visits to the hospital, it was all the easier for her to support this connection. Kevin accompanying us to Europe was a *fabulous idea*, she had said in a call I'd made to her that morning, especially when I explained it wasn't mine.

With Kevin's busy hospital schedule, I had arranged for a driver to pick him up and meet us at the airport. As we pulled up, he was just stepping out of the car and handsome in dark jeans, a crisp white shirt, and British tan leather loafers. Time slowed long enough for me to really look at him without him knowing I was watching through the car's tinted windows. His lean frame reflected strength beneath a well-dressed facade without the bulk of overbuilt muscle. His hair caught the sunlight as it peeked through the otherwise clouded sky and cast a highlight of auburn over the deep coffee-colored locks.

"Good morning," he said as I stepped from the car onto the tarmac.

"Good morning to you." I greeted him with a hand at his waist and a light kiss on the cheek. He stroked a hand along my upper arm, instantly reigniting the flame of desire I'd worked to cool over the past couple of weeks with little success. Something in his gaze told me he knew his effect on me.

"All set?"

He lifted one hand containing a leather duffel and a garment bag slung over his shoulder and flashed a smile, then turned to Mary Ann. "It's a pleasure to see you again, Mrs. Forrester. Thank you for allowing me to join you."

"Nonsense. Only my doctor calls me Mrs. Forrester. Mary Ann, please. It's a lovely idea for you to keep a couple of ladies company."

"It's an awfully long way for you to travel just to accompany me," I said in nearly a whisper after we'd taken our seats, trying to keep our conversation from Mary Ann's prying ears.

"I confess. It's for entirely selfish reasons that I'm here. If this was my only chance to close the gap in our schedules, I wanted to take it. Besides, it's been a few years since I've been to England, and traveling this far is also a great excuse for not having to be on call," he added, smiling.

"I suppose it is. What brought you to England in the past?"

"Business, primarily, but my family traveled a great deal to the UK when I was younger. I spent a few years in Scotland and Ireland."

"Did you learn the language while you were there?"

"At the time, yes. Irish and some Scottish Gaelic. I still recall some of it, but it's a bit rough."

"Fascinating. I'd love to hear it sometime." His mention of Gaelic reminded me of the image I'd received. I couldn't ask him to decipher the meaning of the lettering in the printed version of the symbol resting securely in the locked briefcase in my home office. I couldn't risk showing him the image or explaining the mission that still sounded a bit farfetched even to me, the person supposedly chosen to fulfill it. I'd just have to go the long route to deciphering the message.

His eyebrow lifted. "I understand you speak, what is it, four languages?"

"Yes, but not fluently anymore. How did you know about that?"

He put his lips closer to my ear. "Mary Ann," he whispered. "She was a little forthcoming with information when she was worried about you."

I could feel the pink rising in my cheeks. "Of course. In the hospital."

He smiled across the aisle to her as he pulled a magazine from his bag.

"She shared because she likes you," I added. "She isn't usually that free-spoken with people she doesn't know well."

"Good. I'm fond of her, too." He gave me one sidelong glance before turning to his magazine.

There wasn't going to be any foreseeable moment for us to spend time alone with the short schedule. But I was pleased for the chance to learn whatever more I could about Kevin, even if the information was in tidbits.

We landed, checked into our rooms—three, because Mary Ann had already booked two and quickly added another after I'd spoken with her that morning.

We met for dinner downstairs in the elegant restaurant of the hotel. Conversation flowed easily on the topics of travel, planning this particular event, and the general lack of free time we all had, while Mary Ann tried to figure out what Kevin liked to do with the little bit he had. She laughed and fired back witty humor as quickly as he dished it out. I couldn't remember a time when she was so comfortable and happy, especially before a big event.

An unexplained connection passed between Kevin and me each time our eyes met. Time apart had not had an effect on that feeling. I was being pulled into whatever web he was weaving. But there was going to be no time this evening to see where things ended up as I remembered the speech I would be giving the next evening. Although procrastination wasn't a friend of mine, I'd toyed with the idea through dinner. In what felt like too soon, the dishes were cleared, and coffee was on its way.

"If you'll excuse me, I'd love to stay but will have to pass on coffee and let you two enjoy what's left of the evening," I said, placing my napkin on the table. "I've got to touch up a few notes for the speech tomorrow."

"Can I walk you to your room?" Kevin asked, standing when I did.

"You're comfortable. Stay and enjoy the evening." *Besides, if you walk me to my room, I might have to keep you for a while.*

His eyes smoldered. *I could only hope for as much.*

As I heard the thought, I knew it wasn't mine. It couldn't have been. My eyes widened slightly in surprise.

"Oh, go with her," Mary Ann said, waving a few fingers in our direction. "I've got to make a call, anyhow, before it's too late." She signaled to the waiter.

"Good night," I said.

"Good night, darling," Mary Ann replied. I bent to kiss her on the cheek. "Pleasure to have you with us," she said to Kevin.

"Thank you for having me."

"She loves this, you know," I said to him as he stepped beside me. "Seeing us together."

"That's a bad thing?"

"Not at all. Just been a while." My heart began to race as we stepped onto the elevator. "A while since she's…I don't know…seen me happy."

"Are you happy?"

The temperature needed adjusting to a much cooler setting. "Even keel most of the time. But with you, I'm happy. Yes." I just couldn't seem to find the control.

"I feel the same way with you." He angled his head toward me as the doors opened.

*Trapped. Almost. And liking it.*

"What can we do about this? You're very busy. I'm very busy. We had to take a trip together to Europe for an impromptu date," I said.

We stopped at my door. As I turned to face him, he was smiling.

"What?"

"Oh, I think our schedules will work out fine. One way or another." His stare pinned me against the door. The gentle touch of his fingertips glided along my jawline. "May I kiss you?"

"I'd be disappointed if you didn't." I closed my eyes as his lips reached mine and tenderly placed a kiss. A sweep of his tongue and my breath caught and released. A wave of sensations ran from my neck on a fast track along the length of my arm.

*Remember?*

He eased back on an exhale. "I'd better say good night."

"Me, too. Good night."

I put the key in the door as every sensation screamed for this simple walk to the room to continue. If not for the electrifying sensations, then for the puzzling question to remember. Remember what? Again, it was a thought that wasn't mine. He turned and continued down the hall, leaving a void where one shouldn't be.

Behind the door, I inhaled deeply. He moved me to depths I couldn't identify, all with a look, a kiss, and in this case, a thought. Had I really heard him or just imagined it? I replayed in my mind what I'd thought as I was excusing myself from the table. "Yes, I know what I heard," I said aloud. That meant he had heard me. It would be impossible for both of us to have the same extrasensory ability. Wouldn't it? I dismissed the thought, never having experienced another exchange like it with him in the time we'd become acquainted. But residue from those last words clung in the back of my mind, refusing to be denied. I dropped the key on the table, glanced at the notes lying on the desk, picked them up, shuffled through them, and thought about Kevin.

# 13

Saturday morning was turning out better than expected. After I met Mary Ann for a light breakfast of tea and scones, she hurried off to make sure things were in order for tonight's event. Instead of letting me help her, as was my usual duty, she had insisted that Kevin and I take a couple of hours to see London. We settled on visiting a few of the historical sites, including the Tower of London and the British Museum, before finding a quick lunch in the city and a walk along High Street. The large windows of a few antique shops displayed miscellaneous trinkets resting on a small stand. Detesting shopping about as much as small talk, I passed by the shop windows with my hand in Kevin's, giving nothing more than a glance of curiosity to what was displayed. As we strolled along, commenting on certain items, one antique shop stopped me cold at the flash of copper resting on white linen cloth.

"Have you ever seen anything like them?" Kevin asked.

I glanced at him and back to the three engraved coins the size of silver dollars that had been placed behind a couple of sets of antique engagement rings and wedding bands. An eighteen-carat-gold skeletonized pocket watch was resting open next to the coins.

"No. I don't think so. The detail is exceptional. How old do you think they are?"

From the corner of my eye I could see him staring at me. Was he referring to the rings? One of them contained an enormous stone, and God knew how old it was. Unlike Mary Ann, I wasn't a hopeless romantic. I refused to consider any such trinket despite its beauty for fear of what it meant, losing one's self for another or inevitable abandonment. Sure, it meant love, too, but always at the cost of something else, in my eyes. And my eyes wouldn't be blind, not in this lifetime.

"A century, possibly two. I couldn't say exactly." His attention never wavered.

*I will never be married. I will never be married.* The thought played again and again in my head as if some internal alarm was chiming.

"The medallions look to be from the sixteenth or possibly seventeenth century," he added.

*Thank God he shifted focus.*

"They're remarkable."

One of them appeared to have some of the same markings I'd seen in the fax sent to me. I needed a closer look to be certain.

"That watch is definitely eighteen hundreds. Look." He pointed to the small tag on the side that was peeking out from underneath.

"Incredible," I said, noting the price. "I believe that's the equivalent of thirty thousand dollars."

"It's priceless to the right buyer. You could buy it if you were inclined," he said, nudging me.

"Something tells me so could you. And besides, I wouldn't. I'm very selective with the artifacts I purchase." *Very rare, unique, old pieces mostly.* "I think I'll just admire it from the window."

He laughed lightly and took my hand in his. As he did, a flash image of a ring being placed on a finger flickered through my thoughts, distracting me from going inside the shop for a closer look at the copper disks. It was as though I was looking down at my own left hand in the vision. A sensation of joy followed at the same moment, causing my eyes to burn with the threat of tears. Was Kevin having another effect on me? I had to get to the bottom of the sensations I only felt when I was with him.

"Speaking of time, it feels late." I glanced at my watch, as did he.

"It is. We'll have to hurry," he said, pulling me past the window.

We took a shortcut through an alleyway, heading toward a few cabs clustered near the sidewalk on a corner a block away. A sudden heightened awareness filled my senses. My skin prickled with electricity and the hairs on my neck rose in response. I glanced side to side but saw no one. Kevin dropped my hand.

"Stay close," he said.

"What is it?" And then I saw them. Four men dressed in black rounded the corner in our direction. Their eyes fixed upon us. The lips of the man out front curled, as if he'd found his next meal.

"Well now, what do we have here?" A man with an oversized head upon no neck and jowls like a bulldog cocked his head toward us. His eyes skimmed Kevin while taking in my length from head to toe. I met his gaze and saw something flash.

"You ought not to be lingering in the alleyways, don't you know?" another said in a British accent. A tattoo of one end of a snake lifted from the collar of his shirt, reaching the bottom of his earlobe. "You might come across a crew of hoodlums." Another of the men huffed in response.

Two of the men split up, one going to Kevin's side and the other to my right.

"It would be best if you found your action elsewhere," Kevin warned.

"I disagree," one of them said, and from what I could gather, he was the leader of the group. "There's something about your mate that's caught my eye."

I glared at him and saw his eyes shift to the same yellow I'd seen in the little boy a couple weeks earlier. Kevin stood at least four inches taller and was broader across the chest. Still, the man had some height and bulk to him that made him appear as though he was used to bar brawling. The man to my side took one step closer and reached a hand out toward my shoulder. I jutted my elbow into his jaw, leaned to my left, and launched a right kick into his stomach. He crumpled like a groaning sack of potatoes.

"Ah, she's a feisty bitch, too, ain't she?" the leader said, chuckling in a raspy tone. He glanced at the slumped form of his partner trying to regain composure. "She's too much for ye, matey," he said, turning his attention toward me. "That's more my style."

Kevin took a step closer and reached inside his coat. "I said to be on your way."

He didn't have a gun. I would have felt it, having pressed against him at least a few times during the day. But he threatened the man with something all the same.

"We only want to have a little fun," one of the other men said. "Besides, there's something about your lady that…" He stopped, interrupted by the sound of footsteps from behind them.

"I heard you the first time," Kevin said, his tone dropping in further warning. "I said be on your way."

The man turned as my jaw fell open at the site of Aria and Juno.

*What the hell? What are they doing here?* I tried to step around the man I'd kicked to stop them from approaching but was prevented as he'd managed to get to his feet between us. A meaty hand grabbed my arm. I brought an elbow up and slammed it into his forearm, effectively freeing the grip. Another member of the gang attempted to come around Kevin's left side. In one swift maneuver, Kevin looped an arm around mine and turned us away from the man approaching. With his other hand, he pulled something from his coat. From the corner of my eye, I saw Aria reach inside her long black leather coat and pull out a sword, just as the heavy thud of the bar brawler nearest Kevin hit the pavement. Juno pulled out a dagger and aimed it straight for the heart of the first man still standing in his line of sight. Under Kevin's firm grasp, I was led out of the alley.

"Wait, I know them." I tried to free my arm, unsuccessfully. "We can't just leave them."

"They can handle themselves," he said.

I glanced over my shoulder and saw Aria's sword slice into the shoulder of one of the men a moment before he turned into black dust.

*Jesus. They are real.* They appeared to have things well under control, but how was Kevin so confident? My mind was racing, trying to put all the pieces together.

"Demons?" I said under my breath as we slid into the seat of a waiting cab. "How do you know them?" I asked, referring to Aria and Juno. He didn't look at me.

"Langham Hotel, driver," Kevin said, turning to me. "I don't."

*A lie.* I knew it the moment he spoke the words. Silence passed between us, dividing us as though thick, black smoke had settled between us.

Arriving at the hotel, I pushed open the cab door without another word and headed straight for the elevator, leaving Kevin to handle the fare.

I sat stunned alone in my room, wondering what had happened. No knock came. Probably best. Kevin had to know I was upset. Why were Juno and Aria in the same alley that Kevin and I were? How had the day shifted so quickly?

I reached for the note cards for the speech I was giving later, as a distraction to all the feelings running through me, but I couldn't focus and tossed them back on the desk. How was Kevin involved in this? I had to get to the bottom of it, and I would tonight. "Pull yourself together, Sara," I said to myself. "There'll be a chance to find out soon enough."

Mary Ann was counting on me to deliver a successful speech and encourage donations. As distracted as I was now, I was thankful I'd delivered a similar speech once before. I had no plans to let her or the numerous attendees down. They counted on these events to help organizations that fed and clothed people, funded research to find cures, and provided clean water to areas not having access to it. I couldn't let Kevin's secrets screw this up for the foundation. Tonight's attendees and proceeds from the dinner and entertainment to the tune of 850 dollars a plate would get exactly what they expected. And every seat had been sold for a guest list of just over five hundred. No distractions. Not tonight. Tonight was business, but so, too, was what had happened earlier.

*I'll get it worked out.*

I glanced at the clock and hurried into the shower.

Several minutes later, as I slipped out of my robe to dress, I caught a glimpse of my reflection and paused, wondering who was staring back at me behind a fresh, lightly made-up face and an elegant enough updo. It was clear once, but that was before Ardan, before I had fought shadows and encountered demons in my world that looked so much like ordinary people. The person staring back at me looked as determined as she always had but somehow different.

"If you were told you could save the world, but didn't entirely believe it, could you continue with life as you know it and assume responsibility for the loss?" I asked of my reflection in the mirror. "Or would you take a chance and trust without having all the answers yet, abandon everything you know, and have enough faith in yourself to see a mission through to its end, whatever it may be or whatever it might demand of you?" The answer was clear, hidden well under the mask of a billionaire's daughter.

"Damn this thing," I said, returning my attention to the current struggle with the side zipper on my dress, trying to release it from one of the threads it had caught on its zoom upward.

I wouldn't relinquish my passion for helping others. I'd just do it in a different way, on a much larger and dangerous scale. That was the only thought that eased my mind. I would be fulfilling my life's work, just not the way I had originally planned. "Finally," I said as the zipper was freed from its entanglement.

A knock at my door derailed any further contemplation of what had happened. *It can't be five thirty already.* Mary Ann, Kevin, and I had agreed to meet to walk to the dinner hall. I glanced at the clock on the bedside table. It read five thirty-two. I slipped the note cards I had made neatly into the clutch purse and opened the door.

God, he was handsome. Despite my anger and confusion over the earlier event, Kevin's bold look reminded me how much more exciting my trip was because he was here. Without him, I'd just make my usual rounds and spark up friendly conversation, drink wine or champagne, and nibble on hors d'oeuvres until most of the guests had called it a night. The issue I had yet to deal with tonight was just a bump in the road, but one that felt like a speed hump large enough to grind the underside of my car if I wasn't careful.

"Ready, darling?" Mary Ann asked.

Kevin smiled.

"Of course. You look beautiful, Mum."

I glanced at Kevin and placed my hand into the inviting crook of his arm. "You're ravishing," he said, leaning into my ear.

"Thank you." I angled my head toward him. "I didn't think it was possible for you to be more handsome." I squeezed his arm and caught a faint smile.

"Does that mean you're no longer angry with me?"

"Still deciding."

From a sideways glance, I caught the corner of his mouth turning upward as we entered the ballroom.

Lights twinkled from each crystal in the chandeliers dangling above our heads, like an array of large, sparkling diamonds floating in air. There were cascading flowers in stone planters that spotted the bare walls. We were seated at one of many lavishly decorated tables close to where a stage had been erected. I leaned into the back of my chair and absorbed the ambience. The sound of sparkling silver against porcelain was like a brief musical recital during a dinner choice of beef Wellington or roasted Jidori chicken.

Introductions and speeches were delivered while everyone was working on dessert. And soon, it was my turn to take the podium and thank the organizations that provided a resource to women and families that so often found themselves in fear for their lives. The speech seemed well received judging by the surprise of many audience members at some of the jaw-dropping statistics. Closing comments turned the mood to a lighter side, inviting guests to enjoy the party and remember the importance of the evening. It was, after all, a business engagement. A very fine and elaborate one, to be precise.

As I gazed at the crowd, nearly every face was smiling or engulfed in conversation. People were enjoying the music the live band was playing. I leaned into Mary Ann, seated beside me. "You outdid yourself on this one. It's so beautiful. Looks like a real success, too." She clinked glasses with me and took a sip of wine. To my left, a guest engaged Kevin in answering a medical question, something regarding blood disorders. Though that wasn't the most appropriate table conversation, most of our circle of guests had finished their desserts.

"Yes, I believe we have happy donors tonight," Mary Ann said, beaming as she glanced around the room.

"You have them at most events, but this one, for all your hard work, has extra sparkle. Great choice in music as well."

"Oh, I can't take credit for that. Remember Susan Belltran?" I nodded, remembering meeting the cheery woman with blond-gray hair in her mid-fifties at the last event. She enjoyed handling the entertainment selections of such events. "Well, she's much better than I am at selecting just the right thing for the occasion. I'll let her know you like her choices. Excuse me, sweetie. I've got to go mingle a bit and be a good host," she said, putting a hand on my shoulder.

"All right," I said, taking the hint to attend to my duties. "I'll be over to join you in a moment."

I turned my attention to Kevin. As Mary Ann stood from her seat, Kevin found an opportunity to politely exit from his description of symptoms of polycythemia, or thickened blood due to an excess in red or white blood cells. He smiled at Mary Ann and dropped his gaze to me, raising his brows.

"Need to be rescued?" I whispered, taking a sip of my wine.

"If you wouldn't mind."

"Would you please excuse us? I'd like to introduce Dr. Scott to a few of our guests," I said to the remaining invitees at our table.

"Thank you. I didn't think I would be called to work this evening," Kevin said after we'd stepped out of earshot of our guests at the table.

"So much for slipping out of your on-call duties," I said. "You never know what you can be dragged into at these things. Besides, you were kind enough to travel all the way to attend this event with me. And"—I paused to spot my first mark of the evening—"one rescue deserves another. I couldn't very well leave you to the wolves." We eventually made our way around, visiting with the guests, thanking each person for his or her generous contributions, and joined Mary Ann to say hello.

The lights dimmed, signaling the close of the evening with a few slower songs. As Kevin and I turned from a conversation with a couple retiring for the evening, I glanced at the remaining guests on the dance floor.

"May I?" Kevin asked, lifting a nearly empty glass from my hand. "Certainly."

I hadn't realized until he set the glass down that I had just been asked to dance. A warm sensation extended a slow path upward and I felt the heat of it as our bodies brushed together. As my date to a few of the previous benefit functions, Tyler Mason hadn't preferred dancing. That had suited me fine.

Kevin took my hand in his and led me to a spot on the dance floor while I prayed for graceful steps. I was exactly where I wanted to be—with him. But instead of being relaxed and comfortable, I was hoping I didn't put a finale on this evening by falling over him so that we both needed a doctor. It was a natural musical ability to feel rhythm that was developed when I was young, having learned piano, that I leaned heavily on now. After a few steps following his lead and the realization that I might survive dancing, I wondered where to begin unraveling the mysteries I was finding in Kevin.

I wanted to find the flaws in someone up-front, early in a relationship, to determine if I could cope with them or if a clean cut was in order. The only flaw I could find in Kevin was that he was keeping a secret about Juno and Aria, but not for much longer. How much more did he know, and did I have enough time in this dance to broach the topic?

"You don't like this, do you?" he asked, returning my attention to the task at hand.

"Dancing?" He nodded. "It's not really one of my strengths. Sorry it's so obvious." I shrugged. "You would have had a better dance partner if you had asked Mary Ann."

"I don't know about that," he replied, pausing as his eyes lifted to Mary Ann, who'd twirled past us. "I'm quite enjoying having you as a partner. You just seem a little distracted, and no doubt from this afternoon's encounter."

*Okay. He brought it up.*

"It's not as if I could tell you were bad at it, dancing, that is.

In fact, you're much better than you think. I might even believe you took lessons."

I laughed a little. "Well, if that's coming through, then you're more perceptive than the average person. If you only knew that I'm praying I don't mess it up or, worse, trip you." His smile grew larger, warming the cooler side of me that said, *Stay focused.*

"This is supposed to be fun." He paused, watching my expression. "No worries, at least for tonight, okay?"

"Okay," I fibbed. He pulled me a little closer as if to reassure. The scent of his cologne lifted lightly over his collar and chased my thoughts from dancing to wondering if my lips could trace the scent at his neck.

*Do you remember me?*

"Excuse me?" I pulled back slightly to look at him. He allowed the distance but kept one hand pressed on my lower back.

"Sorry?" he asked.

"Did you ask me something?"

"No." His eyes softened, lulled from drink or the quick sensual exchange that passed between us as our eyes met. I wasn't sure.

"Hmph." I returned to my position with his lips near my ear. It had been a whisper of a question but one I was sure I'd heard clearly. The incident earlier in the day, however, was the one pressing for attention. *Enough waiting. Ask him about it, damn it.*

"Explain how you know Aria and Juno." I felt his breath against my cheek as he pulled away to look at me.

"Why don't you ask me what you really want to know, Sara?" A couple of steps in silence. "How much do I know?" I almost stumbled. He felt it and pressed his hand against my back more firmly, holding me against him, our faces mere inches from each other. My eyes searched his and his gaze never wavered. "I'll answer it for you in one word. Ardan," he replied.

I breathed in, darted my eyes left and back to his. "You have a knack for leaving me speechless. My friends would kill to know your secret."

He flashed a quick smile. "The song is over." He stepped out of the embrace with my other hand still in his. I glanced around to see people mingling onto the dance floor for another song that had begun.

"I'm not finished," I said.

"One last dance it is." He pulled me close as we began moving again.

"What exactly is your role?"

"Tonight, it's dancing and, with any luck, seducing you." He pulled back and slipped his fingers along my neck and shoulder, sending a tingle down the same side. Every ounce of my being said, *Trust him.* But I'd been hurt to my core following that feeling once before. I needed something more before I would follow my conscience again. But my heart wasn't listening to the warning. There wasn't enough proof to trust anyone again. I was under his spell as though I had always been, and that draw pulling me into him was as natural as breathing.

"You don't need luck, but let's see how far you get with a little honesty."

"We need a quieter place to discuss the matter. Are you able to leave Mary Ann to her own devices?"

I glanced over to see she was in conversation with a donor who regularly attended her events. "Things are winding down. I don't think she needs me anymore this evening."

We took our drinks to the empty lounge outside the ballroom and sat on a sofa tucked in the corner of the room, angled near an enormous fireplace. I slipped my shoes off and folded my leg beneath me to hear his explanation. As I did, the soft, sinking feeling of the plush cushions and flicker of firelight cast shadows over us, sinking me into a relaxed state. I took a deep breath and settled into the back of the sofa, facing Kevin. His arm draped across the back with his hand resting close to my shoulder.

"Aria, Juno, and Elise have been engaged in a mission to protect you since you returned from Ardan."

"They've been following me?"

"Looking out for you is a slightly better way of putting it. Juno, you remember, is with Special Forces. He is our primary source for knowing"—he paused—"a lot of things, but especially the increased danger closing in. It's all a matter of your safety, Sara." My thoughts flashed back to what Cerys had said about being the only one who could hold the three keys of enlightenment once found.

"Back up a minute. *Our* source for knowing? How are you tied to this mission? What's your role?"

For a moment, nothing was spoken, but plenty had come together in seconds. He'd known all along. He was part of the mission as Juno, Aria, and Elise were. "To protect you."

"And if I'd never had the accident?"

"That was never a factor. It was inevitable that in some manner you would have ended up in Ardan and our paths would have crossed eventually."

"It was predetermined," I said. Nothing wavered in his gaze. Hearing the words aloud somehow made it real. His eyes drifted, concentrating on a few strands at the end of my hair that he looped around his index finger, and in one blink, they returned to mine. My eyelids grew heavier under the effects of wine and firelight.

"Yes. Predetermined is one way to describe what is happening." But the depth in his eyes said so much more.

*Let me read you.* He was holding something back, something that felt painful and yet passionate. I sensed a desperate need, a longing. I was finally able to tune in to his feelings.

"There is more here than your desire to protect. Unless I'm wrong." I had been before, but only once when I trusted that I was loved and cared for by my own parents, only to be let down. I was eight at the time. My accuracy in sensing another's emotions had been fine-tuned over the years. I wasn't about to let that pain hurt me again.

"You're not wrong." He paused as his thumb stroked the length of hair he had held curled between his fingers. "It's late. I promise we can finish this conversation later. C'mon." He stood, picked up my shoes in one hand, and held the other out to me. As much as I wanted more answers, I wanted them when I could put full concentration toward them. Damn the effects of the drinks and a long night working in his favor. Had he even answered my question regarding how he knew about the mission? I didn't think so. He wrapped his arm around me as we walked to the elevator. I should have been angry that he was keeping the whole truth from me. But I couldn't give any attention to it now. I was distracted and yet felt as comfortable with him as being nestled in the softest bedding on a lazy Sunday morning.

"Would you like to be sure the room is secure?" I said, arriving at the door.

"Tempting." He raked a gaze over me.

"But you have Juno to be sure all is well. I forgot." I heard the edge in my tone. What was holding him back from telling me everything, or just taking me in one heated moment? Was I more attracted to him now with all his dark secrets? Was he only with me to protect me? All the sensations in my body said no, but…

He took my lips with his, closing off any other thought, making every attempt to burn the doubt from my mind. As he did, the question *Do you remember me?* sank deeper with each press of his mouth.

# 14

At the break of daylight, I tied my hair into a sleek ponytail and downed the rest of the coffee from room service, hoping to awaken a little energy from my sluggish state before I ran one errand. I had to get back to the antique shop Kevin and I stopped at yesterday.

"Wait here. I'll only be a couple of minutes," I said to the taxi driver, handing him a fifty-pound note.

As I passed by the window, I noted the ring with the giant stone was gone. *It must have been sold to a fool in love last night. Good for the shop owner and the happy couple.* I stepped up to the door and peered through the glass. A small light was on in the back, but the shop otherwise appeared closed. I knocked, then pressed the lever of the door to find it open.

"Hello?" I called, shutting the door behind me. The bell at the top jingled at my arrival, in case I hadn't been heard.

"Ah, I thought you might return," a cracked voice from behind a counter stacked full of books replied.

"You're open then?" I said, trying to match a face to the voice. "Not for an hour yet, but for you I make the exception." An old woman, no taller than four and a half feet, stepped from behind the stack of books and smiled. Her face had more lines than I'd ever seen and in every place that once was smooth, like a sweet, almond-colored prune. Her hair was a tight, curly light blond, adding an additional height of three inches or so.

"They said the Light Carrier would come and so you have." Her eyes were like a hawk's as they landed on the silver ring I wore.

*They?*

"However did you arrive unaccompanied?" She reached for my hand and held it between hers. Soft, paper-like skin covered what I sensed as experienced, articulate fingers.

"It was easier than you might think." A late night. An early morning. Juno wouldn't be out unless he never slept. And as far as I knew, Kevin had been as tired as I the night before.

"Come. I have what you're looking for." She released my hand and turned toward the small lamp glowing in the corner. The scent of roses lifted in the air around her as I followed. On the far corner table, incense burned a spicy aroma of cinnamon and clove.

"How could you know of my interest in the medallions?" I couldn't have stopped for more than two or three minutes to gaze. In that time, I'd never seen the shop owner.

"Those," she said, glancing over her left shoulder to the window, "are for show and to entice the Light Carrier to find what she seeks. We're not all working on opposing teams, my dear." She winked.

The walls of the small room in the back of the shop were layered with shelves and stacked with boxes of every size, shape, and color, stretching almost to the ceiling. She pulled a rolling ladder to one side and stepped midway up. "Now, let me see. Not here, or here." Her fingers skimmed over the numerous boxes until they stopped at one very ordinary wooden one. She pulled it, brushed a hand over the top, and blew the dust in a cloud that settled as a layer of fine mist over the other boxes.

"Yes. Here we are." I waited as she climbed down with the small square package tucked under her arm. "This is for you. It's been waiting quite some time." I glanced from her to the box she held. She unsnapped the two fasteners on either side and lifted the lid.

To my surprise, one of the symbols matched exactly the image I'd found on my computer. Next to it was one unrecognizable, with what looked like an Egyptian symbol of an Udjat, or the Eye of Horus as it was known in Egyptian mythology. A white light glittered across the stone medallions, so ancient in appearance, yet every carved shape was chiseled to perfection as if it were new.

"You're pleased. Good, good."

"It's what I somehow knew I would find here. The Professors said they would be delivered when the time was right, but I didn't know…" I shook my head, wondering just how they had gone from Ardan to a dusty old wooden box in Europe.

"Their power is not active until the third and final symbol is joined to them. But anyone aware of your quest will sense the individual power they carry. You must guard them well."

"Of course."

"Come," she said, waving a hand for me to follow. She moved across the small room and through a curtained doorway, pulling the chain that hung from a light bulb on the ceiling. Opening two wooden doors at the end revealed an array of weapons. There were guns of all shapes and sizes, daggers, too. Throwing stars and swords hung along the inside wooden panels.

"I have been provided the weapon of choice by the elves," I said, remembering my sword.

"Of course you have. This," she said, pulling a small ring off the top shelf, "is to guard against others detecting the power of the symbols. It will hide the symbols' energy, but only if it's worn by the Light Carrier." She held the ring between her thumb and index finger. "Your right hand, my dear." I lifted my hand to waiting fingertips. She took my pinky finger and slipped the ring on. It fit as though it had been sized for me. I gazed at the light brown stone with a black cross in the center. "It's chiastolite, a protective stone known for its power to guard against negative energies."

"I see." I studied the light and dark colors of brown that blended like a confection of caramel and chocolate. "What do I owe you?"

She held my hand between hers and turned her face up to mine, meeting my eyes, and smiled. "A lock of your hair will do nicely."

*An odd payment for something so valuable, if it does what she says.*

"Those of us who aid the Alliance find that creating unique weapons and the magic that supports them are best done with the genetic material of our living members." I nodded once as she reached across to pull scissors from a small basket and snipped a small angled length from one side.

"Now, you should be getting back before the Last Great Warrior seeks you out. I suspect he's already wondering where you are," she said. "And since I have no business with him…" She waved a hand in the air as if to dismiss further thought.

"Last Great Warrior? What do you mean? Juno?"

She smiled and shook her head, sending the curls into a small frenzy. "Never mind, my dear. In time you'll know."

"Yes, I hope you're right. Thank you," I said, tucking the box inside my coat. A tug at my hand kept me from leaving.

"Guard them well and succeed in your mission. You are provided the tools."

"I'll do my best."

"No." She held my hand tighter. "You will do better. Pull from yourself all the strength you are not yet aware that you have. Believe in it and succeed. You are the only one who can."

"I will do all I can."

"Of course you will." She patted my hand before releasing it. I turned toward the exit. Her words of strength sunk deeper into my conscience. I pulled open the little door. The bell gave another cheery ring, shattering the heaviness that had been placed upon my shoulders again.

"Always my pleasure, love," she called from behind me as I shut the door.

The sun broke through scattered clouds, making a full appearance in the sky. The cab I'd paid handsomely to wait was gone. I stepped to the curb to hail another, but before I could stick my hand in the air, a black car came screeching to a halt in front of me and Juno stepped out.

"How did you…? How could you possibly…?"

"Sara, get in. Please." He stood holding the passenger side door open. "There is no time to waste standing on an open street waiting for the next run-in with evil."

I ducked into the car. He made a U-turn and sped off in the direction of the hotel.

"It's good to see you again, Juno. At least this time I'll be allowed to talk to you."

"It's good to see you, too. You're in danger. He was right to pull you away," he said, referring to Kevin.

"How much danger could there be if I can walk the streets of New York?"

"You shouldn't. Tarsamon has engaged his forces. The demons that you have run into don't fully know of your abilities and we would like to keep it that way, at least until we can get to the first location of the keys."

"Which is?"

"To be determined only by the Light Carrier or..." He stopped and glanced at me and returned his eyes to the road.

"Finish your thought." I tuned in to the same sense of him not wanting to say too much, the same feeling I'd detected in Kevin last night, just before he walked me to my room. "Did you mean the Last Great Warrior, perhaps?"

"The point is, we've got to get the last symbol, get to the next location, and somehow keep Tarsamon from realizing the points that have been met in the mission, namely your recent acquisition."

"God, you're good. It couldn't have been two minutes since I stepped outside her door that you were here, and yet you know of my business inside?"

"Lady Mara is a connection we all have. It was expected you would do business with her."

*Ah, so that's her name.* I realized at that moment I had never gotten it from her.

"How could you expect that I'd do business with someone when I didn't even know I was coming to Europe until a week ago?"

"All I can tell you is the knowledge is provided to us."

"Preplanned, right?"

"Sometimes, yes."

The vagueness was annoying. We didn't speak for a few moments as the car sped toward its destination.

"Where is Aria? I would've liked to have said hello to her. And Elise, is she with you, too?"

"They're near. You'll get the chance to see them again, and another member soon." He stopped the car in front of the hotel and turned to me. "Please understand this mission is in full force. You are the only one who can fulfill it, so please don't underestimate the danger and keep your guard up."

"Will do. Thanks for the ride." I pushed the door open and headed for the hotel entrance. I glanced over my shoulder, knowing Juno was waiting until I'd entered before pulling away.

I made my way into the elevator, through the empty hall, and slid the key card into my door.

"We missed you at breakfast." I turned to see Kevin standing at my back, dressed in a slim-fitting sweater the color of midnight and jeans, handsome as ever. He followed me inside.

"There was some last-minute business I had to attend to."

"I see you're already packed." His eyes glanced to where my carry-on rested near the vanity. "You were up early."

"Did you want me to invite you to come with me?"

"Not at all. I have no business at the shop." He sat in the chair next to the window. Juno had wasted no time calling Kevin. If I wanted to be secretive about anything, it would take some real dedication to the effort.

"I'm sorry. I do enjoy your company, but I don't need a twenty-four-by-seven watch. I'm capable of handling myself." Instead of getting angry as I expected, he simply watched as I gathered the last toiletry items from the bathroom counter.

"If I were here for a 'watch,' I would have stayed the night. I wanted to see you again." He leaned back in the chair he'd selected by the window, resting his elbows on the arms, crossing one ankle over his knee, and linking his fingers together over his stomach. "Is it bothering you that I do?"

Damn him. It was. I didn't like feeling as though I was being watched, even if I was attracted to the watcher. I didn't want to get used to anybody. And he was just the person I was being drawn to with every moment that passed with him. I didn't know how to answer, so I didn't. He stood, took the few steps to where I was placing the last items in my carry-on.

"I was afraid knowing about my involvement in the mission might change some things for you. I hope that you won't stay angry too long." He cupped my jaw and swept his lips over mine once, testing. Maintaining my resilience was growing increasingly difficult. My lips defied further attempt and gave in to the kiss. He drew me in, taking the kiss deeper before pulling back. "I'll see you on the plane, darling."

Our flight left early, and before I knew it, I was being awakened by the gentle stroke of a hand over the top of my head.

"We're home," came a soft voice. I had dozed on Kevin's shoulder, recovering from the lost sleep from the previous evening. I sat up and pulled myself together.

"She can sleep through anything," Mary Ann said, leaning across the aisle to him. Apparently, we had already landed and were hedging toward the gate.

"Thanks for the use of your shoulder," I said, glancing to him. I rubbed the sleepiness from my face. The warmth in his expression ran through me, alighting my nerves yet again in a most pleasant manner. How did he do that so easily? He kissed me on my forehead, reminding me of a vaguely familiar sensation I could not bring to memory.

The car driving us home rushed through the evening as if the driver realized he was late for an appointment. The streetlights flashed by in a cartoonish blur, shortly before the driver pulled up to the curb of a towering apartment building on New York's Upper East Side. Kevin kept an apartment in the city he said was a short twenty-minute drive to his office. I had not yet had a chance to see it but was hoping to soon. After all, we had a discussion to finish. I was also curious how he lived, entertaining the thought his living arrangements were as neat and tidy as he always appeared. We said a simple good-night and exchanged a quick kiss while the driver pulled Kevin's bag from the trunk.

When I arrived home, I slipped into an oversized T-shirt and crashed into the soft, airy bed, leaving my luggage still packed by the door.

A last thought of Mary Ann passed over me and with it a moment of regret, as I considered how she and Robert would take the news that their only daughter had abandoned a well-paid-for education for, um, saving the world with her allies? They would think my accident had surely impaired my ability to handle reality for sure. "Perhaps a delayed reaction," I could hear them say, as they sought the advice of another professional in desperate need to know why their daughter had left her senses.

Maybe they'd remember the decisions I made were straight business, emotionless. Being relatively free of emotion gave me an edge in difficult matters, never thinking with my heart but instead doing what was right by keeping a clear head. That didn't make me a cold and heartless woman, either. I was compassionate and understanding. After all, I still remembered what it felt like to be rejected and abandoned by my own parents, and as such, I understood emotional pain. My childhood had built a wall to protect me from anyone who might emotionally try to hurt me in the future. On the flip side, my experience and ability to feel what others felt gave me understanding and the capacity to relate to them. Even now as I lay awake reflecting, Kevin was quickly becoming the wrench in that logic by forcing emotion I carefully protected.

What if his interest in me wasn't all about protecting me? His kisses were convincing enough. I threw back the covers and went to my office to scan the internet, looking for anything to take my mind off of him.

As I entered through the large double doors, two objects caught my eye: A long rectangular package rested across two arms of a chair in front of my desk, while a rather beautiful plant sat in place of my laptop, budding a single, enormous, deep red flower. A card was neatly propped in front. I went to the larger object first, peeling back the paper on one end to find another cover of heavy cardboard. Though plain in color, this package felt anything but ordinary. There was a tab in the center. I felt along the seams and the edges. The entire package was stapled shut. Pulling the thick tab caused most of the staples to pop. With some additional effort, I forced the last few that kept the cardboard lid from fully opening.

I folded back the protective plastic followed by a soft cloth cover. Inside was a polished wooden case, colored in rich mahogany. What drew my eye past the beautiful polish of the wood was an intricately carved design in the center. It was compass-like, round with a single arrowed point on one side. Bordering the edge were symbols. They looked to be Ogham symbols, an early medieval alphabet referring to sacred trees that contained a symbolic meaning for the essence of an individual. Three triskeles converged in the center of the ring. I traced the beautiful design slowly with my fingertips, wondering just how it had arrived and from whom.

I pressed the intercom button connecting me to security.

"Yes, Dr. Forrester?"

"Who delivered the large package in my office?"

"It was delivered by personal messenger service. We stopped them at the gate." I could hear the rustle of papers.

"Did they say who it was from?"

"No. The messenger stated that the package needed to reach you directly. He gave specific instructions it was only to be opened by you, and that you would be expecting it. Would you like me to remove it?"

*Expecting it, huh?*

I skimmed an eye over it, deciding that, if it were a bomb, it would likely have exploded at the pulling of the tab. "One moment." I inched the lid up ever so slowly. "Nope. It's okay. I'd forgotten about this package. Thanks."

Deep inside the box rested the blade I had used in Ardan. It was perfectly protected in its case, gleaming brilliantly at me. The blade was as smooth as glass, not a knick or groove where it shouldn't be. A few of the same details found in the carving were copied into the hilt of sword. It was a masterful creation, flawless in beauty and design.

In Ardan, I had used it only as my tool, never fully taking time to marvel in more than its precision. The sword began to glow a soft yellow haze, then white with blue flecks, as though waking from sleep. I picked it up and the glow began to fade, finding its rightful owner. I admired it for several minutes, feeling the weight in my hands as comfortable as I remembered, before setting it back in the case.

Sitting down behind my desk, I turned my attention to the blank envelope and flipped it over in my hand before forcing a finger through to open it.

"A small way of saying thank you for a very lovely weekend with you...Kevin."

*Interesting.* It was unusual to receive a plant as a gift, especially from a man. But this was not an ordinary plant. The greenery faded behind the giant red bloom. I preferred to watch a flower endure its natural life cycle from its original source, but Kevin couldn't know that. I responded in a quick but kind email.

*Kevin, beautiful choice. Given the option, would have stayed longer with you...Sara.*

# 15

It had been a long flight from New York to the meeting location in California. Thankfully, I was allotted the time to recover by having the first meeting with C-05 set for the following morning.

A sleek black limo and a driver by the name of Tellmin arrived to pick me up at nine a.m. His salt-and-peppered hair gave him an older, distinguished appearance. But a closer glimpse revealed he couldn't be much older than his early forties. No visible lines existed to reveal a difficult life. Then again, I was in the land of beautiful tanned bodies and Botox. I tucked the long black coat I wore beneath me and slid into the back seat as he closed the door.

Not a word was spoken on the drive, until we arrived at a mirrored building locked down like Fort Knox and Mr. Tellmin said, "Here we are." A series of codes opened several doors as we passed the main entrance and turned directly left down a flight of stairs, one level below ground. I was directed to wait in a large office. As I did, I slipped off my coat and strolled around the room, noting the brown-leathered wall and long black onyx desk, tapping a fingernail on it as I glanced around the room. There were no pictures to hint at the personality of the user of such a space, making it seem as though anyone in the office was as interchangeable as one of the chairs. I turned my head in the direction of the sound of the door opening.

"May I offer you coffee, water, or other beverage, Dr. Forrester?" a woman in a suit offered.

"No, thank you. I'm fine."

"Very well. Your contact will be in shortly. I apologize for the wait, but he is wrapping up a meeting that has gone over."

"Not a problem."

The moment the door closed, my phone chimed, indicating a text message was waiting. I pulled it from the outside pocket of my brief-case and glanced at the message. *Find the unlocked room now*, it read.

*What?*

After receiving the image of the symbols and now this message, it was clear someone had a connection to not only my computer but to my exact location and what I was doing. How could they know right now was the perfect opportunity to reach me? Aside from the security breach on my computer, a concern obviously, I was even more suspicious.

*Now*, the message flashed again.

There must be several unlocked rooms in this building. How in God's name was I going to find one particular room in this massive facility of secrets?

"Where?" I typed back in the small window.

"Left down the hall, below the staircase, to the right of the auditorium." The message blinked once at me on my screen.

Like the Gaelic symbol I'd received days ago, both images faded from view. I closed out the screen, slid the phone into my pocket, and cracked open the door, peering left, then right. I might have a few minutes and not much more. *Left, down the hall.* I repeated the instructions I'd read until I found myself passing what looked like an auditorium and was standing in front of a black door that resembled where one might find a janitor's closet, beneath the stairs and tucked in a rather dark corner out of sight.

*All the more reason why it would seem suspicious if I were caught.*

There was a key code box next to the door, but it wasn't lit green or red. Should anyone be inside, I would simply explain I had become lost trying to find the restroom. It was a plausible circumstance given the complexity of the location of offices in this building. A wave of indecision came over me as I considered what I was doing. I would never have thought about entering the private office of someone, practically breaking in. What if the door was locked? Having come this far and now facing the door, I couldn't turn away.

I pressed the lever, finding that the door was indeed open. My best guess was every room in the building had a code required to enter. Why was this one unlocked?

Upon entering, I closed the door with a gentle push and waited for a half second before switching on one set of lights from the panel on the wall. A corner in the back of the room illuminated enough for me to gaze at the multitude of information. The walls were covered with notes and references to Ardan, including the names Tarsamon and Soltari in bold lettering pasted in one corner. In the middle of the room was an enormous length of paper strewn across two large tables. I walked closer to see it was a map of some sort, like a treasure map with drawings and symbols spotted across it. *Celtic Region* was written in script in one area of the map over Scotland with asterisks appearing to mark specific locations, indicating the perceived location of key number one. In an area south of the US was another marked *Key two or three?* It had to be C-05's office or the heart of his operation, I thought, as I mulled through more of the documents. Markers had been placed on a map of Egypt and another on the Yucatan Peninsula, all on a separate table opposite the map of Scotland.

There were several sketches of circular shapes, with different images and symbols in them. My fingertips gently moved over a few of the pages and stopped when I spotted my name in heavy bold print on a larger piece of paper. Arrows were drawn off of several Mayan, Egyptian, and Celtic symbols that pointed back to my name. Someone was definitely at work here, with a fair amount of information coming together. But there was one item in heavy, bolded red ink that I lingered on longer than the rest—an arrow from my name to Tarsamon. A sick feeling filled my stomach. I lifted the paper to search for any clues that would lead to the meaning contained in the writings.

*Leave now, quickly.* I heard a voice from inside my head speak with urgency. Perhaps it was my own intuition or fear. Without wanting to take any further risk of being caught, I decided it best to heed the warning, shutting the light off and easing past the door that closed in a quiet whoosh behind me. I made it to the exit of the auditorium and into the hall as the woman who had offered me coffee rounded the corner in my direction.

"Dr. Forrester, may I help you?" Her eyebrows closed together as she likely tried to determine why I was so far from where I should be waiting. I, too, had wondered what would cause me to chase a mysterious message from an unknown sender.

"Oh, yes. I'm sure you can. This place is a maze," I answered. Her eyes narrowed further, despite the pleasantry of a smile that remained across her lips. "You see, well, this is embarrassing, but I seem to have gotten lost searching for the restroom. I knew I should have made a right turn instead of a left," I said, gesturing with a wave of my hand.

"Well…" She paused. "It's not the first time someone has become lost in these back hallways. I would have been happy to direct you."

*I'm sure you would have, just not to the place I needed to go.*

"My apologies. I didn't see anyone to ask."

She eyed me speculatively. "Please follow me. I'll show you the way. C-05 is ready to meet with you." I followed the woman in the direction of the office, with a brief stop at the restroom for a deep breath before returning to the office.

"Good morning, Dr. Forrester. It's a pleasure to finally meet you." A man of lean build and approximate height of five feet eight with short white hair extended his hand toward me as he came around the desk. "I apologize for the delay." I caught a glimpse of an old scar that ran from his temple past his ear. A flash of pain hit me at whatever memory he carried of it, yet there were no details of how he obtained it that I could pick up in the momentary sensation.

"Not at all. Please, call me Sara. You are C-05, I presume?"

"Yes. At last I meet the one referred to as the Light Carrier. Seems I'm a little late in meeting with you. Please." He gestured for me to sit at one of the chairs angled in front of the desk.

"I'm sorry, I don't know what you mean?"

"The other members of your team have already found you."

"It would appear so. But I understand I have yet to meet all of them."

"Well then, I may be able to assist." I watched as he moved with precision, organizing documents in a folder on his desk. He was meticulous. It showed in the starch of his collar to the crease in the gray Italian slacks, as well as every movement. "But first, let's get down to business regarding the symbols, shall we?"

I smiled. "I was hoping you might provide me the details contained within them. It's still quite the mystery to me." Without really knowing why, I felt as though I should say nothing about my recent acquisition at the antique shop in London. Better to see what C-05 had to share.

He stared for a moment. I cleared my head to focus on any feelings I could read from him. "You seem surprised," I added, crossing one leg over the other.

"In a way, I am." He leaned back into his chair, brought his hands together, and steepled his index fingers above his lip. "I would have thought for certain your aides in Ardan would have led you to the symbols by now."

"I don't mean to disappoint you, but perhaps I don't have the allies you believe me to have."

His fingers fell away from his mouth. "On the contrary. I'm not disappointed, but rather surprised." He leaned forward, his arms extended over his desk, hands folded.

*Hiding something.*

"How is it that you've come to know of Ardan?"

"Sara, we're all connected in some way to the powers that govern the mission. Like you, I was called to Ardan to practice my skill and assist in the quest ahead."

"And what is your task?"

"To ensure the mission is completed. That you and your team remain on the right path."

*Might explain the details in the room.*

"The symbols are the primary source of energy to lead us to the keys. Of this I'm sure you're already aware. If the efforts of this team are successful and the keys of enlightenment are obtained," he continued, "we expect to snuff out the darkness with the power contained in each key. In essence, the success would create a world of cohesiveness, acceptance, and understanding, a world free of judgment, but also retain it as a place of learning."

"Maybe you can help me uncover the specifics of what I should be looking for?" After all, there was one remaining symbol that I wanted to discover the meaning of, even though I'd been advised the third would stay in Ardan.

"Only you, as the Light Carrier, are given the ability to identify with what source will direct you once the symbols are near." *The antique shop.* "No one else is able to guide you to them, at least not in this world. None of us who have been sent to assist in the quest have the details of what the symbols look like. It's a matter of protection." I did remember the Professor speaking of this as the reason for hiding the details, and yet I'd happened upon that unlocked room with plenty of information. "And I'm quite surprised to hear you have not been led to or obtained at least the first of the medallions yet."

"Perhaps the time is not right for me to find them?" The need to guard the fact that I had the first two medallions was a growing sensation. But why? If C-05 was part of this team, why did I feel the need to be guarded? That feeling didn't exist with Kevin when he'd advised me of his role. Then again, I had not met with Lady Mara and obtained the two medallions prior to our discussion.

C-05 stood from his desk and rested his hands at his waist. "Perhaps," he replied. But I could sense he didn't believe that the timing wasn't right.

"Is there any other way to determine the location of the keys without the symbols?" I asked.

"A great deal of research has been done based on prior knowledge." He glanced up from the floor and crossed his arms. *Guarded.* "I understand much of that knowledge has been withheld from your memory, probably to keep the symbols safe from anyone untrust-worthy trying to pry into your thoughts."

*Pry into my thoughts?*

"Still, we do have some clues. But without the symbols, the gate to the first location cannot be opened."

"I understand. I'm sorry I don't have any information to provide."

"Not to worry." But everything about his body language said oth-erwise. "I expect it will come soon. I did want the pleasure of meeting you, Sara. And there is not much that can be done about the lack of information at the moment, now is there? When you do receive in-formation or come into contact with the symbols, please let me know and I'll move the mission forward." He handed me a card.

*Forward, as in under your control?*

"Of course," I said. But even I heard the doubt in that simple response.

I didn't agree. If the power of the symbols was at its greatest when all three were brought together, it didn't make sense that I would en-trust that power to someone else. I didn't even know who C-05 was. Knowing his name, his real name at least, might set us on a more solid foundation and maybe establish a hint of trust. It didn't help that I couldn't hear his thoughts. He and Kevin were the only two people I had ever had such an experience with. But something was different with C-05 that I had not felt with Kevin. An edge of... A chime rang over his phone, pulling me from my concentrated effort to identify the emotional air around him.

"Please excuse me for one moment. There is someone I'd like for you to meet and he's just arrived. Do you mind waiting?"

"Not at all."

My eyes shifted right just as the door was about to close. *It couldn't be.* I caught the glimpse of a man who looked like Kevin. Our eyes locked for a split second and my breath caught in my throat. *He wouldn't have come without saying something, right?* I stood and reached for the door handle to satisfy my curiosity. My phone buzzed in my pocket. I debated answering or pulling the door open. A second thought of how ridiculous it might seem if I hurried out the door to see two strangers overcame me, and I opted instead to glance at my phone. The sender of the text was blocked.

"Meet me for a drink tonight, 6:30 p.m., your hotel lounge."

*What the hell? Whoever is keeping track of my whereabouts and timing is too good at their job.* "I don't meet strangers for drinks," I typed and paused, considering it might ease my conscience if I agreed to meet and instead pressed send.

In not more than a second, a reply shot back. "I'm not a stranger, Sara."

Now I had to know. Juno? Maybe Aria? She had been with him in London. Perhaps the sender was Elise. I hadn't run into her yet. If the text had been from Kevin, his number would have identified him. *Shit.* I slipped the phone back into my pocket, irritated by the distraction. I had no choice but to meet the anonymous message writer. I paced the room, unable to sit, as though I were a caged animal.

Within a matter of moments, the door opened. Behind C-05, a man about six foot two entered. I could swear his platinum-blond hair added extra illumination to the shady, masculine office. His electric-blue eyes met mine and were now scanning me for a read, as he flashed one of the sexiest smiles I'd seen in some time. Did he know he wasn't hiding anything from me, that I was reading the energy around him, too?

"Sara, I'd like you to meet Matt. He's part of the Special Forces unit with Juno."

I extended a hand. "It's a pleasure to meet a colleague of Juno's." My curiosity was looming. I didn't get the same suspicious feeling I did from C-05.

"Please make yourselves comfortable. I'm sorry, Sara, for keeping you waiting, but an urgent issue was just pinged to me on my way to meet Matt. Seems my assistant is unable to attend to it. I'll only be a moment." I nodded as he slipped out the door.

"Dr. Forrester, I've heard a great deal about you with regard to this mission," Matt said.

"It seems to be a theme with the other members, or so I've heard."

I smiled, taking a seat with him. "How long have you been engaged with this mission?"

"Only a few months, and not nearly as long as Juno. He and I work very closely to assist each other. We don't have much time." He glanced over my shoulder at the door. "Your suspicions of C-05 are shared by the rest of us."

"The other members?" He nodded. "How could you know of my suspicion?"

"I have a similar ability as you, to read thoughts and telecommunicate. You're in a great deal of danger with the uprising of the shadows."

"You've seen them, too?"

"Yes. They aren't fully active yet, not on the hunt. They are learning the environment, getting a feel for the energy of people. But if they get wind of who you are, it would be like blood in a pool of sharks. By the way, guard your thoughts. He can hear you," Matt said, angling his head in the direction of the door C-05 had exited. "Just as I can."

"How much do you know?"

"Only that you are suspicious. Don't bother trying to figure out why you can't pin down the reason C-05 is hiding details. And he is. It simply doesn't matter. Trust what you feel, always."

"Why would he be working against us? I thought the pure of heart are the only people welcome in Ardan."

"It would be more correct to say those who aren't pure of heart, mainly the shadows and Tarsamon, are obligated to stay in one territory of Ardan. It's an area of the realm equivalent to what you'd consider hell, I suppose. But Tarsamon has outgrown the substantial area granted to him. And we don't know yet that C-05 isn't pure of heart. But none of us in this mission hides anything from another member."

*Want to bet?* I couldn't help to think of what other secrets Kevin might have.

Matt shifted in his seat and crossed an ankle over his knee. "We work as a team, always."

"I see."

"Do you?" he asked. I met his gaze. "Do you know why you are incapable of inflicting revenge, feeling hate, or fear?"

"I can't say I'd ever given it any thought. What does that have to do with this mission?"

I rolled his statement over in my mind and decided it was true enough. I had no desire to ever make anyone pay for any harm they did to me. I thought of my biological parents. I didn't wish anything bad for them. What I had experienced was just a fact of life for me. I might carry emotional scars from it, but I was nobody's victim.

For centuries, people had been passing on their hurt and anger to others and hurting one another. Perhaps morality and integrity had taken a larger blow in the last several years than even one or two generations before, increasing the anguish felt and, without being aware, opening a door for evil to enter. Trying to heal emotional suffering and the effects of a fractured integrity had been my life's work. That is, before I'd entered Ardan.

"I've heard you are a thinker." He smiled, warming the razor-like edge held in those blue eyes. "Our inability to seek revenge is what sets us apart as pure of heart. All of the others—" The door opened and C-05 entered. "Yes, I think I remember Robert. A news story regarding a company battling legal issues to hang on to their company."

"Indeed. He can be ruthless," I said, switching gears along with him.

"Well, it was certainly a pleasure meeting you, Sara." Matt stood and extended a hand. We'll see each other again soon."

"Yes, I hope so." I shook his hand, and at the release, his eyes left mine and went to C-05. "Tonight, seven o'clock at Le Martine?"

"Looking forward to it." C-05 said goodbye, and before he could sit down again, I stood.

"I really must be going. I've agreed to another meeting while I'm in town. Should we set another appointment?"

"I would have enjoyed a few more minutes getting to know you. I'm terribly sorry for the interruptions but am glad to have had the opportunity, though brief, to meet you."

"Yes, it was a pleasure. I do wish I had more details to provide."

I placed a hand on the door handle. His hand reached above mine, fingers wrapping around the edge.

"Be sure to let me know the moment you have information, won't you?" He stared with such intensity it could have unraveled me. But I wasn't easily intimidated or moved by a stare, except perhaps those from one dark-haired physician.

I forced a smile. "Of course," I answered, sensing the invisible cloud of deception growing darker between us.

# 16

s I opened the door of the facility to leave, I was met with a mild breeze off the ocean blowing inland from the coast. The scent of salty sea welcomed me out of the stale air of the building. I spotted the car waiting out front to take me back to the hotel. An eerie vacancy of life, however, sharpened my gaze in search of the driver. Not a single person was coming or going.

I stepped off the curb to see around the car when a sudden force hit me from behind, sending me straight into the pavement. I shifted to my side as three faceless shadowy figures surrounded me. Empty darkness in a cloak of black. Hoods drawn over what should be heads.

"We know who you are, Light Carrier. Call off your mission." It was as though I'd been transported to Ardan minus the forest.

But I hadn't. Those figures were in my world. The reality hit me that I could die facing shadowy puppets of death without a weapon.

*The shield of light.*

I pushed myself to stand. "I won't," I replied. "The mission has been set into action by the will of your lord, Tarsamon."

An evil hiss escaped from the group of three.

"Sara." The call from behind dared me to turn away, to take my eyes off the three shadows in front of me.

"You've declared war," the voice continued.

"So be it. The souls who've chosen to come to this world to become more enlightened will get their chance."

"You forget the energy you tempt."

I felt a pinch at my throat as some invisible force tried to remind me of the strength I'd evidently forgotten. Instinct took over and I lifted my palm to the sky. The blue-white sparks crackled to life. But as the flame grew, the hooded shapes collapsed in a heap like tossed laundry and spun upward in a cloud of black before I could ever strike. In their place stood Matt and Juno. They tucked their swords inside their coats and the city came to life as if nothing had happened.

"You didn't think you'd be doing this all alone, did you?" Aria's voice called out from behind me. I turned this time.

"Watch your arm, Sara," Elise said, standing beside her. I glanced at my left arm to see a fair amount of blood trickling down from the elbow, a cut from the sharp edge of stone on the pavement. "Here." She handed me several tissues that I quickly pressed against the wound.

A smile stretched across my face at seeing them but quickly faded at the realization that one person was missing.

"Are you okay?" Juno asked, his eyes scanning my length.

"Yeah, but where did you come from? I never saw you, or them."

"They used a shield that made their dark forms invisible to us, like a bubble, while concealing the world from your view," Matt replied. "We watched your movement to know where to strike."

"We have to get you out of here," Juno said. "You're sure you aren't hurt anywhere else?"

"Yes." I swiped at the blood on my arm that had already begun to slow its descent. "This is nothing. Their visit was a warning to call off the mission. I don't think they intended to battle."

"We don't really know for sure since you didn't have a chance to toss that flame at them," Aria said. "You may want to make carrying your sword a habit. Besides, long coats are trendy this time of year." It was late October, and as if to confirm the fact, a gust of wind picked up again.

"So I see." My gaze skimmed over the small group. "It's good to see you again. It feels like forever, another lifetime, since we were together."

"Technically, it has been that long since when we last fought together. But let's save the reunion for another time. We really have to go," Juno insisted.

I nodded and followed him to his car. As much as I tried to reassure him I was okay, Juno waited a couple of hours in the hotel to be sure all remained safe. As we sat at one of the tables in the restaurant, he claimed he and Matt had received a vision of an altercation to take place outside the building prior to the actual occurrence, which had diverted Matt from his plans to join Juno, Aria, and Elise.

"Were you the one who sent me the anonymous message to check the room beneath the stairs?"

"Yes," Juno replied. "We've had some suspicions about him, too, but I needed you to see firsthand."

"See what firsthand?"

"Shortly after I last met with him, I saw a vision of him sorting through items. While I'd expect him to be researching, I wouldn't expect him to have tied your name back to Tarsamon." He shook his head as his gaze descended, recalling the memory. "The energy around the vision wasn't the same, either. It was gray." His eyes met mine and the confusion I was sure was in them. I didn't see auras, so I couldn't relate to what he meant by gray energy. But I had an idea about how it might have felt. "Something has happened to change things, but I don't know what," he added.

"I know he wants me to, but I'm not sure about sharing anything regarding this mission with C-05, and I'm not entirely sure why. Until we know for sure, have no suspicions, I don't think it's safe to trust anyone outside our immediate circle—you, Aria, Elise, and Matt.

"Is it your intention to exclude Kevin?"

"I don't know." I shook my head slightly. "I don't know enough about him and this mission. That makes me uncomfortable."

He nodded. "You have to trust what you feel. It's what leads the course, what direction we'll take."

"I will."

"You are aware that Kevin is…" He paused a little too long.

"What?"

"An integral part of this mission."

His words were chosen carefully, as if he had contemplated saying something else but had changed his mind.

"So is C-05, supposedly, and we don't trust him right now." I took a sip of my iced tea. "But if you say he is, it must be true."

"I assure you, there are no doubts with regard to him."

I nodded. "On another note, the last medallion, which I hope to find in Ardan, will make all three extremely powerful when brought together. C-05 says he wants information when I get it about these symbols. I believe he wants them. But I don't see why I would put that kind of power in the hands of someone else."

"You wouldn't."

"Taking that concern a bit deeper, why would I be turning over these symbols to C-05 if I'm leading the mission?"

"Good question." I could see in his eyes his mind was ticking away at what might be going on, tossing over the theories he had, and arriving quickly at one conclusion. Anyone who obtained all three symbols could destroy this mission.

"You'll do what you think is best. The rest of us will protect your decision as we move forward. Right now, we're putting this mission with you, not C-05. But he doesn't know it yet."

I nodded and took another sip of tea. He explained the team would be staying close, and like me, all of their duties had shifted to this mission.

"Am I free to go to my room and catch up on some sleep?"

"Sara, you're free to do whatever you need to. You'll just have a mighty force following like an unseen shadow. I know how you must hate the idea, but don't doubt it's necessary."

He didn't say, but because he and the rest of the team were where I was, I suspected they were staying in rooms very close to mine.

"I'm not arguing after what I've seen today. I appreciate that you have my back." I dropped a tip on the table, smiled, and headed to my room, wondering where the missing member of this team might be.

# 17

"Crap," I said, glancing at my watch to see it was 5:50 p.m. I stopped the treadmill, dragged a towel over my face, and tossed it into the nearby bin as I exited the gym and hurried to my room. I needed to get myself from sweaty and smelly into something presentable in a hurry to meet the non-stranger at the six thirty agreed-upon time. *What the hell? Why not ditch the drink and the unknown, order room service, and surf the internet? Because the curiosity is killing you.*

I stepped into the steaming spray of water and soaped my hair with the basil and lemon shampoo I'd thrown into my bag for the trip and hurried through the rest of the shower, only slowing long enough to be sure not to cut my legs shaving. Five fifty-seven. I hung the towel on the hook behind the door. It was a relief I didn't have to drive anywhere to meet the mystery person. I took a deep breath and chose one of the two dresses I'd brought in the event a dinner invitation might be extended with C-05.

The sleeveless mahogany-colored dress contrasted well against the creamed-coffee shade of my skin. The small translucent brown bead embellishments at the dropped-scoop neckline gave the dress a little more to look at than the typical conservative attire. The fit was close without revealing too much, and the length, a couple inches above the knee, kept the look mildly reserved. I quickly blow-dried my hair, leaving it to hang rather neat and long behind my shoulders with a slight curve just below my collarbone on one side. I preferred classic elegance to high maintenance. One sidelong glance and I decided my effort was good enough.

There had been just enough time to get ready and still spare a few deep breaths to get into a calm state of mind after rushing to be on time. I slipped on thin, strappy heels and headed out the door toward the elevators.

I entered a lounge with a perfect blend of masculine and elegant decor in contrasting shades of deep brown and cream. Lighter beige walls were complemented by small circular tables and wooden armchairs upholstered in a neutral checkerboard pattern. Opposite the lounge was a separate sitting area with a large fireplace against one wall that welcomed intimate discussions on the cozy, curved beige sofa with matching oversized chairs. A magnificent, hand-carved wooden table had been placed in the center of a white shag rug between the sofa and chair. I scanned left toward the bar. A large tapestry hung behind numerous bottles of alcohol on the shelf above a mile-long marble countertop. A warm glow sparkled off the numerous glasses perfectly lined up, like shiny new toys awaiting their guests.

There were only a couple of patrons in the place on this week-night. I opted for one of the more private, small circular tables against the wall, closer to the bar, to wait.

"May I bring you a cocktail, miss?" the waiter asked. "We have a lovely Chardonnay this evening."

"I'd like a vodka martini, please. Two olives," I replied, smiling up at him.

I wouldn't let my mind linger too long on the slight annoyance of not knowing who I was meeting, soon to be soothed with a few sips of alcohol. I breathed in the sea air lifting through an open double door beyond the lounge area and felt my body relax further into a state of calm. My attention was drawn beyond the doors to a veranda, facing a sunset over the ocean. A light breeze swirled through the entrance, gently brushing the sheer cream-colored curtains, causing them to billow the entire length from ceiling to floor before settling.

"Hello, Sara," came a voice so flawless and welcoming, much like the sunset outside. I turned my head to see Kevin standing beside me and I couldn't help the smile that crossed my face. I stood to greet him. He leaned in to hug me but held some distance. "It's a beautiful one tonight, don't you think?" he asked as his gaze lifted to the shades of pink and deep orange that swept across the sky.

"Yes, quite." I paused to take in the beauty and sudden comfort that surrounded us. "Please." I gestured to the seat next to me. "This lounge is so comfortable. And to think I considered ditching this meet to stay in and order room service," I added. My eyes drifted around the room and settled on him.

He took a seat in the chair angled to face mine. "And stand me up?"

"You didn't reveal your name, remember?" I sensed caution in his approach and, with it, my invisible wall of defense going up. He had to expect that.

"Yes. And I do apologize, but it was necessary to maintain some anonymity given your meeting with C-05."

"Why? I may be new to discovering your role in this mission, but it wouldn't surprise me if he's well aware of our connection."

"Of course. C-05 is gifted, shall we say, with a second sight that allows him to detect emotion and read thoughts as part of his repertoire of abilities he carries. Any relationship we may have is best kept out of his direct line of sight."

"And that's why Matt asked me to block my thoughts." Thinking of Matt reminded me of the man I locked eyes with in the hall for a split second. "It was you that I saw in the hall, as C-05 stepped away. Why didn't you mention to me you were coming here, to California? Why did you try to deny knowing Juno and Aria in London?" There were more questions filling my mind. As they did, my blood began to heat with the knowing he'd held back information from me for quite some time. How much more might he be hiding?

"I have business with the team on this trip. I didn't think it was the appropriate time to get into a discussion about Juno and Aria before an important event for you in London. I also didn't think we'd meet up with any shady people, either." He shifted so that his leg was closer to mine. Silence passed between us as he stared through the double doors. "The last time we were together, you mentioned not wanting someone to watch over you twenty-four by seven."

"If you cared to keep your distance, may I ask why you wanted to meet with me?"

"Excuse me, sir, may I bring you a cocktail or wine?" the waiter interrupted.

"Scotch on the rocks, please."

"Yes, sir."

Kevin's gaze returned to mine. "I wanted to meet with you because I like being in your company." There was honesty in his answer but also a sense that he was testing the waters. "And I believe we need to clear the air." I leaned back into the soft cushion of the chair, legs crossed. I tucked one side of my hair behind my ear and folded my hands into my lap.

*Well?*

"I want to try something as a matter of privacy. Let me know if you hear this," he said. I was naturally curious and listened closer. *I have to share information with you regarding parts of this mission.* He looked directly into my eyes. I laughed slightly, not meaning to embarrass him. A confused look came over his face. For all he did know about me, he did not know that I was well versed in telepathy, having experienced it to a greater degree in the last several days.

"I hear you clearly," I said, and his expression smoothed. "Answer one thing for me first." I remembered the feelings I had for him before I became aware of his involvement in the mission.

"No," he answered before I could ask. *My feelings for you are separate from this mission and were not in any way part of an attempt to get close to you because of the work we need to do together.* He sent the thought to me.

"Like C-05, you also have the ability to read my thoughts, don't you?"

"I see you prefer speaking aloud," he said.

"Not necessarily. I just think it would seem a little odd for both of us to be sitting here in public just looking at each other as if we were some old, married couple who had nothing more to say."

A smile flashed, just as the waiter arrived with our drinks.

"Would you like me to charge this to your room, sir?"

"Thank you, we would like to run a tab. Room 2104, Forrester," I answered, glancing at the waiter, who nodded in reply.

*A tab? At least I have her attention long enough to run a tab,* Kevin thought, not realizing I'd heard him. He must have dismissed that I was tuned in to his thoughts or underestimated my abilities.

I couldn't help but think back to when I met him and the conversations we'd had. It was clear that being able to read my thoughts, he had been aware of everything I knew or that I felt about him. Heat began rising up from my chest, extending to my ears at the realization I had been transparent all along.

"It's not an accident that we are paired together, Sara," he said, pausing to take a sip of scotch. "And it certainly wasn't an accident that I was your attending physician in the hospital."

"Who, then, is playing the role of matchmaker?"

"You don't understand."

"Perhaps you should explain," I said, taking my glass in hand and returning my gaze back to his.

"We would have been paired together, anyway, like Matt and Juno, because our abilities are similar," he said. "You can hear another person's thoughts and so can I. It's just a bit clearer for me than you, and only because I've honed the ability to listen and block over time. You also feel what others feel, as do I. Just as Matt and Juno are partnered for their similar abilities, we are also paired in a professional manner, you might say, working as doctors in our respective fields."

"Okay. I still don't understand how any of that has to do with your interest in me."

He swirled the dark amber liquid in the glass. "You're in a great deal of danger now that Tarsamon knows you've been called into action." He swallowed another hearty sip. "My purpose in this mission is to ensure your protection and aid in the quest. My interest in you personally is completely unrelated to this responsibility. The feelings I have for you extend longer than you know and are as strong as those you have expressed for me, privately of course." He raised an eyebrow and locked his gaze to mine, perhaps in search of what I was feeling.

I couldn't help the smirk that appeared at the feeling of being exposed or the heat pulsing in my neck, knowing that he knew more than I was willing to reveal. I dropped my gaze to the drink I held and pressed my lips together in a smile. *Do you remember me?* The question he'd asked me in London returned. The answer was still as clear as the hazy night sky settling over the ocean.

"I see."

"Sara," he said. "Please look at me."

I took in a soothing, deep breath and a slow sip of my drink and met his penetrating stare. "Now that everything is on the table, responsibility and emotion, where do we go from here?"

"That depends on you. I have a purpose to serve in this mission that provides involvement with you but it can remain platonic if you choose. Are you interested in more than a working relationship?"

The mood had shifted, as though we were both walking a tight wire. One wrong word and either of us could slip. I wanted him, and he had to know that I did. I hesitated, stroking the stem of my glass with my thumb.

The fear of allowing someone to become close to me crept up my spine and threatened to swallow me whole. It was a fear that had been fed silently since being given up as a child and one that could only be dealt with when confronted with the possibility of love. I considered what it would be like to be involved as if we were business partners and pushed the thought from my mind almost as quickly as it arrived. An internal struggle had begun. Did I protect my emotions from the very thing I feared, getting too close to him, or allow my strong desire for him to grow and trust it would be all right? I understood the risk I took in trusting anyone.

"You probably already know the answer," I said. "At this point, it would surprise me if you didn't." My eyebrows flicked upward and the corner of my mouth turned up. He waited, needing to hear me say the words. "I honestly can't say no. Of course I'm interested in more."

I felt him relax, though his body didn't move.

"It's safe to assume you aren't angry anymore?" he asked, still studying me.

I smiled. The block I attempted at the shifting mood between us, similar to the filter to block unwanted conversation, was working to keep my emotions from being read by him. "My anger is easily cooled, especially with honesty."

He leaned forward, gently taking my free hand between both of his. At the same time, a flash picture of being wrapped in his strong embrace, under soft white sheets flitted through my head. Before I could wonder why those visions always seemed to occur when he touched me, he spoke, distracting me from further consideration.

"I'll remember that. I'm sorry if I hurt you by not telling you of my involvement sooner. Your responsibility in this quest was preset and I couldn't interfere with the timing by coming to you before you were meant to know. You have to know that," he said, piercing me with his gaze. He was struggling with something. I could see it now as I had the night of our first date.

"I understand that now. What I don't know are your intentions moving forward."

"My intentions are completely honest, and I wouldn't waste time with this conversation if they weren't. I do have more that I need to share regarding my role with you in this mission. But…" He sighed and looked down at our hands, stroking a thumb over the top of mine. "I must admit I'm more interested in my personal rather than professional time with you," he said. He looked up at me. "Perhaps we could arrange to satisfy both."

He'd been prepared for me to walk away from any romantic involvement and still maintain a commitment to the mission. It had been his goal in meeting for this drink to confirm my feelings, one way or the other. Like me, he had a desire to put the issue to rest. I felt as though I was standing on more solid ground with him in a matter of minutes.

"Well," I said. "I think talk about roles and the mission is best left for a more private venue."

"Agreed."

"There has been a development that I will share with you later," I added, thinking back to the office I'd found. "But I must ask if you trust me."

"I have no reason not to, Sara."

"Then I'm going to have to request, if you discover any information regarding a symbol, that you not share it with C-05, not immediately, anyway, and that you not let him know I have asked this of you."

His eyes narrowed a bit. "You suspect C-05?"

"I'm not sure. Perhaps it's nothing. But I'd prefer to explain later, in private. It doesn't feel safe to discuss here."

"I understand. Juno has expressed some concern with regard to C-05 as well."

Over a cocktail, all had been resolved. We were starting this relationship again, closer somehow.

The thought of privacy reminded me of the trip I wanted to take in the next couple of weeks. I was sure Kevin and I didn't need to go quite as far as the Bahamas for privacy.

"Would you be interested in considering a visit instead to a home I have in Cape Cod?" he asked, still holding my hand. "The weather this time of year would be less rainy."

"You really shouldn't do that," I said, trying to mask the surprise I was certain stretched across my face at his reading of my thought.

"You must understand the importance of blocking any uninvited listening. Besides, you can be confident your thoughts are completely safe with me."

"I haven't determined that just yet."

"How about the Cape?"

"I don't know. I need a moment to consider it."

This time before I thought any further about the proposition of traveling with him, I blocked my thoughts by imagining a mental barrier between us. He smiled, recognizing it, and let go of my hand as he glanced toward the sunset that was now no more than a hint of deep orange being blanketed by the dark of night.

Kevin was the most intoxicating man in my life that I could remember. I glanced at him over my glass as he waited patiently for my response. He had been a friend to me over the last couple of months, one who never pushed his intentions. It would be foolish to let someone like him go over a secret we both ended up having anyway. I liked what was developing. For once in my life, I'd found a man I wanted to delve into. It took no more than a couple of seconds to consider his offer.

"I'd like very much to join you at your place." Even as I answered, the wave of risk, having a relationship I'd never wanted, was changing tides and pulling me out with it.

He smiled and dropped his gaze to the table, stroking a finger along the top of my hand, leaving me to wonder how this entire situation had turned very much in his favor. I couldn't mind too much. Spending time with him would provide a chance for me to learn how he'd arrived on this mission and perhaps dig deeper to find what I detected as pain hidden in those sultry brown eyes.

"Well then, we have an evening so far that consists of a single cocktail," he said. "Would you like to have dinner with me, or perhaps you'd rather call it an early evening?"

"Let's have dinner." Getting fully caught up on rest was well beyond my reach, anyhow. My desire for more of his company along with a good meal won out over any residual fatigue. The ambience of the lounge and the drink had lulled me further into a comfortable, peaceful state of mind. I could have easily just closed my eyes and fallen asleep in the chair, but I welcomed more time to uncover the mysteries of why I felt him to be so familiar, so comfortable.

"I promise not to keep you out late," he said as a smile crossed smoothly over his face.

I glided a hand over his. "If I wasn't up for dinner, I would have declined."

He placed a hand gently on the small of my back on our way to the exit, reminding me of the night we shared that first passionate kiss. Gooseflesh traveled the length of my arm in response. I wanted to be close to him, in a way that I had never wanted to be close to anyone, ever. In a strange way, that sensation frightened me, too.

I settled into bed shortly after nine, thinking about how I could find the last symbol and how exactly the connection between the physical world and Ardan worked. My eyelids grew heavier until I gave in to them.

I turned at the soft crunch of footsteps behind me. *Cerys.* The familiar tingling sensation raced down every nerve ending. He reached for my hands.

"Sara, you will need protection as you travel between worlds. Your friend is that protection. Keep him close. Darkness is entering your world at a faster pace. Remember, no fear."

"Are you watching what takes place here?"

"We can see all. Members of the Alliance aid you."

"I don't know who they are. How will I lead us to the keys?"

"With strength and fortitude." It wasn't exactly the answer I was searching for. "The symbols will provide the path to the doorway. Have faith, trust. You are guided by much higher powers than you remember."

He placed his hand on my cheek. I leaned into the warmth, wanting to feel the weight of it against my skin, to know the reality of him. I covered his hand with mine and he kissed my forehead, instantly waking me. I wanted more time to speak with him, to ask about the last symbol. I sat up, rubbed my eyes, and squinted at the clock. *Three a.m., again.* I fell back to the pillows and stared through the dark at the ceiling for several minutes, praying I'd fall back asleep this time.

On the flight home, my thoughts slipped back to the memory of C-05's office. A roughed-out image of one the symbols I'd received at Lady Mara's shop had also been drawn on the chart strewn across the table. *If C-05 had so much information, though, wouldn't he—*

"Can I bring you anything to drink?" asked the flight attendant, interrupting my thought.

"No, thank you."

C-05 was well informed of the very pieces our team was in search of, and yet he needed us to locate them for him. Enlisting the team meant C-05 was not one of those selected to carry a symbol. That also meant he was not what my guides had considered pure of heart. I could be wrong. Could someone not entrusted with the symbols still be considered pure of heart?

My doubt about him began to grow as I considered everything piece by piece. Yes, it was definitely better to keep the symbols separate and out of his hands. I leaned my head back on the seat, with more than doubt stirring in the pit of my stomach.

# 18

From the moment I stepped off the plane, evidence of the shadows' presence, the very same that had been attached to the man in the market, had grown. They were clinging to people as they passed by me in a rush, oblivious to the incubus they carried. I remembered Cerys's words in my head cautioning about the growing evil on Earth. The shadows that were stalking buildings weren't visible to ordinary people still going about their routines. It was probably better that way, due to the fear or panic it would cause, fueling the dark energy that sought to consume them. But what were the fiendish shadows waiting for? Were they really learning the environment? Fear was exactly what they wanted more of. They fed off of it. Showing themselves would give them all they wanted, much faster than waiting.

I rounded the corner from the coffee shop to see another of the large black shadows crawling above me toward the roof and another clinging to a man with a scowl on his face. Some of the shadows were like small, angry children attached to their adult, clinging mostly to one side, occasionally peering out from behind their host through squinted yellow eyes.

"They can't hurt you," a voice from behind me said. I turned to see Elise had fallen in step beside me.

"You guys really are at every turn."

"Your protection is what the Alliance has ordered, and ensuring the deliverance of the keys of enlightenment is what we've selected as our role in this life. There is nothing else for us."

"You had lives before this mission, just as I had. Don't you miss it?"

"Not as much as you might think. Giving up the daily grind in a cube farm for the opportunity to assist on a mission to save lives is more rewarding. Do you? Miss it, I mean?"

I was headed back to my office for one last appointment with a severely depressed patient who had not wanted to be moved to another doctor, flat out protested saying she had nothing to live for, and would only try if I agreed to meet once more with her.

"I'm on my way to a last appointment now. There hasn't been a chance for me to miss work yet.

"Why can't they hurt me? The little black shadows," I asked, shifting gears. I glanced at my watch. With a few minutes on my side, I found some shade on a bench near my office and took a seat. I lifted the cup of green tea to my lips and blew on it.

"Your energy is untouchable to the shadows, until they gain strength. The demons that you have encountered are the only ones that are drawn to you, to us, for now. But even they won't hunt you until Tarsamon orders it."

I swallowed hard. "Which will be soon, if what I'm feeling from you is accurate."

"You're getting closer to having all three symbols. And when you do, you will be granted access to the portals that lead to the keys, making it increasingly difficult for Tarsamon to stop you from extricating him from this world. I'd hunt you, too."

"I suppose. But he could have killed me by now, so why hasn't he?"

She shrugged a shoulder. "We think, are hoping, he's underestimating your ability to commit to the mission. He may think you to be as weak as any other human. I don't believe he ever thought you'd take on the task."

"I've hardly begun. Right now, I've got to get to this appointment." I jerked my chin in the direction of the office building. "Will you be staying with me all day?"

"Ouch, Sara. I thought we were friends."

"We are. It's just that, I mean, you're welcome to stay, but this is my only appointment."

"I know, I know. You like your space. I'm gone."

"Elise." I snapped my head right, then left. As quickly as she had stepped in beside me, she was gone. *Kevin. He shared my comment of not wanting the twenty-four-by-seven watch with the team.* I let out a deep breath and left the shade of the bench toward my office.

The people with an attachment appeared angry, with hunched shoulders, a Quasimodo appearance. Many were grumbling, most often to themselves. For those people who did speak, only negative talk came from them.

A tired-looking man, seemingly unprovoked by anyone, emerged from a car mumbling obscenities and cursing anyone who passed him. His brows were furrowed from the moment he had opened his car door. My gaze lingered on him as I crossed the street, wondering about the dark shadow and waiting to see if the man exercised any sort of control over the figure weighing on his mental state. The general slump of his body indicated the demon was winning control. Other passersby appeared to chalk his behavior up to another bad start to the day as they continued on with their own busy lives. *Very interesting, and grisly.* I stepped up on the curb, wondering how he would affect others through the day with his ill temper, passing on his ugliness. Was that how the shadows were spreading, from one bad encounter to another?

"What the hell are you looking at?" shouted one man with fierce intensity as I glanced in his direction. His outburst caused others to peer in his direction with bewildered expressions. I sipped my tea, fully aware he would have liked to deck me over a simple look.

I wasn't able to tell if the shadow reflected how each person felt or if it was the cause of the miserable nature. I tossed my tea into the trash and entered the double doors of the office building.

My patient had arrived early. Waiting in the lobby, she continued staring at the entrance after I walked in, expressionless. Her shirt was sagging at one shoulder and her hair appeared as if the last attempt at fixing it was a week ago. A stack of magazines sat in her lap with the look of utter boredom plastered across her face.

"Good morning, Lauren," I said. As she stood, a shadow peered from around her. It didn't appear as menacing as the others I'd seen attached to the people outside, but then this patient was depressed, not angry. She plopped on the sofa against the wall while I headed to my desk. "I'll just get a few notes from our last visit."

"Don't bother. You won't need them."

"Oh? Why is that?" I looked up to meet her stare. A sensation came over me that she wasn't here to discuss her depressive symptoms. The shadow that hung behind her peered out once again, listening. Its eyes were not the angry yellow peering through the slits of eyelids I had seen earlier, but were instead weepy-looking, almost mocking the woman it hid behind. I could sense heavy, energy-draining feelings from her and put up a block to avoid the sensation.

My skin crawled as the figure quickly retreated again behind her. I realized that the intervention I was about to provide was going to hit a solid wall and be unable to break past the demon barrier.

"I didn't press for a meeting to discuss me." Lauren brushed the hair from her face. "I'm lost and will be forever. I've at least made progress in understanding that much." She placed her arms behind her head and leaned back.

*She's given up.*

"So, what can I do for you?"

"It seems as though there may be something I can do for you."

I felt my brow reach a highpoint close to the hairline, as I listened to a level of confidence I'd not heard from her before now. I kept the distance, choosing to remain standing behind my desk.

"I've been asked to help you understand that you are meddling in things that will only get you killed." She pulled her hands from behind her head, placed them in her lap, and leaned forward. "And Dr. Forrester, I would never want to see anything happen to you." At this, I came around my desk and leaned against it.

"What are you talking about, Lauren? Who is it?"

"He said you would know." Her face changed, and the twist of fear fell over her as though she'd been draped in it. "I've seen him in my dreams. He calls himself darkness. No, no, that's not right. He did have a name. What was it? What was it?" Her eyes darted to the side while she tapped two fingers against her cheek trying to recall. "He said it only once," she paused and looked up at me. "Tarsamon. I fear for you, Doctor."

I stroked a thumb over my chin, keeping my eyes on her. Maybe Aria was right, I should be carrying my sword regularly. "There is nothing to worry about for me. I'm quite capable of taking care of myself. I think you need some rest, and not of the nightmare sort."

"But he was very adamant."

"I'm going to prescribe a mild—"

She stood from the sofa. "You aren't listening." Her voice became stern.

"I hear you quite clearly. I assure you. But whatever nightmare you've had that might've included me is not anything to be alarmed about." But I was surprised that Tarsamon had gone so far as reaching out to a patient of mine to deliver a message. Why? Couldn't he reach me as he had once before?

Lauren's expression changed. Her eyes narrowed. "You. Will. Die. They will not save you, your precious team." The tone was gravelly, and I knew it from Ardan when the dark mist had settled around my ankles and the same voice had spoken. It had possessed Lauren. For how long, I didn't know. Tarsamon had used her to deliver his message.

"I understand what you've said." I paused to see if her expression would change and it did. *If you can read my thoughts, know that I don't fear you.* I walked toward the door. "If you change your mind and would like help for your depression, I recommend any one of the doctors in this practice." I opened the door and waited for her to leave. She glared at me with a wicked grin on her way out the door.

I sat in my car waiting for the light to change, still disturbed that Tarsamon had used someone as vulnerable as a patient to get to me. I turned the ring on my finger that the old woman had given me in the shop in London. Would the two symbols be safe if I kept them here instead of Ardan? Could Tarsamon break the protective barrier that the ring instilled against another worldly force detecting their energy? I punched the accelerator toward home to finish packing for the trip to the Cape and wondered if the other members of the team in this mission were experiencing the same visual examples of discord. Elise hadn't mentioned any possessed individuals speaking to her. But why would she if I was the single threat to Tarsamon's attempt to consume the energy of this world? I slammed on the brakes as a cab darted in front of me.

*If I didn't need to pack, I could have stayed at the apartment in the city.*

I tapped a finger on the steering wheel in thought. *C-05.* Could he have anything to do with the patient sent to my office? *I might not trust him, but if he is involved with the evil, it just shifted this quest to another level… No.* He would begin to wonder why there was no information coming from our team or, more specifically, why I hadn't delivered a single symbol to him. He was already perplexed by it. How long did I have before he came *looking* for information? A call to him suggesting I was close to uncovering the meaning behind one might stall him long enough for me to locate the last symbol and then be able to lead as a leader might, with decision and forward thinking.

When I arrived home, I grabbed the piece of luggage I'd already begun to pack for the trip to the Cape and finished adding the last few items, mostly sweaters and jeans, some loungewear, and a couple of items to go out in. I didn't know what, if anything, was planned. I expected easygoing and relaxing since it was the beach. I double-checked the weather forecast on my computer to see temperatures were expected to be even colder over the coming week. I adjusted the contents and mentally marked one more item off my to-do list.

I recalled the flash of Lauren's face and those three words that had slid from her lips as the last memory I had before sitting in bed with my laptop. The fear consuming me now was not Lauren, but the moon that had disappeared from its position in my window, and the realization it had been replaced by a black figure leaning over me in the dark of my room.

# 19

"I couldn't tell her who she is to me, who we are to each other outside this damned world," Kevin said. He wanted nothing more than to spill all he knew to Sara and help her remember. "Hell, I've explained the danger that she's in and she asked me to step back." He thought of their discussion in London. At the time, it had been better for him to leave her hotel room before he scooped her up and spilled everything, blowing his agreement with the Alliance. He swiped a hand through his hair as he wore a path for the third time toward the window overlooking the city in the living room of Matt's apartment.

"It would make things a lot easier if she knew the truth of who you are to her." He handed Kevin a drink. "Maybe she would be less resistant. Or should I say more open? Either way, it'd be easier for you. For all of us."

Kevin shook his head and stared out the window, as if to see Sara somewhere below. "Explain that to the Alliance. They wouldn't allow it when I requested it, would've revoked my *privilege* to protect her on this mission. It took everything to convince them to let me join her." He turned from the window and sat on the sill. "No," he said more calmly. "She chose this, too, believing our connection would hinder the mission. Too much emotion, concern for one another. So she won't remember." He swallowed a gulp of the bronze liquid and felt it warm his throat. "The Alliance agreed."

"Then you've got a bigger challenge than to protect her, just trying to get close to her to engage your part of the mission," Matt said. "Do you think if Aria told her of your past together, maybe work it in how Aria and Sara knew each other on other missions, Sara might believe her?"

"I can't risk it. The Alliance was clear she's not to know, until they deem it necessary. *If* they deem it necessary," he corrected.

"So how are you going to stay close enough to protect her? You can't remain in the shadows the entire mission. Does she know how strong your abilities are?"

"Not entirely. All she knows is that we share the same. She doesn't know the distance I can hear her thoughts or the other gifts the Alliance granted me in coming to this world." He took in a deep breath and expelled it in one quick release. "I've got some ideas. I don't know if they'll work. And I've been able to stay close without her knowing. But I can't stand back doing nothing while you and the team come to her rescue, as you did in California."

"She's a tough one to crack this time around, for sure. But easy to read," Matt said, recalling his brief meeting with Sara.

"It's her weakness, one I hope to help make stronger. I've just got to approach carefully. She's like a frightened tiger. I don't need her lashing out if I get too close."

"Good luck taming the tiger." Matt smiled. "I could read her defensive wall the moment I said hello."

"It's good for one thing. It's kept her single until I could find her. I swear I'd put odds on the Alliance intentionally instilling the emotional defense to keep her from believing us to be as close as we are."

"Yeah, likely," Matt said, remembering an experience he'd had once on a mission with his love, Aria, in another realm they had teamed up to save. It had been during a battle in a world more advanced than Earth. There was no quest for hidden keys or anything to set them back. But back then, she had nearly snapped his neck a moment before he'd gained the upper hand in one swift move and thrown her to the ground. They'd fought almost to the death before she remembered him. He was still convinced it was sheer luck that she had.

"There's been word from Ardan that Tarsamon is getting closer," Matt said.

"I've seen his version of things in this world. The way he's been engaging the shadows and demons by attaching them to suck the life energy out of the humans." Kevin downed the rest of the drink.

"There's that." Matt paused. "But I mean getting closer to Sara."

Kevin met Matt's gaze. "How?"

"Juno and I got word today that he used a patient of hers to coax her to meet. When Sara agreed to a last counseling session, he gave her a warning, or what we'd consider a threat." Kevin walked back to the kitchen. "He used a human to send his message to her."

"I didn't get any indication that he was near when I was outside her office earlier today. No sense of danger."

"Neither did Elise. She was tagged to follow her today. Because he slid his energy in under the guise of one of her existing patients, you wouldn't be able to sense the danger if he blocked you, or any of us, from tuning in to the emotions or thoughts exchanged between them. And why would you? You wouldn't be interested in what was shared between Sara and a patient."

"Why do you think he didn't use that moment to strike her down?"

Matt blew out a breath. "The visions Juno and I have seen show him in conversation with some other, unidentifiable person. He says she's not strong enough to fulfill the mission, in part because the Soltari voided memories from her. I hate to admit it, but while a certain lack of knowledge does make her a bit weak, the veil is protecting her from our number one enemy. For now."

"I think I'll need to step up my plans. Thanks for the drink," Kevin said, setting the empty glass on the counter. He grabbed his coat and put it on with haste. "Before I forget, Juno is already aware, but—"

"So am I," Matt interrupted, zeroing in on his thought. "We'll be leaving soon. I got the message earlier today. Go do what you have to do. Juno's on property watch at Sara's tonight."

"She's got security on premises."

"It sucks. Not built for demons."

Kevin shook his head and closed the door a little harder than intended. He sat in his car under the glow of the overhead streetlight, closed his eyes for a moment, and connected with Sara. How he wished he were crawling into that bed with her, not only to keep her safe but to help her remember the way they were together.

"Soon enough," he whispered. Tomorrow he would be with her and all would begin to change. It had to. He shifted the car into drive and pulled away from the curb. As he did, the connection he'd made with her was broken, by another force. He pressed down on the pedal and raced in the direction leading out of the city.

# 20

I turned my head into the tip of a blade angled against my neck and froze. The glow of the screen saver on the laptop that had fallen beside me illuminated the figure standing over me. It had no face to make an identification, but the outline of the shape resembled a human form. What if it wasn't? If Cerys or Eldor could reach me in my sleep, then why couldn't one of the shadows?

*The sword. Where is the sword?* I tried to roll to my side and reach for where I had left it standing, between the nightstand and the bed, and felt the knife's point press into my neck. As it did, my mind filled with images of a demonic world, without light or beauty, and full of anger. Tarsamon's world. Though I had not been there, I'd been instilled with the knowledge of it. This thing above me had to be inserting its visions into my thoughts. I imagined a curtain of light that would block the intrusion and fought to create it.

"Release the medallions," a deep voice said.

"I don't have them," I whispered. And in truth I didn't. I still wore the protective ring Lady Mara had given me, but that gave me little comfort after the warning I'd received from Tarsamon. It had only been one night earlier that I'd visited Ardan and delivered the two symbols to Eldor for safekeeping until the third was found. Good thing. I stared up into the black hole of darkness above me as I slowly reached an already extended arm closer to the edge of the bed.

"We know they are in your possession. Get them."

"You have no power with them." *Just a little farther.* The tips of my fingers reached the hilt.

"Power is not sought from them, but to remove—"

With a flip of my wrist and an accepted minor pierce to my neck, I had the sword in hand and swung. A hiss rang out. The shadowed figure dodged. Yellow eyes glowed in the blackness. *Demon?* I rolled off the edge of the bed and heaved a crosscut at the outline.

"I don't feel like talking," I said, lifting the sword again, angling it in front of me.

The moon returned, cascading a dispersed stream of white through the open window. Was that how the shadow had entered? A flash of metal that wasn't mine reflected in the light. *The figure brought someone with him.* Was that a sword or dagger? I wondered, as I considered the next best maneuver. The dark visions cleared, leaving me the ability to create the white energy that might end the creature, human or demon.

I followed the movement of the shadow. Another flash of metal, higher than the last, fell to the opposite side of the demon from where I stood. I took a step sideways. The lamp on the table crashed to the floor as the blade followed its movement. Sword, I thought in answer to my previous question. I stepped toward the blackness for another strike and a low growl sounded. I lifted the sword to strike. A heavy arm reached from behind across my chest, causing me to abandon the figure and fight for release.

"Sh."

Whoever it was had pulled me out of striking distance. The second figure moved with precision toward the first and into the dark so that neither could be seen. The spacious bedroom appeared suddenly small as steel against steel rang out two, then three times. The demon approached the balcony and I shot toward it, not wanting it to get away.

I brushed past the second figure just in time to see the yellow-eyed shadow fall from the balcony and disappear into the night air. "Damn it." The arm reached around me again and I struggled again to free myself. "It's not dead. It'll be back." But he held me against him until I quit fighting. The switch of a flashlight revealed Juno. Dressed all in black, he looked like a jewelry thief on a heist. With a sword.

"Call off your security. Their motion detectors identified the flight."

I did as he asked.

"For you to kill it would have brought more of them to you. It's why the demon engaged in the fight. Watch the glass." He directed his light to where the lamp had fallen.

"Why didn't it just kill me when it had the chance?"

"It's trained to fight. Prefers to steal the energy found in its victim. You're under the protection of the Soltari. In Ardan, a demon can't take energy from you unless he's ordered to do so by Tarsamon. The Dark Lord isn't seeking to start a war with them. Not yet. This demon came for something else."

"It wanted the medallions. How did it know?"

"A simple thought by you, unless blocked, can be read by those who are capable of telepathy."

*C-05*. He was the only other person who had asked me about them.

Juno stepped away. But before I could wonder, he was back pressing a cloth against my neck.

"How did you know?" I asked, taking hold of the cloth.

"Know what?"

"That I was… That it was here?"

"It's my job to know when you're in trouble." He flipped on a light in the bath and holstered the flashlight. "I need to go but I'll be back."

"I can't stay here. That demon didn't get what he came for."

"You're safe tonight. I'll be close by. We'll need to work out better security going forward, though."

I stretched an arm across the cool emptiness of the sheets and the morning light streaming through the window. I rolled onto my side.

Maybe it was nothing more than a vivid dream. I glanced over at the nightstand to see the shards of glass scattered across the table and floor. What some might consider vivid dreams or nightmares were all too real for me. If Juno had been here, there was no sign.

Through half-closed lids, my eyes drifted to the clock that miraculously had not fallen to the floor in the scuttle. "Shit." I tossed back the covers, abandoned the morning tea, and raced for the shower. I was due to meet Kevin at the airport in exactly one and a half hours. That should have been plenty of time for almost any appointment if I wasn't forty-five minutes outside of the city.

*I've never been late for anything, and this of all things!* "I can do this. I've got a fast car, and God willing, the cops will be scouting speeders closer to the city," I said to myself, lathering shampoo with haste through my hair. *Thirty-minute drive into the city if I hurry. Damn.* A little voice in my subconscious nagged at me that I was inconveniencing myself for a man, reminding me that's why I preferred to be single. I brushed the thought away and realized for the first time that voice was wrong, at least in this moment.

After a careful, heavy-footed drive in the McLaren avoiding speed traps to the airport and a smooth flight, Kevin and I arrived mid-morning in the Vineyard and caught a quick lunch in Osterville. We pulled up to the pitched, shingle-roofed home with a cozy covered patio in front and perfectly manicured lawn. White flowering bushes butted up against a wooden fence, while Dogwood trees lined one edge of the property. From the outside, it was a picture straight out of a home and garden magazine. A large gray cat with jade-colored eyes was sprawled on the front lawn, ears tipped and eyes glaring as if we should seek approval before crossing the guarded territory toward the house.

We entered through double doors to a grand room with cathedral ceilings and perfectly polished hardwood floors. A long, overstuffed sofa and two chairs with ottomans, off-white in color, were placed in a U shape in the center of the family room just off the foyer. The furniture contrasted well with the dark floors and taupe-colored walls. Across from the sofa was a large fireplace beckoning to be lit to warm an already cozy space. A few pieces of distressed wood furniture were spotted throughout, adding a touch of rustic charm.

Steps ahead on the left was a library with bookshelves that stood from floor to ceiling in a darker, merlot-colored wood. My eyes grazed over the titles on the shelves, holding everything from Thoreau and Walt Whitman to a few copies of *The Physician's Desk Reference.* An antique desk was placed in the middle on top of a beautiful, floral, champagne-colored area rug. On the opposite wall of bookshelves were four swords, each hanging at an angle in a decorative fashion.

"Do you use them or are they collector pieces?" I asked, gesturing toward the swords that hung majestically on each mount.

"Both. I'm skilled in the use of Highland broadsword, and these are well-used, valuable examples of the skill."

My eyes continued to roam over the walls. "What can't you do?" I said under my breath.

"What's that?"

"Nothing, really. It's just that I have yet to find anything you can't do." He smiled and remained blocked, feelings or thoughts locked deep away. I would crack that lock. In time. I was an expert at getting to the heart of the psyche of a person, usually to help solve a problem. In this case, the problem was mine. He provided only information I needed to know when he wanted me to know it.

I followed him a few steps down the hall through a set of double doors to the master bedroom. It was a spacious but comfortable area with a chaise lounge in one corner of the room and an afghan thrown over it more for looks than comfort, I suspected. The bed, covered in all white down bedding, faced an entire wall of windows capturing the view of the manicured lawn and steps that led down to a small private beach. There were two additional bedrooms of moderate size that were decorated in the same comfortable and tasteful manner as the master, minus the lounge. As Kevin took me through the home, I could feel him watching me.

"Your home is very beautiful." My eyes glazed over every detail, ceilings to floor. "How do you pull yourself away to come back to the city?"

He laughed softly. "It can be difficult, but change of pace is often good, either way. You can see why I like to use this as an escape."

"I can, yes." There was a slight feeling of nervousness between us, mine or his I wasn't sure. Had Juno told him what had happened last night? Probably. Maybe the feeling was all mine. I liked him very much but couldn't avoid the feeling that I was somehow in a lair, or like Alice, falling down the rabbit hole. *Silly.*

"So, do you think you'd be comfortable here for a week or so?"

"Oh, I think I can manage." I paused from taking in the scenery to look at him. "There is nothing I would change about this home to make it any more inviting." It wasn't the home, as comfortable as it was, that was causing me some internal distress. It was a sudden fear of letting him get too close, a desire to create distance that clashed with a fantastic need for him. I wasn't crawling out of the hole, either, and that was frightening. I would fight dark demons or shadows with the use of energy or a sword, talk with spiritual entities that I had come to know as real. But emotions and trust were more difficult beasts to battle.

"Perfect," he said. "I think this meets all the needs for privacy we were looking for."

*All…* My thoughts drifted back to the reason he'd offered the use of his home—to explain parts of the mission and the members involved.

"That it does." I wasn't blocking his ability to read my thoughts, though perhaps I should have. It wasn't good to be so easy to read. Or maybe it was, and I should give in already. Tempt the rabbit and see where he took me? If I did, would I still remember who I was and still retain my focus regarding the mission?

"Can I get you a drink, wine, water, or something else?" he asked.

"Water would be great for now, thanks." We sat in the cozy living room on the big sofa.

"What's your understanding of these shadows attached to people?" I asked.

"Shadow men are what they're called in Ardan. They're one of several demons in Tarsamon's arsenal. They attach to people who do not choose to grow from whatever challenge or hand they've been dealt in life."

"That must be why I see them hanging on some people and not with others."

"Once they are attached, though, it is difficult to remove them. They begin to drag the person down further into depths of despair until the shadow is controlling the individual," he explained.

"Why do they remain attached? What do they want?" I turned to face him as he sat beside me.

"The life-force. The energy found in a person. The shadows attach first, after a brief time of assessing that the person they are attracted to can maintain the fear and anger to sustain them. They discover if the person, or the host, does not wish to challenge or face the thing that keeps them discouraged. You know that feeling about something you must do but you don't want to be bothered by it?"

"Yes." I knew it all too well with Tyler and not wanting to face him, instead wishing he'd just give up and go away. So far, he had. And I hadn't been bothered in any way by it since.

"That feeling creates negative energy in and around the person that others can sense. The shadows are attracted to the energy and feed off of it. The greater the negativity, the larger and more menacing the shadow becomes as it absorbs the person's strength, leaving them weak and ripe for illness."

"How did they get here, or have they always been?"

"This is the passage that was opened to let them in. You may have heard about it in your travel to Ardan. The shadows have not been visible until recently, but it is suspected they have been growing in numbers, a lot like a disease that mutates and spreads. More than just the shadow men are coming, with Tarsamon leading the entire force."

"I've met him, Tarsamon."

"If you had, he'd have tried to kill you, Sara. You may not remember, but you equal his strength. It's the number of his forces that concerns us."

I shook my head slightly. "He didn't try to kill me. He was trying to be persuasive the two times I spoke with him. Wait, three. That's right." I thought of my patient and how Tarsamon had possessed her in a weakened state of depression.

"Persuasive? I don't think you remember how evil he is."

"I know my memory was blocked so I could function in this world."

He nodded. *If you only knew how much.*

He'd let the thought escape. Was it intentional?

"You"—he hesitated—"and another have seen the post-world, a world that has been through this before."

"Who is the other person?"

"You understand that the battle is being fought on two sides?" he asked.

"Of course. Light over darkness. You mean Tarsamon is the other you're referring to. Did we fight against each other in Ardan?"

"No. At one time, he was part of the Alliance. You and he were the most persuasive of the members but never really saw eye to eye on the decisions brought to vote, many of which often fell in your favor. He has a great deal of knowledge about how we are directed. He may even know of the keys' locations."

"The Scottish Highlands and Egypt." I had managed to dig up enough information on the two stone medallions I'd received from Lady Mara to at least determine the origins of the images in the center of the symbols. Kevin nodded.

"How long before we begin to find the keys? Do you know?"

"I'm not exactly sure, but soon." He stood and moved toward the fireplace before turning to face me. "Which reminds me. You have something you have been carefully guarding."

"I have lots of somethings carefully guarded. You'll have to be more specific."

"I saw a few of the markings for one of the symbols that night when we were at dinner, before you knew I could read your thoughts. It was a brief image, I admit, and I wasn't able to see all of the details. But the first one you were given is the first location we need to go to."

"I didn't have them then, didn't even know of the one that has a reference to the Yucatan," I said, recalling the markings in C-05's unlocked room. "Have you shared this with anyone? C-05 specifically?"

He stepped away from the fireplace and reached for the bottle of water from the table before sitting next to me again.

"Of course not. I'm not trusting him, not with Juno's doubt. Just tell me the medallions are safe."

I was using every sense available to feel his honesty and weigh it against my ability to trust.

"They are. I left them in Ardan for safekeeping. You didn't expect me to hand them over?"

"No. But I also didn't expect you to be an open book. I can read you as though I were looking through the clearest glass."

Kevin reached for my hand, placing it in his, and locked his gaze with mine. "I want to get past the issue you have about trusting me. My block is completely down. You can see straight through me."

I did see through him, his desire to know about the symbols and to not reveal the secrets of the mission, even to C-05. But there was more. I began feeling on a much deeper level than I could have imagined. It warmed me to feel the tenderness, strength, and wisdom he hid deep within his soul. There was a great deal of love, too, for a woman, that went back very far in time, and it came with a loss for which I felt his sadness. I wanted to ask who she was, but the words slipped away as I was pulled deeper. I could see he shared the same strong desire to protect the symbols that would lead us to the keys, and the eventual end of the mission. There was also something else he perhaps did not want me to see, but it was how I knew for sure he was completely open for me to read.

I gasped, startled at the brief vision of his mother's pained face, gagged, as she sat with hands tied to a wooden chair in a partially lit room. A blow came from the back of a heavy hand that sent her head lifting up and lolling to one side. A wave of sadness flooded me. I knew the woman hadn't survived the beating. The vision switched to another image showing a stream of blood trailing down Kevin's side from a gaping wound. Feeling as though I was intruding, I pulled my hand away in a knee-jerk reaction.

"I'm sorry," I said in a choked whisper.

"Don't be. I want you to know you can trust me with information.

If that means revealing some very personal memories so that you do, then I will." He reached for my hand again, but this time I didn't see the images that frightened me.

"What happened to you?" I put my free hand to his cheek.

He closed his eyes for a split second before meeting my gaze. "Another time."

"Okay." I lowered my hand. "The symbols are being held by a trusted partner in Ardan," I said, pulling them to the forefront of my memory. "You must understand it is safer to keep them separate until we need them."

"Until the guardian of the key is found. We will keep them away from C-05. You have my word, Sara." I studied him carefully.

"There is more about you I don't know regarding this quest, isn't there? What is your role?"

"I've told you. Above all else, it's to protect you." He paused. "I've located the last symbol, the Mayan medallion. But it's not here."

"What? Where is it? You didn't bring it back here, right?"

"No. I'll share it with you once I'm convinced you have mastered the ability to block your thoughts from being read," he said.

"That hardly seems fair after you've seen the image of the symbols I've received." He raised a brow. "Fine, I'd likely do the same."

"You have reason to suspect C-05." Kevin's brows narrowed as he studied me. "Does he know that you have collected two of the symbols?"

"Not yet." I remembered the demon shadow in my room the previous night. "At least I don't think so, but he might. I just don't trust his decision to bring the symbols together."

I had developed suspicions after I was led to what looked like a think tank, but blocked this thought from Kevin's perusal for now, until I could be certain about C-05. Kevin might already know, anyway, if Juno had shared the information with him. My suspicions might be nothing more than a precaution.

"Tell me more about the dark world," I said.

He leaned back into the sofa, clutching my hand, resting it on his chest as I sat beside him. "We are able to enter the other side of

Ardan, to see the darker side in action and learn how it functions, what drives it, but it's extremely dangerous." He hesitated again, deciding whether to continue down the same line of communication.

"Have you been there?" I asked.

"A few times," he said. "There are things you would never dream of, demon figures that can move faster than you, trolls that tell them where you are and what you are thinking. They try to find your weakest point and tear into that mental image to latch onto you. The key is to be mentally focused, strong. Have no fear or they will find it." His eyes glanced down at the hand he held and back to my face. "It isn't all mental, though. That's just the easiest point to reach you. They are physically strong. You must move quickly and use a great deal of force when battling them. If they latch on, every moment puts you at a disadvantage. That's why your defenses, your shield and your strength, must be impenetrable." He shifted a little on the sofa. "Mentally, you are built as strong as ever. Your childhood experience of having to survive not being loved for a key period of your life left scars that have made you emotionally strong. You can think through any critical situation without the influence of emotions to distract you. You were built for this quest."

"How do you know about my childhood?" I asked. Was that the knowledge he held that might surprise me?

"Sara, I'm well aware of who you are and what scars you carry."

"Then you also realize those scars create a problem, an inability to emotionally bond in this world," I said. This time I looked away and toward the brilliant blue sky outside. He took my chin with his fingertips and drew it back to him.

"It's only a problem for those who don't care to try and understand. If they don't, why give them your precious gift of love and attempt an emotional bond to begin with?"

"True. But sometimes you just have to take the risk and trust people." *Did I just say that?*

"I hope you remember that." Still holding my chin, he lifted it so that my lips were close to his and waited. He touched them gently to mine in a single kiss, a simple example of his understanding.

As each moment passed with him, I was more convinced I was falling down a hole of desire that in time often led to commitment. I didn't want that complication in my life. Ever. But right now, it felt better to be close than to cling to the safety found in self-preservation. His touch was the only one that gave me pause to consider giving in and letting go to follow the rabbit down the hole.

# 21

Kevin's eyes searched mine as he shifted back against the big cushion on the sofa. That pained look was in them again. He wanted to tell me something. I could sense it the way a hunger pang signaled early starvation. What secret was he keeping?

*I could show her.* The thought skipped through my head like a stone across water.

"What is it you want to say but won't?" I asked finally.

He flashed a smile, blinked, and looked at my hand he still held.

"Another time," he whispered. He glanced back to me. "You know, I didn't learn everything about you by reading your thoughts."

"That's a relief. Mary Ann provided inside information, I suppose?

"She would never share everything. She protects you in that way. But she spilled a few things from your childhood."

"Seems I'm at a slight disadvantage with you having more information about me than I have about you," I said. "Suppose we find common ground."

"What do you want to know?"

*Where do I start?* "How did you learn so much about Tarsamon? And how did you know I was the one who would lead the quest?"

"I was advised, you might say, just as the other members of the team were told about the elements of this mission. I also remember the 'persuasive' evil that is Tarsamon. This isn't my first experience with him. I've traveled to many other realms besides Ardan, as have you." He paused. "And while you may not be consciously aware of the memory, the knowledge of who he is and what he is capable of is with you."

The thought of hearing Tarsamon's voice shortly after I'd landed in Ardan returned and how my reply, though unfamiliar to me, was in every way a reminder that the knowledge of him was present in my memory, somewhere.

"I know the beauty that exists in more advanced realms," Kevin said. "And how Tarsamon's intent can destroy the potential for a young world like Earth before it can fully develop. He's been waiting a long time for this opportunity."

"It doesn't make sense that I wouldn't have the memories of these other realms like you have."

"The guides provide necessary information to aid us on any mission the Soltari sends us to complete. It must be confusing, even frustrating. All I can tell you is the Alliance can provide facts that can help answer those questions for you. On this quest, I have been given information about you so that I can do my job. But I have to confess I didn't know about the McLaren in your garage until that night we went out. I must say, it didn't put me off discovering you have a thrill for speed."

"Hm." My eyebrows wrinkled and a half smile began to break from the left corner of my mouth.

"Speechless again?" he said, laughing under his breath.

I shook my head. "So, you have known about me for how long?"

"Oh, let's see, that would be about ten years ago that I was engaged in this mission." He paused, and I could see in his eyes as they went distant to remember another time. "I didn't know exactly when I would find you. It wasn't until the night of the accident when you were brought into the ER that I knew." His expression was now focused and serious. "I had all the confirmation I could ever need when I saw that." He pointed to the silver ring Cerys had given me.

"You can read this inscription?" I asked.

"You're surprised? It identifies you as the Light Carrier, one who will bring forth the power of the keys of enlightenment: love, to see things in their own beauty, the light of understanding, and acceptance of all things as they are."

"Do you think C-05 can read it?"

"If he could, you'd already know it. He's had plenty of opportunity to question it but has not, according to Matt and Juno."

"Then he's not one of the pure of heart. I was told only they will be able to read the inscription." I paused, letting a moment of quiet settle between us, my hand still in his.

"Kevin, I need to go to the side of Ardan where Tarsamon resides."

A look of concern came over him. "You will remember the knowledge and strength that you carry. You don't need to go. Trust me, it's much more dangerous than anything you can imagine. My visits were to exercise my strengths to prepare for the quest. They are not a place meant for you, Sara. Your practice in Ardan is sufficient to rebuild your skills."

"I think you may be overprotecting. It's important that I trigger the hidden memories to know what we are up against."

He waited. "You already do. The knowledge is with you. It's just not needed yet." I could see him turning over ideas in his mind—how he could keep me from going, who I would listen to that could speak to me, and finally settling on reminding me how to protect myself.

"That'll help," I said, before he could say what he was thinking.

"You're getting much better at reading thoughts to aid you. I'll have to keep that in mind. Have you been told why certain memories are locked away?"

"No," I replied. "I suspect there are things that would change the outcomes if they are known before their time. It's becoming a hindrance, though, not remembering specific information I need to fulfill my task. I have to get stronger. The dark world has already begun to move into our world."

"I can't make you stronger, but I can show you how to protect yourself here. Do you remember the use of light and how you can use that as a shield?"

"Yes."

"You have a light, an aura that surrounds you." He paused, seeing the confusion I felt masking my face. "You can't see this in others like you see the shadows?" I shook my head as he continued. "Yours is a brilliant shade of white with blue flecks. Try to imagine this around you like a sort of halo that encircles you and imagine extending it out beyond you nearly another foot, then two. Push it out with your hands." I did as he suggested.

"Good. That's good. You remember how. Whenever you feel threatened, extend this light beyond you and hold the image in your mind. Expressing energy in this manner in the physical world will tire you quickly. So, have a plan to exit when you use the shield," he added.

"Okay."

He stood from the sofa. "It's getting a little late. Are you hungry?" The time had really flown by since we had arrived. The sun hung lower in the sky.

"I could eat. And you?"

"Famished. I've got a stocked fridge but I'm no cook." He stood with the door of the refrigerator open as he eyed the contents.

"Sorry, cooking usually results in some tragic kitchen disaster that I have learned to avoid," I said.

"Well, there are some pretty good restaurants around the corner, but we'll have to make it quick if we don't want to be stuck experimenting in the kitchen," he said. "They'll close early tonight with it being off-season."

"I'm good with that." I stood and reached for my coat as we headed to the front door.

"I promise something nice for tomorrow," he said.

"Think nothing of it. Quick and easy is fine by me."

"There's a casual place just up the street that serves the best lobster bisque. We may only be able to get sandwiches, but they'll be good." He glanced at his watch.

The restaurant was cozy and casual with the expected seaside fare. My eyes passed over the nautical theme that covered the walls. Different-sized blowfish, shark jaws, and netting hung wall to wall. We did a serpentine through the ropes that formed a waiting line and past a large Atlantic fish, resting on tons of crushed ice, to a counter and placed an order. I skimmed the enormous chalkboard menu that hung on the wall above our heads, noting seventy numbered items.

After dinner, we wandered past the shops to the beach. I bundled my coat tighter as an icy breeze blew past us off the dock, chilling my nose and cheeks.

Kevin opened up to me a bit about his family and how his dad had remarried a few years after he'd lost his mother at the tender age of eight. The only single piece of information he shared about the tragedy was that the evil man who had hurt her had said he wanted him to suffer the loss of one he loved. My heart broke for him. My mouth fell open slightly and my eyes filled with tears. The fear and horror this little boy had felt careened with the sadness of losing her.

"You were eight when you were pushed away," he said, referring to my biological parents giving me up. He lifted a lock of hair off my cheek and tucked it behind my ear.

"But I didn't suffer like that." I swallowed hard, choking off the sadness I was feeling for him.

"You carry your pain, too." He turned and held my hand as we continued along the sand. He shared memories of his parents vacationing on Martha's Vineyard when he was small. He'd fallen in love with the locale even more over the summers when his father and stepmother visited with him over summer breaks. It was when he was a teen that he decided to one day own a home on the water and away from the largest of the crowds that the summers there attracted. Something in him sharing such personal connections and memories moved me. I found his hidden sense of innocence combined with honesty and the strength he carried most endearing.

Like me, he was an only child. Though he mentioned the tragic loss of his mother, he didn't share the details of that most painful event, and I hadn't expected him to. Still, I couldn't help but be curious what the circumstances were that caused him to be in such a place to witness what he had and if he'd been hurt physically at the same time. The conversation touched lightly on my family life when I was young and some with Robert and Mary Ann.

By the time we returned to the house, it was late. The rooms had been picked up, though you couldn't really tell unless you were looking. The water bottles we'd left on the table were gone and there was a fresh bowl of fruit on the table just inside the front door with two new bottles of water. The luggage that had been at the front entry was gone.

"You have turn-down service?" I asked.

"Sure, why not?" he replied, setting the keys on the table and smiling as I slid out of my coat.

"It's nice."

"I would think you'd be used to luxuries like that."

"My house and the so-called luxuries are priceless relics and cars. Services? Not so much."

A few dim lights had been turned on and the gas fireplace was burning low. The home looked more charming than when I'd first seen it that afternoon.

"If you'd like, the service leaves a collection of soaps in the bath if you want to freshen up." He kissed me on my forehead. "Make yourself comfortable. I'll be back in a moment," he said as he headed in the direction of the office.

"Thanks." I wasn't certain if I should shower or just make a quick change of clothes.

I went into the bedroom to find two robes waiting on the bed. I sighed as a knot in my stomach began to form. Although I had expected this night, I felt surprisingly nervous. I pulled my hair up in a clip, selected one of the verbena-scented soaps provided, and quickly showered, rinsing off the day's travel. The chill of the evening walk on the beach melted under the steamy hot water that penetrated deeply, creating a flush of pink on my skin and instant relaxation. Skipping the bulky, plush robe, I settled on one I'd brought, a simple black silk chemise and matching robe with a narrow cream stripe that ran through it. I ran a brush through my hair, letting it hang loose.

As I entered the softly lit living room, the faint sound of music spilled from the wall facing the sofa. Kevin had changed into drawstring pants and a black T-shirt that outlined a broad chest and narrowed waist. He approached with a glass of wine in hand, extending it to me while picking up another.

"If you'd be more comfortable, we can watch some television instead," he said.

"This is just fine, really. Did I miss that you have a TV in this room?" I glanced around, as if it would magically appear out of thin air.

"It's hidden behind the wall panel."

"That's nice. This is comfortable the way you have it." I smiled and took a sip of wine, finding a spot in the middle of the sofa and curling one leg under me.

He sat closer to me than earlier. I wanted to wager if we would even make it through a single glass of wine. I knew my limitations, gambling under the circumstances with a man I had quickly fallen for and one who had as much interest in protecting the relationship for the mission as for his personal reasons. I could feel him balancing desire with circumspection, to be sure he didn't move too quickly and risk me pushing him away due to my own fears of attachment.

"To privacy," I said, lifting my glass to his and pressing my lips into a smile.

"And enjoying it together," he added.

"This has been one of the nicest days I can remember in a while," I said, taking another sip of wine that immediately warmed the center of my stomach, making nice work of loosening the nervous knot that had begun to form earlier. "You're right. This is a much better idea than the rainy Bahamas."

"I'm sure your place is as comfortable."

"Mary Ann's décor is definitely beautiful, but not as warm and cozy," I said, glancing at the soft glow of light from the fireplace playing on the walls. I never felt as though I could curl up on the stiff sofa or lose myself in crisp, tight bedding, not the way I could on the fluffy down comforter waiting in his master suite.

"I'm glad you're comfortable here. It makes it that much easier to seduce you," he said, going straight for the kill. My stomach gave up on the knot and trembled instead. I shifted a little and ended up no farther away from him. He laughed a little.

"What's funny?"

"Just wondering if you think you'll make it through that glass of wine," he said, seeming to enjoy the look of mild surprise I felt blooming over my face.

He had been listening to my thoughts again. I'd have to be careful in the future, but this seemed harmless enough.

"Before what?" I asked, though he was well aware I knew exactly what he meant. He set his glass on the table and turned to me.

"Sara, I've waited a long time for you," he said and paused. "I'm finding it difficult to sit beside you any longer without touching you. May I?" he asked, reaching for my glass.

"Yes. And no, I'm fairly certain I'm not making it through this glass of wine," I said, my voice almost a whisper.

Testing the waters, he stroked the top of my hand lightly, sending that familiar tingling sensation racing up my arm. His fingers followed the path of sensation on my arm, stopping at my shoulder to loop the end of my hair around an index finger.

He brushed the hair from the corner of my eye as I watched his face. "Well, you can finish one, even two glasses. I won't push." My solar plexus quivered. He knew just what to say to ease past the emotional boundary that was assuredly in place.

"Are you always listening to my thoughts?"

"Lately, yes." His fingers still toyed with my hair. I couldn't tell if he was teasing or nervous.

"Then you must know I don't believe you would push."

"Ah, but I do have to be careful," he added.

His eyes locked with mine long enough that I could see them cloud with the urge to consume and the battle it took to restrain that desire. I placed my hand on his chest, above his heart, and felt the beat increasing steadily, mirroring the rhythm of the pulse in my fingertips. He shifted. The warmth began to move from my center and spread quickly south as he wrapped one warm arm around my waist and held himself above me. His lips touched mine softly at first, testing, before taking the kiss deeper, as if he'd waited too long and was intent on replenishing what he'd missed.

I'd satisfy that need, with the same desire driving through me with every pulse of blood through my vessels.

The robe was adding to the discomfort with the sudden rise in temperature. He slipped his fingers under the collar, pulling the corner aside, exposing the strap of the chemise and my bare shoulder. His soft mouth lingered in smooth, wet kisses down the side of my neck, slowly to my collarbone, and then across to the exposed shoulder, where he pulled back and paused, glancing longingly into my face, as if to be sure it was all right to continue. The control he was fighting to have so evident in the crease of his brow. His eyes gleamed with golden fire rising from depths of brown. I became aware of the quickening of my breath with each movement, and with the connection between us halted in a frozen fire, I reached to cup his face and bring him to me.

He kissed me thoroughly before easing back and resting his forehead in the center of my chest, just above my breasts, as if reconsidering. He released a deep and heavy sigh. Whatever he was thinking was not intended for me to hear as he continued to block me from reading him. But I didn't need to hear his thoughts. I sensed his concern and wanted to ease it for him. My fingertips reached into his hair and smoothed it back, extending farther down the nape of his neck.

I bent my head so that my lips were close to his ear. "It's okay," I whispered. I wanted to know what he felt like, wondered about it several times alone. He picked me up in his arms and made his way to the fluffy down covers over the bed that had already been pulled back, waiting for us to find our way beneath them.

He held all of his weight above me and continued the kiss, slow and searching, pausing briefly to free the tie that fought to deny him access and hold my robe closed. My hands slid up under his shirt. I felt him shiver just before I lifted it over his head. As I placed my palms at his waist, I felt something that contradicted the normal pattern of skin. The image I'd seen earlier of blood making a path south returned. I resisted the urge to pull my hand away. Instead, my fingers delicately traced the scar from his waist up near his armpit, curving toward his upper chest.

"How did you get this?" I whispered, searching any thought or feeling for an answer.

"Not tonight, love," he said into my ear. He glided a thumb over my cheek.

I dipped my chin under his arm until I reached the line I'd felt and pressed my lips to the healed injury, knowing the story that lay behind it had left its own invisible scar.

He turned and lifted me onto him, gently rolling me to the side, his eyes fixed on mine, watching every expression in the dim light of the room. He reached past me and switched off the light, leaving a stream of moonlight coming in through the wall of windows across the bed. I moved to slide out of the robe as he reached for what was left and let it fall to the side of the bed. His hands glided over the length of my body against the silk chemise, taking in the outline of my breast to waist, then down my hip and thigh, where he delicately but with urgency removed the black silk material that stood in his way. I sensed his restraint at the desire to grab greedily. He slowed his movement.

My hands reached up and across his chest, extending to his back and inching down. A tremble went through him. My fingers slid slowly down to his hips. I tugged at the drawstring pants that had come untied in our movement. He kicked them to the side to join the robe on the floor. I stroked a hand over the taut stomach muscles and lowered my lips, finding sweet, tender spots as I explored what I had wondered about for the last couple of months.

He rolled once more, holding just enough of his weight to me to feel him pressing against my lower half. My skin responded to every kiss, every touch. Tingles ran a path like electrical current from my neck, across my shoulders, and down my sides, alive with the energy he was passing through me. He placed one hand against my cheek, staring into my face.

"Sara," he whispered. "I have missed you, my love."

I was too lost in passion to consider what he meant. His tenderness was consuming as he slid into me and I rose to meet him. He held me closer as we moved in one beautiful motion, meeting thrust for thrust, as if moving to a precise and fluid musical rhythm all our own.

"So long I've waited for you," he whispered at my ear.

My head tilted back as I released a breath to the moonlit ceiling. His arms tightened around me and he rolled once more as I took him in deeper, until long-awaited pleasures were fully expended, filling the room with quiet gasps and soft moans. From the heat of our bodies, the aroma of citrus and amber wood mingled across my senses. I was discovering him, his movement, his scent, his caress. My heart raced as the air flowed into my lungs to calm the storm while I lay close beside him. His hand slid over my waist and he pulled me gently against him, taking in a deep breath at my hair where his face pressed before drifting to peaceful sleep.

# 22

The morning brought with it the hint of sunlight creeping through the wall of windows. I turned over, my face pressed into Kevin's chest and my eyes still closed.

Kevin stroked my hair and kissed the top of my head. "Sleep, my love. I'll be back soon," he whispered. I kissed his chest. He pulled the covers to my shoulder and quietly left the room.

Within minutes, I woke to the sunlight streaming through the wall of glass, not to be ignored. The heavy robe that had been left on the bed last night lay crumpled in a heap on the floor at the end of the bed. I reached for it and stepped into the bath, quickly running a brush through my hair and another over my teeth before stepping onto the patio to the private beach behind the house.

"Sinking toes in sand." I scrawled the message on a random slip of paper found in a drawer beside the bed and placed it on the pillow. As I slipped on a pair of dark jeans and a sweater, I noticed a red rash on the inside of my forearm. It stung like a blistering sunburn, instantly reminding me of the intense dream that night.

I'd fallen asleep thinking about the dark world that Kevin spoke of, the world where the demons were, to learn about how to defeat them. The mark was the evidence of a successful travel to the darker side of Ardan. The landscape was not the same as my previous travels, though. At first, I'd thought I arrived elsewhere.

I remembered trying to stay hidden against the walls of several buildings that had seemingly popped up out of nowhere. It worked only until ominous creatures had begun chasing me, one right after another, through pitch-black streets. The only light was a faded orange glow rising up in certain areas. A solitary streetlamp in a foggy night.

As the flesh-colored beasts with no face would catch up to me, I'd fight them off with my sword, darting and lunging as they tried to swarm me. At one point, I found myself doing tumbling aerobatics as I leapt to the rooftops around me, running across them to increase the distance between us. Running was not the same as being on Earth. It was faster, with longer strides and lengthier distances with little exertion. That didn't deter the beasts, who matched my pace. I was left with only seconds to escape before they were with me again.

As I looked down from the rooftops, I could see some of the demons running in the streets, waiting for me to leap or fall to where they gathered for my impending doom. Only once had I become stuck on the rooftop with three of them, recalling one had tried to grab at my arm. I managed to break free and sink into a hole in the top of the same building. I don't remember exactly how I left that dark world, but it had been after narrowly escaping their clutches. I didn't wake up instantly, as I often did after going to Ardan or when Cerys visited me. Instead, I'd slipped out of the dark world and into a dream state. Could the hole I dropped into be some sort of transport?

I sucked in a breath as my fingers traced the edges of the sensitive skin. I couldn't show Kevin the mark. He'd already been concerned when I suggested going to the dark world. It would only worry him to see the burn. Besides, it was no larger than a silver dollar and would soon disappear. Next time I would have to remember to use the shield of light. I must have forgotten about it in my attempt to gain information, lost in the effort of escape. The burn stung again. I pushed the sweater to my elbow and let the long sleeve of the robe lightly cover it. *Good thing it's cold. Makes this easier to hide.*

Sliding open the door to the patio, I headed across the lawn to the steps that led to the beach. The crisp sea air rustled the nearby trees and whipped my hair around my face before settling. I chose one of two wooden deck chairs planted in the sand and sat with my knees drawn up to my chest with the robe at my ankles, reflecting on the tranquil waves of the ocean and taking in the salty breeze, cleansing the city air from my lungs.

*Wonder what time it is, anyway.* I'd lost track somewhere around ten thirty p.m. the night before. Hearing footsteps behind me, I turned to see Kevin and smiled.

"How are you this morning? Rested?" he asked.

"More than rested. *Finally.* I'm at peace." I rose from the chair and stood on my toes to meet him eye to eye, kissing him lightly. "What are you busy doing?"

"A little work while you slept, I thought. I hope you don't mind." He wrapped his arms around my waist as he stared into my eyes.

"Of course not. I'd forgotten how much I've missed the beach." Another breeze caught my hair and lifted it. As I reached around him, my arm stung wickedly again. I hid my response to the pain behind a long blink.

"What is it?" he asked.

I cleared any thought from my mind and shook my head. "Nothing," I said, trying my best to sound honest.

"Stop blocking me, Sara. Your arm flinched."

*It did?*

"Let me see."

I missed the reaction that had given me away. It was hardly enough to be called a flinch. And yet he hadn't missed a beat. He pulled back to allow me to show him.

I held my forearm out and eased the sleeve up, exposing the mark to the cold air. Unlike a burn that was healing as time went on, the red patch on my forearm was beginning to hurt more, not less. He pushed the sleeve of the robe up to my elbow.

"Here, sit down," he said, leading me toward the chair, where he began scrutinizing the red mark that started as a four-inch patch but was now taking the shape of something similar to a cross. "You didn't have this last night. Where did you go?" He paused, searching for the answer in my eyes. "You need to tell me, Sara." His brows narrowed, reflecting the potential seriousness of the issue.

"I went to the dark world. I know you warned me about it yesterday, but I had to see for myself." I sucked in air between my teeth as the wind reached the exposed tender spot and stung again. "Sorry."

"I didn't expect you would go so soon." His eyes left mine to focus again on the mark. "You can't go to Tarsamon's realm alone. Anyone who knows that place rarely does."

"It's just a burn. It will go away in a day or so, I'm sure," I said, trying to reassure him.

"Not this one. They marked you, like when one brands an animal. That's why it's hurting more, because it's changing as it's being created." He placed his palm over the entire shape and wrapped his fingers around the rest of my forearm, causing the burn to sting that much more. I winced at the pressure being applied. "This may hurt a bit but it should help." He pressed down and held his hand in place. Within seconds, his hand became as hot as the branding iron I imagined in his description. I sucked in another breath and held it, this time visibly wincing in pain.

"What are you doing? Stop. It really hurts."

He pressed his hand into the painful area.

"Hold on a little longer. I'm trying to remove it."

I watched him in silence, glancing at his face with its focused concentration on my arm. I'd thought I understood what his abilities were but soon realized there was much more to Dr. Scott than I was aware.

"What else can you do?" I asked, trying to take my mind off of the stinging sensation. He looked up at me. His hand was beginning to cool, much to my relief.

"That's about it." He smiled, leaving me uncertain if he was referring to the burn or his abilities.

"It actually feels much better. Thanks."

His hand fell away and I could see a faint pink patch, instead of the image that had been forming.

"That will clear soon enough," he said.

"Now tell me about the entire trip there and what happened," he said as he sat in the chair next to me. He leaned forward, dragging a hand through his tousled hair and resting his forearms on his knees.

"I got there, to Ardan, so easily. I don't even know how." My eyes left his and floated to where the chair leg met the sand.

"If someone doesn't have a message for you, it's a combination of desire and curiosity that led you there. Your energy called to it for the experience you sought, and so you arrived in a place we often avoid."

"I just wanted to see what was in the dark world. I had no intention of fighting the demons, dogs, whatever they were. It was as if they knew who I was with the number of them pursuing me."

"That's because they do know who you are. And never think you can go and escape without a fight. You have to understand the Dark Lord drives the nature of the creatures, trolls, and all evil to work to find and possibly kill you. It's easiest for that to be accomplished on his ground. That's why you're not safe there. If those forces are successful, there's nothing standing in their way of manifesting evil into human nature at a much faster pace." He watched my face for a response.

"That sounds utterly crazy."

"If you believe in the abilities you have and those you've seen in the rest of us, your team, then why would it be crazy to believe that there is a darker force at work, one that wants you dead?" He leaned back into the chair. "You do believe in the quest and the importance of the symbols?"

"Yes, of course. But why would anyone want me dead? I'm not a threat. Not yet anyway."

"Aside from Tarsamon, you are the only other soul who can change the course of what is coming. You are a threat to the darkness. They didn't know how much but may know more now after your visit. Do you remember hearing of the Soltari?"

"Yes."

"It's a powerful entity. Soltari means to understand one's nature. The Soltari has set in motion a mission planned thousands of years ago. Those of us who will aid you in the quest have abilities that set us apart from others."

*Like healing the burn on my arm?*

"Yes," he said, answering the thought. "That's one of my strengths."

"Doesn't the force in dark world want you dead as much as they want me?" I said.

"Yes. They would like all of us to be wiped out, but you are singled out because you are the one who can hold the keys. What you have to understand is that, for now, you can't travel to that world alone. I will go with you if you insist on going," he said.

"I do. It's the best way for me to understand what we will be fighting."

"That knowledge is already with you. You just don't remember. You need to trust that you know." His brow wrinkled over one eye.

"I'll tell you the next time I decide to go."

He shook his head slightly. "Remember something for me whenever you travel. You are felt before you are seen in that world. Your energy is sensed. Hiding behind walls or in shadows is like blowing a whistle as you are trying to conceal yourself. Your particular energy is very strong, easily felt by others in the realm."

"Okay, but why don't I remember these details like you?"

"You know of them. It's being kept from you and I can only guess why."

"I'm going to Ardan tonight to get some answers. If you want to join me, you can."

"Those who give you guidance will only speak to you and how what is to happen relates to you. Just be sure to tell me when you decide to travel to the dark world, okay? You must be kept safe."

"Of course. I didn't mean to cause you to worry."

He clasped both hands around mine and pressed his concern aside with the flash of a smile. How dangerous could finding a few keys really be?

The angst of the discussion was forgotten in a day spent exploring the Cape and another better than "nice" dinner. I didn't really care what I shared with him. It could have been boiled potatoes. But the awareness of how being close could hurt grew with each laugh or brush against him. The connection developing was much stronger than any other I'd ever experienced. And with it, another layer of brick was added to my wall of protection, safeguarding my trust, my feelings should it not last.

I wanted to press my fears of the past into the shadows, run full force into this mission with Kevin. But the tender spirit hiding behind the wall said no. I would have to trust the guides that led us to be together and try to silence the internal voice acting as the protector of my emotions.

We sat together on the plush rug in front of the fireplace, examining the remains of the now blush-colored burn from the morning. The shape of the cross was gone.

"I'm sure it will be completely undetectable by morning. You don't need to worry," I said, gently prying my wrist from his hand, only to find he held it a little tighter in his grasp.

"Only if you don't return to the dark world will I not worry."

Irritation inserted its ugly finger into my perfect day at the feeling of being trapped. Did he expect me to promise I wouldn't go? Like it or not, I needed to follow what felt right, to learn what evil we would battle. And that meant I would visit the forbidden realm where Tarsamon resided again.

"I can't promise that. I'm stronger than you give me credit for. Besides, I'll be leading this mission, right?" He nodded. "That means I won't have anyone tell me what I can and can't do." I glanced away as he released my wrist. At his silence, I turned back to meet his heated stare.

"I expect that you won't," he said calmly. "Understand, you're only making my job harder by putting yourself at risk."

"Did someone say it would be easy? Because I'm getting a clear picture that it won't. If you don't want the responsibility—"

"You're a stubborn woman," he interrupted, "who knows better than to push me, Sara. It's not who you are. This has nothing to do with wanting the responsibility."

I could feel his temper rise and fall quickly. "Maybe we should just stop this thing between us right here. I don't need any complications."

He stared at me in disbelief, as the momentary silence hung thick in the air between us.

"If you knew everything that was at stake…" he said under his breath but just loud enough for me to hear. "You don't need to put up defenses with me. I'll move at your pace," he said louder and with control. He knew me too well to merely have been informed by a few guides. He couldn't have felt my attempt to push him away before I did. Hell, I hardly realized what happened, until he identified it as a defense tactic. And I couldn't deny it. It was my MO when I began to feel too close. But how did *he* know that? I took in a deep breath and let it out at once.

"What is it between us that I don't know?" I asked, pausing. "Don't you think I can feel it? Something draws me to you, and it's much deeper than just a physical attraction."

"Good. Follow that feeling." He paused. "I want to tell you so much." There was a momentary flash of pain in his eyes before he concealed it. "I've taken an oath not to reveal certain information before it's planned. Telling you that much is quite nearly breaking my promise."

"To whom?" And then it came to me. "The Soltari?" He just stared, but the answer was clear in his eyes. "Why don't they want me to know?"

"It was planned for your protection. You agreed, at the time," he said. "Trust me, okay? You don't need to be defensive with me."

"I'm sorry for that. I told you I don't trust easily." It was so much easier, safer to hold him at bay. "I meant what I said about doing what I must."

"Understood. And old habits die hard," he said. "But I'll see what I can do."

There was a familiar fire rising from behind those brown eyes that fixed on mine, as hot as the one flaming in the hearth in front of us. He reached a hand to my cheek. I closed my eyes. Somewhere locked deep in my soul, there was a brief chiming of a warning to push him away as he moved closer. But I didn't move, consumed by the heat and the attraction that willed me to him. The internal voice quieted, and I realized I had just crossed over a boundary I had created. I allowed his approach, melting into his touch as his hand glided from my cheek to cup beneath my jaw. With my eyes still closed, I felt his lips gentle on mine.

Tonight he moved in slow motion, savoring every inch of skin that he paused to kiss. His warm breath and soft lips urged me to give without hesitation, while I received what I so desperately needed to soothe the emptiness in my soul. Upon reaching the deep scar on my thigh, he slowly and gently stroked it with his fingertips, coming back to my face every moment or so for the hard-pressed kiss of my mouth on his. I was breathless beneath him with each new place his hand purposefully traced and then followed with his lips. The memories he was creating were not only enticing but meant to bond, leaving me to wonder if he had heard the warning and knowing, if he reached deeper, he could stifle that voice forever.

Much later in the evening, I dozed to the comfort and stillness in the room as the fire crackled its warmth around us. An eerie sensation crawled up my spine upon entering the familiar forest in Ardan. Clouds of white mist glided between tall trees, lighting the darkness as it moved. I called out this time, not waiting for anyone to appear.

"Are the ones called Soltari here?" I asked, lifting my voice above the thick trees in hopes that I would be heard. "Where are you?" I heard footsteps coming toward me but couldn't tell from what direction. *They know I'm here. I'm sensed before I'm seen.*

I narrowed my focus on the scenery as the sounds of several soft footsteps drew closer. A faded band of white was beginning to encircle me. As it became more visible, I could see that it was a fairly large group of figures that now surrounded me. The faces were transparent, clear in a frame of white, but the bodies were lucent shadowy figures that stood hanging almost motionless in the air.

"How may we be of assistance to you, Sara?" A single voice reached out but I could not recognize which of the faces had spoken. I turned slowly in a full circle.

"I seek to remember the details that have been hidden from me." There was no answer, and so I waited.

"You understand your ability and your purpose to fulfill," came the reply. "That is who you are."

"Which of you do I speak with?" I asked, searching each visible face in the crowd of white that hung like a thick fog all around me.

"You speak with us all. This is a collective voice that sounds like one to you," came the reply.

"There are details I wish to know that must be revealed so that I am able to lead," I began. I turned, gazing into another set of peering faces. "My world is growing darker and full knowledge is what I seek." There was another pause as if the group was contemplating an answer. High above the trees, a light buzzing sound began to resonate like a swarm of bees that transformed into a communal hum among the transparent figures.

"Your ability to recall is limited purposefully. You cannot leap beyond the stages to proceed at your desired pace as a human," the voice replied, this time slow and precise.

"To lead my team in this mission, I must have more than basic knowledge of my abilities. I cannot move to the next stage without more information." How else could I lead a team or even form a plan? "Uncover what you hide from me so that I may proceed without the risk of failing."

Another long pause came as I tried to sense any telepathy being shared, without success. I must have been blocked as the Soltari made their collective decision. In the physical world, I could sense the next direction an individual would take and react accordingly, but not in Ardan, not now, anyway. Important minutes were passing. Would there be any answer before I woke?

"Very well," came the reply after what felt like forever. "Your request is granted upon first sunrise. However, certain details and the stages must be revealed to you systematically to protect the mission from discovery by those who work against you."

"Thank you." The white shadowy figures came closer and began to rise above me, joining into one enormous, lucent shadow that hovered briefly. In an instant, they vanished as one.

I was startled awake at my return from Ardan, finding myself in a much softer place than the fluffy rug in front of the fireplace.

"Are you all right?" Kevin asked in a whisper. His arm had been draped across my waist. He lifted it gently off of me.

"Yes. Sorry I woke you."

"It's all right, love. Where did you come back from?" he asked.

"I went to see the Soltari."

He shifted gently, turning to face me. "Did you see them?" he asked, sounding surprised.

"Yes. I asked that they provide details that have been hidden from me." Through sleepy eyes, I could make out his face in the dim moonlight that filtered through the sheer curtains in the room. The gleam outlined his broad shoulders and narrowed waist to where the sheet rested over him. He stared at me for a moment not saying anything.

"What is it?"

"Well, it's just that no one has ever actually seen the Soltari."

"And why is that?"

"It takes a great deal of their energy to combine into one collective mass, so they rarely do it."

"Well, they did this time." I yawned. "I didn't mean to wake you. Go back to sleep." I reached to stroke his hair. He eased closer to me, intertwining our legs, replacing his arm over my waist as his fingers began stroking my back. I began to ponder a new question. Why it had been so easy for me to meet with an entity that "rarely" gathered the energy to do so?

# 23

The cloud of confusion that encircled me like a heavy mist passed on with the start of a new day. A sense of newfound ambition filled me with the clarity of my task revealed and why it was important. I was no longer Sara Forrester, someone who could hear one's thoughts or feel their emotions. I was the sole person with the strength to hold the power of the keys when brought together. The burden of responsibility was mine, shared also by the team that had chosen to aid in the endeavor.

Knowledge had been imparted regarding my strength and determination being unmatched except to one, the Dark Lord that would soon seek me out. As I became stronger, he'd have to adjust his plan.

The energy in my body, too, had come to life this morning, like a live wire that had finally been fully electrified. I remembered my skill and prior knowledge of the dark demon world. I had battled them before to fight for other worlds with a team similar to the one that was with me now, though I could not see their faces in my memory.

I knew what I had to do. I had to meet the one entity that matched my strength and had the same drive to win as fiercely as I did, Tarsamon. We were the same in strength, determination, and desire. Only one of us could claim the future.

Tarsamon and his evil legion sought the life-force of humanity, to sink it into a plague of darkness and pain. That energy, this world, would provide expansion for the power he'd obtained. If I saved the world, kept it from Tarsamon's grasp, would it still end up on the same course it was on, with fear passed from one person to the next? The very fear that had opened an entry to Tarsamon? I had to believe one of the keys, the acceptance of all things, would impart a reduction of that fear.

As I lay comfortably in the soft feather bed, sunlight streaming through the beautiful wall of windows and the crevices of my mind, I smiled at the newfound knowledge. The one piece still missing was that of how I knew Kevin, leaving me with some sadness at the fact. I stretched, turning my head to see that I was alone. Before I could wonder why, Kevin entered the room.

"Good morning. I see, or rather hear, that your request was fulfilled. Would that be correct?" he asked, smiling at me. He'd been listening to my thoughts again. I would need to remember the block to keep them private.

"It appears so." I sat up and flipped my legs over the edge of the bed to face him, tucking the sheet around me. "You have to stop reading my thoughts."

"I'll use any means to keep informed as part of my duty to protect you. May I suggest you consider practicing a block if you find it an intrusion?" he said with a casual air.

"I'm comfortable. I should have nothing to hide."

"Ah, but we both know you do," he said, making his way across the room.

*What?* I remembered the one piece of information regarding C-05 I hadn't shared. Before I could muster a reply in defense, he spoke.

"I have something I want to give you." Reaching into a drawer, he pulled a medium-sized square box out of the lowest drawer of the table next to the bed. It was a rather ordinary white box, with a silver bow tied on top.

"It's so thoughtful of you. But you know I don't need gifts."

"This is different."

My curiosity heightened as I slipped off the bow and removed the lid. Inside the white velvety box was a silver bracelet. I carefully lifted it out to see that two diamonds were placed on either side of a medium-sized sapphire stone that rested in the center. The bracelet was gorgeous, with four silver bands that were interwoven to hold the precious stones in place.

"It's beautiful."

"I know how you feel about gifts, but as I mentioned, this is a little different."

"How?" He was blocking me from being able see any more than he wanted me to know.

"It's just something to remind you of our time here." I could sense that was true but that there was something else he was not telling me.

"Thank you," I said, admiring the sparkling silver against my skin. It surprised me how comfortably it fit, as if it were a second skin I hardly felt on my forearm. I reached up, placing a hand on his cheek, and kissed him.

He held my face for a moment before letting go. "We have to go," he said.

"Where are we going?"

"It's a surprise but it involves the use of swords, so dress comfortably."

I showered and dressed quickly, pulling my hair back. As we drove for a good hour away from the beach town, thoughts of the mission returned. In between light conversation, I reflected on what needed to be accomplished and how the team could move forward with my lead instead of C-05's.

"You aren't thinking of replacing him just yet, are you?" Kevin asked, again tuning in to my thoughts. When was he not? Could I get used to his presence in my thoughts? Not likely. Privacy was still mine to keep.

"Just thinking. Not really planning anything yet."

He nodded in satisfaction. Blocking him then, I wondered if he would feel the same way knowing what I'd found in C-05's think tank. Why had my name been linked back to Tarsamon's, anyhow?

We turned onto a dirt road just off the main highway with dogwood trees flanking each side, finally arriving at a desolate area sprinkled sparsely with chestnut trees. "Just beyond this grouping of trees is a clearing, not too far, where we can practice."

"Practice?" I asked.

"You'll be fine. You'll see." Kevin pulled two rather plain-looking cases from the trunk and began heading toward a clearing ahead of us.

"Just over here," he said, lifting a case and pointing with an index finger.

"Let me help you," I said, taking one of the cases from him and feeling its weight heavy in my hand.

Upon opening the box, I found the European longsword of similar length and blade type as the one I'd used in Ardan. I lifted it carefully from the case. Sword gripped tightly in both hands, I held it upright in front of me and safely away from Kevin as I adjusted to the grip and weight in my hand.

"How is it that you have a couple of spare blades at hand, and fine ones at that?" I asked.

By this time, I gathered from his description of the dark world, the knowledge he shared and his purpose to protect me meant he was not only a doctor but also a trained warrior of some sort. *Last Great Warrior.* Lady Mara's words flitted through my head. "You must practice often," I said, looking over the beautiful blade I held.

"I collected these for practice. They aren't of as stellar precision as those we've used in Ardan, but they will suffice for purposes of practice here." He came to where I stood, facing me in a defensive hold. "Let's see what skills you have in slash and thrust."

I almost laughed at the thought of approaching Kevin with a sword, tucking the urge to do so behind pressed lips. "You really expect me to initiate an attack?"

"Better to dive in. Don't you think? Believe me, Sara, you're not going to hurt me."

"Oh, it wouldn't be on purpose. But as long as *you're* confident, very well." I began moving slowly to exhibit a slash, then a thrust, and kept at it for several minutes.

"You're doing quite well, but your opponent will not move like that when fighting. Increase your speed."

As I did, my breath drew in faster under the physical demand of the sword. I pressed on for a few more minutes, turning and blocking his thrusts, while Kevin met every approach of mine straight on, with much less effort than me, until I was nearly gasping for breath. He pushed me through each maneuver, causing me to deny fatigue and calling out, "Faster" when my movements began to slow. "Tarsamon's forces aren't going to wait for you when a real fight comes. They'll look for that weakness."

The strenuous exertion over time began to eat at my nerves. *Just the right moment and I'll take your head off.*

He laughed, hearing the thought, giving me more momentum to fight. The required concentration to meet his strikes made it impossible for me to block any frustration or thought from his perusal.

We practiced techniques for hours, taking much-needed breaks, for my sake, allowing a chance to recover from the breathlessness exertion in this world caused. Kevin hardly broke a sweat with only a gleam of perspiration on his forehead.

"Your internal energy is combined well with your external environment as you shift. The movements are fairly smooth and appear almost effortless," he said. "You only need a few more techniques."

"Almost effortless would mean I wouldn't be gasping for breath after a few minutes." He laughed lightly. "Is Highland broadsword the only training you've had in this world?" I asked, placing the sword into the case.

"I've made some effort to learn about techniques used in other cultures, particularly those of Asian influence," he said. *That explains the internal versus external energy comment.* "You only need practice and you'll get used to the effort soon enough."

"I had no idea you had such a plan today," I said, smiling at him.

"Well, I didn't want to give you the chance to say no by telling you what we would practice. Although, I suppose you still could have declined." He glanced at me as he pulled onto the dirt road leading to the highway home. "But after the gift of the bracelet, I felt the odds were more in my favor," he added with a smirk.

I had forgotten about the bracelet resting comfortably just above my wrist and gazed with affection at it, noticing how it sparkled as it caught the light in the early setting sun.

"I don't recall being *asked* to go," I said with a smile. "Still, gift or no gift, I wouldn't have turned down the opportunity to be challenged."

"I didn't think so."

On the ride back to Kevin's home, I was careful to block any thoughts from his focused attention, fully suspecting he was aware of my effort to do so. He'd blocked me plenty of times. I wasn't betraying this new relationship by doing the same.

Those thoughts I preferred to keep private kept returning me to the dark world with the demons and other hellish creatures. How was I going to properly prepare to fight the evil in my world unless I challenged my strengths in their world? The time to exercise my abilities was not when the battle was coming through my door. I needed to know my strengths and weaknesses against the evils that had found me once and might again.

That evening was similar to the others in that I had come to welcome the approaching darkness that brought with it an intimate connection. Kevin lay quietly beside me, drifting off to sleep. My hand stroked gently along his side in affection, finding the scar again, and along with it a moment of quiet to contemplate the cause. Because I had seen the image of his mother just before another vision with blood streaming from the wound, I wondered if the gash had occurred at the same time, when he was only a small child. I cringed at the thought and felt my stomach turn over as I swallowed both the feeling and the image away. It didn't feel right to ask again about it and I wouldn't, knowing he would tell me in his own time.

"It didn't happen then," he whispered.

"You don't have to tell me if you don't want to." I could see the outline of his body in the faint moonlight that filtered into the room as he lay on his back, staring upward, his thoughts taking him beyond the walls of the room.

"It's all right." And I could feel that it was. He lifted my hand to his chest, covering it with his. "Remember I told you I discovered Ardan several years ago?"

"Yes."

"My reacquaintance with the two sides of Ardan was discovered after a fight in the dark world. I had a dream where I had met with the Alliance and was told the mission was being engaged."

"Did you always have your memories of past battles and who you were?"

"Yes. I've always known. I went to the dark world for the same reason you have, to know what I would fight one day as the person I've come here to be in this life." His hand glided over mine and gently squeezed. "I nearly lost against a fierce group of demons. There were three." He paused, shifting on his side to face me. His eyes, however, were looking past me in thought, back to the fight. "Until a fourth had crept behind me," he continued. "I slipped. Just one wrong move. I managed to get out of the way but not in enough time before his claw came down along my side. I couldn't fight, was reduced to fleeing instead, and managed to escape that part of the realm with the speed I'd been given. At first, I thought I woke from a dream with all the light streaming in, but discovered I had remained in Ardan, too weak to move. That's where I met the elves and discovered their ability to heal." He paused. "Eldor found me on the border that separates the dark world from the side the immortals reside. He extended to me the gift of healing, but only wounds and the like."

"Only?"

"I can't affect any dark magic or the evil Tarsamon carries. I'm a warrior. A protector. I don't deal in spells and magic."

He described how the elves had applied herbs and covered the wound with a bandage, while words mingled with white smoke rising above him in the air as he fell in and out of consciousness. He had woken the next morning in his bed, sheets soaked with blood and a thick, tender red line as a painful reminder of the visit.

"The wound was sealed. No stitches were needed," he said, his attention returning to the dark room we shared. His thumb glided across my cheek.

"And still, you went back to the dark world?"

"Much later. After I had developed advanced fighting techniques and practice in the better half of Ardan, outside Tarsamon's reach." Silence passed between us.

"I do understand your desire to go there," he said, stroking a few fallen strands of hair away from my face.

"I must go, tonight." His recount of events had given me a chill enough to reconsider, briefly. But my decision was solid. I had to go. I couldn't learn without doing so.

"Why tonight?" he whispered.

"Because the last battle is fresh in my mind."

"I'll teach you. You're risking too much going there. You may be learning, but they are fighting to end the battle there."

"Yes, likely." I paused, considering. "You asked me to tell you when I'm going and I am."

"You're not strong enough to survive them, my love, not yet."

"I have been strong enough to fight them in the past, on other quests, and I will try again. You said yourself, all the knowledge is present."

"Your muscles, this body, needs to remember what will be demanded of it. That comes with practice."

"I must get stronger. There is no other way."

Silence filled the room. I could feel him contemplating a way to change my mind. "I can't stop you if you're set on going but you won't go alone. Agreed?"

I nodded. "I'll meet you there."

"Be very watchful. They are like dogs seeking out a scent."

"I'll be careful." But I felt that did little to ease his worry. He kissed my forehead, and all was silent. I curled into him as we dozed to sleep with an aim for the dark world.

# 24

I arrived in heavy brush, nothing but pitch-black surrounding me and Kevin nowhere to be found. *I must have fallen asleep first.* Picking through tall blades of dead grass, I headed in the direction of the buildings where I'd fought the demons, the familiar orange light my target.

My ears prickled with heightened sensation, listening for the sound of faint footsteps or animal noises in the distance, hoping to be able to catch the glimpse of a shadow or movement before my enemy found me. My extrasensory abilities were keen to the danger lurking in the darkness and the awareness of time. I found the blackened empty streets and the glowing orange from a single streetlight above, a beacon to what hunted.

I needed to get to the top of any one of the buildings but couldn't recall how I had done so in the past. As if in answer, a strange sensation came over me, a feeling as natural as the instinct of a cat that I could leap from the ground to the rooftop. Thinking or feeling I could jump that high was one thing. Actually doing it was another. And time was ticking away. The last time I'd been here, I'd arrived and left from the same entry point on the roof.

I glanced to rooftop ledge. *Long, straight line. Solid. Stucco, maybe?* Placing my sword back into its sheath I crouched and pushed off the ground. Following a tumble headfirst and an uncomfortable press of the sword into my back, I landed at the point along the building's edge I'd gazed at a moment earlier. *Nothing in the streets below.*

I scanned the building tops and the vacant streets with Kevin's caution echoing in my ears. Nothing ominous was visible, save the looming darkness on the edge of the dusty orange-glowing streets. The buildings where light reflected off the dirty, cream-colored walls were landmarks to run to in battle. I committed to memory the path they made for as far as I could see. Should I have to run, at least I'd have a mental map of the layout.

A sudden overwhelming anxiety filled my body, an indication evil was approaching from the depths of the darkness. My blood pulsed faster in my veins as my heart kicked into action. Yet the stillness remained like a placid lake moments before the kids of summer camp dove in. The light was strangely soothing in an otherwise dark and vacant hell. I hated it for the target I'd become under the false comfort of orange glow. There was no place to hide, nor a way to watch from a distance. *You come here, you'd better be prepared to fight.*

*Where is Kevin?* It felt like several long minutes had passed. *Doesn't matter. I was going to come alone anyhow. Just remember how to use the energy.* I reached again for my sword. Being caught by surprise would be detrimental in a matter of seconds. As I gripped the sword, I noticed the bracelet he'd given me. I must have fallen asleep with it as comfortable as it was. With any luck, it wouldn't be the only thing left of me when I finished here.

A movement caught my attention on the border of the brush and street, beyond the glow of an empty city. It looked like a dust storm of black shadow headed toward me, engulfing the lighted streets in darkness like a biblical plague. As the dust began to settle, outlines of bodies began to show and the faceless, flesh-colored demons wasted no time crawling with urgency up the wall of the building I was on. Their extended claws scraped along concrete and mortar as they slid back before finding a better grip to approach. Some of them remained below in the streets, their bare faces angling upward, waiting as though a meal were likely to be delivered off the edge, out of thin air.

I imagined the shield of white light extending beyond me at least two feet as Kevin had instructed and as I had practiced in Ardan, while trying to ignore the lesions splotched across what looked like animated dying flesh approaching. My fear was edging toward the surface. They could smell it too, as though a feast of rancid meat was waiting, causing them to push each other out of the way to get to it.

Clutching my sword tighter in my right hand, I held open my left to see the crackle of white-blue flame come to life as I set up my arsenal of defense and waited for the demons to approach. Their claws, as sharp as eagle talons, clicked along the flat rooftop as the first few climbed over the edge. I hurled the ball of light into the first group of creatures, listening as their cries of pain transformed to a terrible hissing noise. Once hit, they transformed into a black mist that rose above and faded into the sky. That noise only fueled their seething with fury and excitement at the chance to kill. *That must be what Juno meant about killing one—only brings more to the party.*

There were more creatures this time. I hadn't stayed long enough then to get a good view of what I'd be up against. Some of the demons had with them hounds with tainted yellow eyes fixed in my direction. With the excessive muscle in the legs, particularly the hindquarters, and overly sharpened, longer teeth, the dogs were bred as weapons.

Kevin was right about me not coming here. I wasn't strong enough yet. But how could I know for sure until I fought them? Yeah, maybe it was too risky of a decision not knowing what I was fully capable of yet. I pushed the thought from my mind, knowing it would only weaken me to think of what I should have done or what I might not be ready to handle. I was here now. Time to fight.

The beasts drew closer, cautious of the energy I held as a defense, sniffing the air and following the scent. The dogs snarled beside them. It wouldn't take them long to learn how I fought. Then what? I'd been taking small steps backward, not prepared to face an army. *Gotta keep them at bay and find the exit. Shit, where did I exit? A hole in the rooftop. But where, which one? What building?* I scanned the rooftops before refocusing on my enemy.

Why hadn't I thought to ask the way out when Kevin and I had been talking? How could I have overlooked exiting? Probably because it was never an issue. How long could I run to find the escape route? Kevin's words, *one wrong move,* repeated over and over in my head.

The dogs coming close enough to touch the white shield of light yelped. The demons drew back briefly before approaching again, this time with more curiosity than fear. The shield had done nothing to deter their ambition to kill, only stunning them momentarily as they came harder and faster toward me. *The dogs must be stronger than the demons.* In their recoil, I swung the sword with such ferocity, landing blows across three of the beasts, angering the other creatures close by. Snarls ripped across the night sky from below as the beasts in the streets, also making their way up the wall, answered the call. Streams of drool dripped from the corners of the dogs' mouths in front of me. I swung again, taking out six demons and four more hellhounds.

The shield I carried began to change in brightness. The demons that had encountered the light radiating from it and backed away beyond the reach of my sword made a new attempt to break through the shield. They weren't shocked in the same manner as the first encounter and none of them were dying. Had they become immune to the electrifying effects of the first touch? *Need to strengthen that defense but how?* I didn't know how long it would take to completely break down the protection. There was no opportunity I was willing to give to find out. I lunged forward again, swinging in a half circle. I shifted the blade and swung in the other direction followed by a backward somersault, creating a small distance between us. After that, neither the hellhounds nor the demons, free running and those that held them, hesitated. They flung themselves in a forceful, bloodthirsty doggy-demon pack at me. I pushed back with my shield, shaking only a few. This was a fight that brought with it a triple dose of what I'd experienced last time. *Got to get out.* Directed by instinct, I somersaulted over the street below and onto the building closest.

I whipped around to see the beasts snarling, ravenous for blood. Could they make the leap? The faceless demons in the street were already making their way up the sides of the building where I stood. Another group of them with a pack of dogs ran below, watching

which direction I'd go. I was just bringing my fight to another location and not really outrunning any of them. I'd need another plan
and fast. There was only so much energy I could create that could be
sustained in this world before it burned out. With no way to reclaim
it, it wouldn't be long before I not only ran out of strength but out of
time. This was a place to come and accomplish a specific goal and get
the hell out. It was all too clear I'd put myself in a no-win situation.
*Maybe the portal back is inside one of the buildings? Can't be. Wasn't last time.*

The orangey glow grew dimmer as something black as Hell's own
shadow flew closer. All I was doing now was allowing the rest of the
army of evil time to catch up. I would be overcome in a matter of moments. I scanned the rooftop for the exit. Not finding one, I looked
to the streets below for another alternative only to find the cluster of
beasts had grown in size, frantic with hunger and seething with desire to tear into flesh. I was clearly outmatched. *Run! Where is the damn
portal back to my world? I can't hide.*

The acrobatics, swordsmanship, light, and energy I had practiced
wasn't enough here. Kevin had been right. If I got through this, I'd
find some balls to tell him so. *You couldn't just listen to him.* My shield
began to dim, weakening in the constant state of struggle. I tried as
I had in the other world to recall my energy, imagining the light becoming bigger and more powerful around me, using everything I'd
practiced.

In response, the shield's blue-white energy grew brighter. But
with the increased demand for energy in place with no reserves, my
thoughts grew more negative as the dark force of this place filtered
through my shield. Why had I been so determined to come? If only
I hadn't been so stubborn, so determined… If I died here, the world
would end without me being able to get the keys to save it. *No, no, no!
Damn it, Sara. Stay focused!* I pressed the negative thoughts away as I
fought left and right, taking out the demons that had made their way
to where I was, then ran again in a desperate search for the portal.
*Why can't I wake up?* Those at my back hit the shield first, giving me
the time to at least turn to strike, slashing again. Seconds dragged on
like minutes, with me lunging and striking. I leaped above them to

a ledge, creating only a fragment of distance between us, and ran as fast as my body would allow. But the creatures continued their mad rush, keeping pace at my heels.

A distraction warmed at my arm. *No, they couldn't have broken the shield and reached me. Not yet.*

I was moving quickly. I wasn't tired, just pissed off. And unlike my previous battle to get out of Ardan, the realization of likely dying here was hard to ignore.

"Damn! What is that?" I said. My arm, where the bracelet rested, was becoming warmer, until it was disturbingly hot. I couldn't stop moving or break my concentration to glance at the area, knowing that would surely allow the creatures to break through what resistance I had left. Refusing the distraction, I ran for another building, scanning each rooftop for the exit. Could I make it back to where I had come in? Maybe the portal was there. *And if not? Can't consider it.*

As I took one more leap, I caught sight of another dark wave of shadow that was coming from the opposite direction of the first. *Two walls of hell? Shit.* Just ahead of it was the hint of a bright light moving like a bullet from the brush, billowing past the shadow cloud. It moved so much faster than the darkness and it was all headed in my direction. I didn't have enough reserves to take the additional shadow group or what other thing was being sent this way. *Got to get out, just get out.* I turned, taking another swing, just as one of the demons landed inches from my face with only a thin membrane of shield separating us. I heard the heavy breath and snarl of it on the side of my head. "Aarrgh," I shouted, pulling the adrenaline necessary to kick the massive beast off my leg as my sword came down at its neck. A blast of light filled my vision, and from the corner of my eye, I saw something slide to my side. *Get off the ledge. Run like hell. Head for the brush. The elves. It's the only chance to…* My thoughts went blank and all I could see was blackness. Something grabbed my arm and the fire that had previously scorched above my wrist burned again and was suddenly gone.

My body didn't hurt and there was nothing, except that I felt so very heavy and weak. I couldn't see anything except blackness. *I must have died. I let them down. All of them. And Kevin.* I tried to move but it was as if each tiny shift was like moving ten tons of weight.

"Lie still," I heard a voice say quietly. I couldn't identify who had spoken. I tried to peel my eyelids open to see who it was and gauge where I might be. It was useless. I was completely immobile.

"Where am I?" I asked. My voice came out scratchy, broken.

"You're safe now," the voice whispered.

"Kevin?" No answer.

I sensed frustration and relief in the air.

If it was Kevin, I didn't know if he could forgive me for visiting the dark world, going against his warning and risking both our lives and the rest of the world. I didn't know what had happened, only that now I had to trust the voice that said I was safe. The void of emptiness was all that remained in place of the fight, along with its companion— complete and utter silence.

# 25

ow long had I been here? Where exactly was here? Was I still safe? I let out a breath. Memories of the last few days began flooding back to me. The bed I was lying in was as soft as when I had curled into Kevin and had fallen asleep. The throbbing in my head warned me to refrain from any attempt at movement. Despite it, I lifted my arm and let it fall onto my stomach. As I lay on my back, with a mild sense of accomplishment at the effort, I wondered why so much weakness. I felt the bed move next to me. I turned my head and peeked under my lids to see Kevin sitting beside me, blocking out the sun as he looked down at me. He stroked my forehead and brushed his fingertips over my hair.

"How are you feeling?" he asked.

"Better than last night." I wanted nothing more than to shut out the light.

"Well, that would have been a fast recovery." He took a deep breath. "You've been out for two days."

"What?" I replied, surprised at the amount of time that had passed and that I'd not awoken for any basic necessities.

"I was concerned about getting fluids into you, thinking I might need to start an IV sometime today."

I nodded as the memory rushed back to me of the dark world.

A pain shot through my head, punishing me for not listening to him. I felt foolish and embarrassed for not heeding his warning.

I tried to sit up, helped by two large hands under my shoulders, and leaned back into the pillows resting against the headboard. "How did I…" I began.

"How were you fortunate enough to escape?" He asked the question before I could.

"Yes. And I'm so sorry."

"Here, drink this. It will help you recover your strength," he said, handing me a bottle of electrolyte-enhanced water. "I got to you a split second before they wore down your shield."

"I didn't see you."

"You wouldn't. I was moving too fast. A second more and…" His voice trailed off. "It was too close, Sara."

"I know. I'm sorry." *Sorry that I didn't listen. Sorry you had to rescue me. Sorry I almost ended everything for the need to know.* "There was a light I saw ahead of the second large shadow. That was you?" I asked as the memories began coming back to me slowly. He nodded once. "I remember it felt like a long while since I'd arrived. When I thought you might not come, I wasn't sure how to get out. I realized at some point I was in over my head and was trying to figure out how to get back here." I was already feeling better after a few sips of the water, finding strength in my voice.

"You fought a good, strong fight because you carry the knowledge of how to fight, but you're no match for them. Not yet. Besides, the demons were also stronger because you had been there before. They were learning from you and that is why, my love, your shield wasn't going to hold."

"So I was strengthening them instead of becoming stronger myself. Great. How did you know how I fought? You weren't there with me. Was I talking in my sleep?"

He laughed softly. "Well, you do talk a little, but not in this case. I can see what you can see."

"You can see what I can see?" I repeated.

"I don't want to explain how. It doesn't matter."

"I'd like to know."

"Do you like the bracelet?"

"I love the bracelet. What's the connection?"

"Can you promise to wear it?"

"Of course I'll wear it." But I wasn't promising anything until I at least heard an explanation.

"This gift is very unique," he said as he touched my arm where the bracelet remained. "It allows me to find you when I'm not able to be with you, when you are in danger."

"I thought my energy could be felt without the need to see me and that is how you knew where I was."

"True. That is one way of locating someone, by sensing his or her energy. Think of this like a GPS device that helps me find you more quickly. It also provides a sensory-like picture of what is around you."

"You're tagging me? What is this gift when I'm not in danger?" I asked, uncertain if I should be angry or understanding.

"Well, I believe you said it's a beautiful piece of jewelry."

"Yes, I said that. What do you say? Is that all it is?"

"Yes. You have my word. It works when there is danger and no other time." He sounded sincere. I didn't sense any deception at work. If I came out of this experience knowing anything, it was that I'd better trust his word.

"I won't lie to you, Sara."

"You didn't exactly tell me what this was when you gave it to me, either."

"I didn't want you think I was *tagging* you, causing you to refuse it."

"Yes, I probably would have," I answered. "After last night, I can understand why you gave it to me, especially after you warned me about going to the dark world and I went anyway. I'm sorry for risking your life, too."

His face softened at my apology. "You've already apologized and I'm not angry. Besides, I've been given fair warning by my guides that you might be a wee bit of a challenge to protect. This bracelet helped me to get to you in time. It's a strong personality that is called to lead this mission, not one that follows the desires of others, especially mine. I understand why you did it, but you understand that I must keep you safe by any means?"

"Yes, and I'm glad it's you." I reached for his hand resting on my forearm. "I have to know how you avoided the demons? There were so many of them this time."

"I move much faster than they and I've had a lot of practice shielding myself from them. Now is not the time to fight them and definitely not in their world, where they outnumber us." He paused, lifting my hand into his. "As for today, I think you should get plenty of fluids so we can leave tomorrow for the city, once I'm sure you've regained most of your strength."

"That's fine. I'd like to go down to the beach and take in the sea air one more time."

"I have some work to wrap up that won't take me long and then I'll come join you, okay?"

"Okay." I smiled back at him and began pulling myself out of bed, ever so slowly, heading for the shower.

As the warm water pulsed down my back, the muscles in my body began to awaken. The welcome heat pulsed life through my veins. The rising steam filled the air with the scent of the fragrant citrus soap, rejuvenating my body and lifting my spirit. I threw on a snug-fitting tank and layered it with sweats for warmth, bracing against the frigid ocean breeze that blew in as I opened the back door.

It didn't matter how cold it might be, the ocean air was just the cure after being immobile for a couple of days. With the bottle of water Kevin had given me in hand, I headed across the manicured lawn to the deck chairs plunged in the sand. The sound of the breeze lifted over the ocean and its cool fingertips nipped at my cheeks, imparting a shiver through my body at the drop in temperature over the last couple of days.

Out of the corner of my eye, I saw a flickering light dancing in the chair next to me, as if someone was playing with a mirror and reflecting it on the back. Shifting my gaze in the opposite direction provided no answer to the question of origin. The beach was practically vacant this time of year. A man and woman with an afghan wrapped around their shoulders sat huddled a fair distance away. I glanced back at the empty chair. The reflection of light, now white with a slight orangey hue, had grown larger. Convinced this was no mirror trick, I leaned back and continued to watch as it danced across the slats into a sparkling form.

"Sara, my love." Cerys's image was transparent, with only muted color. But distinct features defined him clearly as the vision I'd come to know.

He reached for my hands. "I have something to show you," he said, brushing a transparent hand over my eyes for me to close them.

A chill ran through me and I shuddered in response. A rushing light pulled me deeper, like a vacuum toward something familiar, orange and dark. *The evil world, the one I barely survived two nights earlier.* My breath caught in my throat and I tried to gently pull my hands from his.

"I have to leave. They'll know I'm here. I'm not strong enough to fight now." The bracelet was in the house, left on the counter from my shower. Kevin wouldn't know how to find me.

"Remain calm, Sara," he said, still holding my hands. "You are not in the world from which you just returned. You are only watching. They can't sense you from here. Only in dream state. You are completely safe," he explained. I watched as the demons gathered around, listening to a barking voice, the words unclear.

"You're certain they cannot see us?"

"Quite certain."

I walked undetected through the grim, cave-like opening dimly lit with torches scattered along the walls. Shorter creatures with leathery, bluish skin and bulging bellies bumped into the numerous dog-like beasts, reminding me of trolls. Their heads, smaller than their bellies, held putrid yellow-green eyes as though bad peas had been thumbed into fat dough faces. Black and gray string-like hair hung in tangles down their backs. They grunted with displeasure as they pushed through the crowd. There were several hundred creatures in the space I was occupying in spirit and thankfully not form.

Shadow figures floated smoothly over the deep crevices in the wall as if molasses were flowing up and down the cave. They began to chant unintelligible words directed at a large, black-as-night shadow whose presence engulfed the large space he had assumed to make a speech. His slanted red eyes pierced across the room.

I recognized the leader of the dark world well. Tarsamon had assumed a form that was acceptable to his followers, and so unlike the well-dressed image of the civil man I had spoken with. In that conversation, he'd tried to convince me to give up the mission and the world to him. To the examples of evil surrounding him, he spewed his hatred for the light and the people of Earth, speaking of his intentions to overcome humanity.

The language, a slur of heavy linguistic sounds and harsh intonation, was unlike any I recognized, but the meaning flowed to me as if I were fluent in whatever speak this was. His venomous dialogue provided specific details of how he wanted to use the energy in the physical world and consume it for himself to give to his followers, expanding the malevolent rule to create a larger empire of darkness. Too long, he said, had the Soltari ruled and restricted the evil energy to suit their desires and fit that energy into what they'd called *balance* on Earth. Fists rose in the air and screams that would account for cheers spread like a wave through the great cave forum.

My recovering body filled with complete disgust for him and the pain he wanted to bring to people who struggled daily on Earth. He drew strength in his claim to end the suffering and absorb the energy from the already weakened state of the humans. I watched with repulsion as the army of followers bellowed for more of his brand of hatred, quieting briefly as Tarsamon spoke of the light to be brought forward by our team. This mention evoked loud growls and sneers throughout the crowd that translated to mean light would never be allowed. The faces of the dark and vengeful creatures burned into my memory with the most residual effect being the strong sense of death to my world. My visit and subsequent escape had only fueled their anger, vowing there would be no escape if given another chance, followed by the promise that I would be back. I had no intention of returning, ever. Any battle we fought would have to be on Earth.

As Tarsamon continued speaking, I was most intrigued with the strength he carried, not unlike my own, that was persistently expressed to his followers every couple of sentences. Though not yet ready to fight, I could see clearly what I would be up against in a battle. Getting a clear view of my opponent was beneficial, but how was I to fight a demon as strong as this one? Tarsamon had as much drive and desire to collapse my world as I did to triumph over his poisoned intentions.

He planned to use the negative energy created by fear to control people. God knew there was plenty of it to feed an army, but to grow one? Through fear and anguish, he would reduce each human to feel less and less, causing them to crawl inside themselves and erode the hope life gave them. A storm of violence and suffering would come, as the evil forces plotted to latch on and consume the energy of each human until they were no more than a shell of their being. That couldn't be allowed. Tarsamon would count on those who would not act against another person to tire and cripple in desperation and depression at the loss of life, causing each to become ill through a reduced immune system that could no longer support such emotional pain over time, if they didn't commit suicide first.

His voice rasped out a request for patience as the self-serving desires of the repugnant humans, as he called them, continued to grow while the slow infiltration of forces mingled through the population on Earth, darkening both sky and ground with the shadow of evil. Countless snarls and shrieks filled the room. I realized, as leaders on countering sides, our strength and determination were all that was matched.

My desires rooted from aiding others, like those in the crisis center and the couples in my office, responding to the pain. Tarsamon wanted to use this suffering to tear them down further and consume them. *Who's self-serving?*

The cave began to narrow in my mind's eye to a vision that was becoming smaller. The light that had taken us to the dark world as witnesses began pulling me backward. Back to the beach, and returning me, my conscience, to the deck chair, still holding Cerys's hands. I sat in silence for a moment, contemplating the enormity of the situation.

"You can't go there to practice your skills. The symbols will remain safely hidden in Ardan. For how long, I can't say," Cerys said, breaking the silence.

"What do you mean? Do the dark forces know they are there?"

"They weren't meant to be kept in Ardan. Their power is strong, detectable even in a believed safe haven. Your recently acquired ring can distract the power of them for only a short time. Long enough for an escape."

I glanced at the gold and brown colors on my finger and back to him. "We'll leave soon. I was told we would travel to the location of the first key for the symbol identifying Scotland. Is this true?"

"The first symbol you receive directs you to the first location. That is all I can share. Only you as the Light Carrier direct the path."

If that's so, how did Kevin know before I did that we would travel to the location of the first symbol received? And yet without any way to explain it, Scotland felt right.

"The elves will provide the additional protection you need and any weapons to guard the keys while on your quest. We need you to succeed."

"I understand," I said, feeling the pressure of responsibility deepen. "Thank you for bringing this to me." A transparent, sparkling hand glided across my cheek. As he stood, his image carried toward the ocean and faded into the hazy sea mist.

*I've got to get back home.*

With the shadows already establishing residence, who knew what else had changed. Tarsamon was in the action phase of his plan, leaving less time to strategize on our side. The soft sounds of bare footsteps on the deck behind me distracted me from further thought.

"Don't let me interrupt," Kevin said. I turned to see him smiling at me. "Is this seat taken?"

It was an awkward question to ask. Obviously, no one was there. "Of course not. Why do you ask?"

He sat on the edge of the seat and linked his fingers together. "Visitors."

"How much did you hear?"

"Nothing. Had to be a guide by the way you leaned forward to an empty chair."

"Maybe I was just leaning over in contemplative thought?" He smiled. "Do you know who I was speaking with?"

"No, and you don't have to say." He scooped up a small shell in the sand. "Your communications with spiritual entities are meant only for your ears." A moment of waves crashing to shore passed between us.

"There's a man I knew a long time ago who directs me as a spirit now."

"I see. And did he direct you in a good manner today?" He looked up at me from the shell he had been turning between his fingertips. His brows lifted.

"I believe so." His eyes narrowed in the corners, searching for something more. "Here, let me show you." I replayed the memory of what I had seen and heard so he could listen to my thoughts and get the visual.

"I see how that information provides fuel for the mission." He paused. "You love him?" His eyes locked on mine just like they had done on our first date at dinner, and I realized he not only picked up the message but also the feelings that were shared when Cerys was present.

"I think so, yes."

He paused. "You answered honestly."

*Why wouldn't I?*

"I know that what we have shared is not threatened. I feel that from you and I understand what you wanted me to know. Thank you." A gust of icy wind blew between us, as if signaling the beginning of separation.

I wrapped my jacket tighter around me and took his free hand in both of mine. "This is difficult for me to say, having come from a place where love was not expressed. The love I'm developing for you is deeper than any I have shared with anyone, and I only want it to continue to become stronger. Nothing threatens that, certainly not a love that was held in another lifetime." I wanted Kevin to know just what he meant to me and to be clear of the role Cerys had in my life.

While I didn't cling to any past feelings, to deny they existed when Cerys was present would be a lie and not how I wanted to continue with Kevin.

"There's no need to explain, Sara. He aids you now and I am grateful for that." There was no sense of resentment or jealousy. I didn't expect that from Kevin. "Your feelings, residual or not, would never change what I feel for you, ever. Though, you will have to share more with me about the contents of C-05's office. I didn't realize he had as much information as you found, or that you were capable of such risky behavior by entering such a space." He tossed the shell to the lapping waves.

"How deep does your ability to read thoughts really go?"

"As far as necessary, given enough time," he replied. "I only caught a glimpse of what you saw and it's most concerning."

"Happy you agree. By the way, I was led to his office at the time by an unknown contact. It is certainly not in my nature to snoop."

"So, C-05 knows the location of each of the three keys. You realize what you saw puts you at a greater risk? If I found out, C-05 must know, or at the very least suspects you know more than you led him to believe."

"Actually, I'm counting on the fact he knows nothing regarding me and that room. You found out because I let you in, sharing a visual image with you. I blocked him and continue to keep that barrier in place."

"I suppose it's possible that he's unaware of your knowledge, but don't underestimate his abilities, Sara. Your unknown contact concerns me as well."

"It shouldn't. Juno confessed to having led me to the room. He doesn't trust him, either."

"Perhaps." His fingertips grasped at the stubble forming around his jaw. It appeared he hadn't shaved in the two days I had been unconscious, and it was the first time I noticed his normally tidy appearance looking a bit scruffy. Not that I minded. The unkempt look gave him a rugged appeal I began to find extremely desirable. He glanced up to catch me watching him.

"You need a distraction," he said, taking my hand and standing.

"On the contrary. I have one." I stroked his bristly cheek with the back of my fingertips and smiled up at him.

A single eyebrow shot up. "Mm-hm. A different one. For a little while, anyway. You're still recovering." He pulled me against him and wrapped his arms around me before we turned and headed back to the house.

The wintery day progressed lazily with the warm comfort of the fire crackling around us in the living room. Clouds filled the sky and colored it in gray-blue haze. I stretched long on the sofa and rested my head in Kevin's lap. His fingers glided across my forehead and down my cheek, as we discussed Scotland as the location we'd find the first of the keys. In total relaxation, I started to close my eyes at the sound of his voice.

*Remember us, darling.* Another thought, not my own, skipped through my head and was gone as quick as the snap of the fire.

"Why don't you tell me?"

"Hm?"

"Tell me what it is you want me to know."

"I don't think I said anything."

"We both know you didn't. So?" I tilted my chin up to see him gazing down at me.

"I can't. Simple as that." He paused, and his brows drew together in that pain I'd seen in his eyes twice before. "Not now. Please don't ask. It risks too much for me to share."

"So the best I can do is try to remember something between us? That's hardly anything to go on. But I won't ask again." I didn't want to be the cause of what pained him by pressing him to share whatever it was he kept guarded. Still, the curiosity of it had taken hold, like a seedling that was fighting through the soil to reach daylight. I had to see, needed to know and ease that pain for him.

"Promise me you'll come back here with me," he said.

"I will." It wasn't like me to give in so easily to the wants of others. But bonds had been created over the time spent with him this past week, a closeness that wasn't going to be broken by the protective internal voice that guarded me from getting close to people.

Kevin and I said our goodbyes at the airport where we had met to fly to the Cape. As I settled in for the drive home, my attention turned sharply to getting all three symbols from Ardan and heading to the first location of the keys. Or, I reconsidered, would collecting the three medallions cause them to come after us? I glanced at the ring Lady Mara had given me to hide the energy of the symbols. Did it really have the strength to protect all three? *Only for a short time.*

The evening crackled with the sensation of danger, except that I couldn't yet see it. As I pulled into the garage in the courtyard, a black sedan being held in the driveway by two of the security guards caught my attention. An immediate feeling of agitation and urgency came over me as I sensed the vehicle's occupants and an unknown connection to them. Despite the brief warning from one of the guards, I waved a hand in dismissal and made my way to the driver's door to see Juno and, beside him, Matt.

"It's okay, Tom. I know these men," I said.

"Dr. Forrester, you understand I needed to…" he began, believing me to be upset.

"It's all right. You're just doing your job. Thank you.

"Juno, Matt, good to see you," I said through the car window. "Park your car in the drive just over there." I pointed to the bricked archway off the side of the house and walked over to meet them. "What is it that brings you all the way out here?"

"Can we talk privately?" Matt asked.

"Of course. The house should be empty. I just arrived myself." I led them down the hallway to my office. A soundproof room with the ability to shut off cameras by location. "Please, make yourselves comfortable in here. I'll just be a moment."

I quickly checked to be sure my assistant wasn't roaming the house and returned to my office to call down to security. "Tom, we will be meeting privately in my office. No need to be alarmed by the blackness you'll see."

"Are you quite sure, Dr. Forrester?"

"Absolutely. No need for concern."

As I crossed the room to my desk, I glanced at both men. Juno sat eagerly on the edge of his seat, while Matt displayed a wrinkled brow and lips pressed firmly together.

"We're secure for you to speak freely," I said.

"Sara, we tried to reach you while you were away but were unable," Juno said. *When I was knocked out? Did they try Kevin?* "We've seen some unusual coming events, aside from the shadows already visible," Juno began.

"I don't know how much time there is to bring the team together, but we have to move quickly," Matt added. "Do you have the symbols?"

"They're safe but not with me."

"We think Tarsamon intends to move faster than expected, to destroy a great number of individuals, create a depression among those who remain, and weaken them," Matt explained.

*Destruction is the first stage.* It made sense. Mass devastation first, then consume the remaining humans while they were weak. Faster and required fewer resources.

"Have you seen what form of destruction will be used?" I asked.

"That's just it. We didn't see the specifics but received a call from Aria shortly after. She deals with weather, nature. That sort of thing. It's got to be something like that." Juno leaned back in the chair.

"How much time do we have? Did she say?" Both shook their heads in response. "When did you receive this premonition?"

"A couple of days ago. Because of the concern regarding C-05, we wanted to keep the issues within our small group. When Kevin didn't respond, we became more concerned and decided to see you." *So they had tried to reach him.*

"Good. That isn't too much time that has passed, perhaps allowing us a chance to act. My apologies you could not reach me. I was detained in a rather unexpected manner," I said, referring to the dark world. The last memory of my escape flooded back to me. My vision reached Matt and Juno as they exchanged a brief glance.

"What happened?" Juno asked.

I paused, leaning into the desk, resting my elbows on top. "I've seen the darkest energy that drives what comes, our nemesis and his army."

"You fought them?" Juno asked. "Alone?"

"Yes and no. We have to get everyone together immediately. Can you notify Aria, Elise, and Kevin? Ask them to meet in Ardan at the Professors' gateway, the old ruins, tomorrow evening." I leaned back from my desk watching both of their faces. "And if you can't reach someone, let me know." I exchanged cell phone numbers with them.

"Consider it done," Juno replied. "If Tarsamon has set his forces to move faster into this world, they will be headed for your door. We'd appreciate your guards' clearance for full access of the property.

"Anything you need is granted. I'll let security know tonight. There's plenty of room to make yourselves comfortable, too."

Both men stood and turned to leave. Matt stopped at the double doors of the office.

"You should also be prepared to leave soon."

I nodded. "I've been advised. Thanks.

"It's officially underway," I said as I closed the door. How could I get my hands on that last symbol in Ardan? Mayan. That's what Kevin had said. Would I receive the symbols when the time was right? Could the skills of the other members of the team intervene to stop the unnatural disaster being plotted? The one thing the members of the team had in common, aside from our extrasensory gifts, was the ability to manipulate energy. Anything was possible, no matter how unlikely it appeared.

Intervention in the destruction was a puzzle, with all the pieces in front of me to solve. If only those pieces, the symbols, the locations, and the keys, could be placed just right to see the picture before the clock on life finished ticking, sounding the alarm our time was up.

# 26

I hit send after finishing the email notification to a few friends that I would be away on a long excursion, downed the last of the remaining iced tea in my glass, and reached for the phone to dial Mary Ann. *Got to get to the bottom of why she's been on my mind, and to say goodbye.* It could be that she wondered how things with Kevin and I were going. But her curious nature about my life didn't ever plague me with thoughts of her. Something was definitely in the air and I needed to close the nuances to regain total focus.

Before I could press the button to autodial Mary Ann, a knock sounded at my office door and the face of my assistant peeked through.

"Emma, what can I do for you?"

"I'm sorry to interrupt. Your line was busy, and a man is here who is quite adamant about seeing you. Now."

"Is he a patient?"

"No. It doesn't seem so, but he says he knows you. Wouldn't give his name, either. I don't know how he got past security. I've asked him to wait in the foyer while I check with you."

"I don't have time for a drop-in, no matter how urgent. If he's a patient, tell him any one of the doctors—"

"Already tried that." She turned as a man approached from

behind. I stood and rounded my desk but hesitated as he pushed beyond her into my office.

"Would you like me to call security?" Emma asked.

"No. It's all right." The air in the room grew colder at the sight of C-05. My skin prickled against it. Emma nodded and closed the door, while I kept my temper carefully controlled, awaiting a reason for the unexpected visit.

"Sara, I apologize for dropping in. I won't be but a few minutes but felt a meeting was urgent," C-05 said.

"Why not call? I would have been happy to schedule a meeting. Can I offer you something to drink, perhaps?"

"Maybe another time. Thank you. I tried to call."

*I doubt it.*

"But got your voicemail."

He took an empty seat in front of my desk, leaned back, and crossed his ankle over his knee. My block was up immediately upon recognizing his face, hoping it wasn't too late to block the thoughts I'd had moments before he barged into my office. I turned back to my desk, attempting to wipe any residual expression from my easy-to-read face.

"What brings you here, and with such urgency?" I asked. "I hope nothing is wrong?" I leaned back in the chair, resting my elbows on the arms, my fingers laced, studying him, and not surprised at being unable to pick up a clue from him. The ability to block was an effective tool, when applied properly. I was no expert, not the way C-05 and Kevin were, but I managed to maintain a level of control that appeared to be undetectable.

"I've missed something, I believe. And you may be able to help me," he said with an air of easiness in his voice. Caution hung thick in the air as if it were a humid summer's day.

"Really? Do you mean to say you've *misplaced* something?"

He shook his head. An icy stare washed over him as he pursed his lips into a tight smile that didn't seem at all very friendly.

"I fail to see how I could help you in finding whatever it might be you missed." Recognizing I was being scrutinized, I became aware of my own body language, keeping my arms open, while my eyes held steady with his.

"Oh, but I think you can. You see, it has come to my attention through our thorough security staff that you entered a room near the auditorium during our last meeting that contained some pertinent information."

"Hmm." I paused, reflecting. "Oh, yes, when I got lost looking for the restroom. I certainly hope you are not missing anything?" I knew to leave my expression blank as I glided over his perceived accusation of wrongdoing on my part.

"It doesn't seem so, that we can see. But what exactly were you doing there?" His eyes narrowed in focused concentration.

"As I said, I'd gotten lost, and thinking that door might lead to a restroom, I entered." It was possible, though not likely, they had security cameras in his office. None had been immediately visible. With C-05's limited information, I was willing to bet all he had was that I entered the room and maybe a time stamp on how long I'd been there. "I assumed the information was just the research you were working on to help the team and gave it not another thought. What is it you think you missed, exactly?" I hoped it would not come to his attention as a result of the security footage that I had passed at least two restrooms on my way to the office.

His eyes shifted between my own, searching for anything readable. The silence grew as I masked every emotion and thought from his careful examination.

"Perhaps only a minor oversight on my end."

*An unlocked door? No camera in the room? How I assumed control over this operation without your knowledge?*

"I assure you, I have every confidence you have the mission (*as you see it*) under control."

"I'll investigate further and resolve it with my assistant. Thank you for providing me clarification. I'm sure if you had any questions about what you'd seen, you would simply come to me and ask."

I nodded once and forced a pleasant closed-lip smile. "I'm sorry my confusion caused alarm for your staff."

"It's quite all right. We need to investigate anything security deems questionable." *I only hope they can determine how you might've found your way to such a concealed area.* "I won't take up any more of your time."

He stood, headed toward the door, and paused. "Oh, any luck on the symbols yet?" One hand held the office door as he turned, angling his shoulders to face me.

"Just a few hieroglyphs. Still working on the meaning behind one. We think we may have something soon." I doubted he'd chase the bone, but also couldn't care too much.

"Good. Again, my apologies for intruding. Thanks for your time."

"Not a problem. Though I don't know that I did much to help you."

"Oh, you did."

I sensed his visit was only to rattle me because, in fact, I had provided him nothing useful, to my knowledge. I expected he was curious why no one had come forward with any information or the actual symbols. I'd heard his thought about the "concealed area." It was probably intentional to see if he could get me to slip and reveal more than I cared to in a simple look. His decision to surprise me was an attempt to catch me off guard so that I might let down my block long enough for him to detect what I felt based on what I'd seen. That only meant he did have something to hide. And I'd need to know why before I ever decided to trust him.

Moving to the task at hand before I'd been interrupted, I pulled my cell phone and dialed Mary Ann as I headed toward the garage.

*What a change a mere week could make.* A noticeable increase in the number of dark shadows attaching to people had occurred since I'd returned from the Cape. As I drew closer to Mary Ann's home, I noticed how much larger the shadows were. Rather than mirroring the size of small children, they were almost as big as the human they hid behind, increasing the sulking appearance in the people to whom they clung. Those individuals without the dark demons ignored the angry or depressed people that walked by them, undisturbed by their emotional dilemma.

I pulled into the drive and felt my mood lighten at the thought of another one of Mary Ann's home-cooked meals.

"Sara, over here," she called, standing to greet me from a cluster of flowers. She always seemed to be working in her garden. God, how I would miss her. I didn't know how long I'd be gone searching for the keys, but traveling to three different places in the world didn't mean a short trip. And if I wasn't successful… I shut the car door and smiled from ear to ear, giving her a big hug.

"Careful, I don't want to cover you in soil," she said, wrapping an arm around me, taking care not to pat my back.

"You're always busy with something. Do you ever rest?"

"This isn't work. This is pleasure," she said, yanking off the gardening gloves and tucking them in her other hand as we headed into the house. "You want something to drink?"

"Maybe in a bit, thanks."

"I'm going to wash up. Make yourself comfortable," she called as she headed down the hall. I sat down at one of the barstools in the kitchen, where she had a television tuned to a national news channel. I hadn't heard any updates on current events since I'd been away with Kevin.

A flash of *Breaking News* was running across the bottom of the screen. Three hurricanes were approaching the south coast of the US and another two were headed up from the Gulf of Mexico, one in front of the other. As hurricanes often did, they were gaining speed and intensity as they moved toward the coast and were expected to lose some of their gumption after they reached land. The reporter was so engrossed in the wind speed and size of the storms that it was all the focus of the program, stating it was like nothing he had seen in his twenty-two years as a meteorologist. The hurricanes were expected to make landfall in the next three days. *Could that be the cause of the destruction Juno, Matt, and Aria foresaw?*

"What's the emergency?" Mary Ann asked, eyeing the television.

"Oh, five hurricanes are making their way up the coast with such intensity never seen in history," I explained in my best effort to sound like the meteorologist. I swiveled off the stool and headed to the bar to make a cocktail. "Can I make you a martini?"

"Sure, sweetie. Then you can tell me about your trip. You look so refreshed."

*Refreshed? Strange.* After all I had experienced, I should look completely exhausted. I brushed the comment aside and finished making cocktails.

"Where is Robert this week?"

"Back in England ensuring the acquisition of Mellon Industrial Corp. He's been working on it for months. He won't be back until later next week. You'll have to come over when he returns since he hasn't seen you in a while. I'm sure he would like to catch up."

"Sure. I'd love to." The truth was, Robert was as satisfied catching up on the details of my life second-hand from Mary Ann as hearing them directly from me. It was Mary Ann who liked to see our small family together, trying to get Robert to give details about some of his trips as a means to bring us closer.

Robert wasn't indifferent to the concerns of others, just preoccupied with making a living instead of enjoying the fruits of all that labor. It was easy to respect his work ethic, but neither Mary Ann nor I could help but feel he was missing out on life. I handed Mary Ann her drink as we headed into the living room area.

"So, how was the Cape?"

"It was cold but so beautiful."

"I bet that made it romantic, too." She winked at me over the top of her glass.

I took in a long, deep breath and let it out quickly. "You're so terrible about trying to squeeze details from me." I smiled, shaking my head.

"Oh, come on. I get nothing but other people's sorrows, for the most part. Surely you can spare some of your heartwarming new love for me."

"I hate to disappoint you but..." I began.

"So don't. Tell me. You're practically glowing just thinking about him."

"I don't glow." She raised an eyebrow. "He's responsive, sensitive, strong, intelligent," I began.

"That's boring. Tell me what he's like with you," she said.

I told her about the house, things we had done on the island, and visiting the Vineyard.

"When are you going to see him again?" she asked.

"I don't know. Soon, I suppose. I just spent a week with him. He'd probably like a break, don't you think?"

"In London, that man had eyes for you as much as you did for him. It wouldn't be soon enough for him to want to see you again. I'm sure."

"I don't know about that. I'm not the easiest person to get close to."

"I believe I'll agree with you. But if ever you found anyone patient enough to wait, I'm quite certain he's the one."

"We'll see." I took a slow sip of my drink.

"By the way, I ran into an old friend of yours." She paused. "I was picking up a file at Robert's office. Tyler was hanging around and asked about you."

"What does he want?" I heard the annoyance in my tone at the mere mention of him.

"It seems he's trying to determine through other sources if you would be willing to see him."

"What? I have really had more than enough already. That boy stormed away from me when I was honest with him. I'm not interested in giving him a second thought." I shook my head.

"I knew I shouldn't have said anything. But at least I can answer positively if he were to ask again."

"If he asks about me again, just tell him you haven't spoken to me lately. You don't need his badgering."

"He's a depressing subject anyway." She sipped leisurely, staring at the olive in her glass. "I've been wanting to ask you something." I waited. "Actually, I wanted to tell you about some strange nightmares I've had and wanted to get your take on it. I'm getting them more often, and I think maybe I'm just under stress at the center. I don't know. I've never had anything like this before."

"I'm no expert at interpreting dreams but go ahead."

"Okay," she said, shifting on the sofa, angling more toward me. "In these dreams, there are all these people around, some familiar, some not. There are also dark gray figures that slide between everyone, like smoke. Some even have them holding on to them, long fingers curled over their shoulders. You know?" She curled her fingers to show me. "Anyway, everything turns black, even the sky. It's very frightening, especially when they start coming at me."

"The shadows chase you?"

"Yeah. You know those dreams where you keep running from something?"

I nodded with a shrug. "Do they ever catch you?"

"Not yet. I usually wake up before anything more happens."

I sat for a moment, contemplating her words and at the same time understanding why she had been in my thoughts recently.

"Is anything else happening in these nightmares? Do you recognize where you are?"

"No. But once, in all that darkness, there was this light that shined. I couldn't see who or what it was. As the light moved, the shadows let go of people and turned into a mist that disappeared, right into the sky."

I'd be leaving soon to recover three objects I had no clue how to find. I didn't know how long I'd be gone. And now, a new concern for Mary Ann was forming.

"That is frightening," I said, pausing to consider how to tell her some of what I knew without sharing all. "And right now, it's only a dream."

She angled her head toward me. "What do you mean, right now? Of course it's a dream. It can't be anything else. What I'm wondering is why am I having them?"

"I don't know. Have you been under more stress, feeling depressed or angry?"

"No more than usual, I think."

"This is going to sound strange, but I can also see these shadows you describe attached to people."

"Oh, you've had these nightmares, too?" she asked. "You're right. That is strange, Sara."

"Yes, well," I said, deciding it best not to share that the dark gray apparitions had been seen during the day. "In my dream, I fight them. They are just as frightening as you describe."

"We're having the same dream, except you fight and I run? Have you been feeling okay? What's stressing you out, sweetie?" She patted my leg.

*Nothing much except that these dreams are nothing short of reality for Kevin, a few people you haven't met, and me.* But I couldn't tell her that much. Why frighten or worry her to a level she might not be able to handle?

"Trust me. I'm fine, just a little tired."

"I'll bet," she said. Her brows lifted and the corner of her mouth pulled up.

I brought my fingers to my eyes, trying to rub the fatigue away, and shook my head, smiling. "Stop, will you? Kevin isn't the cause of my restless nights."

"Aw, sorry to hear it." She smiled. "Okay. Seriously, why are you having bad dreams?"

"There is a belief held by some that when you dream, you are really visiting another universe, a sort of parallel world that is different in some ways than the one in which you live." I could see the expression on her face resembling the time when she and I stared as a glassblower contorted liquid glass into twisted shapes without dropping the delicate creation. She was deciding whether to believe what I was saying, just as she had once wondered how the artist could create a sculpture from a bubble. "Have you ever heard of two people sharing the same nightmare?" I asked.

"Never."

"What I'm going to tell you may be hard to believe, I know, especially since you weren't convinced I could feel what other people feel or hear their thoughts as a child." I paused. "Think of something specific that I would not know."

"Sara, honey, I always knew you were sort of special but you don't have to prove you can read my thoughts. I'm an open book. If you say it's so, then I'll believe you." She paused to take another sip of her drink.

I hated the use of the word *special* when describing someone. To me, the term meant someone having tolerance for something they were either unable or unwilling to understand.

"But for the fun of it, go ahead and try," I finished her thought aloud. Her face froze. "Are you in my head right now? Two-seven-five-six-four-three, the account number I just transferred funds to this morning." I spoke the words as quickly as I heard them in her head. Her mouth never moved. Only now, there was nothing to say. Her mind was blank. Her eyes widened to the size of dinner plates and her mouth fell open.

"Can you do that with anyone?"

"I think so." Kevin and C-05 had been the only exceptions. "I blocked a lot of it because it was too much noise to hear everyone. I tuned them out, you could say, until recently. Since my accident, the ability has become stronger. And the nightmares have been occurring. I've heard of others with similar dreams that believe these shadows are a predictor of something coming." I thought of the team who would join me on the quest.

"I'd rather just like to think we have an unusual coincidence. I'm not going to believe a similar nightmare means anything more than that." Mary Ann reached to put her glass on the table beside her. "Is that what you really believe?"

*Go for honesty here or make her feel better?* "There is some substance to that belief." *Careful, Sara.* "I think," I added under my breath.

"Are you sure you're feeling well? You were in a horrible accident. Maybe it changed you in some way." Her eyes fell distant and glided toward the floor. "They didn't think there was any brain injury, but what if it's some sort of delay?"

"Mom," I said, putting a hand on hers. "You've met Kevin and trust him, right?"

Her eyes lifted back to mine. "I do. Just tell me you haven't joined a cult."

"Really? I'd have to tell you that?" She stared, her face as blank as an artist's sketch pad. "Of course not! I didn't believe it myself at first. All I'm saying is enough evidence to support the reality of the prediction has been provided that I can't ignore it. And now you're telling me of these same shadows." Mary Ann shook her head. "Kevin is one of the first people I met who believes the same. I assure you I am in my right mind. Five other people I've met have had similar dreams as you're describing to me."

"You're scaring me, Sara. I trust your decision in selection of friends. But if what you say is true, what's really happening?"

"You see those hurricanes the reporters are going crazy about in the news, five of them all at once?" I pointed in the direction of the television. "It's predicted that there will be mass destruction coming."

"Who predicts? And that is if they make it to shore in full force. Hurricanes being destructive is nothing new."

"No, but how often do you see five of them together at once?"

"I call it a potential catastrophe. Sara, tell me you're not suggesting this is the beginning of Armageddon?"

*Depends on how you look at it, I suppose.* "Of course not." I shrugged a shoulder. I knew well enough what was coming was a battle for life that could be attributed to an Armageddon-like event. "We'll deal with what comes if it comes. Okay? For now, it's a very odd coincidence." *Who says a white lie doesn't help a situation? No harm done.*

"Exactly."

"By the way, I'm going on a sort of research mission with Kevin and will be traveling a fair amount soon."

"Really? What are you researching?"

"Some new, life-saving cure." *Three keys to saving the world.* "I don't know much about it yet."

"Keep in touch and let me know how you are, will you?"

"Of course." I didn't have the heart to tell her of the appearance of the shadows in our world or the mission to find the cure. Besides, there was time before Tarsamon put his entire objective into action, I hoped.

"When are you leaving?"

"It's up to Kevin, but I'd guess within a week, maybe two." It would depend on how long it took me to get the symbol Kevin had hidden away in Ardan.

I could never have imagined that my visit would have erupted in such a turn of conversation for Mary Ann. She was used to hearing about tragedy and had developed a tough skin for hearing gruesome real-life stories from the work at the center and in the hospital. That toughness would serve her well in time, should we be faced with a clash between light and darkness. I sipped from my glass as a brief, quiet moment passed in our conversation.

"Maybe you and Kevin could come for dinner before you leave," she suggested, tossing a glance at me over her shoulder as she filled her glass with ice. "I'd love to have Robert meet our doctor friend. Might get him to let go of Tyler a bit." Her voice echoed from the kitchen.

"Robert will question him to death, I'm sure. Do we have to do that to Kevin so soon?"

"Better to get it out of the way," she said, coming back into the room. "Besides, I don't think Kevin will have any problem with Robert and his questions. He seems to be able to handle himself quite well. But…" She paused. "I'll let Robert know not to grill him, okay?"

"I'll see what I can do." I smiled. "His work keeps him very busy."

"Not too busy to take you away for a week," she said, smiling at me.

I followed her toward the kitchen. "C'mon. I've got to pull the lasagna."

Mary Ann had a full staff, including a chef, but wouldn't let anyone get in the way of cooking her old Italian family recipes.

"By the way, where did you get that bracelet?"

"You like it? It was a gift." I leaned against the counter, my drink cupped in both hands.

"It's gorgeous, very unique." She took hold of my forearm gently to turn it for a thorough look. "I thought you hated gifts."

"I do, but this was sort of a surprise that I couldn't turn down." I looked at it thoughtfully, remembering what Kevin said when he gave it to me.

"Of course, from Kevin. I see why you couldn't turn it down." She opened the oven and pulled out the steaming-hot dish.

We settled at the small table in the expansive kitchen for dinner, continuing our conversation on a much lighter front than when I'd first arrived. The TV rumbled on quietly in the background.

I glanced at the news program, again, as I stacked the few dishes we had used by the sink. The meteorologist was still as fascinated by the whirling wind speed as he had been at the beginning of the hour.

"Just leave it, Sara," Mary Ann said, referring to the stack of dishes I had collected. "It'll be taken care of later." At that moment, Mary Ann's butler stepped from the hall into the kitchen.

"Please, Ms. Forrester, won't you make yourself comfortable in the living area? The chef made a chocolate torte earlier if you are so inclined, or coffee perhaps?" he asked.

"No, thank you. I've got to get going."

"Very well. Good evening."

It was nearly eight p.m. and I had other things on my mind, especially after viewing the weather report. I picked up my purse that I'd left at the entry and put an arm around Mary Ann. "Thank you for the wonderful dinner. You know, you don't always have to cook Italian on my account."

"It's your favorite. And unless I cook for you, you'll eat that raw fish." Her nose wrinkled as she reached to hug me.

"I'm sure Kevin would like to come for dinner and meet Robert. I'll remember to ask him soon."

"Good. We'll both look forward to it. I'll see you later."

"Love you," I shouted from my car as I closed the door. I eased onto the road for the twenty-minute drive home, noting fatigue was settling in early this evening. I realized I'd never really shaken it since I'd returned from the Cape.

The flashing light on my phone glowed like a beacon in the dark room as I entered the house, indicating a message waiting.

"Sara, I received the most interesting invitation for tonight and wanted to discuss it with you. Please, call me this evening," Kevin said. The message had only been left about an hour ago. *Why hadn't he tried me on my cell?*

For a moment, I felt like a child in trouble. *How silly.* It wasn't like Kevin to be bothered by such a small thing as not contacting him directly. That's an expectation I could count on from Tyler. I had often adjusted my reactions to appease Tyler's insecure nature, in effect enabling his behavior. I supposed old habits were hard to break. This feeling of mine was nothing more than residue left over after scraping Mr. Ego to the side.

I still had yet to experience what really moved Kevin to any depths of annoyance, with the minor exception of my emotional defenses. Even then, he was rather patient.

In addition to having abilities similar to mine, Kevin could also move very quickly and had some ability to heal. There wasn't a single indication of the burn he'd removed from my forearm. I had already given in to trusting him, convinced that he wasn't a threat. The exception, of course, was falling for him and finding myself involved in a relationship I hadn't wanted. I was too tired to give it any more of my attention and picked up the receiver. Just before I could push the button to dial, the phone rang.

# 27

**H**ello?" I answered, without waiting for the caller ID to deliver a name.

"You had to know it was me, Sara." Kevin's voice flowed into my ear.

"Not exactly. I was just about to call you and—"

"I beat you to it," he interrupted, sounding pleased.

"So it seems."

"I needed to speak with you before you gave in to your fatigue."

"I'm not going to ask how you knew that might happen."

"Because you already know."

My suspicion that he was more advanced in his ability to feel than I was aware was proving to be accurate. I slipped the bracelet off for extra measure. I might be falling for him, and hard, I admitted. But I was still entitled to my privacy.

"Let's say that I do. So, you have an invitation to discuss with me?" I asked as cheerfully as I could muster through an increasingly sluggish state.

"Yes. Matt reached me about your desire to meet in Ardan."

"Aria had some information to share that relates to Matt and Juno's predictions."

"Yes, I know. Their concerns aren't something you need to worry about. We can handle it."

"What is that supposed to mean? We're a team or we're not." There was a stretch of silence, and in it I contemplated just hanging up and falling asleep. I didn't have the energy to argue about Kevin's protective nature or why he thought I didn't need to meet with everyone.

"You're right. We are a team. But you have your role and we have ours." He paused. "Ah, now I remember, the guide aiding you. I'm not sure how you refer to him."

"I suppose by his name, Cerys." I took in a deep breath.

"I hope Cerys has not directed you to participate in battle? Your role is to stay safe so you can hold the keys once found, not risk your life, *our future*, to help protect us." Though he hadn't said the words *our future* aloud, I'd received the thought as clear as if he had. What was the purpose in not speaking of it? Of course *our future*, everyone's future, was at risk. "There is more at stake than you may realize."

"I've had quite enough of not knowing. I'm operating on what knowledge I do have. Look, I don't mean to be short-tempered. But I won't be standing around waiting..."

"It's all right." He paused. "The team is already experienced with battling Tarsamon's forces. This quest is not their first encounter with them. You don't have a second-rate group here, Sara."

"I'm sure I don't. But I won't stand around and wait for direction as someone leading this quest. The team's concerns are my concerns." For the first time, I knew I'd hit a point of frustration for him.

"I will be there with the others tonight. I'm going to let you go now. See you soon, love."

"Good night."

It was a sensible decision to hang up before my temper grew. I wasn't in any mood to debate issues after having a day that had included C-05 and new worries over Mary Ann. I crashed into bed within moments of hanging up with Kevin, with the aim of reconnecting in Ardan.

"If you want to end her quest, the time is now. As I've told you, the last warrior is helping her to become stronger. They will have all three symbols soon. I feel it. Then she may be out of your grasp."

"She is never beyond my reach. The end goal is bigger than the quest and the time is not right. Not yet.

As I moved between realms, I caught the sound of a familiar voice and one other, though I could not identify them by name and saw no faces to match with those speaking. Instead, only complete darkness had surrounded me before entering Ardan. It was the first time I'd heard a message while shifting between worlds. A cold shiver ran down my spine, knowing the *her* being referred to was me.

Upon arriving, I recognized the ancient ruins illuminated against the stormy gray horizon and made my way straight for them, moving again with ease. Everything was as I remembered it to be, from the ivy that draped the walls to the stone pillars that lined the entrance.

The familiar group of five was waiting in front of the old passageway where I'd first visited to meet with the Professors. Matt's spiky blond hair contrasted against the blue-black sky like that of a welcoming beacon on the edge of a rough sea. His piercing blue eyes reflected back at me as I drew closer. I directed my attention across the line. Aria's red hair caught a rare breeze and blew to one side, glowing like a five-alarm blaze in the depths of night.

"Thanks for coming on short notice. It's crucial that we pull together for the predictions that Aria, Matt, and Juno have made." I glanced toward Aria and Elise. "Are these hurricanes within your power to intercept and weaken?"

"Elise and I have seen the level of destruction that is coming," Aria began.

"We think we can take each of these storms, one maybe two at a time, but five? We can't be sure," Elise added.

"You are the strongest of our group with the ability to manipulate those elements of nature. Reducing the effects of such intense storms, anything you can do is worth the lives you'll save. We'll help however possible.

"We've known from the beginning of this quest that the possibility for people to die was likely. While Tarsamon is placing his forces to begin consuming the energy in our world, I don't believe he plans to battle yet."

"He'd be more concerned in stopping you if he saw you as a threat," Juno said.

"Let's say that he did and sent his forces to come after me. What would the Alliance or Soltari do?"

"The Alliance, acting on behalf of the Soltari, would move to strike down every existence of darkness, instead of trying to align the balance between the dark and light forces," Kevin answered.

"Exactly. And Tarsamon wouldn't risk that unless he'd grown his army to full capacity to handle such a battle."

"That may be true," Elise said. "But we don't know where he's been building his forces. They could be in other realms outside Ardan. Aria and I have noticed our abilities have become more powerful. The Alliance would only need to increase our strengths if they are aware that the dark forces have become stronger."

"The same is true for us," Matt said, gesturing to Juno. "We've also noticed the ability to control the emotions of those around us has intensified. It's much easier to do and requires less concentration than before we met. This means all energy is strengthening for an encounter between the forces."

"Not before I find those keys."

It wasn't just the destruction of humanity that Tarsamon sought but also a real possibility that he intended to obliterate light everywhere in all realms, just as finding the keys would extinguish Tarsamon's ability to spread darkness across Earth. Although his forces might be getting stronger, I had a gut feeling he was more concerned about intervening in our attempt at finding the keys.

"It's a fine line," Matt said. "If Tarsamon sees you as weak, he'll put more focus on the building of his forces on Earth and the consumption of humans. At the same time, if he has information that you've obtained any of the symbols, I'd expect him to set his priority toward stopping you."

"Does Tarsamon have access to you in Ardan?" I asked. While I'd been provided insight from the Soltari concerning the mission,

I'd noticed certain elements pertaining to individuals, and not just Kevin, had been omitted from my request for knowledge.

"Tarsamon resides in a small realm of Ardan considered an isolation area," Kevin replied. "He is barred from entering our location and blocked from any decisions made by the Alliance, including any plans we create to enforce their directives. I believe he may be able to view all while we are in the physical world."

"And yet when I first arrived in Ardan, Tarsamon spoke to me, and a small group of his demons had arranged for an impromptu greeting."

"That's right," Juno said. "We aren't sure how he managed that, being that you were under watch by the elves. Also, if he can see all that's happening on Earth, it means if we practice anything there, we will be revealing the abilities we've been granted."

I thought of Kevin's and my practice in the Cape.

*Sara, Tarsamon already knows who you are and your ability as a skilled fighter.*

I shifted my attention to Kevin. *Get out of my head, will you?*

"What we've discovered is that Tarsamon has knowledge of only one defense, the shield of light that is used as protection. He's not familiar with our ability to manipulate dark energy," Matt explained. "So far, that's our strongest weapon in defending our position, at least until that force grows beyond our capability to handle. Because he can see into our world using the shadows he has placed there, it's possible he has knowledge of the symbols, depending on how well the information has been kept hidden by C-05. It's a race to protect the symbols until we can open the gateway to the realm where the first key is hidden and before Tarsamon consumes Earth any further."

"We need protection from being seen by Tarsamon in the physical world, especially as we travel." I paused, thinking about C-05 and how my suspicions of him might somehow be connected to Tarsamon's knowledge. "I'll meet with the Soltari. It's beyond our capability to carry a cloak back with us when we leave Ardan. That cover would enable us to use our abilities to manipulate negative energy to stop the storms. It's also possible that the security of our communications here in Ardan may be compromised as well. Matt, would you and Juno be able to check into this, maybe with Eldor?"

"Of course."

"We can't be expected to guard two realms *and* locate the keys," I added. "I'm going to see about the additional protection we need. I'll get a message to you if I'm unsuccessful. Otherwise, I'll see you at the first location." I glanced at Juno. "That's been arranged?" He nodded. "Good, thanks. Connect with me if there is a problem that deviates from this plan and we'll adjust our strategy. All agreed?" The team nodded their approval.

With four other members on assignment, that left Kevin remaining. As I stepped toward the door, Kevin fell in beside me.

"Thank you," he said.

"For what?"

"Understanding that my only assignment is you. And until Matt or Juno comes back with confirmation that Ardan is secure, I'll be your shadow in both worlds."

"I believe I've heard something similar from Juno. And for some reason, I think that would be the case even if Ardan was secure." I smiled. With the Soltari in mind and the ability to travel by a single thought, Kevin and I stepped through the door of the ruins.

The place we arrived was darker than the last. Had there ever been light here? A group of dismantled buildings stood in similar size to those we'd just left. As Kevin and I drew closer, the weathered old walls began to fade in and out, revealing the shadows of trees scattered in the distance. They were void of color and leaves. It resembled an eerie graveyard, minus the headstones. Were we on the border of Ardan and Tarsamon's isolation area?

The transparent walls shifted to solid form again, in an undecided state of being. At the front steps of the building, a huge fog-like mist pushed out from the walls in a huff and slowly began to surround us. "We are expected." I could feel the heat of Kevin's body as he stood inches behind me.

"There are many individuals contained in this mass," Kevin whispered, leaning into my ear.

"This is what happened last time," I said in a low voice, watching as the formation of a thick cloud moved around us. Transparent faces I'd seen in my previous meeting randomly appeared within the cloud of white mist.

"You seek our assistance?" The voice spoke as one entity. A single voice in a crowd.

"Yes."

"You have also brought the Last Great Warrior." A spiral of white swept across Kevin's face and behind him. Knowing it was rare for the Soltari to show themselves, I wondered if it bothered them that I had not come alone. "Allies that support the outcome in favor of the light are welcome," it answered. "How may we assist you?"

"In our physical world, we are visible to the dark entity known as Tarsamon. I seek for the members on this quest to remain concealed to the Dark Lord's visual acuity of our abilities while on Earth."

There was a pause as the answer was being constructed. "You will be fighting him and the dark forces he brings soon enough. What additional purpose does this serve?"

"To allow us more strength by preventing Tarsamon from preparing to defend against our abilities. If we can buy even a little more time to get closer to the keys, it will be worth having that protection."

Another pause.

"We recognize your need to remain concealed. The light in your world must remain for any chance to save humankind." I waited for the voice to continue, to answer the request brought to them, until I could not stand the silence any longer.

"What is your answer?"

A long, low hum emanated from the misty fog once more, then ceased.

"Your request is granted." A pause. "We cannot guarantee how long you will be concealed in your world. The Dark Lord's strength grows by the day." Another pause and hum. "Do not divide your forces as the evil grows."

"Understood."

The mist swirled around my right hand. "The stone in the ring you wear will shroud the symbols' energy for a short time. Guard them carefully when they are delivered."

*Delivered?*

"They are what the Dark Lord seeks to rid you of." I remembered the visitor in my room that had sought to take them.

"I need all three to take to the location of the first key."

"They will be provided."

"How will I know when to leave if I don't...?"

"Trust in those who aid you."

I turned to look at Kevin, whose eyes were fixed on all of the faces visible in the white mist, a host of hovering entities with no visible bodies. He watched them like a predator to prey, waiting for the next fraction of movement.

I lifted my gaze as the faces began to fade, combining into the spin of the cloud, like a tornado collecting its valuables. At that moment, a shot of white pierced through the single mass straight for me, stopping inches from my face. The features of a misty white mouth and eyes formed in the oval cloud.

"We lend you our strength on your path," the entity said. The face lengthened into a vertical line and fell over me in a wave. I lifted my hand to see white mist flowing from the ends of my fingertips. Had it entered my body? My head grew lighter, as though it could float like a balloon into the awaiting white cloud. And as quickly as it appeared in front of me, the entity withdrew into the vertical white cloud to join with the others, fading from view as though an invisible hand in a glove of night had covered it.

Kevin's eyes were bright.

"We have to go," I whispered. I touched him gently, not wanting to startle him. He blinked a few times. "There is just one more guide I must try to visit." I wanted to reconnect with Karshan to know how to reach him should a battle begin but had no idea where I would find him in the vast forest. "Karshan, are you near?" I called out, remembering how he'd said to summon him and his pack. Kevin picked up on the image in my thought.

"You speak to them?"

"Of course. Don't you?"

"I've never had an experience that would provide the opportunity."

"Well, you might this evening if he's here."

I turned at the rustle of leaves behind me to see a rush of peppered gray fur race past us between the trees. One angled its head in my direction and our eyes met, a black sparkling light in the evening shadow. The large gray wolf departed from the pack and stepped toward us.

"It has been too long, my friend," he said. His lips pulled back, extending longer, showing more teeth.

*A smile?*

"It has. My apologies. I did not want to disturb you until necessary."

"Whom do you bring with you?" he asked, leaning forward and lifting his nose in the air near Kevin.

"This is my companion, Kevin." Kevin nodded to him.

"A wise and noble choice to be paired together," Karshan said approvingly. Could he sense Kevin's strengths? "You must hurry. The dark forces are moving."

"The symbols are here in Ardan for safekeeping. Do you know if all three are together?"

"I would have no such information. My pack and I guard the boundaries of Ardan from roaming dark forces. For you, we will provide additional protection."

A menacing growl sounded in the distance. I lifted my gaze over his shoulder to see a pair of saber-toothed cats approaching. Emerald-green eyes glowed in my direction. They were long extinct from my world, and I felt my eyes widen at the sight. Kevin stood silently beside me, his hand touching my back.

"They run with great speed, providing an additional resource to you," Karshan said. "Perhaps an asset in your world, where things move much slower than here?"

"Indeed," I said.

"We have insight as you travel the path to the keys. Go now. The daylight comes soon." Karshan turned and disappeared in the thicket of trees in two leaps, the cats close behind.

"I had no idea you had connections with them," Kevin said, interrupting me from my trance as I stared after the wolf.

"It's good to finally be able to surprise you with some knowledge about me. I was convinced you knew everything."

"Where it concerns you, so was I."

A thought of the team swept through my head. "Did you catch that?"

"A sense of urgency?"

I nodded.

"It can't be. Not in Ardan. We must be mistaken."

"Both of us?" I asked.

"This way," Kevin said, pointing in the direction he felt the energy coming from. While there was no concept of time in Ardan, I knew we had to hurry. As members awoke from their sleep, they would carry with them the urgency that had called to us and any injury sustained during their sleep.

We stopped at the edge of a hilltop. A landscape that mirrored Tarsamon's dark world was waiting, as if the very foundation had been plucked from my memory and placed at our feet. I froze in response, feeling the unexpected fear of what I had experienced in the dark world begin to consume me. I jumped at Kevin's hand on my arm, firm and reassuring.

"I want you to stay here."

"The hell I will."

"The dark forces are looking for you in Ardan."

"Or the symbols."

"Either way, we have more reinforcements here that can handle this."

"It doesn't make any sense that they would come for me here. I don't have what they want."

He turned me to face him. "It doesn't matter why they are here, just that they are. That means right now being close to any dark force is not the safest place for you."

"The team needs me to help fight with them."

"I swear if I could carry you back to your bedroom, where you're sleeping, and tie you there, I would."

"Lovely thought." I flashed a smile.

He wrinkled his brows. "Look over there." He pointed to the streets that separated the buildings where I could see Juno and Matt. Elise and Aria were on the rooftop under the orange light. They were moments away from where we stood, watching. My initial fear began to fade, replaced with the strong desire to fight and kill what threatened the mission and the team. The elves were moving in, arrows loaded into bows. Farther in the distance, I saw Karshan and his pack racing through a black cloud.

"I will not stand here and watch!"

"Come with me." Kevin slipped an arm under mine and, with his strength, lifted me a few inches off the ground and raced toward the action, only to deliver me into the hands of Eldor.

"Take her to safety until this is under control."

"It won't be long before the sun will be waking all of you back to your world," Eldor called out above the shrieks of demons around us.

"Good," Kevin said. "It'll be less time for her to seethe with anger."

"So help me God if you think time is a deterrent to my anger. Let me fight with them."

"Sara, no," Eldor urged and swept me back in the direction of the hilltop.

He turned to face me. "They don't want you anywhere near this. Don't fight that anymore. Your strength and ability are for defense only, not to protect them. Your calling is greater than a battle. Remember that as you go through this quest." He turned back to watch. And I sensed in him a craving to be fighting with them, while still holding a duty to guard.

"Why is Kevin there if his only mission is to protect me?" I flicked a glance to where Kevin was and back to Eldor.

"That's what he told you?" He continued to watch the battle, his forces gaining control. "As the Last Great Warrior, it is his primary duty to guard you. But he is the leader of the team that fights for your safety on this mission. If he lost his team, he knows he would have a much more difficult task on his hands and a greater risk of losing you."

My anger slid away like a silk sheet at the realization of Kevin's full responsibility.

I turned my gaze back to the fight at hand to see Elise's shield was nothing more than a thin line wrapped around her, indicating not much energy remained.

"Push forward," someone shouted.

"Use other forms of fight," Juno called out.

Within moments of hearing Juno, an annoying buzzing sound could be heard growing louder. I was certain distraction was the intent of whatever was now being cast into this battle. The demons faded as the sky changed from black to a mingled shade of deep orange and blood red. Eldor created a shield around me the color of gold as a cloudburst of dark forms began a rainstorm upon those below.

"Are we invisible to them?"

"Your energy is undetectable by way of the field around you."

I scanned the valley below. With the elves, the defense was almost equal in number to the onslaught of shadows raining down. I caught a glimpse of Elise struggling, her knees bent under the pressure of a consuming cloud of phantoms. She was fighting to get back into a standing position. It would be a matter of moments before she would collapse at the mercy of the shadows, unable to battle further.

I clenched my fists at my sides. "Elise," I called out, frustrated at not being able to help her.

"I can't," she shouted. "I see it but can't focus on it long enough to make it real," she said, referring to her own weapon that had faded from her hands, leaving her with only a shield. She barely got the words out before the dark shadows broke through, engulfing her in a single black cloud.

Kevin blew past the others toward Elise, Juno at his back, and crouched down in front of her, extending a single hand to block the next strike. From his hand, a shield of light formed and extended around both of them as bright as the glare off a window. I could see he was saying something to her that I couldn't read in thought. The shadows swarmed the ring Kevin had created until nearly no light could be seen coming from it. The breath in my chest came in and out faster in my eagerness to fight with them.

The entities had taken the battle to Ardan. They were learning our defenses.

I could no longer see Elise or Kevin, nor a single ray of light that shielded them. Every few seconds, I saw Juno battling near the two. I covered my arm over my eyes as a burst of light exploded into an array of showering beams, igniting upon what I guessed was seventy-five or so blackened shadows, leaving them in misty dark forms that mingled like lost souls lifting into the air.

The remaining wraith-like figures began to retreat and lifted above our heads. Like the ones I'd battled, they hovered briefly before combining in a single black mist in the sky. With a sudden force, the cloud dispersed into the orangey glow until nothing remained.

"Tarsamon underestimated the energy of this legion of fighters this time," Eldor said.

"Let me go to them."

"Not just yet."

I turned to find the others and spotted Juno grasping his shoulder with the opposite hand as though he'd been struck. Elise and Juno were the ones who had endured the greatest impact. Matt moved as swiftly as Kevin, like a blur as he joined the others. The shield Kevin used around Elise was gone. He placed his arm under her shoulder for support as they moved in our direction. Eldor's ring of protection disappeared and I raced to them.

"Are you all right?" I asked Elise.

"Yeah, I'll recover. I'm just pissed they got through my shield and I didn't have the strength to fire anything back or even move away." She shifted her arm off Kevin's shoulder to stand on her own, leaning more to her left side. "It's been too long since I've had to fight like that."

"They're stronger," Juno said.

Aria slipped her sword into its sheath. "What were they doing here?"

Eldor arrived beside me. "A few of the demons were found by the lookouts, trying to enter two homes in the trees. When they were pursued, additional dark forces stormed the lookouts and began a frantic search, we think for the symbols. They've since been moved and are in safekeeping, to be delivered upon the order of the Soltari."

"Thank you for your assistance," Kevin said to Eldor.

Eldor nodded and, with the same speed as Kevin and Matt, raced toward the army of elves.

"I wasn't aware that we had located all of the symbols," Juno said.

"There wasn't time to discuss it," Kevin replied. "Make sure we are prepared to leave for Scotland, in search of the guardian of the first key, upon waking. I can't imagine Tarsamon will call back his forces."

"What about the people the shadows have already attached to or that they are trying to attach to? What about right now?" Aria asked.

"We don't have a choice but to leave people to fight the negative energy for themselves," I answered. "If the people aren't strong enough to make the choice to resist fear and negative energy, there is little we can do to prevent further illness. We can't destroy the shadows attached to them without killing the person."

"A catastrophic event often helps to remind humans of the value of life," Matt added. "It's one way to close the path to the dark force."

"It's too late for that," I said. "The force that has started consuming them is deeply seated. It's why we are on a recovery mission for the symbols."

"Sara, we have to hurry. Sunrise is coming," Juno said.

"All right." I directed my attention to Aria and Elise. "As far as the hurricanes, they are in your capable hands?"

They nodded. "We'll do what we can to take them out," Aria said. "At least we can have an effect on that wave of destruction."

"If you need additional help, our abilities can be combined to add strength to your force."

"I believe it's possible Tarsamon may have certain people in our world who are working with him, watching to see what we are capable of," Juno said.

"If we are truly cloaked, all they will see are the storms dying out, without knowing just how it was accomplished," I said.

"What about C-05?" Matt asked.

I shrugged. "If our suspicions are correct, the truth of who he is will show sooner rather than later." I glanced toward the sky. Though there was no change in color, I could feel our time in Ardan coming to a close, as the familiar pull to leave crept upon me. "The daylight has arrived."

# 28

I was jolted out of my sleep to the sound of the security dogs barking outside in the yard. From the proximity of the noise, they were in the courtyard just on the other side of the wall to my bedroom. Anyone who decided to cross onto the property was no match for the two well-trained Dobermans, Ares and Kona, and the continuous security watch on the grounds. Finding confidence in that, I pulled the covers over my shoulder and sunk my face deeper into the pillow to catch a few more minutes of lazy slumber.

The faint sound of a man's voice leaving a message on my answering machine floated into my room and shifted my thoughts to who could want something this early in the morning.

I flipped the covers back, failing to fall back asleep after the noise, and made a beeline downstairs for a cup of tea, nice and strong. As I returned for a shower, I caught my reflection in the vanity mirror and stopped. Beyond that face was a soul with a memory that was coming back. That person had a history older than the keys themselves. And I was going to know everything about her. Turning away from the mirror, I rubbed the tiredness from my face and glanced out the window. Several clouds moved to block the few beams of sunlight that had streamed in, leaving the sky in a gloomy shade of gray and a feeling that it was much colder outside than was expected this time of year.

All that had happened the night before in Ardan made the

morning already feel like it had nearly been three days that had passed, as if this mission was a constant job, visiting another world at night and searching for meaning during the day. I would have welcomed tucking myself under the layers of warmth in my bed and dozing for a few more hours. Since I was wide awake, I was going to find relaxation another way before I had to leave. God knew when I'd get another chance to take any of the racy collection of cars out for a drive again.

*Weather.* I flipped on the television to see what changes the hurricanes had made overnight. After hearing the local forecast that today was expected to be crisp and clear with the high around fifty-seven degrees, indeed colder, the program provided an update on the hurricanes, stating they had all moved closer inland, without much change in direction. The meteorologist was saying something about two more days to landfall and people were being advised of evacuation notices in certain areas should the hurricanes follow the current path.

I sipped the tea and turned on the shower, setting my sights for a drive to release an accumulated burden of responsibility, replacing it with a welcome adrenaline rush.

The Ferrari 458 Italia sat in the garage, calling to me each time I pulled in the courtyard. There just hadn't been time to test it out, until today. I'd be leaving soon for Scotland. Juno had already locked down the plans in the last few hours, according to the text message I received from him while making tea. I'd likely be heading for the next two locations of the keys in succession, and I'd be damned if I didn't get at least one thrill out of the 458 first.

Dressed in my Saturday special, a T-shirt, jeans, and driving moccasins, I threw a scarf around my neck and pulled a matching knit hat over my ears, leaving the rest of my long hair to fly where it wanted as I headed for the garage. Tom, one of the security guards, was outside in the courtyard giving commands to one of the Dobermans as I approached the garage, a set of fifteen bays lined with an array of older and newer top-of-the-line exotics.

"Good afternoon, Dr. Forrester. Taking the car out for a drive?"

"Yes, it's a fabulous day for a little steam letting. How's the training of the pups coming along?"

"Slower than expected. This one's got attitude." He arched an index finger at Kona and turned it over to stroke under her chin, the first sign of affection I'd witnessed from him.

"That's representative of strength. A little time and she'll be loyal."

The dog glanced to me, ears lifted on alert, perhaps for a possible dart into the car and a chance to escape.

"Maybe one day you can take me for a spin in that, or better yet, let me take it for a spin?" Tom said, lifting a chin toward the McLaren P1.

"Perhaps." I smiled, settled into the seat, and shut the door.

There was nothing I liked better than to get out on the roads and test a sport car's speed and handling under my own grip. It was nothing short of exhilarating. Besides, I would be busy enough trying to see how I could help Aria and Elise as the storms rolled closer to shore in the next day. Whatever happened between now and then was out of my hands. A thought of satisfaction that progress was in motion had me settling into the sport seat. The smell of the car's leather filled my senses while the power beneath my hands took hold and chased every other concern away. I turned onto the road leading past my house and away from the city, punching the gas once and making it to sixty in just a hair over three seconds. The only thing on my mind was good old-fashioned driving performance and exhilaration.

It must have been about twenty minutes into the drive I guessed when I caught sight of a car in my rearview mirror. It was rare to find anyone on this stretch of road, with most travelers this far out preferring to stay on the main highway. I glanced back again. *Wrong color for a cop.* I had only punched the gas a couple of times after coming out of a corner and was enjoying the feel of the car. Whoever it was would just have to sit back while I assumed ownership on this stretch of road. I glanced at the speedometer to see I was keeping a steady eighty-five miles per hour. It certainly wasn't pushing anything for this car at that speed.

Another check of the mirror and I could swear the car I'd seen was closer than just a moment before. I tapped the gas and the car responded instantly, as expected, gunning me to ninety-five in nothing flat. I looked back again to the see the car was nothing more than a speck blipping in and out of view, satisfactorily farther behind. Feeling a bit happier about the distance I'd put between us, I lifted my foot off the gas to take a turn coming up and goosed it again before hitting the straightaway and maneuvering into another turn. *Awesome steering. So precise.* I held my position tight as I downshifted and rounded the next S-shaped turn, enjoying the freedom that took me far from the responsibilities that waited.

I enjoyed another mile or so before I glanced back again to see the car was now only a few hundred feet behind me, a silver, sporty-looking thing. It was obvious that it wasn't some lost soul out for a drive. The next straightaway and I'd lose the little car.

As I neared the next stretch of road, I pressed the pedal to gun it, but the other driver had made the decision a split second before me, whizzing past just before the next turn came into view. The Audi R8 that had practically thumbed its nose at me was only fractionally slower than my 458. It wasn't going to fly by me. All I needed was a little compelling competition to light my fire and I was on its tail.

There was only one person with an R8 that color and who I knew might have a reason to be out this way. I hadn't had the opportunity to identify the driver at the pass. But if I was right, I'd give him a run for it. If I was wrong, no harm in a little fun. He sensed my anticipation for play as I remained on his tail until a straightaway came into sight. He cornered each turn close to the inside shoulder and moved out wider when called for, holding me at bay for a pass. I didn't allow any more distance between us, keeping pace with him at every turn.

The longest stretch of road was just ahead beyond the last hill on the right. I was counting on that fraction of faster speed from my car to make the pass. As I accelerated, so did he. I didn't want to look at the speed and break the concentration I had, full of focus to get him behind me.

We were side by side now, and making sure the road was clear, I glanced right, finding it no surprise to see the half smirk gleaming at me through the dark tint as I looked back to the road and pressed down on the pedal, making the pass with ease. There was a turnout just up the road a couple of miles where I planned to refuel. I let off the gas slightly, approaching the turnout. He had already been right on my bumper from the moment I'd passed. I slowed to a stop and stepped out of the car.

"Well, I can't say that I'm surprised," I said, smiling at him as he exited his car. He was dressed in jeans, dark Italian leather driving moccasins, and a crisp white shirt.

"Really? Not even a little?" Kevin asked, a playful note in his tone.

"Perhaps only because there's someone else on this road. I might be impressed, though. I know what that car can do."

"I'm sure you do, with your collection and all." He raised an eyebrow in my direction. "It can hold its own when compared to that." He tilted his head to where my car was parked. I was standing inches from him now, my face close to his.

I looked into his eyes that always had a way of piercing me with their intensity. Today they looked playful as he held his sunglasses in hand. From what I could read, he liked the thrill of the drive.

"How did you know about my collection?"

"Your security guard let me know you were taking your 458 for a run and showed me the collection when I stopped by to see you. Impressive, especially for a woman."

"Some security I have," I said jokingly.

"Don't be too angry with him. The dog had taken off through the garage and he had the doors open to go after it."

"New pup in training. And what do you mean *for a woman*? Don't go and get chauvinistic on me. I'm starting to like you."

"Starting? Hmph. You know exactly what I mean. You're no ordinary woman. You hate shopping."

"How did you know I—"

"Mary Ann again. As I was saying, you're no ordinary woman. You drive that machine like a professional driver. And I haven't known any woman with a car collection enviable by most men." His free hand slid around my waist, drawing me to him, every indication of his excitement for my atypical traits evident in the press of his lips against mine. His tongue slipped across mine and delved deeper. When I eased back slightly, he held a palm against my back, urging me against him. I placed a hand on his chest and he relaxed his hold, letting out a breath.

"Sara, so much passion and still enough restraint. That, I don't understand." His lips pursed together into a smile as he stroked my cheek with the backs of his fingers. It reminded me of a warm and sensitive memory tucked far away. It reminded me of Cerys.

"Well, I'll let you wonder while I pursue my other passion, driving this beast. Come back to the house so I can find out why you came all this way to see me, anyway. I'm guessing it wasn't for a long drive." I smiled as I broke away from his hold to finish filling up my car. I settled into the seat wondering just why I wouldn't let him hold me as long as he'd wanted. *You know why. Don't let anyone too close, ever. And damn if it didn't feel so good in that moment.* With a new frustration stoked, I turned onto the road for home.

# 29

Kevin had nearly forgotten why he'd come all that way to see Sara. First the playful thrill of the drive, then the kiss. He'd only intended a soft, sweet graze across the cheek. They were, after all, at a fuel station. Before he'd realized it, he was well into a hot-blooded kiss.

It frustrated him, but he loved that about her, how she could distract him with her passions, especially those she didn't know she lit in him. The way her hair had brushed across her lips at the very moment she wanted to defend females against another potential chauvinist... Soft and strong. The contrast ignited his fire in an instant every time.

It was when she'd pulled back that he realized she was not just a responsibility for him. He had fallen completely under her spell once again as he had done so many lifetimes before. Her independence, strength, and grace captivated him, not to mention the beauty she didn't even know she had. It was more than distracting. He saw it as a potentially dangerous weakness. And one that, if not managed properly with self-control, would put her life, their future, at risk.

After concentrating his efforts on creating a successful life for himself, the image of a woman in his life had not occurred to him as anything more than a pleasurable convenience. There had never been time to contemplate anything more. That had changed when Sara was rushed into the ER that rainy Saturday evening. Everything he'd known had ceased to exist once he'd realized who she was. He fully expected it would take time to fall in love again in this life, to learn her all over again. But it hadn't taken quite as long as he'd thought. She was as exciting and sensual as he remembered in the past lives he'd shared with her. And she wanted him. He knew that much. But he sensed her hesitation along with the desire. A small distance she kept, as though an imaginary line had been drawn in the sand between them, reminding him of his second mission—to help her recall the bond they shared that carried them from one lifetime to the next together.

She would let down her guard completely once she remembered him. He was sure of it. For now, bound by his oath to the Soltari and the Alliance, he had no choice but to move at the pace predetermined by those who governed this mission. He cursed under his breath, knowing the truth he had to keep would tear at him.

It was that promise that had proven to be a growing thorn in his side. According to the Soltari, love had no place between them on this quest. But he had the strength and willingness to push the boundaries of the rules set forth for him to be here with her and to fracture the emotional walls she'd built to ensure her safety. He had just found her, was making the connection with her he desired, and needed, to maintain the love they had kept for thousands of years. If only he could balance that desire and the urge to close the distance between them and keep it from distracting him from his purpose on this mission, to ensure she obtain the keys.

He caught up to Sara within a moment's time, again playing the cat-and-mouse game, trying to edge her out around the turns all the way back to her home. In all the excitement during the drive, the simple thrill of her, he wouldn't let himself forget the reason he had come to see her, and with it understanding the true nature of his agenda would have to wait until tonight, when she was on his turf. *After all,* he thought, *taming the tiger takes skill in the art of patience and finesse.*

# 30

We pulled into the stone-paved driveway in the rear of the house that opened into a courtyard. Kevin was nearly at the door as I stepped out.

"Where did you learn to drive like that?" he asked.

"Robert and his attempt to scare me out of the thrill of fast- paced driving sent me through a Formula One training program." I pressed the latch of the door to the house. "It had the opposite effect."

"I see." He flashed a smile as we stepped through the entry.

"Make yourself comfortable anywhere," I said to him. I was getting hungry and had lost track of time in all the fun. I glanced at my watch to see that it was about four thirty p.m. "Would you like a beer, glass of wine, or something else?" I reached for a couple of glasses from the bar.

"Actually, I'll pass on the drink for now, thanks. I was wondering if you would like to come back to my apartment in the city for dinner. That is, if you don't already have plans this evening."

The limited food stock in my kitchen and the thought of his company made the offer hard to pass up.

"I'd like that. Do I have a couple of minutes to change?"

"Take your time," he said, sitting on the edge of one of the sofa cushions.

I hurried up the stairs to my room and pulled the knit hat off my hair, fluffed it back into something more attractive, and slid into a pair of casual black pants and a fitted top. I noticed the bracelet Kevin had given me resting on the shelf in my closet and slipped it on. As I came down the stairs, I was surprised to see him waiting.

"Was I too long?" Ten minutes couldn't have passed.

"Not at all. I was just wondering when you might take me on a tour."

"I can give you a quick walk-through. Not sure there's anything interesting, unless you like old artifacts."

"I have a particular interest in such things. By the way, if you'd like, you're welcome to stay this evening."

I could hear the hope in his tone that I'd say yes to this second invitation. He had to know it was a definite consideration, given that his apartment was well within the city and almost an hour drive from here.

"That would be nice, thanks. C'mon up." I waved a hand for him to follow. "I was going to give you the formal tour, but we can start upstairs, since it's closest."

He waited patiently in the spacious bedroom as I grabbed some essentials and a change of clothes for the next day. From my closet, I could see him gazing at the furnishings, the two overstuffed chairs that decorated a separate reading area, and the view I woke to every morning. He peeked through the window before glancing in my direction.

"Beautiful taste," he said, tracing a finger along the sheer white draperies. "Did you decorate it yourself?"

"Most of these things, the furniture and bedding are my choice." I stepped from the closet into the room. "But I'm not so talented when it comes to window treatments, paint, and fixtures."

"I like it." He strolled over to my bedside table. "Did you choose this piece?" He lifted a small, ornate wooden box to get a better look at it.

"Yes. I have a fascination with well-carved decorative boxes. There are a few scattered around here." My hunger pangs were increasing. I waited for him to finish looking at the box and then directed him through the other rooms in a somewhat rushed manner. My hands were beginning to tremble visibly for lack of food.

"What's bothering you?" he asked as we proceeded down the hall of the first floor. My stomach protested as we moved in the opposite direction of the kitchen.

"Are you hungry?" I asked.

He laughed lightly. "Why didn't you just say so?"

"I was about to but wanted to see how long I could hold out." I smiled. "I'm happy to finish showing you my place. I just need to grab—" I was interrupted by the phone just then. "Excuse me," I said, stepping into my office. I picked up the line at my desk.

"Hi, honey," Mary Ann said cheerfully.

"Hi. I have a friend over right now. Can I call you tomorrow?"

"Sure. It wouldn't be Kevin, would it? Because that would make me all too happy for you."

"You know better than that. Who else would be important enough for me to call you back the next day?" I said in a hushed tone, turning away from the open door.

"Did you get my message?"

"Not yet. I've been out driving. I haven't even had a chance to eat, let alone check messages."

"Ask him if Wednesday night works to come to dinner, as long as it works for you, too."

I sighed. "I'll work it into the conversation later, okay?"

"Thanks, sweetie. Don't forget. I love you."

"Love you, too. Call you tomorrow."

I hung up the phone and grabbed my long black coat off the chair and a couple of peanut M&Ms I had evidently forgotten on my desk. "I apologize for the interruption," I said, closing the door to the office.

"It's not a problem." He swept a lock of hair on my cheek aside.

"Would you like to get going?"

"Would you like to eat first?"

"These will hold me," I said, showing him the two remaining candies in my palm.

"I thought I smelled peanuts. I'll cook something for us when we get to my place."

As we began the long drive to the city, I wondered about two things: why he had come to my house earlier, and the fact that he had once told me he didn't cook.

"So, you're cooking?" I asked, opting to set aside his reason for coming until later.

"Yes. Are you afraid you'll go hungry tonight?"

"Not really." I smiled. "I'm looking forward to it. I could damn near eat anything in sight at this point. Even if you were a bad cook, I'm certain it would go over well right about now."

He laughed. "I'll get you something to hold you over."

"I thought you couldn't cook, you know, back at the Cape?"

"I only said that because I wanted to take you to my favorite seafood restaurant."

"It was worth a white lie. Just for the record, I didn't fib about not being able to cook. I promise, though, if you do come for dinner, you'll be well fed."

"I don't doubt that. That is, if you invite me." He angled his head to meet the instant surprise I felt, then smiled and returned his attention to the road.

After exiting the elevator to the top floor and following the hall to the end, I stepped through the entry into a spacious, well-decorated apartment that in no way matched the Cape Cod residence. A sparkling view of the city caught my attention first as it beamed through the massive picture window in the living area. A white leather sectional and a few decorative pictures on the wall added the only hint of color I could readily see. I turned toward the kitchen with its modern, Scandinavian-style cabinetry. The floors were bamboo throughout and glowed with a brilliant shine in a mirror finish, reflecting the recessed lighting above. The only similar feature to the Cape home was a fluffy white rug in the living room. I felt Kevin's eyes on me, sensing if I liked it. Though not my favorite style of décor, it was pleasing in a masculine-and-polished versus masculine-bachelor style.

"What a beautiful apartment."

"Thanks. Have a seat anywhere." He pulled a glass tray from the refrigerator that was loaded with different cheeses, crackers, strawberries, and a few clusters of grapes. "I'll be back in just a moment." He disappeared down a long hallway.

*Note to self: Hire that personal chef Robert wanted me to before Kevin comes for dinner.*

Since he had an appetizer prepared, I wondered if he already knew I would say yes to his dinner invitation, until I remembered he had used a service in the Cape. Maybe he had a personal chef. With the hours he kept at the hospital, when did he have time to cook? No matter, the array of snacks was exactly what my famished body needed for sustenance. I plucked a strawberry from the tray as Kevin returned. He opened a bottle of wine and poured two glasses. I took a seat at the island in the kitchen while he pulled out a few items from the refrigerator. The two sips of Zinfandel quickly went to work on my empty stomach, lulling me into quick comfort. I glanced past him into the living area to see the warm light accenting the pictures on the wall and a sculpture in the corner.

"Is there anything I can do to help?" I asked. I genuinely liked to try to cook. I was just bad at it. Capable of prep work under the watchful eye of Mary Ann, as a younger person, I felt I could offer some assistance.

"No, I've got it. Just relax."

Wine in hand, I strolled to the sculpture to get a better look. The three-headed figure appeared Mayan. There were a couple of colorful masks between the pictures on the wall also representative of the same culture. My gaze fell back to the carving. From my education on various civilizations I recalled this one as a bat, very similar to that found on one of the symbols.

"You're correct," Kevin said, answering my thought. "It represents different meanings depending on the culture. But the symbolism I prefer is the guardian of the night."

"And the masks?"

"Used for all sorts of events. The one on the left is a jaguar and represents an otherworldly gatekeeper that can move between this world and an underworld."

*Like Karshan.* "They're beautiful.

"What was your reason for coming to see me?" I asked, changing the subject. I still couldn't read his thoughts, either because the wine was affecting me or he didn't want me to.

"We'll talk about it later."

I was more curious but decided to let the conversation unfold at his pace. "Then tell me, what fabulous thing are you cooking this evening?" I headed back to the kitchen. The aroma of sautéing garlic in olive oil lifted from a pan and filled my senses. "It already smells wonderful."

"When I get the rare chance to cook, I love to use a few of the recipes my grandmother shared when I was growing up. I hope you like scallopini."

"Anything Italian is my favorite." He looked up at me from chopping pancetta and smiled. "What? Don't tell me you knew that, too. Mary Ann?"

"Do you eat Italian a lot?" he asked.

I shrugged. "Not unless I'm at Mary Ann's and that's not often." I shifted in the seat and turned my glass a full circle. "You know, she's quite fond of you. Wait until she finds out you cook, too." I paused as I thought about it. "Oh my God, on second thought, she's likely to want a battle of the pans cook-off." I remembered then that I was to ask him to dinner Wednesday.

"I'm free Wednesday for dinner," he said, reading my thought.

"Well, that was easy. Are you sure? You haven't met Robert yet. He may question you right out the door. Though I warned Mary Ann and she promised he would be pleasant."

"I'm not worried in the least," he said. "He just wants to be sure no one is out to steal his daughter and his wealth. I completely see where he would be coming from by being inquisitive."

*And defensive.* "You're kind. I, on the other hand, see him as a kind of bulldog that needs to trust a bit more in my choice of company or companion. I've never given him any reason to doubt me."

*Which am I? Company or companion?* I heard his thought and looked up from watching him cook to meet his eye. "He's not doubting you," he said. "He's being protective. You should worry if he wasn't."

"True enough, I suppose." I couldn't argue with that. Kevin and Robert would be fine. But the thought of Robert and his ability to fire questions at someone and not think twice about how it made anyone feel immediately got my hair up. It was just how he was, all business all the time. When they finally met, I'd have to remember to hold my tongue.

Kevin looked up from two plates of food he had neatly created. "Let's eat." Reminded of how famished I was, I'd need to take extra care savoring the flavors. The wine had done a decent job of staving off the hunger, until the aroma of food wafted under my nose and I swallowed a bite.

"You're a fabulous cook. Thank you for this."

"I'm glad you like it. It's one of my favorites."

There was a slight awkwardness in the air that I couldn't quite place. We had been in each other's company long enough that any lingering discomfort came as a surprise. The conversation had breaks of silence, indicating he was trying to find a way to say whatever was on his mind.

I set my fork down and leaned closer. "What is it you've been wanting to discuss with me?" I paused, searching his eyes for a clue. "Is there something you want but are afraid to ask?" The thought of Kevin being afraid of anything seemed ridiculous to me. I was relying on every sensation as informants to what he was holding. Perhaps *afraid* wasn't the most accurate description of what I was picking up from him.

"Hold that thought," he said as he rose from the table and pulled another bottle of wine.

"If we finish that, I'm sure there won't be any problem with you getting whatever it is you want," I said.

He smiled wryly as he topped off my glass.

"Sara…" He paused, taking in a long, deep breath. "You know as well as I that I don't need wine to get what I want from you."

"No, I suppose you don't. So, now I'm easy." I smiled back at him, thinking back to our trip.

"Oh, I wouldn't say that." He exhaled. *No, this is for me.* He wasn't blocking me right now from hearing his thought. I tried to delve deeper into why he needed more drink that was connected in some way to the awkward sense in the air around him, to no avail.

"Come with me," he said, picking up his glass of wine in one hand and gently grasping my hand with the other. I scooped up my glass and followed him to the sofa, where there was a gas fireplace lit just opposite, adding comfort and warmth to the room. The ambience and wine did a fine job of distracting me from my curiosity, momentarily, as I began to feel a strange sense of tension rising up in him. I waited, letting him take the next encounter at his pace.

"I want to ask you something," he began. His eyes searched my face for an expression indicating it was safe to proceed.

"I gathered that much. You can ask me anything." It wasn't like him to find difficulty in a question or the need to preface anything. He usually just said what was on his mind.

"You know that things are beginning to change and the safety of everyone in this physical world is coming down to our ability to obtain the keys."

"Yes."

"Your safety in particular is at a greater risk."

I studied his face for an indication of where he was going. This better have nothing to do with leaving me with Eldor last night. I'd already resolved my initial frustration with his decision to do so.

"Matt discovered that C-05 is aware of you having two of the symbols. Because he hasn't come to you directly about them, we think he may be acting as an informant to Tarsamon."

*Not what I expected him to say.* I thought about C-05's visit and his attempt to surprise me. Had he been able to see deeper into my psyche, to know I had two of the medallions? How else could he have known?

"Why? What would C-05 gain as an informant?"

"We don't know yet. But we have reason to believe Tarsamon will soon set his sights on you, instead of the symbols. We think they want info on the third medallion before they'll come after you. Juno and Matt have increased surveillance on your property." Kevin's comment reminded me of the voice I'd heard just before I went into Ardan last, something about *ending her quest.*

"In every mission, each of us is driven by a promise, a kind of reward granted by the Soltari. This fuels our ambition and desire to see this mission to completion. We carry as much strength as you, but you carry the ability to hold the power of all three keys and take us to the end of the mission," he said. "And to the reward at the end of it all."

"I don't have a promise from anyone."

"You wouldn't. The Soltari asked the Alliance not to grant it to you." He paused, pressing his lips together. "Because it involves me. I'm taking a large risk in telling you that much. So, I'll need you to trust me."

"I already said that I did." I shifted a pillow aside. "I understand the importance of what I'm here to do. You know that I have become stronger since being engaged in the mission."

"That's just it. Part of the upper hand we held was that Tarsamon believed you to be weaker than you are. I'm concerned they will try to come after you soon," he said. I paused, considering what he was saying and Juno's desire for him and Matt to stay close to my home.

"I understand your concern, even share in it." The air hadn't cleared yet, and I suspected we were close to uncovering the source of his discomfort. I eyed him, waiting for him to come out with it.

He grasped my free hand. "I need to protect you at all costs. Will you come stay with me at my home?" I looked long into his eyes, filled with determination. Distress began to wash over me. A conflict. A challenge had been placed before me, the love I was feeling versus the preservation of my independence, my strength.

I shook my head slowly. "I can't do that right now." I wasn't ready to sacrifice my freedom for the sake of protection and for a relationship that I'd essentially already committed to. It wasn't that I had other prospects to discover. I couldn't imagine anyone I'd rather be with but Kevin. But no was all I could think at the moment, as though the word had been burned into my soul since birth on the issue.

I could see in his eyes he had anticipated my answer to refuse but held out hope otherwise. Something told me he wasn't a man to be caught without a backup plan for any situation. He felt as strongly about me staying with him as I did about not doing so. It just wasn't the right time to take that step, regardless of the need to protect me.

"I knew you might say that. I still had to ask," he said.

"I understand."

*I'll find another way.* I heard his thought. "Will you at least wear the bracelet?" he asked.

"Sure. If it protects me and gives you some additional peace of mind, of course I'll wear it." I pushed up the sleeve of my shirt to show him and leaned forward, kissing him once, softly, at the corner of his mouth. I could feel his frustration fade, but he didn't turn toward my kiss.

He was still thinking about something, and the slightly furrowed brow suggested he was trying to figure out how to phrase it. "You want to ask something else?" I probed.

"If I can ask you anything, and I think I can, I would love to get your professional opinion on something."

I felt my guard go up, careful of where the conversation was being taken. He had too willingly accepted my refusal to stay with him. I had expected some argument on the subject. But I was also learning that just as I thought I had a handle on what to expect, I didn't. Not with him.

My skin prickled with the sensation that this was going to be a deep question, relying on me to delve into some area of discomfort I preferred not to. Still, I never shied away from challenge. I set the glass of wine on the end table behind me to allow full focus. *Bring it on.*

"Yes?" I invited.

"I'd like to know your thought on what keeps you from letting anyone close to you? If you were the patient, what would be your professional assessment?"

I realized I had been holding my breath and released it in a small gasp, reflecting my obvious discomfort with the topic of conversation. "You seem to know a lot about me already. My childhood, as an example." He'd probably gotten the much of his information through conversations with Mary Ann during my stay in the hospital. I doubted even Mary Ann, as open as she was, would reveal the details of that ugly time of my life.

"I know you were adopted by the Forresters, but why?"

"That's not a well-kept secret. Mary Ann could tell you why better than I can."

"Fair enough. What I really want to know is what keeps you from fully trusting anyone or allowing them to get close to you? It sounds like you had a good life with the Forresters."

I was under his microscope and I wasn't going to be able to avoid it. The topic of trust had been a brief conversation in the Cape but one he had not forgotten. He really wanted to know how he could break the lock that kept anyone from emotionally bonding to me. It was sweet, expected. But it wasn't going to happen, no matter how hard he scraped the surface.

"It isn't the life with the Forresters that keeps me from giving you any more than a few days together. It's the life I had before Robert and Mary Ann rescued me. It was very painful and has left hidden scars that run as deep as the visible mark you have on your side. As I mentioned back at the Cape, there's an inability to emotionally bond." The memories of my past were trying to spring forward. I pressed them back to focus on the words and the hope they were enough to satisfy his curiosity.

This feeling of vulnerability in the discussion of my personal life was disconcerting. Even though I was young, the pain of being neglected and not wanted still left residual scars, scars that forced themselves to the surface, especially when faced with commitment or trust. I hadn't wanted to discuss the topic with Tyler, and now I found myself wanting to avoid it again. Though admittedly, Kevin was already much closer than Tyler had ever been at cracking that lock. And as I sat in front of him under his keen eye, I believed he was very aware of the fact.

I knew exactly why I wouldn't live with Kevin. I was still working through the fear of being abandoned that had resurfaced its ugly head, after realizing my feelings for Kevin had begun to run deep by letting him get close. It was my baggage. We all carried some. I'd discovered long ago I could be educated enough regarding behavioral issues to earn an MD in clinical psychiatry. But nothing, not even rational explanation and education, could heal the emotional pain of such personal experiences.

He took my hand in his and lifted my chin. "I do remember you saying that, but I don't believe you. You can't tell me you aren't emotionally bonding with me, Sara. I can feel it from you." His gaze burned into me, seeing straight to the very scar I carried, trying to smooth it. And like a child with a tender wound, I didn't want anyone touching it.

I tried to pull my chin from his gentle grasp but his thumb held tighter. "I don't want you to relive any pain, but may we at least consider that you can trust me not to hurt you? If I have to wait so that you believe me, I will." A single tear welled up in each of my eyes, not at his words but at the distress I was beginning to cause him and the struggle I felt to let him in that fought so vehemently against the need to keep the distance.

He had the patience necessary to handle this task, and he was certain of what he wanted. Protecting me wasn't just a job to him. I didn't know what promise of "reward" waited for him at the end of this quest. What I did know was there was enough between us now to know he had another goal, to bring me around to trust in him completely and to share love with him, possibly forever. I sensed he knew he had to work carefully around my deep-seated pain, tossed in some dark corner of my soul with the hope it could be forgotten forever. I couldn't help but wonder if he would become pushy like Tyler Mason had when his patience ran out. I felt my guard lift higher at the thought and still something in the back of my mind said, *let him in*.

"All right." I closed my eyes and hoped I could allow myself to trust him. I took a deep, cleansing breath in and blinked the tears away that fell one at a time down each cheek. His thumbs brushed away each one as he cupped my face, placing a kiss between my eyebrows.

*I never left you. If only you remembered.* His thought came through to me again. The more time I spent with him, the less confusing it was to hear them and to distinguish them from mine. But what did it mean? His hands left my face and grasped mine.

"It is not and never will be my intent to cause you pain," he said.

"I know. You just touched on a very tender spot. Probably the only one I have." I smiled and shook my head.

"If you don't let me look at it, how can I help heal it?" he asked.

"Okay." I paused. "I'm putting my trust in you."

"I won't drop this precious gift. You have my solemn word."

"Good. Because you have my word, I'll kick your ass if you do."

We laughed and shared a couple more jokes to ease off the sensitive subject before he lowered his eyes and held my gaze.

"Well, you turned me down on one request but I have another," he said. The corners of his mouth lifted and so did the heaviness that had consumed my heart. He kept his eyes locked on mine. "And since you said no once, I'm kind of thinking I'm due for a yes." He was careful not to offend but like our drive, he knew I liked the game.

"Maybe you are. Maybe you aren't. We'll have to see. What's your request?" I asked, detecting a lighter agenda on tap.

"Come with me," he said and paused. "Please."

This time he took my hand and led me down the long hall of his apartment through two black double doors that led into his bedroom. Another fireplace was burning in the corner, reflecting a glow on the polished hardwood floors, warming the caramel-colored walls. He sat me on the edge of the bed and reached for the glass of wine I held.

"May I take this?" he asked.

"Sure."

He watched me with eyes that were soft and alluring. I closed my own, trying to escape the gaze and the noticeable way every sensation was becoming fine-tuned to the point of a needle. Given the circumstances, I didn't need to know what he was thinking, but I questioned why it was happening after the sensitive nature of our conversation just a moment prior. I suspected the bond he worked to create in the Cape was to be reinforced closer to home. Though he wasn't letting me see that far into his psyche to confirm any such suspicion.

He stood in front of me with my face at his chest, my cheek pressed against his shirt as I inhaled a deep, slow breath of him. He smelled wonderfully masculine with only the faint scent of some intoxicating cologne that had worn off through the day. He stroked the length of my hair a couple of times. My arms instinctively moved around his waist and my hands reached up his back, feeling his warmth. I glanced up at him.

"What is it?" I whispered.

"Just a moment." And then I had the image of us he wanted me to see in my mind's eye. It was one of us embraced in passion followed by another, involving his shower. He whispered something in my ear, sending tingles down my arm. But my concentration was completely on the picture he had sent so that I didn't quite hear the words. It sounded like a question. I wasn't sure, and I didn't care. His touch was distracting me from my other heightened senses. He gently pulled my hair aside with one hand, leaned in, and pressed his lips just below my ear once, then again. A second set of tingles ran down my side and we both knew I was under his control. Once he began, my own self-preservation was forgotten. Need took over. I began to unbutton his shirt at eye level and worked my way down, pulling the rest of it free from his jeans.

"Yes," I whispered, planting my lips gently on his bare chest.

"I thought you might see it my way," he whispered into my ear, easing me farther onto the bed. His lips continued a path down my neck as we proceeded to create the blazing image he had implanted in my mind.

# 31

I blinked my eyes open, seeing the first streams of morning light playing off the wall, and felt the weight of Kevin's arm over my waist with his body curled against mine. The wind whistled at the window, a nature-like alarm beckoning us to rise for the day. I was bundled in crisp sheets and a heavy quilt, and the memory of last night's dream replayed in my mind. I shut my eyes again to see it more clearly.

Eldor glided toward me in the dark forest of Ardan, his movement fluid. A dim bluish-gray light shone as he approached, illuminating the grassy space between us. A purposeful gaze met my eyes as he greeted me.

"Sara, there are developments."

I nodded, accepting his open hand in welcome.

"What has happened since we last spoke?"

His strong hands closed gently over mine in a warm greeting. He led me across the grassy field to a tree with branches much like the willow that had sheltered me once as I tried to escape Cerys, before I'd been gifted with the memories of who he really was.

"Tarsamon has crossed the boundary into the territory of Ardan he is forbidden from entering. This is a signal of his defiance of the Soltari and his intent to increase efforts to stop the mission."

"Are the medallions safe?"

"They remain so, yes. I have come to offer details regarding the sword provided as you proceed on the mission, and also to give you some important information regarding one of your own."

"One of my own?"

"Yes. But first, may I have your sword?" He turned to face me as I pulled the sword from its sheath and placed it in his waiting hands. He gripped the hilt and thrust it into the ground halfway, then turned and led me toward a few boulders that were only a few feet beyond and sat.

"This sword is no ordinary blade. It is not only crafted to meet with your personal skill in bladed weaponry but has been blessed by the Soltari, offering you additional protection. It cannot be touched or held by the bare hand of anyone other than you and its creator. And should it fall into the wrong hands, the blade can never be used to harm you." His gaze shifted from me to the sword. "You see, it will always try to seek you out if it's not in your possession." I followed Eldor's gaze back to the sword as it began to glow a white-blue light, similar to what Kevin had described as my aura. "It will not fight in the hands of any other person. It knows its owner." The light continued to glow at ground level, as though seeking to move beyond its locked place in the soil.

"Where is Tarsamon now?"

"He was in pursuit of the medallions. But when he learned they were placed beyond his reach, he turned his attention toward you. We haven't found any trace of him or his forces in Ardan in over a day, not since the last fight."

"I see." *So, it's true. His focus has changed.*

"There is just one more thing." He paused and held his gaze with mine for a long moment. "You must allow him to protect you. It is his purpose and he knows how to fulfill it." I thought of Kevin asking me to stay with him until the danger was over, but it wouldn't be over until we found all of the keys and restored the balance to Earth.

"It risks his life for me to be where he is," I argued. Though it wasn't my primary reason for saying no to Kevin, the statement was true enough.

"Ah, Sara. The care you have for him is why the Soltari didn't want you to love again in this life. Your concern for him interferes with your focus. If they become aware that your attention is not fully on the mission, they will divide you both. Your survival is paramount to the end we all seek." He stood and walked toward the sword. "A bit of advice if I may; though you lead this mission, you'll have to trust what he says." He glanced back at me from the glow of the sword. "I must be going."

"What information do you have about one of my own?"

"Yes, yes." He angled his head toward me. "Unfortunately, one you may have trusted no longer believes in the strength of your mission and has chosen to move to the dark world, aiding Tarsamon. He believes the dark entity's strength will overcome your abilities. It seems he has lost faith before giving you a chance. His weakness may be his demise."

"Why? Who is it?" I asked, standing to meet him eye to eye. I had one man's name in mind.

"It's because he has visited the dark world. And though he knew of such things, it wasn't until he experienced how evil it was that he became too fearful, causing him to make a conscious decision to move to that side. I caution you. You already know who it is."

"But I'm not certain," I said, thinking of C-05.

Eldor took my hand in his. "You are. You only need to trust your intuition as a guide." He lifted a palm in the air, as a moving picture formed in a frame of white mist showing C-05 kneeling to Tarsamon. The fear that consumed the man in the vision filled my senses. C-05, who I'd seen strong and sure, now hung his head almost to his knees. I sucked in a breath and nodded to Eldor. He took only a few steps before his image faded into the darkness. The sword was left glowing with its white-blue haze in the place he had thrust it. Gripping the hilt, I lifted upward and slid it out of the ground as if pulling a hot knife through butter.

"Good morning." Kevin's low, smooth voice distracted me from further recollection of the dream.

"Good morning. Did I wake you?"

"It's hard not to hear you, love. You're sort of an open book unless you choose to block me, and you usually don't."

"In my thoughts again, are you? Maybe you're just nosy," I suggested, looking up at him through sleepy eyes and smiling.

"Mm, that's not it. I'm quite sure." He kissed me on my forehead. "What would you like to do today?"

I thought for a moment. "I'd love to stay, but I think I need to head home." It was late morning, and the hurricanes closing in on the coast were on my mind.

He laughed softly.

"What?" I asked.

"Nothing. It's just going to be a busy day for me, that's all." He picked his phone up off the nightstand, punched something into it rather quickly, and set it back in its place.

"A note to Juno?" I guessed.

"I have a job to do that protects us." He glanced from the phone back to me.

He had been listening to my thoughts, but for how long I didn't know. Perhaps he had been awake through my whole recall of the dream. If he had, then he knew Eldor had advised me to let him protect me. And by leaving, I wasn't. So be it. I needed to do what felt right for me. I'd never compromise that for a man. And after Eldor's suggestion and information about the Soltari dividing us, I needed to sort out why I was really keeping the distance. Childhood baggage or another reason?

"I know you need to get back," he said. "It will be miserable out with all this wintery-like weather." Another low whistle came through the eaves. "The wind is blowing wickedly." I felt his fingers slip down my back and it caused me to shift closer to him. "Let's consider another option, shall we? We stay in and keep each other warm right here awhile longer." He wrapped his arms tighter around me. He was so warm. And the comfort I found in his embrace was luring me into a soft and sensual place against him. I eased my head back to see him better.

"As nice as that sounds..." I began.

He placed one finger to my lips. "Don't say anything else."

I lifted the corner of my mouth and pulled my head back slightly as his finger fell away. "I wish I could stay but I've got too much to do. The hurricanes have al—"

His lips came to mine in a soft kiss, preventing any other words from escaping.

"I understand," he said against my lips. "I'll get with Matt to arrange—" A chime interrupted him. The fingers that had been stroking in a gentle up and down sweep across my back stopped and the arm draped over my hip was removed. He reached for his cell phone next to the bed. "The hospital," he sighed.

"I'll take a cab back," I offered.

"Take my car. It's too long a drive for a cab." He flipped the covers back and headed toward the bath. It was the first complete look at his backside I'd had in daylight.

*Beautiful.*

"Better yet, stay here," he added.

I smiled and got out of bed. "Not going to happen today." *Not sure about tomorrow, though.*

By the time I arrived home, it was nearly one p.m. I was no closer to abandoning last night's question. *I wonder if he'll ask me to stay with him again or just let it go.* Perhaps a good hour of sweat and concentration in the gym would produce an answer to satisfy us both regarding my safety and the independence I sought to keep. I scooped my hair into a ponytail and changed into more suitable clothing before heading across the property.

I was becoming uncomfortably aware of the childhood baggage I'd collected and neatly tucked away in the recesses of my mind that was now beginning to interfere in something good, maybe even compromising to my safety. Perhaps Eldor was right, I needed to let Kevin do what he was trained to do and push my fears aside, no matter where they originated.

I knocked on the door of the security building. I'd been working with Tom over the last couple of months on jiu jitsu training. The technique was just another weapon I wanted to develop in my arsenal of fight and survival strategies.

"Dr. Forrester, hello. How can we help you?" Paul said as he pulled the heavy door open, allowing me to step through farther into the entry. A blast of wind found its way into the opening, sending several papers resting on the edge of the desk flying into the air. I stepped inside as he quickly shut the door. The disruption caused heads to turn. My eyes scanned beyond Paul's shoulder, seeking their mark.

"I've got it. Thank you. Hey, Tom, do you have time for a little jiu jitsu practice today?" I asked.

"Sure do, Dr. Forrester. I was actually on my way over to the gym in just a few minutes."

"Great. See you there."

The wind had picked up, gusting through the trees, whipping the long ponytail into a frenzy, and reminding me that once I was done working out with Tom, I would try my ability at transforming strong winds to calm. I might have one role in this mission, but it didn't mean I couldn't help where or if I could.

A certain energy was carried on the breeze as I headed across the neatly cut lawn to the gym. Something seemed off, not quite right. Though I couldn't quite tell what specifically was wrong, I knew from previous experience that whatever was coming would be requiring some sort of attention in short order. Without the ability to pinpoint the distraction in the air, I filed it in the back of my mind and wondered if Juno or Matt were sensing the same.

As the head of security, Tom was one of only a few people I allowed myself to trust. He made all the decisions regarding who was hired to assist with security after extensive background checks and his own personal markers were completed for identifying *fruit loops*, as he liked to call them.

Tom's term referred to a potential newbie who might have been capable of watching monitors and walking the property, but who he had determined had a few screws loose somewhere that did not meet his approval. He was a hard-edged, strong man in his mid-forties who reminded me of a strong father-figure type, at least when he worked with me in training.

"I don't put up with any lip from any employee, you understand,

and have no qualms about dropping those I don't like, especially the lazy ones. If there's a question about it, I'll be happy to explain," he said during the interview, illustrating how he liked to work. We had been on a first-name basis since beginning the jiu jitsu training. He only referred to me as Dr. Forrester outside the gym, preferring, he said, to maintain the level of professionalism he liked to keep.

"May I ask you a personal question regarding Dr. Scott?" he asked.

"That depends on what it is."

"How much do you trust him?"

"That's easy." I moved into another position, thwarting his attempt at a chokehold. "I unconditionally trust him with my life." *I just won't live with him.* "Why do you ask?"

"He had specific questions about the security here yesterday when he was looking for you. I know he's a very close friend of yours, but I didn't give him any details."

"Good. That's what I pay you to do." I smiled and paused as I pressed into another maneuver. "I bet that had to be uncomfortable conversation for a minute or two," I added, trying to imagine Kevin frustrated.

"It was, briefly. He was persistent. That's why I thought I should ask you about him."

"I'd be worried if you shared information with anyone outside about the security you keep for me. Juno and Matt are the only two I've given additional clearance for." I slid out of a hold position and looked directly at Tom. "Without explaining in detail, let's just say that I am positive Dr. Scott is extremely concerned about my safety and I assure you he is only interested in how I am protected here, much like a personal bodyguard might be. Perhaps that might help ease your concern a bit."

"I see. Has something happened to cause additional concern?"

"If you mean does he have doubts about the security I have, no. I assure he just wants to be sure it's locked down tight. Let's keep going," I said, indicating my intent to continue with the training.

"As long as you are certain there is no threat."

"I'm quite certain I know more about Dr. Scott than most people, and to answer the question you are about to ask, yes, his background has been checked out thoroughly. He's safe."

"How do you do that, know what I'm going to say?"

"I just sense it. It's really not that big a deal." Suspecting I had eased his concerns, I switched to a position to pass the butterfly guard, focusing more on the training and less on Kevin.

I headed for the main house for a much needed shower. As the hot, steamy spray soaked into my skin, softening the muscles that had begun to tighten, I contemplated the Soltari pulling Kevin and me apart if they became aware of my concern for Kevin's safety. "How ludicrous," I said aloud. *A punishment if I fall in love. Totally absurd. Wait.* I reconsidered. *Maybe it's a punishment for distraction from the quest.* But people fulfilled all sorts of tasks every day distracted by love. But not tasks that risked billions of lives and whatever reward Kevin held so close. I grabbed the shampoo and set it down again, realizing I'd already soaped my hair. *Who's distracted?*

Sufficiently scrubbed and dressed, I opened the double French doors of the bedroom to the balcony that looked over the manicured courtyard below. The sound of water trickled from the fountain into the clear surrounding pool and played like a musical interlude. Its peacefulness was a stark contrast to the ominous thick clouds to the east.

In the opposite direction, the sun was beginning to set on the horizon, the orange-yellow sky fading with the coming evening. And as I gazed at it, I felt as though those lovely colors where ticking away with time, perhaps to be lost forever. A chill settled over me as the hairs on my arms and neck rose in response to a heightened sensation mimicking the one I'd felt earlier that afternoon. The dark sky was coming in fast, riding on the wave of billowy clouds like a surfer to shore. The gray clouds beneath the huge black streak hung low, heavy with rain. They mingled with a haze of lighter gray, moving like thick puffs of smoke.

My hair whipped around my face with each gust of wind that caught it. I closed my eyes to create the image, thought of what I wanted to happen, and thought of the time I'd spent with Aria in the beginning of my introduction to these abilities in Ardan, rocking the lake and lifting it in the shape of a saturated tornado.

With my eyes still closed, I pictured the wind easing in intensity, even as it continued to blow with ruthless endeavor, whistling past the eaves. I concentrated harder still and opened my eyes, narrowing them to focus at the invisible energy whipping currents in multiple directions. My conscience was elevated to becoming part of the wind that blew, joining my energy with it as I had done when I'd found the tree with Juno in Ardan and melded myself into its form. The power of such energy blew across my skin and touched me to my core, as nerve endings tingled with anticipation of some unknown and possibly unpleasant sensation carried high on its breeze. As if in answer, the black puffs began moving closer. The cumulonimbus clouds swirled until the fading colors of the deep orange sunset had disappeared behind dark forms. And then to my surprise, the mass of energy settled into a quiet and calm mass above me, so much more ominous than minutes earlier.

The wind picked up once, as if to show me it was still in control and then ceased altogether. The process to move the strong winds to stillness only took a matter of moments, but I was surprised at how forceful the energy was, requiring me to join forces with it rather than remain a bystander on the sidelines of its power. This was my first such attempt at manipulating energy in this world. And though I was pleased at the success of it, an unknown darker presence still lingered. My gaze shifted across the grounds and back to the sky. *Who or what am I sensing? Were Aria and Elise not successful?*

I turned back from the balcony and tuned in to the Weather Channel to see the recent status of the hurricanes being discussed. Three of the five had been downgraded to a tropical storm. I breathed a sigh of relief. There was at least another day and a half before the remaining two hurricanes reached landfall, enough time to for Aria and Elise to work their magic. I clicked off the TV, noticing the bedroom had grown darker with the evening sky. The lingering feeling of something being wrong returned as I made my way across the bedroom to fumble for the light, bumping into the duffel bag of necessities I'd packed upon learning Juno had secured our flight to Scotland.

As if the answer could be found outside, I went back to the balcony, listening. The air cracked with the too-still sound of quiet. The air smelled like fresh rain, with a cold crispness that lightly stung my cheeks. An icy breeze sent a shiver through to my core. I wrapped my arms around my shoulders and leaned into the railing. It was a different feeling than that of the hurricanes, or the urgency that would have brought about the evacuation warnings. A faint whisper on the breeze called, "It comes," feeding the disturbing sensation. I turned and almost stumbled back at what I swore had been an image on the threshold of my bedroom door. It was gone now.

"Dr. Forrester, you have guests. They say it's urgent." Tom's voice coming in loud over the security intercom caused me to jump a foot out of my skin. I stepped inside and pressed the call-back button. A heavy pounding on my front door sailed up the balcony to my bedroom at the same time.

"Let them in," I replied. I grabbed the duffel bag and sword and raced downstairs to open the door, dropping the items at the foot of the staircase. Juno, Matt, Aria, and Elise stood expressionless, all business.

"They're coming. We've got to get you out of here now," Juno said. "Where's your sword?"

"It's right here," I said, pointing behind me. "What's happening? Who's co—" The sentence died in my throat. From over Juno's shoulder under the security lights, a shadow peeled off the wall behind them. Juno pushed me backward through the door as the others turned to fight. I saw another shadow lift from the ground and approach.

"Your sword, where is it?" he shouted, shaking me from my state of shock.

"Here." I grabbed it from the case next to the duffel bag and slipped on my boots.

"Let's move. Stay beside me until Kevin can get you safely out of here." *Kevin? Did I miss that?*

"Where's C-05?" I asked. "Did you see him? A car or something when you came in?"

Juno turned and glanced at me, a bewildered expression on his face.

"Damn it. I saw someone or something upstairs," I said, frustration biting at my nerves.

"The shadows. He led them here. The longer you're here, the more shadows will be called to you."

I raced with him toward the door. One step outside and I felt my arm yanked into the darkest corner of the entry. Juno spun around as I ducked in time for him to stab above my head into the demon shadow that had grabbed me. *Shield of light. Create the shield. Where the hell is Kevin? God, let him be safe.*

I glanced up to see several more shadows and joined the others battling the onslaught of shadows raining down upon us. There had to be at least a dozen swarming the entry. My shield held strong as I slashed into one. I felt another pulling at the light that surrounded me. A huge cloud of darkness lifted and rolled over me like a wave. I pressed the hilt of my sword against my stomach and held firmly. The wave slammed me to my back, and as it did, the shield protecting me in its cocoon allowed my sword to pierce through the center of the blackness covering me. It faded into the night sky as I lifted off the ground for another strike. But my mind went back to C-05. Could he be here? I turned and charged back inside, with the gut feeling, if I was going to find him, he wouldn't be caught in that onslaught of darkness outside. I flew up the stairs. Juno's voice was calling behind me, followed by a curse. I pressed the light switch on and saw C-05 in the corner. He turned quickly from watching over the balcony below.

*Hiding in the dark like the coward you are.* "Why am I not surprised?"

"You've no idea who you call a coward," he said, hearing my thought. "I had to see them successful."

"Why didn't you just do it yourself, when you were watching behind me?" I asked, referring to him killing me when he was in the entry of my bedroom.

"You're a marvel to listen to." He waved a hand in the air, his sword in the other. "Your thoughts are"—he paused—"pure and pleasing to me. Your determination so strong. Perhaps I shouldn't have hesitated, but—" A screech sounded from behind him, like that of a bird of prey.

"But what?"

He didn't answer. Instead, his eyes widened and began to change to a pale yellow in the illuminated room. The sound of his sword hitting concrete rang out. An arm reached across my chest from behind and another sword appeared in my field of vision. I was pulled against Kevin's firm body. I glanced back toward the balcony to see an enormous hawk had taken C-05's place in the corner, clutching the balcony railing. The wings opened nearly five feet wide, and with a single whoosh, it turned and went sailing into the night.

"That's not... He's a shapeshifter," I whispered, staring after the bird in disbelief.

"Sara." Kevin turned me to face him. "Let's go. Now." His voice was firm. I turned toward the door as he took me by the elbow and rushed us down the stairs.

"What about the others?"

"When you leave, so will the shadows. Once they realize you aren't here anymore, they'll stop the fight." The bag I'd left at the bottom of the stairs was gone, and so, too, was the sword case. "Stay beside me, then get to the car." I could see his car from the front entrance. He had pulled it just inside the drive. It wasn't a far leap to get to it, but who knew how many more shadows had been called to this chaos since I'd found C-05.

As I stepped onto the drive, a rush of shadows approached. Kevin threw up a shield, causing them to scream as though the light from the barrier between us was burning them. I lifted an arm to strike at a demon that had reached me in steps. It cocked its head just before I brought my arms down and took it off.

"Get in the car," Kevin shouted over the increasing screams that approached us. I opened the door, slid into the seat, and slammed the door as Kevin rushed in beside me. The car lit up like a large glowing ember, with the shield still in force around us. The wheels spun on the drive but no sound could be heard above the shrieking.

As we sped past the iron gates, my eye caught the sight of Paul pressed against the wall as a shadow slid into his form.

"Oh my God," I gasped. I turned my head to see the shadows frantically searching the property. Several were climbing over the walls and rooftop while a few lifted toward the sky.

"He's gone," Kevin said quietly, racing us down the stretch of road. He placed a hand on my forearm. "There will be casualties. Some you know, some you don't." A tear welled in each of my eyes at the thought that I was responsible for the deaths of those around me. "The only way to stop them is to get the keys."

"He was a good man. I thought that made him stronger, able to resist them." *Tom? Did he manage to get away?* I stared past Kevin and my eyes dropped to his hand now resting on my wrist. The realization sunk in that this was what I had to prevent from happening, the end of our world.

"The others?" I asked.

"They'll be okay, now that we're gone. They'll meet us in Scotland." His thoughts were open and I could see the image in his mind of the private plane that was waiting for us.

We hadn't been on the road more than five minutes when Kevin turned to me.

"Quickly, duck down." I turned my glance from him back to the road to see headlights coming in our direction and ducked my head so as not to be seen by whoever was coming. I remained hidden until the car passed. "All right," he said, glancing in the rearview mirror. "I think we're in the clear, for now."

"And who was I hiding from?" I asked, sitting up and looking behind us.

"Tyler Mason."

"He's harmless. Annoying perhaps, but harmless." I received the picture of what Kevin had seen that had driven past us in my thoughts. "Oh," I said. Tyler's car had sped past us, but with a shadow the size of the car clinging to the top of it.

"They are still looking for you, probably believing because you knew Tyler you would have let him in." His eyes remained fixed on the road.

"Maybe. I didn't have any more to say to him. Besides, I would have stopped short at seeing the shadow," I said.

"You didn't have any reason to fear them before tonight, not knowing they now hunt you. Good thing Tyler was late to the party."

"But how could they know I was connected to Tyler?"

"It was C-05's job to have every little detail on every member of this team, especially you. Besides, Tyler's face was plastered across the tabloids just two months ago. Who didn't know?"

"True."

"You aren't safe to go anywhere. I'm only glad Matt and Juno were keeping guard at your home."

Kevin was right. If the additional security of Matt and Juno hadn't been in place, I would have let Tyler through my door, even if only to tell him not to come back, without ever thinking twice about the shadow. I'd seen them all over the city and they had never come after me until tonight. Kevin stepped on the gas, pushing the car as fast as it would go, and grasped my hand in his. "It wasn't a coincidence that he was coming to see you."

I remained silent for the rest of the drive to the airport. Kevin had the accelerator pressed to the floor, as we took the quieter roads to avoid unwanted attention in the city.

On the plane, I leaned my head against Kevin's shoulder. A rush of emotions raced through my head, leaving me exhausted yet fully awake after the encounter. And it was at that moment I knew we had been thrust into the full depths of our destiny on a race to Scotland and to the guardian of the first key. How long would it take to find what we needed? And how fast could the shadows track us?

As the door of the plane slammed shut, so, too, was the decision that I would stay with Kevin. It might not have been the living arrangement I'd expected, but there had been no choice in the matter. He stroked a hand down the length of my hair and kissed the side of my head. It was a small comfort to know that, as long as I was with him, the world had a better chance of survival, perhaps for a little while longer.

# 1

*"Bleeding hearts will never survive. Foolish girl. Faster, Sara, run!" a booming voice said, breaking the silence like a thunderclap. All I could hear now were the gasps of breath that escaped me and the heavy pounding of my heart thudding in my ears. I couldn't run fast enough to catch whatever I was chasing or escape from that which was close at my heels. The fact was I could see neither, but the sensation of urgency still tore through me. I tripped and fell, hitting my head.*

I blinked open my eyes and felt as though I was trying to catch my breath. A trickle of cold sweat beading on my chest and back sent a shiver through me, as I gazed out the window over the foggy landscape.

"The road is a bit bumpy. Sorry it woke you," Kevin said, glancing at me. "Are you okay? You look pale."

"Yeah. I'm fine, thanks," I said, swallowing hard. I slid a hand over the top of my head and straightened in the car seat. My heart was beginning to slow at the abrupt realization I was no longer in Ardan, another world immortals could travel to during sleep, but instead with Kevin on the mission to obtain the first key of enlightenment and, with any luck, rescue humanity. I must have dozed on the drive from the airport. I could see the faint outline of Doune Castle through the clouds at the top of the hill just a little way up the road.

"What scared you? Where were you?" Kevin asked, reading my thoughts.

"I don't know. Maybe Ardan. I didn't recognize the world I traveled to this time."

"We can wait here a few minutes if you'd like," he said, pulling to the side of the road.

"No, no. I'm fine." My head was throbbing with lack of sleep and the need for water. "Better to keep moving. Besides, we aren't going to get less tired."

After the narrow escape from the dark shadows hunting me the night before, neither of us had rested well on the nearly seven-hour flight from New York to Scotland. And now here we were, plunged into the center of our mission to find the guardian of the key, one of three that would rescue earth.

*Better get used to this, Sara. There could be several sleepless nights on this journey.* The gentle touch of Kevin's hand against my cheek pulled me from my thoughts. I lifted my eyes to his, deep brown with flecks of gold winking back at me, reading every thought and emotion. Through tired eyes, I dropped my gaze to his lips and back to meet his stare.

"Let's go," I said.

*A Light Within*

Sara Forrester is plunged into the only role in life she was ever meant to fulfill—the quest to obtain three ancient keys hidden by a powerful governing order across the realms—the Soltari. She and her team race to Scotland to find the sacred Druid priests before the evil seeking to end her quest traces her energy trail and puts an end to mankind. But when Sara arrives, a powerful force lures her to a break in time and space, diverting her intended path.

*Flight of the Feathered Serpent*

When age-old myths of a lost civilization come to life, Sara suspects the very Order she serves might have other intentions—using her to achieve a separate and malevolent purpose. She's vowed that no matter who or what might be working against her and the immortals, nothing will stand in the way of achieving her vital goal.

*Winter's Labyrinth*

Finding the last of three keys hidden in an underworld of spells is the one hope remaining and a task only Sara Forrester can fulfill. Joined by her team, Sara must brave the cryptic City of Souls to release the ancient Egyptian powers she believed to be myths.

Can Sara rescue two worlds and a future she's fought lifetimes to claim with the one man she'd risk her soul to keep before time runs out?

**If you'd like to sign-up to receive exclusive content and special offers, please visit Dana at https://danaalexander.net/**

# ABOUT THE AUTHOR

Dana Alexander is a summa cum laude graduate of Arizona State University who spent her career in Medicare policy, education, and audit before being compelled to write the story of two souls connected across countless millennia and held together by their duty to the Alliance. When she isn't creating scenes, dialogue, and realms for the series, her time is spent with family keeping cool in the ridiculously hot desert with their two huge, swim-loving Labs, Ryley and Brodie.

**Connect with Dana at her website:**
**www.danaalexander.net**